I0776996

Malitu Book Three

Only a Grave Will Do

James Lloyd Dulin

G & D Publishing

First paperback edition June 2025

Cover Illustration by Martin Mottet
Cover Design and Interior Layout by Michael Dulin
Map by Gustavo Schmitt
Copyedit by Rachel Marchesi
Proofread by Dominic McDermott

ISBN: 979-8-9871736-6-4 (paperback)
ISBN: 979-8-9871736-7-1 (hardcover)
ASIN: B0F4VYBJKK (ebook)

www.jamesldulin.com

Content and Trigger Warnings
As a note of caution, this story contains depictions of graphic violence, violence towards children, racism, ableism, colonialism, war, child soldiers, genocide, death of loved ones, suicidal ideation, slavery, survivor's guilt, grief, trauma, and abandonment.

To the people who fill the story of my life:
Dominic, Sonny, and Aneicka.

ENNEA

TOLTIAN
RENEQUA
NORTH ENOCH
PORT RILAN
ASTILE
THE LOST NATION
STRAITS OF TALMO
MYANACK
COLIAN
THE LOST FOREST
TOMAK
DASOON
NOMAR
TAL KINIC OCEAN
IAHIQUE
STONE CITY
SONACOA
PROTISI
N

The Story Until Now

Ennea gave life to the sun, the moons, the spirits, and people alike.
She was the land and its creator. When her people prayed for gifts, she
bestowed the ability to hear The Song and pull on the powers of The Great
Spirits: shadows, water, fire, earth, wind, and plant life. The gifted were
called many things—most commonly, dancers.

However, some dancers abused her gifts. So Ennea bestowed one final
gift, the ability to borrow the magic. Spirit dancers were supposed to
provide balance when dancers misused their gifts, but the stories painted
them as nothing more than villains and thieves.

This land was never free of strife. No land ever could be. However, the
four nations of Ennea were experiencing over two hundred turns of relative
peace when the Gousht arrived.

The Gousht Empire presented themselves as explorers as they prepared
for war. Once they discovered spirit crystals and the ability to permanently
steal people's magic, Ennea's fate was decided. Eventually, they claimed the
Stone City, the most populous city in the four nations, and the war was
finished.

Only the Lost Nation, which hid behind an impenetrable forest surrounding its border, survived the Invasion War. The Gousht occupied cities, enslaved Enneans, and went to work assimilating their new conquest into their empire in the name of their One True God.

KAYLO'S STORY

Kaylo grew up under Gousht occupation. He kept his head down and survived, but everything changed when he first heard the song of other people's magic. He was a spirit dancer.

Within a turn of Kaylo's sixteenth birthday, the Gousht killed his parents, his best friend, and a family who had taken him in.

So Kaylo decided to fight. He and his friends found the Missing, a rebel group only spoken about in whispers.

Commander Zusa led the rebel group on raids, allowing Kaylo to satiate his bloodlust.

Then The Balance revealed a secret to Kaylo. Spirit dancers could destroy crystals and return the trapped spirits to their rightful hosts. It should have been a blessing, but when Kaylo shared his new-found ability with Commander Zusa, he found out the truth. The Lost Nation used the Missing to conscript warriors, stock spirit crystals, and gather supplies for their eventual war against the Gousht. Their rebellion was a lie.

The Missing would never wage war. They were merely a distraction while the King of the Lost Nation collected supplies and conscripted free Enneans.

Before Kaylo could do anything about the truth he had uncovered, the Gousht raided his encampment. They were led by the same priest—The Priest—who had massacred Kaylo's surrogate family.

Despite the pleading of his friend, the water dancer, Liara, Kaylo chased after The Priest instead of escaping. His choice led to Zusa's death and Kaylo's capture alongside a young resistance fighter named Boda.

The Priest brought Kaylo and Boda to the Anilace Mines where he

interrogated Kaylo and stole his fragment of The Seed. Kaylo resisted
sharing his secrets until his interrogator turned his attentions to Boda. The
interrogator beat Boda to the edge of death despite Kaylo confessing every
secret he knew.

The night before Kaylo was set to be executed, the remaining members
of the Missing infiltrated the stronghold to rescue him. The escape plan
turned into a battle. Enslaved Enneans joined the fight, but all seemed
lost until Kaylo reached towards the echoes coming from the mines. In an
instant, every crystal in the mines and within the stronghold shattered.

The Enneans won the battle, and Kaylo had become the Hero of Anilace.

Current Day Ennea

After twelve turns of hiding, Kaylo saved a war orphan named Tayen
from imperial soldiers. He took her in and began training her until more
soldiers came in search of those Kaylo had slain.

Kaylo and Tayen escaped to a freecity on the border of the Lost Forest
to avoid capture by the Gousht. However, the freecity would prove to be
a trap as well. The city's leaders, Hakan and Nix, had made a deal with the
Lost Nation to provide conscripts in exchange for food and supplies. Nix had
a change of heart and tried to help them escape, leading to her conscription
alongside them.

Wal, Kaylo's former friend, was now a commander in the Lost Army, and
his bitterness towards Kaylo had only grown with time. Tayen and Nix were
forced into training for positions within the Lost Army as Kaylo was coerced
into training three spirit dancers.

While in the Lost Nation's care, Nix came across a young girl named
Sosun whom she had traded to the Lost Nation for grain. Sosun had been
forced into servitude, and the Lost Nation did not treat their servants with
care. They took their names, their freedom, and their tongues.

Kaylo orchestrated an escape plan. It worked, but along the way, Tayen killed one of Kaylo's spirit dancer students, Kaylo killed all but one of Wal's guards and left Wal himself bleeding on the training grounds, and Tayen took an arrow in the shoulder.

Kaylo, Tayen, Nix, and Sosun made their way into the Kenke Forest to heal and plan their next move.

Wal was stripped of his rank and imprisoned in a dungeon underneath the Lost Nation's mountain fortress for allowing his former friend to escape.

PROLOGUE

KAYLO'S STORY

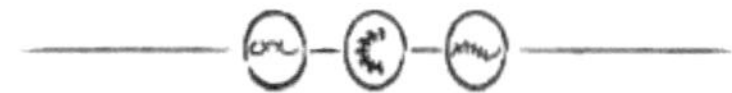

A BREATH CAUGHT IN my throat and came out as a faltering sigh. Gaps in the tree wall surrounding the grounds, collapsed tunnels at the base of the mountain, rows upon rows of unsettled soil marking the one hundred twenty-three graves we had dug—this land would never be anything other than a battlefield to me.

If I had followed Liara or listened to Zusa, my friends wouldn't have died.

Each mound of loosened dirt took on a different shape. Of course, I knew where Adéan and Sionia lay, but the rest of the dead belonged to people as well. They had names, which I would never know. And now, I would carry their blood as well.

"Blood for blood," I whispered to myself as I walked through the courtyard, careful not to step on the graves.

Some of the survivors knelt beside loved ones. Restrained sobs broke through the quiet reverence.

I stopped at near the end of the row and knelt beside a grave like any other save the small ironoak tulip stuck in the dirt. My mother had loved tulips. Maybe Sionia had as well. We never discussed it. Conversations about flowers had seemed frivolous. So I had placed a tulip I carved on her grave because she deserved something soft after this life.

People had mistaken her quiet demeanor for meekness, but she had been the unmoving sort. Her anger never forced her hand, though she had her anger. When she believed in a thing—or a person—she carried that belief like a weapon.

"You believed in the wrong person." I placed my hand on the tulip. It was the closest thing to touching her hand.

"Remember the day we met? I got a blade through the thigh, and you refused to go on without me," I said. "I thought I was doing the right thing by telling you to go. I always think I am. Then you wrapped your arm around me and helped me limp up the hill."

I chuckled to myself.

"Liara says I need to stop playing the martyr. Maybe she's right," I said. "You left without me this time. Why do you get to do the noble thing while I have to carry on? Tell me how that's fair."

"War isn't about fair," someone said over my shoulder.

I jerked back to find Wal standing behind me. Too many fallen tears had irritated the skin below his eyes, but he wore an impassive expression. "We have work to do."

"Wal, are you okay? We haven't had a proper chance to talk since everything happened," I said. "Adéan fought until the end. He saved lives. I know what you're feeling and—"

"All respect, there may come a time when I'm willing to compare our dead and grieve side by side, but now is not that time." His fists clenched into hammers at his side. "The others are meeting, and we need you."

"Okay." I turned back to Sionia's grave, touched three fingers to my lips, then placed them on the dirt. "Rest easy."

Wal was already several paces ahead of me when I got to my feet. As long as I had known him, he had carried himself with a looseness in his shoulders and an easiness in his stride. Tonight, he stretched taller into the night's sky. His shoulders squared off with the ground as if he wouldn't move for any obstacle, as if he bore the spirit of the man he had lost.

The survivors of Oakheart—those who hadn't left—had constructed a small grouping of tents between the graves and the stronghold. The stronghold could have sheltered most, if not all, of them from the ever-colder autumn night, but they kept their distance from the stone building.

If they had been through anything like I had in those walls, I understood. It took me a moment to cross the threshold, and I had only been a prisoner here a few days.

Once inside, Wal didn't slow his pace. We took a different path through the stone-lined hallways, but every turn reminded me of the night Boda and I had been dragged to The Priest's chamber.

I had been ignorant enough to believe I understood Gousht cruelty. The Priest had proven me wrong yet again.

Each time I blinked, my torturer and his oversized hands were there. It didn't matter if he lay dead in a mass grave. He had broken me. And Boda.

Wal rounded another bend, and a set of harsh voices carried through the corridor.

"...charge in like we didn't jus bury ova one hundred twenty bodies?" an unfamiliar voice questioned in anger.

"We have more warriors now." A voice that unmistakably belonged to Talise matched anger for anger. "The couta won't stop because we took back a single mine."

"Taking a mine 'n holding it are two very different tings," the stranger said.

The voices got louder as we approached. Then I was there, waiting beside a new battlefield I had no interest in joining.

When I stepped into the doorway, the group paused. A handful of familiar faces were interspersed between the strangers lining the perimeter of the room.

There may not have been bloodstains and a tree bursting through the floorboards, but the room bore a too-similar resemblance to The Priest's study.

My feet felt heavy. My heartbeat filled my ears. I had to fight not to turn and look for an exit.

He's dead, I told myself. *The prick who bludgeoned Boda is dead.*

And he was. I had made sure of it before I rolled his carcass into the pit of bodies in bloody green uniforms.

Amongst the crowded room, I found Liara's smile. I concentrated on her—the freckle beside her right eye—and the next breath came easier.

"What's this?" I asked, entering into the room.

"A spirited debate." The Sonacoan fire dancer who had introduced himself as Annit wore a calm about him that didn't fit the room. "During your speech, you said that what we accomplished was the start of an uprising—I'm paraphrasing, of course—and people seem to have different opinions as to what that means."

"We aren't an army. If we go out tere actin like it, tere will only be more graves. Tha is if anyone is still alive to dig tem," said a short northwoman leaning on a walking stick.

It was unmistakably the woman I had heard from the corridor. Her voice carried the hint of a Renēquan accent dulled by turns of imprisonment. She may have been older than most people in the room, but she stared around as if to challenge anyone who would disagree.

A young Tomakan with a shaven head, apart from a singular braid at the nape of their neck draped over their shoulder, stepped forward. "The empire's trespass cannot go unanswered. The courtyard is full of our friends and family. Blood for blood."

"See, someone is making some sense," Talise said.

"Cha propose we march in rows to face tere armies?" the northwoman asked.

"We do exactly what we were doing when we thought we were

fighting for the Missing." Talise spat on the ground before continuing. "We disrupt their supplies, ransack their caravans."

"For what purpose?" Liara's voice stood apart from the others in its softness. "The Missing were siphoning resources for the Lost Nation. It did nothing for the people who are actually out there suffering."

"But we could use their weapons against them. We actually could do everything that Zusa said the Missing would do." As Tomi spoke, she spoke to Liara and Liara alone. The rest of us were only witnesses to their conversation.

"No," Liara said to her sister, before turning to the rest of those gathered. "Using stolen spirits would stand in opposition to everything we should represent. We should stand for returning freedom, power, and the land back to the people and the spirits of Ennea."

"Your moral outrage is only going to get in the way." Wal's expression narrowed his grief into a point aimed at Liara.

"Say we succeed and use spirit crystals to exile the Gousht from our shores," Liara said. "Will you give the people back their spirits then?"

"They owe blood, not exile!" Wal yelled.

"I will not enslave a spirit to our cause!" Liara stepped towards the center of the room. "We are only standing here tonight because Kaylo freed those spirits and the dancers in this room turned the battle's tide. I will not keep that opportunity from another. I will not keep a spirit from the binding they belong to."

Wal matched her step for step. "Easy for a dancer to say."

The tension in the crowd forced most people in the room back to the stone wall, but one Sonacoan woman stepped forward against the current. "Differences of opinion cannot be solved by competing to be the loudest voice in the room. That is a clear path to a quick death."

She turned towards me. I had seen this stout, onyx-skinned woman before. In the seconds before I collapsed, she had defended Liara. She broke the earth into a mouth to swallow several soldiers.

"After everything that has happened, I would hear from the young thief, if he has a voice to share." The earth dancer spoke the invitation—even the word thief—with a genuine question in her voice. If she meant to turn or twist the conversation for any unsavory reason, she hid it well.

As the sound of her question faded, a silence wrapped around the moment and a dozen faces turned to me. After everything that I had done, the many mistakes, each with corresponding bodies, people continued to look to me as if I had answers. Why? Because I had broken a few crystals before passing out?

Annit patted me on the shoulder and smiled.

"I only pledged myself before Ennea a few moons ago." My voice wavered as I spoke. "If you're looking for someone with answers, I don't have them.

"The smart path would be to hide and make as good of a life as we can for as long as we can." I held up a hand to Wal before he could say anything. "I can't do that. I owe too much blood. But we can't keep ambushing supply convoys either. It didn't stop the Gousht. We might as well dry the ocean with a bucket.

"The Gousht's biggest weakness is their arrogance. They don't consider us a threat. So, we use that. We take their outposts and strongholds, and free more people. We grow our numbers. But we don't rush forward or use weapons that are beneath us. We train and scout, and we become the army they thought we never could be. An army of misfits who don't have much left to lose."

"Ha!" Annit's boisterous laugh reverberated off the close-quartered walls. "I knew it! This young man was touched by The Mother herself."

"Cha can't be serious," the older northwoman said.

"Why not? People had a chance to leave already. If they don't like our plan, they can take a second opportunity, but the rest of us are here because we want to fight. Let's fight," Annit said.

One after another, everyone in the room added their share to the conversation. Much of it restated an earlier thought in one way or another, and no one bent far beyond their starting point. The discussion ended up being a series of ropes tied in a knot; as we all pulled in different directions, the tension kept us from moving far from where we had started.

When enough hours had passed to wear on the bones of everyone in the room, we left with the loosest of agreements to ponder what had been discussed.

While I waited for a moment with Liara, the others filtered out of the room. Wal barely met my eyes as he left. Talise stared at me with an impassive look. I couldn't tell which reaction was more unsettling.

I caught Liara by the arm as she made her way towards the door with her sister. She motioned for Tomi to go on without her, then waited for me to speak.

"Why did they even include us in the first place?" I asked. "We are some of the youngest people left on the grounds. Surely, there are people with more experience."

"The scary thing is, there aren't." She moved beside me and rested her back against the stones. "Even if some of them have experience fighting the Gousht, they've been locked inside these walls for turns on turns. We are the ones who have been ambushing the Gousht and fighting for the Missing."

"So we're even more fucked than I thought we were."

"Pretty much," she said. "Do you really think we can become an army?"

"No. At least, not like any army that ever made the history books." I smiled because all of this was ridiculous, and I needed to acknowledge it, if only for a moment, with her. "But I do think that a small group of people can do enough damage to be really irritating."

When she found my hand and curled her fingers between mine, everything paused, and the dark humor of the moment fell dead on the ground. "You did good tonight."

"I don't know what I'm doing, Liara. They look at me like I am a hero, but all I did was get captured and be a spirit thief."

"As far as I know, no one has ever broken a spirit crystal before. You broke a mountain of them. To them, you are a symbol of their ability to fight back, even when the odds seem insurmountable. But if you do anything that stupid again, I'm not coming after you." She leaned into me, and her lips held mine for a moment in the softest of kisses. "Do something good with their faith."

Trying to maintain a modicum of composure, I didn't move as she slipped her fingers from my grasp and walked out into the hall.

If I pawed through every moment of my life in search of a single deed, or even a collection of them, that made me worthy of her belief after the choices I had made, I would have come away empty-handed.

Chapter One
Current Day Ennea

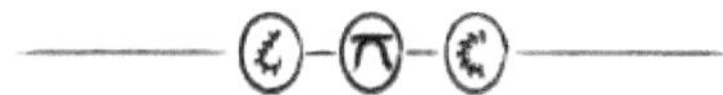

Tayen sat as still as her spirit would let her while Kaylo treated her wound. Pain came less frequently these days. But when she had the mind to listen, her wound repeated the life of her heart, a gentle ache underscoring the rhythmic throbbing.

Her wound was healing, but they were still hiding out in this rush job of a hallow a full moon later. Anytime she pushed Kaylo about searching for the Uprising, he changed the subject or told her she needed more time to heal.

The tight walls closed in around her with each new day. The Lost Nation had been a prison of sorts, but at least she'd had room to move. None of the commanders hovered over her like Kaylo.

She forced herself to breathe. He was only trying to take care of her. Even if he had chosen to do so in the most annoying way possible.

Kaylo finished washing the old bits of ground-up plants from her skin and began applying the new, sour-smelling poultice. As usual, he said nothing as he worked. Her kana either had an unending string of words falling from his lips or said nothing at all.

"Tomorrow will mark a moon since we escaped," Tayen said. "We can't wait here forever."

"Really? That much time? I hadn't noticed. You only remind me every day. Are you going to threaten to leave without me next?" His hands didn't break their steady flow as he spoke. "If your hair weren't getting longer, I would swear the day was just repeating over and over again with the same conversations."

"You realize how much of a hypocrite you are, right? I have never heard another person repeat the same set of words more in my life." She furrowed her brow and drew in her lips, mocking his cadence. "'Slower is better than dead, little shade.' 'Still wounds heal faster.' 'The Uprising is not the answer you hope they are.'"

"One, I don't sound like that. My voice is much more pleasant, like a summer breeze gently kissing your ears," he said as he twisted her earlobe with the gentlest pinch. "Two, I repeat myself because my toka has a hard time remembering good advice."

The bushes at the entrance bristled, and Kaylo jumped up, reaching for his knife.

"It's just Sosun or Nix," Tayen said.

He shushed her, still staring at the entrance with his blade drawn.

Even after Sosun stepped through the singular gap in the ironoak wall, it took him a moment to sheathe his blade. The Lost Nation had its lasting effects on each of them.

Sosun didn't react to Kaylo's overprotective display. She simply smiled, pulling her deep brown cheeks taut.

When they escaped, Nix had to shear Sosun's matted hair to the scalp. The short bristles had begun to grow back in tight red curls. The cut suited the shape of her head.

Without warning, she began signing. One gesture ran into the next as if they were a part of a larger movement—a hand over her heart, a tug at her earlobe, then two fingers circling in front of her lips.

At least she slowed down for Tayen. When she spoke with Nix, her hands moved at pace with her thoughts. Either way, Sosun's facial expressions provided half the translation.

"You heard arguing, which usually means we're done," Tayen said. "Was that right?"

Sosun smiled and nodded, patting the back of her left hand, then brought her right hand perpendicular to her left. *"Well done."*

"How about it, Kaylo? Are we done?" Tayen asked as she signed, definitely missing at least one word along the way.

Settling Tayen's robe back over her shoulder, he looked between the two young women. "All done," he said, gesturing with the words.

He finished by placing the flat of his palm on his forehead, and Sosun began to snicker behind her hands.

"What is it this time?"

"You said you have..." The laughter was caught in Tayen's throat as she tried her best not to cackle in her kana's face. "Shit for brains."

"How am I supposed to learn if Nix keeps on lying to me? It's not funny. I'm trying my best."

Tayen patted his arm with her good one as she lost the fight against her laughter. "I know you are, but I don't know why you keep falling for it."

"Go on. Get out of here and try to get a little bit away before you start giggling between yourselves about this," he said, holding his knife out for her.

Despite the joy his bright-cheeked embarrassment gave her, Tayen pushed herself off the ground, took the knife, and rushed towards the gap in the tree wall. They spent far too much time stuck on the same patch of dirt, and she wasn't about to trade her time in the forest for a few more laughs at his expense.

She blinked away the stinging sunlight and fought her way through the overgrown bushes at the hallow's entrance.

Kaylo had insisted they had to let the bushes grow over the entrance to hide the opening. Sound strategy or not, it left them all with far too many tears in their sleeves. If spring hadn't cut through the cold, they would be freezing because of his cleverness.

Tayen walked her usual path through the forest with Sosun close behind. Above the canopy, the Gentle Dagger carved into the sky.

Despite spending most of her life moving from one place to another to avoid Gousht patrols, Tayen had never set foot on a true mountain. The Citadel definitely hadn't counted.

If she asked, Kaylo would take her before the breath fully escaped her lungs. He would do anything to avoid searching out the Uprising for another day. But time only made her decision clearer.

Revenge would never heal her. It would never bring back Nita or Vähn or her parents. Nothing would. Blood for blood was a convenient line for storytellers. Spilling blood did nothing for the dead.

It might do something for the living though.

Anger can either be selfish or it can be righteous. It can't be both. Chitere had been right about that much.

If Tayen couldn't get rid of her anger, she would have to put it to work—give it to the Uprising. Kaylo had to understand that.

An empty snare dangled from a sapling branch. Rabbit prints littered the soil beneath it. Some animals refused to be caught.

Tayen put her weight on the branch and bent it back into place, hooking the twine rope on the release. She knelt down and scattered some leaves and pebbles around the looped twine.

The routine of checking and setting her traps had given her an excuse to escape Kaylo for a little bit every day. It allowed her time to think—to breathe.

She had gotten good at it too. Most days they had to rely on the mercy of the trees, plants, and what little supplies they had escaped with. But not today.

A rabbit still wearing its winter heaviness dangled from the next snare. With its size, its front paws almost scraped the dirt.

As naturally as she would stack firewood or sweep fallen leaves from the hallow, Tayen drew Kaylo's knife from her belt and slit the animal's throat. Blood streamed from the wound, and the rabbit twitched for a few moments before stopping altogether.

Sosun turned from the violence.

"You know, we're heading towards much more blood than this," Tayen said as she signed the words she knew.

Sosun focused her eyes on Tayen's, avoiding the gore as she signed. Gestures, many of which Tayen had never seen before, moved in firm strokes. *"Violence...yes. Blood...hands...not the only way to fight."*

"Maybe, but the greens definitely deserve to lose their share of blood."

Tayen freed the rabbit's legs from the snare and set it on the ground. "Blessed Mother, this spirit died so that we may continue our journey. Take it. Guide it home to endless fields in The Mist." She lifted three fingers, still marked by the gore of her kill, to her lips, then placed them on the ground beside the rabbit.

The sound of a blade peeling away layers of wood like short gusts of wind stopped as soon as Nix disturbed the bushes covering the entrance. Paranoid may have been an unfair term for someone on the run from multiple hostile armies, but Kaylo wore the description well.

With an Astilean sword in his lap, he waited cross-legged, staring at the entrance to their temporary abode. Curls of discarded wood lay scattered amongst a pile of arrow shafts, which may have been useful if they had more than one bow to share between the four of them.

"Can't you relax for a moment? I swear, if I find another strip of ashburn in my hair from your discarded scraps, I'm taking one of those hands," Nix said before taking a second look. "Wait, you're using a sword to whittle?"

"Tayen and Sosun have my knife."

"I won't have to cut off one of your hands. You'll do it for me. Has no one ever taught you to match the tool to the job?"

"Sorry, I must have shit for brains," he said as he repeated the sign she had taught him.

A smile crept along her face, and she let it. "You can't blame me. You're the one who keeps falling for it."

"It makes them laugh." He shrugged and picked up an unfinished arrow shaft, continuing to shape the wood with a damn sword. "They need a bit of laughter."

"Don't act like you knew."

The rhythmic scraping of the metal over wood returned, and Kaylo kept his concentration on the task at hand.

"Seriously, did you know? You couldn't have known."

"I'm not the only spirit known to routine around here," Kaylo signed. "You probably went south to the river, east at the downed ashburn tree, and trailed back up around the edge of the tree line like you always do. Same path, every time you go out scouting."

"I'm impressed," Nix said. "I mean, I know you're lying, but it's not a bad lie."

"If you want to fuck with people, you need to change up the game. Sure, I'm not the smartest man, but I do occasionally learn from my mistakes."

As he looked up and smiled at her, his face offered a challenge, daring her to call his bluff. Maybe she had grown too complacent. Next time, she would have to find a unique way to pull the chair out from under his condescending ass.

Her leather belt snagged on the same old groove as she tried to slip it from her waist. Which was what happened when one stole belts from oversized corpses. *Fucking lost bastard.* When it finally released from the half-knot, she tossed the belt, scabbard, and sword into her loosely claimed corner of the hallow.

"Enough back and forth." She sat in a mirrored cross-legged position in front of Kaylo. "Whether you like it or not, we are going to have to get moving. We can't stay here, and the kid has healed up quite well from what I can see. You can't hold her back forever."

As Kaylo placed his sword and arrow to the side, his expression lost all of its playfulness.

"The longer you wait, the more she will resent you and the more dangerous it becomes to stay," Nix said.

"Why are you in such a rush to lead Sosun towards the fighting? You care about that girl just as much as I care about Tayen."

"When I let the Lost Nation take Sosun, they didn't take her life. They took her tongue, and they took her freedom." Nix restrained her tone despite the challenge in Kaylo's. It came from a place of fear for Tayen. Otherwise, they would be sharing different words.

"Blessed Mother knows, I can't give her back her tongue—she might not even want it. The servants under that mountain and the culture they built in the shadows are as much a part of Sosun as anything else. But I can protect her freedom."

"There's no freedom in war."

"That's where you're very wrong," she said. "There is freedom in the choice to fight back, and you are stealing that from Tayen every day you stop her from making her choice. You can't keep someone free by restraining them—no matter how well meaning you are."

Kaylo chuckled like the weird fuck he was. "You may be just as wise as you are mean."

"I guess I'll have to set the balance right and find new ways to mess with you."

"Thank you, Nix. Truly, thank you."

"You always know how to make things uncomfortable. Go back to whittling, oh great Hero of Anilace."

Fat dripped from the rabbit into the flames below as it cooked. The scent of juniper berries and rosemary tamed the greasy smell as Kaylo rotated the animal. If this was to be their last night here, this meal would be a fitting send-off.

"Maybe after Kaylo finishes telling us his story, you can tell us about how you ended up with Hakan in Dasoon," Tayen said from over his shoulder.

"I save that kind of self-aggrandizing for those who have practiced and developed their skill over turns," Nix said, eliciting a series of giggles from Tayen and Sosun.

"If you don't have anything interesting to say, you can just say that," Kaylo said.

Over the past two seasons, their barbed banter had become the way they related to one another. For some twisted reason, she seemed to respect him when he found ways and means to be as hurtful and harsh as possible.

As long as it kept their small ecosystem in balance, it didn't have to make sense.

"And then, I wept because I was the worst person ever, and I would never be good for anyone, but also I may be able to save us all," Nix said in a deep whine.

"Being a contrarian isn't a personality, Nix."

"What's a contrarian?" Tayen asked.

"It's someone who sees happiness or meaning, and then decides to hate it in order to seem above what they lack," Kaylo said.

A pebble bounced off Kaylo's shoulder, and he jerked around to find a stone-faced Sosun staring him down. Her hands moved in slow, deliberate strokes so he wouldn't miss her meaning. *Some things are beyond the game. Some things are simply rude and mean.*

"It's okay, Sosun," Nix said.

"No, it's not," Sosun signed. *"We don't have much. If we cut each other down, we only become less."*

Ever since he was a young boy, battling Shay and drowning in her harsh words, Kaylo crossed lines when he fought back. The game and its boundaries made as much sense to him as the rest of life.

"You're right," he said, signing the words he could. "What I said was unnecessary and unkind, and I apologize. As much as we butt heads, Nix helped me see something I was overlooking today."

"What, that you're self-aggrandizing?" Tayen said with a wide smile, but no one joined her. "Sorry, I don't even know what that means"

"Tayen, I failed to protect you because I was protecting your life in spite of what you wanted. Each and every thing I did was to keep your heart beating, but I never thought about keeping it intact." He paused, choking down the knot forming in his throat. "My obsession with not being responsible for anyone else dying…I made keeping you safe about me and my needs.

"In the meantime, I allowed the Lost Nation to snatch you up. None of my justifications can take away your grief for Vāhn or the pain you felt under the army's watch."

"Stop making everything your fault, Kaylo," Tayen said, tears building in her eyes and an edge sharpening in her voice.

"I have been holding you back from your choices in an attempt to keep you safe." He turned back to the rabbit and rotated their meal once again to hide his face. Crying during an apology only served to steal attention away from the right people. "Tomorrow, we will leave. If you want to join the Uprising, I will help you find them."

Boots scraped over dirt behind him, then Tayen threw her arms over his shoulders, hugging him from behind. Her wet cheek pressed against his beard.

"You never meant for this to happen. You did your best," she said.

"That's what worries me. It was my best." He chuckled even as tears fell from his eyes.

"We're both still alive. That's something."

"Little shade, you really should raise your standards."

Chapter Two
Kaylo's Story

Our warriors lay in wait amongst the forest surrounding the Gousht outpost. Before their green and yellow banners, it had been a trading post not far from the northern coast of Tomak. A few families had worked the land and hosted travelers from Renêqua and the Lost Nation. People bartered and slept, exchanged stories and cooked meals to share.

The greens hadn't changed much about the grounds. They used the bones of the homes they stole. The archer perches were new, but the outpost served largely the same purpose. Supplies came and went. Soldiers rested before continuing their march one way or another.

A young Gousht soldier leaned against the railing of the closest perch. He yawned with the rising sunlight as his bow rested beside him.

The Gousht hadn't sent warriors. They had sent bodies to occupy our land because their Emperor felt entitled to it.

Our scouts had been watching them for several span. The routine never changed. Their arrogance couldn't conceive of a world in which their right to rule would be questioned.

Still, if we meant to bloody our blades, we had to understand the battle ahead of us. A single turn of training could only prepare our ragtag rebellion so well.

Boda's leg bounced as he waited beside me like a mountain lion preparing to pounce. If any of the others wanted blood more than him, they had been quieter about it.

The milky white of his now-blind eye seemed to stare at me. He refused to cover the scars, which served as a daily reminder of my mistakes. He said he wanted to make the Gousht see their abuse before he ended their lives, but I had no doubt he took pleasure in how much it unnerved me as well.

Bells chimed from the center of the outpost, calling the couta to their prayers. Our spotter in the tree above signaled to confirm the soldiers had started towards the old communion hall, which they had reclaimed as their new church.

Of course, the archers remained in their perches.

Annit glided through the forest like a spirit and knelt beside me at the edge of the tree line. Burns pebbled his dark skin and underscored his eyes. The marks hinted at a life he refused to speak of no matter how many questions I asked.

Even without the details, it was clear to anyone who spoke to him for more than a moment that he should have been the one leading this little rebellion. He wouldn't hear a word of it.

So, as it had too many times before, the responsibility landed on me— the Hero of Anilace. What a ridiculous moniker.

"Everyone is in place?" I whispered.

Annit answered with two taps on my shoulder before he unsheathed his blade, removing all doubt as to what the gesture may have meant.

His unspoken confidence allayed the loudest of my fears. He knew the blood that was owed, and he knew when the battle required patience. If Annit believed in our plan, that had to be enough for me.

I dug my hand into the dirt to keep it from trembling, but nothing could stop my heart from battering my ribs. Once again, I held lives in my hands.

The Emperor's seal hung from the archer's perch, drifting with the autumn breeze. I stared into the eyes of the snake depicted on the banner. The people who had built this trading post and made this land their home were gone. Whether the couta sent them to The Mist or away to labor in the mines didn't matter. These soldiers had no claim to this land.

My growing anger stilled my body.

As if to bolster my resolve, stolen spirits screamed from within the walls. I focused on the sound, searching for The Thief's echo residing in the core of the crystals. No matter how I searched, I couldn't steal the spirits from their prisons from this distance.

I would have to get closer.

The outpost's proximity to the Lost Forest made it a strategic stronghold for the Empire, also making it the perfect place to strike. No more raiding caravans. No more meaningless targets. If we meant to fight, we meant to do damage.

The pale-faced archer stretched the sleep from his bones. It was almost a cruel thing to take him unaware, but war left little quarter for compassion.

With a nod to Annit, I lifted my bow and nocked an arrow. The bowstring whined with tension as I pulled it back. The air smelled of morning—pine and wet grass. This gentle moment would shatter as soon as I released my arrow.

"No turning back," I said.

Annit's connection to The Flame roared to life, and the sharpened tip of the arrow began to smoke before it caught fire.

"Just loose the damn arrow already." Boda hadn't bothered to whisper, glaring at me with his healthy eye like he wished a stare could slit my throat.

"Follow the plan, and you'll get your fill of blood, little brother," I said.

"Don't. My brother is dead," he said. "Now loose the arrow."

The pull of the bow began to creep along my arm. "Mother, guide us."

As the flickering arrow reached the top of its arc in the purpled morning sky, archers on either side of me released their bowstrings as well.

The young soldier in the tower facing us clutched his chest beneath one of two arrows protruding from his body. His green cloth armor darkened around the wounds, then he stumbled back and toppled over the banister. The distant thud of his body finding the ground whispered through the silence.

A high, tight sound clanked arrhythmically from the eastern side of the outpost, then fell silent. Someone had missed their mark, and the element of surprise had vanished.

No plan ever went perfectly. Raids required improvisation, but for a first engagement, the plan had gone astray far earlier than I had hoped.

Boda launched into a run through the rough growth at the edge of the forest, and I chased after. *The fucking Mother,* I thought. Eager blood found quick death, as the saying went, and I had enough to worry about.

As the warriors I led rushed towards the tree wall, the muscle and tissue around my knee begged me to slow down. The arrow wound had healed as well as it would, but the pain didn't care. I refused it. I could never send my people where I wouldn't go first, no matter how much my scars strained against my gait.

Several echoes surged to life around the city. The cadence of Liara's connection to The River wove its way through the chaos.

Still forty paces from the tree wall, an explosion rang out from the north.

"Wal's early," Annit shouted from over my shoulder.

"Yelan, bring it down!" I yelled, and a shorter Sonacoan woman full of heft and muscle adjusted her stride.

Of course, we had meant to enter without announcing ourselves, but the alarm bell had changed all that.

As Yelan's body rotated, her arms extended like rays of the sun and her echo became a series of ever-quickening thuds beneath the ground.

The grass and soil tore apart in a cascading line, breaking the earth in twain. The split soil careened towards the tree wall, and the rest of us chased it.

A pair of ironoaks broke from the tree wall when the earth split beneath them. They crashed to the ground. Before they had time to settle, I climbed through the gap, and the others followed.

Our training had done enough to keep the lot of us from turning tail from a fouled-up plan. Now, I could only hope it would be enough to survive the day.

Through the smattering of buildings, a cluster of green-shirts stood in front of their church's doors, looking back and forth, pulling weapons from scabbards. I couldn't help but smile. There would have been a certain poetry to burning their holy building down around them, but it lacked the satisfaction of pressing a blade through the heavy, padded armor they liked to wear.

I ran at the front of a stampede of rebels rushing towards our vengeance. And somehow, the pale bastards turned a shade lighter when they saw us.

A priest, clad in his red robes, face veiled from sight, screamed for his soldiers to attack. They had the numbers, but we had come for blood owed.

To the west of the church, a torrent of wind streamed through the buildings. The Wind sang a hollow symphony. Thatching ripped from roofs. Window shutters tore from buildings. Then the wall of compressed air slammed into the disarrayed soldiers, throwing them to the dirt at the foot of their god's house.

A soldier turned to run. "Annit," I called out.

His echo flared and fire crawled along the dirt, creating a barrier, turning the soldier back.

The rebel group from the north clashed with the soldiers first. Metal clanged and people roared their rage into the morning.

The priest grasped a tawny crystal hanging from his neck, and the stolen shard of The Mountain shook the earth for a moment. The small thread tying the spirit to The Mist—the realm of spirits—wavered in the air like spider's silk in the wind.

I clutched it, and the ground stilled.

Stolen spirits would not be turned against us. I would not allow it. Instead, The Mountain raged at me from within, and I met her fury with my own.

When our band collided with the soldiers, Boda dropped his shoulder and crashed into the Gousht woman in front of him.

Annit batted away a sword meant for me, and I angled around him to plunge my knife into the soldier's thigh. The green bastard's eyes went wide before he screamed, then I cut his sound short with my sword.

Stolen spirits sprang up all over the town square that had become a battlefield. The elements formed a chorus of discord—spirits forced to move against their people. Shadows rushed from nearby buildings and began to block the light from the First Daughter.

One by one, I collected the abducted spirits. They thrashed and ripped at my flesh from the inside. No matter how many times their torment turned on me, the pain never lessened. However, one could practice pain, sit and languish in it like old company.

The shadows receded, and I fell to my knees with the weight of the spirits.

Annit engaged two soldiers charging towards me, but a third, a young Tomakan man wearing the invaders' colors, pushed through a gap in the carnage. His red-brown skin separated him from the other soldiers, just as his garb separated him from us.

He overreached when he drew back his poleaxe, which gave me the time I needed to catch the heavy blow with both of my blades. While my spirit struggled to rein in the pain, my body had to keep moving.

In his face, I saw my family. Loose strands of gray hair fell from beneath his helm. He withdrew, and then lunged with the spear mounted to the top of his weapon.

I deflected the strike, but not quickly enough. As the blade ricocheted off my sword, the spear tip dug into my thigh.

A searing red pain exploded out from the wound.

Either the collection of angry spirits fighting their way from my flesh or my kinship with my attacker had slowed my reaction. He pushed his weight behind his weapon, and I screamed.

"No heart for a thief," he said. Even after betraying us to the Gousht, this blood banner pulled the same tired line from our stories.

I dropped the hilt of my sword, grabbed the shaft of his weapon, and held it firmly in place. "No pity for a blood banner."

Pain jolted from the wound and he tried to yank his weapon from my thigh. If I gave in to the pain, I would be dead. The wooden shaft of the poleaxe scraped against my callused hand, but I held firm.

He wore the same disgusted look all the Gousht did when they fought us. It didn't ease as I plunged my father's knife into his gut. Blood spurted as I twisted the blade, then pulled it free from his wound.

The tension on his poleaxe disappeared. The blood banner stumbled backwards, holding his bloody gut before collapsing to the ground.

I watched his chest rise and fall for longer than I should have in the middle of a battle. His strained breaths slowed until they stopped altogether. As the scowl on his face softened, his deep brown eyes stared into the dawn sky.

He and I had probably grown up sitting on the same rough benches in a Gousht church being told the same lies about our people. The green bastards must have stolen him from his home at some point before dressing him in their colors after they broke him.

When I looked up, the fighting had ended. Bodies littered the front steps of the church. The priest and a handful of his soldiers held their hands aloft with their backs against the doors.

Annit knelt in front of me. "Breathe out," he said, then he pulled the blade from my thigh as I did.

Even as the wound throbbed, it settled behind the pain of the spirits caged within me. I allowed their agony to flood my body as Annit tied off the wound with a length of cloth.

"Always the same fucking leg," I said.

"You really should be more careful." He smiled, but there was no playfulness in his tone.

"Thank you for the advice. Now, help me up."

Annit had to slouch in order for me to wrap my arm around his shoulder. The bodies made my journey to the church more difficult. As we weaved through bloody gaps between the dead, some few Enneans lay amongst them. An older northwoman who had lost her whole family to the invasion rested flat on her back with a Gousht blade pinning her to the dirt.

She had insisted on fighting. Her spirit had earned its rest.

"May The Mother hold you well," I whispered as I walked by her, careful to not disturb her body.

Wal rushed to my side as soon as he saw me and took his place under my other arm. "Why do you insist on putting yourself in harm's way? It's not like you're that great of a sword fighter."

"Your words are comforting as always, my friend."

He turned towards the remaining soldiers. "Even the last few breaths they steal of Ennean air are too much."

"I have my questions, then you have your blood," I said, though most of his chest and arms had already been colored red.

Every one of our remaining warriors followed our final steps to the base of the church stairs. Liara stood with those guarding our new captives. She slid her sword into her scabbard as we approached. 'Are you alright?"

Blood streaked across her chest and freckled her cheek. She held me in her gaze, and beside her concern there was tenderness. Without her, my rage would have taken me countless times.

I nodded. "You? Tomi?"

Pain weighed down her lips. "We're fine, but we lost seven."

"I would have a word with their holy man," I said, pulling my weight from Annit's and Wal's shoulders.

Talise and a Sonacoan woman with close-cropped red curls dragged the priest down the stairs. He struggled to get his feet under him, but they never gave him a chance to hold his own weight. Then, without ceremony, they released his arms, and the priest tumbled to his knees in front of me.

This man, for all his adornment, didn't carry the commanding presence of The Priest I hunted. *"The One curse you, you konki shit,"* he said in Gousht.

"She already has." I grabbed the base of his veil around his neck and ripped the fabric loose.

Under his facade, this priest looked weak, blinking away the light. His chin flowed into his neck without division. The mess of silvery-white hair on the top of his head fell into his eyes. He didn't have a scar to show for his several decades in The Waking.

"The priest called Kyernan Janome, where is he?" As I stared down into the priest's ice-blue eyes, his fear looked back at me. *"Tell me or you won't be dead before we start your funeral pyre."*

His non-existent chin shivered and water filled his eyes. *"So, you're his little thief?"*

I lifted my knife to his cheek, just beneath his eye. *"Where?"*

The priest set his jaw in defiance, though his body trembled.

"I'll leave you a moment to contemplate your answers." I pointed to the nearest soldier. *"Show me where you keep our stolen spirits."*

Refusing to break eye contact, the soldier stepped forward. A smear of blood broke the line of his jaw where he had been cut. This man had been more than a simple guard, and he wore the evidence on his padded armor—aged blood stains, patched cuts, tarnished colors.

As he made his way to the shack where the crystals resided, the spirits sang to me from behind the ironoak planks. The soldier's guidance was unnecessary, but he would serve another purpose.

"Open it."

After turns giving orders to Enneans and putting us to the blade, he delayed for a moment—a small defiance. Symbolic resistance could safeguard one's spirit, but it could only last so long. Enneans knew this far too well.

He turned and lifted the latch. The ironoak door swung open to a bare shed with burlap sacks of spirit crystals lining the far wall. A layer of hay covered the floor.

No matter how many moons passed, the echoes of trapped spirits only served to remind me of the connection I lost to The Seed and The Song. The derivative version mocked me with a promise that one of these trapped spirits could be my fragment of The Seed. But that was a false promise. The Priest had added my spirit to his personal collection.

In another pointless attempt, I reached out to the underlying melody of The Thief beneath the enraged spirits. I could hear it, but regardless of how I strained, I couldn't shatter the crystals. Ten paces were more than enough to stop me.

"Take what you want, konki thief."

"Thief, huh? You think I'm stupid, don't you?" I asked.

"No." His stoic face twisted into a question.

"No, you must. You think that we raided your outpost without knowing exactly where you kept these crystals, without studying you and your fellow soldiers," I said. *"No. We have been watching."*

The soldier's eyes widened, and he reached to his side for a sword that was no longer there.

My wound screamed as I leaned forward and shoved him through the threshold of the shack. He reached out to grab ahold of me, of anything, but found his hands empty. The floor cracked beneath his weight. Loose sticks and hay scattered into the air, revealing a false floor. The soldier's pride broke, then his whining scream stopped with a wet crunch as the wooden spikes at the bottom of the pit pierced his body several times over.

Our scouts had done well. The Gousht liked their little traps.

The surrendered soldiers and the priest remained on the steps of their church, powerless.

"Jolrin and Acta, please gather the crystals in front of the church steps for me." Two of the younger warriors liberated from Oakheart moved to their task.

"Now, priest, you have had your moment to contemplate." I walked back towards the red-robed old man, doing my best to not let my pain show. *"Where is Janome?"*

"He will kill you. He will cleanse this land in the name of the—"

"NO! No, I am in no mood for sermons." I leaned in for only the priest to hear me. *"It wasn't your god who brought you to Oakheart. The Thief whispered in your brethren's ears, and twisted you about to her own devices. Your god never could have done this."*

As Jolrin and Acta laid the bags of crystals at my feet, Jolrin took a moment to smile their venom at the old priest before stepping back. They had waited for this moment through their long seasons of imprisonment. I would not begrudge them a moment to revel in it.

"Let me show you." I lowered my voice so the priest was forced to lean in.

Finally, with my hands on the crystals, the small melody of The Thief's song hummed beneath the torment of the stolen spirits. That gentle undertone of betrayal didn't screech in anguish. She had given pieces of herself to each of the stones. Those pieces were never prisoners; they were the guards.

I gathered the threads of The Thief, which bound her to the stones, and pulled.

The sacks shrunk into themselves, and whispers of color drifted into the air with each spirit released. I picked up a single sack and turned it over in front of the priest and his men. Grains of sand streamed from the bag into a pile on the ground.

As if I challenged their god himself, their expressions elongated with shock.

"You do not have the power here, priest. Now, where is Janome?"

The priest continued to look down at the pile of debris. When he did not answer, I grabbed his face and turned him toward one of his men. "Talise."

Without hesitation, Talise drew her axe blade slowly across the soldier's neck. Blood sprayed from the wound and streamed down his chest.

"You'll kill us all." The priest's voice came out as a whine.

"Yes, but I haven't decided how," I said. *"Where is he?"*

"May The One True God forgive me." His shivering consumed his entire body. *"I don't know."*

"Strangely, I believe you." I took my father's knife from my belt and jammed it beneath the priest's ribs into his heart.

The priest collapsed to the ground at my feet. "Find the enslaved, lock these fucks in their church, and give them their funeral pyre."

The fires had finished consuming the Gousht and their church hours ago, yet the acrid smell of burning bodies hung in the air around the city. Say nothing else for their barbaric death rituals, they were efficient—and they saved The Mother the hassle of sorting their flesh.

Far from where we buried our dead, on the outskirts of the outpost, I knelt beside the body of the blood banner I had killed. The thread binding the Emperor's seal to his padded armor gave way to my knife, revealing a clean patch of green amidst the soiled and bloodied fabric.

The rest of our tiny militia had settled down for the evening, but I hadn't the heart to throw a Tomakan body into the flames no matter the decisions he had made on this side of The Mist.

More and more, our people traded in their robes for green tunics and padded armor, but I had never sent an Ennean to the other side with my own blade. His gray hair lay loosely against the grass.

Liara's echo approached me before she did. She stopped beside me while I hovered over the man I had killed. "Are you okay?"

"My leg will heal, again. Wal helped me stitch the wound. He has surprisingly nimble fingers."

"That's not what I meant." She placed a hand on my shoulder.

"He chose to wear their colors," I said, even as I rested a hand on the dead man's chest. "He picked them."

She dropped to her knees between me and the grave I had dug. "This war has forced us all to make hard choices, Kaylo. And I know you have to make ugly ones—I just don't want to lose you along the way."

"I never wanted to be a warrior. I never wanted any of this."

Her fingers swept over the nape of my neck as she pulled me into her arms. She felt soft and safe. "You are what you have to be. Let me be there to protect you along the way."

When the warmth of lips pressed against my neck, I gave up fighting my tears. I clung to her robes and pulled her tightly to my chest. "Don't die," I whispered. "Please. Stay with me."

Chapter Three
Kaylo's Story

As our small raiding party filed through the entrance to our
encampment, I lingered behind. The cluster of tents looked like a
smaller, grayer version of the Jani's tent city. Function ruled every choice.
Without a true forest dancer amongst us, we lined the perimeter of
the small village with nets laced with scraps of plant life. Sparse leather
canopies hung from the trees for protection from the elements with
gardens of simple crops running between them. And yet, as pitiful as the
comparison might have been, it made me ache for the Fallen Rock Clan.

Liara had once commented that the Jani built their encampments to
live as good a life as they could. This encampment existed purely for
survival.

Those who had stayed behind rushed out to greet the returning
warriors. A young woman yelped as she embraced Acta, an eager young
warrior.

Even though Acta stood only a turn my junior, the fool followed me
about as if I were his kana. He asked for advice, and it took my all not to
tell him to find someone wiser to ask.

The woman hugging him, on the other hand, glared at me.

Not all shared Acta's excitement for our rebellion. And that number
would only grow after they counted the missing warriors.

I watched the joy of the crowd temper in waves as people realized the consequences of resisting the Gousht. The seven who hadn't returned had names. They had survived the horrors of Oakheart beside the others.

Even as I claimed the enemy's blood, my debt grew larger.

While the others celebrated and mourned, a single figure broke with the crowd. Hylīane steadied each step with her walking stick as she approached. The turns had not reached her face, but they reduced the black in her curls to streaks amongst a field of gray and white.

"Ta hero returns," she said in her slight Renēquan accent.

"Can't I have a moment to breathe before you begin your lectures?"

"By my count, tere are several who no lonner have tha option."

Where others grimaced or furrowed their brows, Hylīane wore her anger softly. Her eyes narrowed in a small warning, but the rest of her face held still.

"We mourn for them. We pray for their spirits. But no one is greater than what we are trying to do."

"Ta greatness of one cannot be measured," she said. "Cha young ones take too much time ta learn tat."

"Our people are dying!" My control abandoned me, and my voice carried farther than necessary. "There is no outlasting the Gousht. There is no survival without fighting. We are out there trying to save our people!"

"Cha go out tere ta quench cha bloodtirst. Don't lie ta me like cha lie ta chaself."

"What exactly are you implying?" I stepped closer, and the distance between us vanished.

The blackness of her irises held me as she tilted her head to meet my eyes. "Be careful, or tey will see cha for what cha are—a young boy looking ta make the world hurt as much as he does. Tese people need ta heal from their trauma, not ta wield it like a weapon. Cha need the same too, my boy."

A heavy hand clapped on my back. "There is much to discuss in council," Annit said. "Hylíane, can't you see the boy needs a fresh bandage?"

A patch of my robes had shifted into a dark brownish-red hue over my wound.

"Why don't you gather the council? We will report once Kaylo has stopped leaking." Annit's way spoke much about his approach to battle; the warrior angled around the sharp edges of the conversation and slithered his blade towards the heart of it.

Hylíane held his gaze for a moment before tipping her head and walking off towards the larger gathering.

"Is she right, Annit?"

"Yes, but you aren't wrong," he said as he turned me towards the tent where we kept what little healing supplies we had. "If there were right answers in war, the decisions would be far easier."

Under the canopy, I rummaged through our stores for a bit of moonlight hazel and barberries. Dried ingredients didn't work half as well as the fresh ones, but we made do.

I had taken every step The Seed walked with me for granted. No amount of searching for The Song or crossing into The Mist could bring back our connection. If I could only see him again, speak with him, apologize for letting The Priest take him away. But there was only one way to restore our connection.

As I thought about The Priest, I gripped the pestle harder than necessary, grinding the dried bark, berries, and leaves into a fine powder.

"What would you have done differently?" Annit asked, while ripping a new length of fabric from an old set of robes.

"Maybe if they had more training, the archers along the north wall wouldn't have missed their mark."

"Nah, I asked what *you* would have done differently." He sat down in front of me, lifted my pant leg, and began unraveling the old bandage. "There will always be mistakes, and you can't carry the weight of every arrow that flies wide."

The raid unraveled like my bandaging, full of holes and just as bloody. After two full span of scouting the outpost, we knew their routine and the small ways it wandered from its path. The council, at least those who didn't fully object to the raid, constructed a plan that gave our warriors the best chance—and it fell apart before we reached the wall.

"If we didn't push through the mistake, we wouldn't have had another opportunity. They would have raised their defenses and adjusted routines to prepare for a second attempt."

"Go on."

"All three breaching forces made it through in their own way; none of them would have turned from the fight. Wal because...he's Wal. And Talise and Liara know better than to turn back without the signal."

"What about during the fighting?" Annit asked.

"We fought well. Our advantage diminished when the alarm sounded, but the soldiers weren't prepared for us even with the warning."

"Seven died."

"How could I have stopped that? The soldiers had the numbers. I stole their spirits, but they still had iron and steel. What could I have done?"

Tali and Unet had left behind younger siblings in the encampment. After everything that they had been through in the mines, Dasjoni and Pem found each other, only to be torn apart by the raid. Our numbers were small enough that I knew the ways each of the dead belonged to those still breathing.

As I bowed my head to weep for them, Annit lifted my chin. "Nothing. You cannot control death, no matter how much you want to. We pray for the dead, we care for the living, and we move forward."

"Why is all of this on me? I don't want this."

"You have people standing with you, but the survivors of Oakheart look to you because of what you can do. You give them hope in a way no one else can."

"You could," I said. "If there is anyone here who understands how to fight this war, it's you."

"I had my chance, and I failed." He drew back and went quiet.

The sullenness he kept so close behind his smile reminded me of Jonac. There had been a different man before the Gousht clamped chains on his wrists. He rose to the surface when Annit forgot his control.

"Whatever future we have in front of us can't be worn down by the burdens of the past," he said. "Our people revere elders for good reason, but sometimes the next generation needs to decide their future themselves."

As he cleaned and dressed my wound, the weight of our losses dulled the sting in my leg. Small flashes of pain cut through long enough to make themselves known, but they paled beside the bright scars on my spirit.

"What did it feel like to hear The Flame after so many turns?" I asked.

His hands stopped halfway through wrapping my wound. "When someone dies, the way they felt, looked, sounded—all fades away with time. Most memories hold onto the barest sliver of them. Then you find a particular memory in your cluttered mind and it brings them back, and for a moment, you can smell the way their hair held the morning wind. That's what it felt like."

"Why don't you speak in clear answers?"

"Don't ask complicated questions if you don't want complicated answers." He cinched the bandage tight and the pain flared. "We need to get to the council. Remember what we discussed. This wasn't your fault, but it is your responsibility."

Outside, the commotion regarding our return had settled—or rather relocated under the largest tent in the encampment.

The meeting hadn't started, and yet, voices flew through the air sharper than a hail of arrows. The tenor of the jumbled noise made me question the wisdom of joining the gathering.

The few of us who sat on the council worked out the logistics, but the decisions were not ours alone. There were always people to convince.

Annit slowed me with a hand on my shoulder. "None of them are your enemies. They are all your people, and their opinions have value."

"Even Hylīane's?"

He smiled. "Sometimes the most important voices are the ones that disagree with us."

"Just once it would be nice if you would recognize that she can be an asshole."

"I never said she was pleasant," he said. "Now, get in there."

The crowd barely fit into the confines of the tent, but the constrained space didn't keep the council from fighting. Hylīane's walking stick angled up at Wal as he yelled about how she betrayed the dead with her words.

"Don't cha dare!" She waved her walking stick like an untrained sword. "Cha tink cha know loss cause cha buried a few friends along ta way. My whole village died between ta war and ta occupation. My grandchildren didn't understan why all ta buildings caught fire, and tey didn't make it out either."

"Then fight for them," Wal said.

"Stop," Liara said as she stepped between Wal and Hylīane. "This isn't helping. We have to stop blaming each other for the Gousht's actions."

"Have cha learned nothing of cha history? Young folk need ta respect cha elders."

Small conversations moved about the crowd even as they fought, but eyes turned as Annit made his way through the tight spaces towards the center of the tent.

"Is this how you would mourn the dead, Hylīane? Belittle all they fought for?" His tone found notes of compassion amidst the anger in the tent.

"That's what I said," Wal said.

"Boy, don't get me started on the wrong you carry with you," Annit said. "The Gousht are the enemy. If you treat your own people like that, what will we have when they're gone?"

People made as much room as they could for me as I worked my way to the center of the tent. The heat of too many bodies in such a small space and the intensity of their stares unnerved me, but I tried to hold on to Annit's words. *We pray for the dead, we care for the living, and we move forward.*

"Yelan," I called into the inner circle lining the commotion, and found the static face of the Sonacoan earth dancer. "Could you lead us in a prayer for those who passed into The Mist?"

In the turn that had passed, a small crown of coarse red curls had begun to shape around Yelan's head, which made the darkness of her skin glow. She simply nodded, not being one for casual expressions.

"Blessed Mother." Her voice sank into her lower register, carrying the timbre of a song. "Yesterday, seven of our family left this plane to join your spirits. They fell fighting a war that was sprung upon them, and yet, for all its injustice, they met the call."

Autumn winds rustling the canopy only served to emphasize the quiet. Wal and Hylïane had both made their way to their knees out of respect for the prayer.

"Tali, Unet, Pem, Yasier, Shonti, Alēm, and Cirila are your children, our family, and kin to this land. Guide them home. Hold them close. Keep them, for we shall meet them once more."

Gentle sobs interrupted the silence that fell as everyone touched three fingers to their lips and brought them to the ground. A child's cries tore through the rest, and an older Tomakan woman guided Unet's little sister from the tent.

I allowed grief the moment it needed before speaking. Trying to conquer grief like a battlefield would only end up with us turning our blades on each other.

"All of us grieve those who were spirited on, and the ways we react to that grief do not make our pain more or less valid," I said. "Thank you, Yelan."

"Tis a nice gesture, but tere is a reason tose young people are dead," Hylïane said.

"Yes, there is." I rose to my feet and took the center of the crowd as everyone else remained on the ground. "The Gousht are the reason for our grief."

"And who led them to ta Gousht?" Hylíane pushed herself to her feet with the help of her walking stick.

"Disagree with me all you want. You are a member of this clan and the council, which gives you every right to your voice. You are an elder, and I respect your wisdom, but that does not mean I agree with it. And neither did the warriors who died fighting for what they believed in.

"Yesterday, we managed to take away a Gousht outpost and liberate three more Enneans from their bindings. And for that, we lost people." I turned to the crowd rather than Hylíane. "If we continue this path, we will continue to lose people, but I believe that we will lose each other in other ways if we don't. Every Ennean living under occupation is suffering, and you may not believe we can end that, but I do."

"Cha can say pretty words, but cha are after blood, not freedom." She dug her walking stick into the swept dirt with every step as she closed the gap between us. "Tell me cha aren't off chasin cha priest and cha missing spirit."

"The last time I did that, I got a lot of people killed." I found Boda, his one-eyed glare aimed at me as I spoke, which I had expected. However, I hadn't expected to find Talise looking at me with a reflection of the same anger. "The Priest owes blood, and I will take it given the chance, but I am not going to risk anyone else over him."

"Fuck that." Boda stood up as he shouted. "The Gousht owe blood. Why should any of us apologize for taking it?"

"I hate to say it, but the little shit is right," Wal said.

"Fuck off," Boda said.

"What? I'm agreeing with you."

"Shut up both of you," Tomi said in her typical flat tone.

"No, this is ridiculous," Wal said. "The council agreed to fight back against the Gousht. People are going to die. It's going to be sad, but that's the tragedy of war. While the couta still occupy this land—while they still breathe—it's our duty to put them down."

Back and forth they went, as I stepped back to the edges of the inner circle. A couple of the other survivors of Oakheart advised caution. Annit tried to bring the conversation to shared interests. All the while, grief and anger swirled around the tent like a storm picking up speed.

"We destroyed one outpost," Talise said. "We need to do that again and again until they have nowhere left to hide."

"We lost seven in a single day. How long do you think we can continue before no one is left?" Yelan asked without the emotion straining her voice like all the others.

"She's right," Liara said. "We need a better way."

"We have a better way, right, Kaylo?" Wal asked. "There's another mine in Renéqua. We liberated one, we can do it again."

"That might work if the spirit thief could actually use his gift," Boda said.

These people weren't an army. They weren't a clan or a family either. The cruelty of some pale fucks from across the ocean had driven them together in a clash of pain, trauma, and grief. Each one of them responded out of a base instinct for survival or vengeance.

How can I bring these people together? I thought. *The kid's right. I can't even rely on the cursed gift that gave me the slightest claim to authority in the first place.*

Side conversations built around the tent until the noise consumed my thoughts. The louder they got, the more tenuous the ties that bound us became.

I was not the right person to lead anyone, but too many of my families had crumbled around me. It wouldn't happen again.

With a nod to signal Annit, the fire dancer's echo crested into an ever-quickening series of staccato bells, ending in three flashes of fire in the center of the tent.

Everyone turned towards the light in various stages of shock. "Wal, they're right. We can't go to the mines in the Renéquan foothills. And we can't continue to target outposts. We don't have the numbers," I said. "But we can't stand back and do nothing."

"Then what do cha propose, hero?" Hylïane asked.

Words failed me as I opened my mouth to speak. I was no strategist. What I knew of war I had learned trying to survive it. Then I remember my history. My mother would have cuffed the back of my head for forgetting her stories.

"The only advantage Enneans had ever had in this fight was our numbers, and that was before they scattered our people," I said. "Between here and Colian, there are half a dozen occupied villages or mission schools. We free them. We remind the Gousht that there are more of us. Then we take back our city—Colian."

"Cha wanna take back the most occupied city in all Tomak? Cha wanna take their port? Tey ain't goin let cha do tat."

"That's why we take our time and build an army."

"Cha are goin ta get us all killed." Hylïane waved her walking stick about, pointing at me and the rest of us who had served the Missing.

"We decided to start an uprising, and I appreciate your concerns, but we can't simply hide and wait for the world to change," I said. "Everyone should take the day, then we can decide our path forward tomorrow."

The conversation was quelled, and the crowd scattered. But that wasn't the end of it. Different versions of the same debate continued around cookfires throughout the encampment. If anything, the gathering had only stoked the embers of contention within our would-be clan.

Hylïane waited for the majority of the crowd to fade away before she approached me. "Do cha know why I stayed behind after we left ta mines? I saw a bunch of angry young people ready ta die and ta fools who would follow tem. Cha can't liberate anyone from Ta Mist."

"You are afraid, and you're trying to make other people afraid with you so you won't be alone."

"Thief." She spat on the ground and walked away.

I watched her leave. She had been right about one thing: an army of liberated Enneans would lead me to The Priest. I hadn't been lying when I said I wouldn't sacrifice the others to kill him. But I would find my chance. Blood was owed, and I would claim it.

Chapter Four
Current Day Ennea

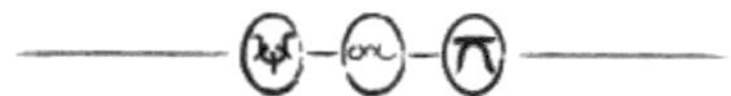

The particular nature of the darkness surrounding Kaylo existed in layers. The first was the most common and the layer upon which the others were painted: an absence of light, not so different from a moonless night. If not for the others, it would have been an insignificant thing.

The second, however, shifted back and forth over the first like shadows moving according to a flame that was not there. Black wisps caressed the still darkness, giving depth to the absence—making the absence a statement of possibilities that went unrealized. So much could have taken up space here that didn't.

Any spirit foolish enough to enter this realm could have noticed the first two layers of darkness. They did not hide, not like the third.

Over the turns, this final layer of darkness had grown out of balance. The ever-present hunger that consumed any light had begun to feast on the darkness as well. It pulled on the part of Kaylo that originated from this place, as if it would feed on the piece of him that belonged to her if it could.

The Mist was, and always had been, a realm of infinite possibilities, projecting a world according to the design of the spirits who inhabited it. That sliver of The Balance living inside Kaylo understood the need for darkness, even if he hadn't the words to express it. In a way, The Balance hid within these three layers just as Kaylo had hidden in his hallow for those many turns.

"Ahh, not so little anymore, little thief." The Balance's voice faded in and out of the surroundings, as if the sound was searching for new ways to approach him. "I seem to remember you promising never to return. We aren't breaking our word now, are we?"

All the pieces of his spirit that didn't belong here urged Kaylo to run, to escape through the endless darkness back into the body he had left behind.

"What does it matter to you?" Kaylo rotated as he spoke, addressing the entirety of his surroundings. "Whether I visit this place or not, you are always with me—our spirits tied together."

Movement stirred the shifting darkness to one side as her voice emanated from the other. "Something is different about you. Not just the turns. No, you've forgotten to hide from yourself," she said. "Oh, that boy used to shake like a flame in the wind when he visited me. Not easy denying yourself when you are looking into your reflection, is it?"

"Seems only one of us is hiding now."

A chill crawled across Kaylo's skin even though he had left his body in The Waking. Shadows made of the slightest variations of black burst to life in front of him, forming The Balance's cloak. Under the hood, a cavernous darkness separated him from her face.

"Hiding?! I haven't left this place. If you wanted to find me, you knew where I would be," she said, and her voice slicked over the words like poison.

"I didn't come here for old fights."

"Then why come at all? We haven't much to talk about, Hero of Anilace. The old questions have the same answers...oh, no. I see. You came because of the girl."

An image of Tayen solidified in his mind, the young girl sitting across the firepit from him with a length of wood in her hand. As she drew her blade through the wood, she bit her lower lip and furrowed her brow.

Rogue braids fell in front of her face, casting shadows on her warm ochre skin. Her hands were almost gripping the wood correctly.

You know what happens when you care about them, The Balance's voice whispered in his mind.

"What has your violence given you?" The patience left his tone as he spoke. "Truly, did your manipulations work?"

"Watch your step, thiefling. I may decide to keep you."

"Tayen deserves a life beyond the mess we created, and you could give that to her—and so many others."

"What about your kin? All I did was balance the scales, but your people never looked to my descendants for anything save a scapegoat. Spirit dancers could have won the day time and time again, yet Enneans let their prejudices guide them. Even as the war dragged on, they exiled and abused your marked brethren.

"I was there when your pet killed Pana. She stuck him and left him to bleed out on the stone floor. He died afraid."

As the hooded spirit spoke, she projected a vision of the dying boy into Kaylo's thoughts. He whimpered with each shallow breath. Blood mixed with waste leaking from the wounds on either side of his body, even as the spear remained part of him. Too many breaths passed, growing softer. The distance between the strained gasps stretched.

"He suffered," she said, as if it weren't apparent. "Your little shade left him all his pain."

"She had to save herself and Sosun. He didn't leave her any other choice." Even as he defended Tayen, his words didn't have enough air to give them proper strength.

"Then you'll understand that I have to protect mine. You could help me change the stories, but you won't. As long as Enneans look at you like a hero, you'll never know what it's like to be their villain."

"There are other ways to find balance."

"Then find them, Hero." She receded into the surrounding layers of darkness, and the black grew hungrier. "But you won't find them here."

———

Moonlight washed down on the trees that formed their hastily made hallow. Stray limbs and leaves interrupted the light, casting shadows. These shadows didn't pull at Kaylo's spirit, but the foreboding hunger he had felt in The Mist lingered on.

Ironically, the rough push and pull of sleeping noises settled him into The Waking.

Beside the fire, Tayen's hands danced, and her echo kept pace with their movements. The hum of a gentle summer fit into the interplay between her gestures and her song.

A cluster of ill-placed shadows remained still against the flickering firelight, then slowly they took shape. The densest shadow amongst them thinned as it stretched into an oval. One after another, the dark shapes shifted and found their places amongst the rest.

Kaylo's back ached with a sharp pain that begged him to move, but he didn't want to interrupt Tayen's dance.

The layers of thinned darkness created depth atop what had been a simple oblong shape. A shadow that she had pulled from under a stone grew darker, becoming a pair of lines arched in a brow. Slips of shade contoured the lines of a face on the dark canvas.

When the tendrils draped over the curve of the forehead, the portrait settled into a girl who could have been Tayen.

"When Sokan rises, it will mark what should have been her thirteenth turn," Tayen said, still looking at the portrait. Then she met his eyes. "You were rocking back and forth in your sleep. When you stopped, I assumed you had woken up."

"When did you become an artist?"

Her hands continued to move in order to urge the shadows to remain in place rather than rush back to where they belonged. "It's not too different from whittling. Instead of stripping away pieces little by little, you build them up. I needed to do something to pass the hours on watch."

"She's beautiful."

"She was an annoying little brat who never wanted to leave me alone, but she had moments when her energy swirled about like fireflies," Tayen said. "She didn't deserve to die like she did."

"No, she didn't."

Gently at first, then in a sudden rush, the dozens of small shadows broke away in every direction.

"Were you mistwalking?"

For a person who had spent so much time hiding from everyone, the people around him figured him out far too easily.

"You don't usually move when you're asleep, then you mumbled something about finding balance," she said. "So, you were, weren't you?"

"It's been a long time. Then again, it's been a long time since I decided to head towards the fighting, so I figured I would try to reach her."

"And she's changed her mind completely? She's decided to destroy the spirit crystals?"

The laugh tumbled out of him louder than he expected it to, then he covered his mouth and paused in case he had woken the others. "Not exactly, little shade. She's more bitter than I remember."

Even when he first mistwalked, The Balance had always carried an edge, but beyond the harshness, there had been a hope. A piece of her had believed that her descendants would find a way to fix the stories by creating new ones. As misplaced and silly as her hope had been, without it she had become something smaller and crueler.

"You should teach me."

"What? No, absolutely not."

"In the Citadel, The Shadow helped me find a path forward," Tayen said. "She's the spirit of wisdom, right? Don't you think we could use some wisdom?"

"Two of the wisest people I have ever known warned me about the dangers of The Mist."

"And yet, you still go there." The volume of her echo swelled, but she held it back. "I'm not asking for permission. I am asking for help."

Over the past turn, Tayen's fire had waned and flared. It ran in parallel with her emotions, and she allowed it to burn as it would. Here and now, she stoked it enough to feed the flames, but controlled the heat of it.

Despite the little wisdom he had earned with time, an ache crept into his chest as he said a quite goodbye to her wildness.

"Don't get old too fast," he said.

"What?"

"I'll teach you, whatever that means," he said, shaking his head. Nix and her fucking wise words about protecting their freedom strolled through his head. "The only reason I didn't lose myself in The Mist was luck, pure stupid luck. You are going to be smarter about it."

"Okay, where do we start?"

"Blessed Mother, I don't know." He chuckled to himself. "You need to give me a minute to think before I start teaching you how to allow your spirit to cross over into The Mist.

"Go get some rest. I'll take the next watch and think on it." With hands on either side of his head, he twisted to one side and the other until his neck popped.

"Just think of how bored you'd be if you never came across me."

"I think about it every day, little shade. Sleep well."

Nix translated as Sosun's hands flowed between gestures with a grace none of them had mastered. "Now that the old geezer has shared another depressing story, when are we going to search for the Uprising?"

"That's not what she said, Nix." Kaylo tore through the steamed fish, prying the meat from bone.

"You need to stop teaching them to sign," Nix said as she signed.

"You're taking away one of my only joys."

Kaylo tapped four fingers on his heart twice. "Joys, not enjoy," he said as he swept two fingers in a swirl over his heart.

"No, fuck that." She turned to Sosun and continued to sign. "Tell him he's wrong."

"Sorry, this time, Kaylo's right. Joy. Enjoy," she signed with a wide smile.

"I hate you all," Nix said before turning back to her fish, which, despite wanting to hate it, she found quite delicious. Kaylo had managed to char the skin, and the meat took on a heavy smoke that went perfectly with the sweet potatoes he had baked in the coals of the pit.

"How about we get back to the question, geezer?" Tayen said, but she hit the word geezer with the wrong emphasis and turned the slight jab into a harsher insult.

"Nix has plenty of great skills to teach you," Kaylo said. "You don't have to learn to be an asshole."

"It's not about having to. It's about finding joy in life." Nix signed 'joy' with extra emphasis.

"Seriously, is someone going to tell me the plan or are you all going to banter about like there isn't a war going on?" Sosun signed.

Despite the relative quiet of Sosun's words, they reverberated throughout the small hallow. Smiles slid off Kaylo's and Tayen's faces.

The young woman, who had grown up from the little girl Nix failed all those turns ago, sat in front of them demanding to charge into war. Sosun was not a fighter. For all her wonderful talents, war would not make good use of her. It would consume her like so many others before her, and yet Nix had agreed to take her towards the fighting.

"I did not mean to make light of your question," Kaylo signed like a child, each haphazard gesture bumping into the next. *"If the—* Damn, how do you say 'Uprising'?"

Sosun didn't hesitate. She balled her fists at waist level and brought her knuckles together.

"Thank you," he signed. *"If the Uprising keep to their ways, they will be watching the lodestones."*

"Really?" Nix said. The lodestones were relics of the Hundred Turn War. The only people who took them seriously were storytellers and pacifists.

"We found poetry in using the stones that helped end a war to start a new war," Kaylo said as he continued to sign. "The stones are meeting points for refugees or different regiments. Can you think of a better way to mark meeting points all over Ennea?"

"All we have to do is find a lodestone?" Tayen asked.

"Maybe. It's been more than thirteen turns, Tayen." Kaylo turned to Sosun. "But I promise you both, I will do whatever I can to bring you to the Uprising if that's what you want."

A strange weight settled over the hallow as it never had before. The anticipation of leaving some small semblance of safety and the knowledge of what waited on the other side of their journey compounded into a silence that filled the space between the trees.

When the meal was finished and they began to pack, Nix settled next to Sosun. *"You don't have to do this, you know? You don't have to run off searching for a fight you can't win."*

The scowl that Nix expected didn't come. Instead, Sosun offered her pity wrapped in a smile. *"You all think fighting against the Gousht is about how well one can wield a blade or dance with the spirits. You're missing the point."*

"What are you talking about?"

"Do you think that all the people living under occupation aren't fighting? Do you think that the Citadel servants aren't fighting?" she signed. *"Violence will never snuff out violence. We need to take care of each other, and build something that will survive the blood.*

"I'm not going to pick up a spear and charge into battle. I'm going to serve a cause with whatever I have to offer. Because I escaped, I owe it to those who didn't."

Nix's lecture about safeguarding Sosun's freedom had been complete shit. If she could find a way to promise the girl another two hundred turns in The Waking, she would, even if it meant stealing away a few choices.

"*You don't owe anyone,*" Nix signed.

"*No, I owe everyone. There was this older Sonacoan woman in the Citadel who took care of me when I failed the trials.*" Tears began to form in Sosun's eyes, but her mouth held a stern line. "*I was so angry, and she helped me understand that I still had value—that we still had value. I learned how to live as a part of something. Everything we could give to each other was given. That was how we survived.*

"*I forgot that for a while. I'm not going to forget it again.*"

Chapter Five

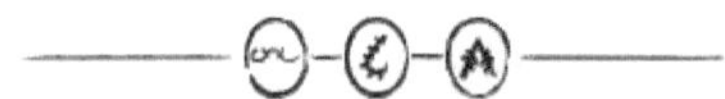

After the war there will be wounds
There will be dead lying on worshiped grounds
The stories will make prayer of their sacrifices
Outlasting their names
They will become a warning or a rallying call
But the stories will not remember the love that broke
The guilt of blood clinging to hands that did not want it
Reasons on top of reasons will fall from the mouths of storytellers
But time turns anger into a reason as quickly as any spirit

As Wal lay atop the least jagged section of his cell floor at the bottom of a fucking mountain, his fingers traced the silver scar running the length of his forearm. Unfortunately, Kaylo's shallow cuts hadn't torn Wal's spirit free of his flesh, which left him waiting for his execution in a cell next to a rambling poet.

If he had been any kind of friend, Kaylo could have at least used a dirty blade and let infection do the work he had been too much of a coward to finish.

"Can you believe Onikan wrote that only three span before he died?" Despite the wall of thick stone that separated them, Lanigan's voice filled the small chamber. "At least, that's what the stories say, and as he not-so-subtly points out, stories have a way of adjusting with the turning of time."

"Do you think I can have a moment of quiet before they kill me?" Wal asked as he sat up, various tendons and muscles clearly unhappy with his movement.

Without the Daughters to count the passing days, he had to guess how long he had resided in his new quarters. The infrequent meals were poor measures. However long it had been had given his flesh enough time to heal, even if the inactivity made his body ache with an age older than he had earned.

The chill of the stone siphoned what little heat he had left in him from the flats of his bare feet.

When earth dancers pulled the Citadel from the ground and hollowed out the mountain into a city, they found imperfect pockets within the rock. They could have smoothed them out as they had every other surface, but the king at the time decided to keep them as they were. All he needed to do was add thick stormwood doors, and he had himself a collection of cells scattered amongst the maze-like interior of the Citadel.

Light from a single oil lantern filtered through the barred window in the door.

Wal leaned his forehead against the stormwood. "Tell me, poet, why are you so fucking cheery? From what you told me, amongst the unnecessary litany of poetry, King Shonar is going to keep you here until the spirits drag you to the other side of The Mist."

Maybe it wasn't fair to remind the poet of their plight, but fair had died long before Wal had the turns to comprehend the concept. And niceties never brought anyone anything of value in this world.

"The size of the cell is only an aesthetic difference," they said, still with a lightness in their voice that didn't belong. "I have been a prisoner in this mountain for twenty-one turns and had to learn ways of living within myself. Though the food isn't quite as good under our current accommodations, I still have plenty of room in my head to escape."

"Don't feel obligated to share all that space with me. If you want, you can keep a few of those thoughts to yourself."

"Kaylo always spoke of you as a more jovial person."

The outer door to their pleasant little alcove screeched and cut Wal off before he could remind Lanigan what he thought about Kaylo. The door's hinges needed oil, but their wardens wouldn't waste a drop of spittle on them. If the sadistic fucks who jailed Wal knew how much the sound grated on the little bit of sanity he had managed to hold onto, they would have found a way to make it worse.

Footsteps reverberated off the stone walls, growing closer.

"Speaking of our lovely rations..." The poet stopped themselves midthought as their guest stepped through the mouth of the corridor into the lantern light.

General Tanis wore standard Astilean purple, but ornate fillagree decorated the shoulders and sides of her leather sannil. Tattoos filled both of her cheeks with the legacy of her kills and service. Absentmindedly, Wal reached up to his scarred cheeks where she had burned away his honor markings.

"They seem to be healing," she said, with a smirk curving her lips.

"You could have done cleaner work. It's all about symmetry."

"I'll keep that in mind," she said. "This is a sorry sight. Truthfully, I don't know who is worse—the King's shame or a commander turned traitor."

"What do you want, Tanis?" The playful melody in Lanigan's voice had vanished, leaving a cold, enunciated tone in its place.

"I stopped by your library this morning," she said, stepping closer. "You must miss it."

"Pages only carry words; they don't imprison them."

"Alright, as much as I enjoy this lovely exchange, can you simply tell us why you're here?" Wal asked. "I told you a hundred times by now, I don't know where Kaylo is or where he's going. He may be the only person I hate more than you. So you can kill me or leave me alone."

Tanis kept her hair cropped low, tight black curls hugging her scalp. Everything about her, from the fall of her robes against her pants to the consistency of the tattooed lines on her face, maintained order—always. So, when her smile broke wide and caught the lantern light in a moment of actual joy, the depths of Wal's troubles started to come to light.

"I choose neither, former commander Wal. You still have too much life in you. That quick tongue still dances around in your mouth like you think you're clever." She unsheathed her knife, the edge catching the light. "I could cut it out, but that would be too easy. No, I want you to break. I want your spirit to die before your body does, so when I release you to The Mist, what crosses the veil will be far from whole."

"Why do you hate me? Ever since I came here, you've always hated me."

"We're done with the quick wit?" Tanis positioned herself directly in front of the barred opening of Wal's cell door. "You don't know your place. You never believed in the great unification of Ennea. Astile was only ever a path to your personal vendetta, and in a warrior, that can be a useful trait. That anger can drive a warrior to great deeds, but even after you earned your markings, you still chased your vengeance. Astile doesn't need people like you, who place themselves above everything.

"Always a witty comment or an eye roll. Even now, you believe you're above this, but you earned this cell when you gave a man like Kaylo the means to escape. Six skilled warriors died because of your arrogance— nine including the archers he killed in the Lost Forest. You made us look weak at a time when we need the warriors who will fight for this nation to know our strength."

As the remnants of Tanis's voice finished reverberating off the stone, a silence fell over them. The weight of it set Wal's legs shaking. His guards had been his friends, and he led them into a battle that ended in their blood.

"How is Shiena?" Wal's question trembled as he spoke it.

"That's all you have to say for yourself? No denials? No regrets? You pained a nation—the last nation of Ennea—and still, only the people connected to you matter?"

"Tell me!" Wal's shout filled the chamber, and tears settled in the crooks of his eyes, ready to fall. "Tell me, please."

The door flew open behind Tanis and two guards with spears ran into the room.

Tanis waved them off, and they stepped back into the dark entryway. "Very well. After allowing the son of a governor to die, Shiena has been demoted. She'll watch the border and waste away like some new recruit in their first set of purples. Pana's mother may only be governor of a small, shit village on the northern coast, but Shiena is lucky she kept her head."

"Fuck you," Wal said through clenched teeth. "You have always looked down on outsiders. Whatever extra reasons you've come up with, you lived your whole life safe behind the Lost Forest. When you left, you were well-armed, accompanied by trained warriors following a carefully constructed plan. That doesn't make you better than us. It makes you lucky."

"Me being better than you has nothing to do with the place of my birth. Some things just are."

"And you are more twisted than a braided cunt hair."

"I knew you weren't ready for death." Tanis shook her head with a false pout. "With The Mother's grace, Shiena may be able to piece together a life from what you left her with. It would be a pity if you were responsible for destroying yet another life."

Pain surged through Wal's bones as his fist crashed into the stormwood door. The sharpness of it focused his anger, until the pain subsided behind a new vengeance.

The smirk that lifted her left cheek higher than the right. Her hollow black eyes. Tawny skin that contrasted with her midnight black curls. For a moment, time took a breath and General Tanis, leader of the Astilean

Army, became an image that would remain with Wal forever—the visage he would lie awake at night and pour his hate into.

"Thank you for proving me right, once again," the General said. "I wouldn't want to keep you from your meal any longer." Her footfalls rang off the stone, then disappeared.

If she meant to waste her opportunity to kill him, she would come to regret it. No stormwood door, no guard, no fucking mountain would keep him from showing her blood to the world.

A squirrelly Sonacoan, maybe old enough to have seen his swearing day, walked through the mouth of the dungeon carrying two shallow bowls of porridge. His tattered gray robes and matted red hair made him indistinguishable from a whole host of other nameless. But he didn't avert his gaze as he had been trained. The young bastard stared at Wal with a version of the hatred Wal felt for Tanis, only muted by degrees.

"What are you looking at, nameless?" Wal asked with his old air of assumed authority.

The servant's hollow cheeks turned his bones into blades under his onyx skin. A series of healed cuts peeked through the tears in his clothing. Before the army had taken his tongue along with his name, this young man might have looked very different. Wal may have known him, or he may have been like any other servant who resented their place in the world.

When he stopped in front of Wal's cell, he spat in one of the bowls and placed it at the gap beneath Wal's door.

"Fuck you too," Wal said, but the servant walked to the next door without acknowledging the curse.

When he placed the second bowl in front of the poet's cell, his hands danced about his chest and face in a series of gestures, then he walked away.

Wal's time in captivity had stolen what little fat had lingered on his frame. The hunger had become a constant thrumming in the background, so much so that the spit in his food didn't turn his stomach. He pulled the bowl into his cell and stared at the viscous globule atop his small rations. It would be simple enough to scoop it out. He'd done it before.

"Tell me, poet. Why did you lose your tongue in front of the General? She make you nervous?"

"Tanis is my cousin actually," they said. "She and I grew up together, more like siblings than anything else. Shonar, Tanis, and I shared more than a childhood—we shared dreams and fears. She actually can be a very fun person. You should see her and her wife dance."

"You're right, she's perfection incarnate. Does the crack of her backside smell of lilac?"

"Do you always have to be so crass?"

The silence that fell between them would have been the perfect place for a bit of colorful blasphemy about The Mother, but Wal was too focused on removing the spit from his porridge. He attempted to scoop it out but lost a portion of his meal to the floor instead.

"When I spoke out against our inaction during the Invasion War, Tanis took it harder than Shonar. She called me a traitor and denied our shared blood. Everything we had been grew more and more bitter as we both refused to bend from our positions," Lanigan said. "She was the first to call me the King's shame."

"You must hate her."

"I mourn her. The safety of the Citadel and the Lost Forest beyond that have kept me from the worst of the occupation. I managed to get through most of this life without losing too many people to The Mist. Instead, I lost them to ambitions. The people I loved did things that destroyed the people they had been.

"A grave is a remembrance of those who have left our arms. There is no such marker for those who have abandoned our hearts."

"Who wrote that?"

"Unfortunately, I have the honor of claiming those words."

The grief in Lanigan's tone managed to steal the strength of Wal's anger from his chest. Wal hooked three fingers and dipped them into his porridge again, finally managing to remove the servant's gift.

Given enough time, he would either find a path to his vengeance or a path to The Mist. Either would do.

Chapter Six

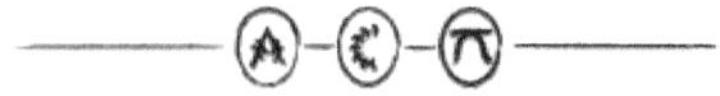

After two days of hard walking, Tayen stopped in the clearing and stared at the lodestone.

She had seen a lodestone once before. She and Nita had run around the tall cylindrical column, playing make believe. The history of the black magnetic stone hadn't mattered. They had known the stories, but in that moment, it became nothing more than a funny stone they chased each other around.

When her father let his knife clink against the surface, the stone held it like magic. Tayen had known how to play with the shadows, but she couldn't make things float.

So many turns later, she stood beside this obelisk-shaped lodestone in the crook of a river. Sokan's falling light cast gleams of iridescent purple running over its onyx surface. It still was magical.

Kaylo strode to the stone and gave it his father's knife. He shifted the blade until it ran parallel to the ground and pointed towards the river. Her father hadn't bothered pointing his blade in any particular direction. It had been a trick to make his girls smile.

After fiddling with the angle of the blade, Kaylo bent down to rub at his knee and grimaced. He had been complaining about it less than when they first met, but she found him like this occasionally. His hands massaged the muscles above and below his kneecap.

The long days of traveling made Tayen's wound ache. She had assumed it would fade with time until it became a scar and a story. However, it might not. Maybe she would be rubbing her shoulder in twenty turns, trying to cool the pain.

"What are you staring at?" Kaylo straightened up with an arched eyebrow.

"Oh...nothing," Tayen mumbled. "What's that supposed to mean, anyway?"

"If they still abide by the old signals, a blade pointing east is a request for safe haven."

"What if you pointed it west?"

"That would be a warning. 'Danger's near.'"

"Seems like a waste of a signal," Nix said. "Danger's always near."

Kaylo leaned against the lodestone and stared down the river. In many ways, he wasn't the man she had met the previous summer. For one, he smelled much better. He also stood differently, upright and open-shouldered.

When Tayen met him, he stuttered and stammered around her as if the wrong word would have sent her running—and it likely would have. Neither of them would run now. As much as she knew he didn't want to go looking for the Uprising, he had paced them through the forest like he had a mission.

"You met Zusa at a lodestone by the river. Is this the same one?" Tayen asked.

"We sat across from each other right about where you're standing." Kaylo closed the gap between them. "I need you and Sosun to go find some firewood. We may be here a while."

"What do you mean 'a while'?" Nix asked.

"Did you think the Uprising had someone watching the lodestones at all times? It's more like a snare. Set it, and check it. It would be a waste of time to perch in the trees watching a stone," Kaylo said. "Come on. We have to set camp before it gets too dark."

Tayen grumbled loud enough for him to hear her.

Without a fire, they wouldn't have much to eat and she would shiver through the night. Even so, she had to fight with her body not to lay prone where she stood.

It was Kaylo's fault if she thought about it.

He had forced her to sit on her ass and heal for over a moon, then pushed them through two hard days of travel. It left her exhausted from spirit to bone. Her feet ached, and her back had become a cluster of tightened muscles.

Kaylo held out a waterskin. "You need to stay hydrated, and it's not good for your muscles to suddenly stop. They need to cool down. Take your time. It's a nice evening for a stroll through the woods."

His smile was the worst part—like her pain amused him.

"I don't like you right now."

"It sounds like we might need some time apart. I have an idea—I'll stay here, and you go get firewood with Sosun."

I asked for this, she thought, doing her best not to throw a rock at his smiling face. Though if she could have picked up a rock and thrown it without aggravating her shoulder wound, she may have.

A few paces away, Sosun waited for her, draping lashed-together waterskins over her shoulder. The gentle glow of the coming night framed her. She pointed at Tayen, swirled her finger in a circle, then beckoned Tayen with a wave.

"How are you not as tired as I am?" Tayen signed as she walked off into the woods.

"When you spend a short lifetime of days running around a giant mountain waiting on a bunch of entitled assholes, a day of walking through the forest isn't so bad."

With that, Tayen's shame throbbed louder than her aches. Had she really just asked someone who had been forced into slave labor for the better part of eight turns how she had built up her stamina?

"I also wasn't wounded with an arrow."

"I'm sorry. That was..." Tayen stopped when she couldn't find the word, only feeling worse for her inability to communicate. "How do you say 'insensitive'?"

A smile spread across Sosun's face as she shook her head. She placed her fist on her chest, dragged it down on a diagonal, then thumped it once.

Tayen repeated the gesture.

"Please don't apologize for the things in my life you didn't do," Sosun signed. *"You're too young to take that on."*

"I'm not that young."

"The elders in the Citadel used to say only children fight for the turns they haven't lived."

There it was. Everyone looked at Tayen, measured her by her age, then dismissed her as if she couldn't be of use. The Uprising would probably do the same damn thing.

Ironically, she had just escaped the only people who had considered her of value on the battlefield. Sure, the Lost Nation had truly fucked ideas about the world they wanted after they drove off the Gousht and what they were willing to do to get there, but they never questioned her usefulness.

She had taken two lives, saving both Kaylo and Sosun in the process. That should have earned her some latitude.

As if beckoned by the thought, Pana flashed in front of her. His bloody hands clung to the spear as he tumbled to the ground. While he lay there, he had seemed smaller.

A sudden clap pulled Tayen from hovering over the boy's dying body.

When she looked up, she met Sosun's narrowed eyes, stretched thin with concern. *"Are you okay?"*

"I'm fine. It's just been a long day."

"You know, when I was young, my brother got sick," she signed. *"The Gousht made the whole village manufacture iron from the mountains and make weapons for them. They didn't tolerate anyone who couldn't pull their weight, so my mother smuggled us out before they got rid of my*

brother like they did with anyone else who fell behind."

The sunset barely offered enough light to see her clearly under the forest canopy. Sosun angled her face away from Tayen's gaze and sniffled.

"My mother thought that we would be safe if we made it to the Lost Forest. Surely, the Lost Nation would help us." She chuckled deep from her throat. *"My brother made it to Tomakan soil before he died."*

Her hands fell to her side for a moment.

"Why are you telling me this?" Tayen asked as she signed.

Sosun wrinkled her nose as if to keep her tears from coming, then she settled into a resolute expression. *"I know how trauma can age you. There probably isn't a child anywhere in Ennea who doesn't. I know how you think you need to carry the world when everything breaks around you, but that isn't the case. You can let someone else take the lead."*

Despite how much they had shared over the last moon, conversation after conversation, somehow Sosun still thought of Tayen as weak. The pressure at the back of Tayen's jaw built as she held her words at bay.

"You chose to track down the Uprising and join the fight against the Gousht. You don't have to act like you aren't scared. We're all scared, and you are allowed to lean on the rest of us."

"Is that what you did?" Tayen couldn't keep the bite from her voice as she spoke alongside the signs.

"My mother and I nearly died before we found Dasoon. Hakan and Nix fed us and gave us a place to stay, but my mother didn't get off her bedroll most mornings. On the days when she actually followed through on her responsibilities in the freecity, she would break into tears when she thought no one was looking.

"Nix helped out—until she handed me off to the Lost Army," she signed. *"I didn't have someone like Kaylo to lean on."*

All the fire in Tayen's belly petered out. Her anger and her pain didn't make her special—not in this world.

She placed her palm against her chest, tilted it until it ran perpendicular to her sternum, then tapped her closed fist against her chin twice.

"I didn't tell you that story for your apologies. I told you because I am worried about you," Sosun signed. "You decided to join the war. Maybe that's the right decision for you, but you have to keep your anger in check. If you can't learn to rely on those around you—those who love you—you won't survive this. At least the person you are now won't."

With the cleanest part of her sleeve, Sosun wiped her face and continued walking deeper into the woods.

If they only had an axe, they could make easy use of the forest around them. Instead, they would have to rely on fallen branches. It would take time, but they would find plenty.

Tayen followed at a respectful distance behind Sosun, bending to collect loose twigs from the undergrowth for kindling.

The Shadow sang a gentle melody, shifting with the shade. The high hum of dusk dwindled beneath the rising baritone of the night, but it wasn't a song of one consuming the other. Notes passed from them like a gift.

The harmony in The Song clashed with the chaos running through Tayen's bones. Without her vengeance, she needed a new anchor. If she couldn't rely on her anger, how would she hold her ground the next time her blood was at stake?

Sosun stopped beside a fallen tree. Lightning had struck it down, leaving singe marks along what remained of its trunk. She had her foot propped against a crack in a branch as she tried to finish what the fall had started, yanking it back with all her might.

Tayen joined her, and the wood snapped and popped with their effort. "I didn't mean to bring up the past," she said, her hands too busy to sign.

Sosun released her grip and stepped back from the branch with an exasperated sigh. *"You didn't. I did. Again, you don't have to take responsibility for things that aren't your fault."*

Like bile, Tayen's anger rose from her gut. She was only trying to comfort Sosun. Why was she making it so hard?

Tayen forced herself to breathe instead of yell. "Where is your mother now?"

A pained smile stretched Sosun's face. *"Nix said that she left not long after the Lost Army took me."*

"Why don't you go find her? She could still be out there."

"Trying to get rid of me, huh?"

"No, that's not what I meant—" Tayen starting signing before Sosun waved her off.

"I'm teasing." Sosun paused and looked up towards the forest canopy. *"Maybe I will, but for now, I need to make a life that serves me for once. I need to contribute in some way that isn't picking up people's shit."*

"Are you angry with her?"

"My mother? A bit," Sosun signed. *"I used to be really angry with her, but then I realized something. So many of us have experienced more trauma than we can bear. We end up blaming the people who couldn't withstand it rather than the people who caused it. My mother just didn't have it in her to be strong when she felt weak."*

The rabbit's hide clung to Nix's knife before it surrendered and opened up for her.

When she and Hakan first made claim to Dasoon, she went hunting every day. Didn't always catch something, but the feel of being alone with the forest calmed her. People had plenty of ways to define her; most of the worst were still fairly accurate, but the forest allowed her to be herself—no need to prove her womanhood, her strength, her care.

Without anyone demanding her time, she had hunted almost every day since they left the Lost Nation.

The river sloshed as Kaylo dipped another waterskin into the rushing water.

Soon, the solitude of being four in a world of too many loud-mouthed cravens would be over. Even if Kaylo could be an annoying fuck, he knew how to keep his mouth shut when necessary. It was a rare trait that far too few people had.

The two of them had set to their tasks with an ease of knowing. As soon as he finished filling the waterskins, Kaylo would line a pit with stones and erect a basic spit roast. By the time the girls returned, Nix would be done dressing the rabbit and filling its chest cavity with the few wild herbs they had found along the way.

These Uprising assholes better have some herbs and salt, Nix thought.

They had been able to scrounge up a good deal better than the bland porridge she'd had to stomach for a season under the eye of the Lost Army, but that didn't stop her from missing the sting of salt against her tongue.

Nix sharpened a few small twigs to sew the rabbit shut while it cooked.

"Full truth, will they come?" Nix said.

The expression of surprise on Kaylo's face settled in her belly like a warm spiced cider. She rarely broke a silence. It took time to train people not to expect her voice, but eventually, it settled in. His shock only proved her training had worked.

"Full truth? If the spirits have a clue, they haven't told me. I haven't seen anyone from the Uprising in over a dozen turns, and I have to think Wal doesn't count."

"So, this is a game? We're chasing your nostalgia or something?"

Kaylo stopped tinkering with the spit and met her eyes. "When I said I would get Tayen to the Uprising, I meant it. You should know better than to question my loyalty to that girl.

"We'll wait. If the Uprising comes, we will find our way through. If they don't, we may have to follow the fighting to find them. Though, I would prefer staying away from battlegrounds for now."

———

Belly full and feet worn, Sosun looked at Nix beside her. Everyone had settled into their silence—too tired to engage, trying to milk every moment of relaxation they could before sleep.

She threw a pinecone at Nix's boots. *"You know you don't owe me anything, right? After we find the Uprising, you can go."*

Nix tore the last hunk of flesh from the rabbit leg with her teeth before tossing the bone into the fire. Light played along the curvature of her face as she stared into the flame.

"*What's this about?*" Nix signed.

"*Tayen kept apologizing for things that weren't her responsibility, and I realized I never said it. You aren't responsible for me.*"

"*Do you want me to go?*" A fragment of pain hid within Nix's hard stare.

Nix rarely showed emotion other than anger, at least not outright. Instead, her displays of emotion lay within the nuances of her glares, stares, and scowls.

Surviving servitude had often come down to Sosun's practiced ability to read the minute expressions tucked between people's larger, bolder shows of emotion. The multitude of angry people the Lost Nation had stolen and molded into warriors gave Sosun ample opportunity to hone her ability, which made reading Nix simple by comparison.

One person. One face to study.

"*You did what you had to so that Dasoon could survive. I understood that, even if it took longer to stop hating you for it. You don't owe me anything.*"

The left corner of Nix's mouth twitched, meaning she had foul words caught somewhere between her lungs and her lips that she wasn't going to let out.

"*Who said I owe you anything? I owe myself.*" Nix spoke to fill in the gaps in her signing. "*I was eleven when The Reaping started. I already knew I was kamani, and so did everyone around me. If I wanted to survive, I had to leave everything behind.*

"*Of course, Hakan had to tag along. Whoever that motherfucker turned out to be, he was family once.*" Nix paused and cracked her knuckles like someone clearing their throat to capture their thoughts. "*No, I owe myself. I spent too many turns thinking about survival, and I ended up losing the person I wanted to be. I am searching for her. You just happen to be walking the same direction.*"

Sosun gnawed on a small rabbit bone, and the taste brought her back to her mother. Citadel servants didn't get many opportunities to enjoy meat, and after turns without it, whatever meat made its way to them turned stomachs more often than not. This rabbit, however, fed her spirit with a warmth she hadn't known in too long. Her body had taken time to adjust to her new diet, but she could finally enjoy it.

"So you're doing this for selfish reasons," she signed.

"Of course."

"You are full of..."

"What is...?" Nix repeated a gesture that didn't have an exact translation in common tongue, twisting her fingers as she ground them into her other palm.

"Citadel servants are responsible for cleaning up after the entitled assholes who lived in the mountain. Let's just say, the pricks left behind some nasty shit for us to clean up." Sosun repeated the gesture. *"Use your imagination."*

"How could they have ever called you servants when you are such poets?"

"Fuck you," Sosun signed, feeling her lips pull into a smirk.

A season past, Sosun couldn't have imagined seeing the world beyond the Lost Forest again. She hadn't killed herself because it would have burdened the other servants. The susu root had dulled her pain. But when she saw Nix, she changed.

At first, she wanted to kill Nix. Wrath had felt new and exciting after being numb for so long. Then somehow, the woman who had started out as a caretaker only to betray Sosun had become the most important thread tying her to this side of The Mist.

For turns, Sosun had known what the next day would bring. Now, only The Mother could guess.

"It won't be so bad walking the same direction as you for a while longer," Sosun signed.

CHAPTER SEVEN
KAYLO'S STORY

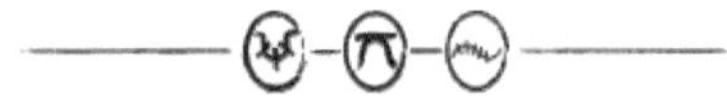

"This sounds like a horrible idea," Annit said, his echo thundering under his soft words.

The clearing mimicked the ten-pace circles Zusa used to make me clear out for our training sessions. Even if the man had been a liar, his methods always found their way towards working. And I needed this to work.

"If people are going to continue to treat me like a leader, I need to be stronger. I can't carry more blood, Annit." Wal, Talise, and Boda milled about, waiting for us. "I can't do it."

"I'm stopping this the moment it gets out of hand."

"Why do you think you're here?" Despite my smile, Annit's expression remained unmoved.

Choosing to walk into an obviously ill-conceived training exercise was easier with the weight of a birch blade in each hand. It had taken a span to carve facsimiles of my sword and my father's knife for myself, as well as the set Boda currently held. The wood offered enough flexibility and strength that the weapons wouldn't break from the heavy contact. Their weight also promised to make any strike sting.

"You sure you want to do this?" Wal asked as his fingers fiddled about with the red crystal in his hand.

"When you're worried about something being a bad idea, I really worry."

So keep it to yourself."

Wal smiled and shook his head in response as the crystal began to glow an angry red in his palm. He always picked The Flame.

"Remember, call the spirits one at a time, and only on Annit's mark," I said.

"Can we get on with it?" Boda cut lackluster slashes and jabs through the air. "You promised that I was going to be able to swing these things at you."

"Little shits with bad attitudes are occasionally right," Talise said.

"Fuck you," Boda mumbled, but Talise paid him as much mind as a gentle breeze.

"We all have responsibilities to tend to, Kaylo." She pushed herself up from where she sat on the outskirts of the training circle, her lips in a tight line of irritation. "If we are going to do this, we should begin."

This was the rebel band that would follow me into battle—a group of people with more anger and hatred than they had the turns to justify. None of them deserved the weight the spirits had placed on them.

I had to become better for them.

With a quick nod to Annit, I set my feet and prepared for Boda's rage.

"Talise!" Annit shouted, and The Mountain's echo surged to life.

The low hum of The Thief sang a melancholy tune under The Mountain's rage. Then that rage became a familiar pain in my gut as I snatched it from the air.

"Yaktan," Annit said, and our training had begun.

While Boda circled the edge of the clearing, he angled his head to keep his unblemished eye trained on me. The Boda I first met would have charged in immediately, but that Boda had been left behind and replaced with a calculated, anger-sized boy. He guarded his body with his long blade and kept his knife hand tucked into his side for an easy strike.

"Wal!" Annit shouted.

The Flame's echo overtook the sound of the forest, before I consumed its fury as well. If I waited any longer, I would be too bogged down in rage-filled spirits to maintain my defenses against Boda. So, with both spirits clawing at my insides, I burst forward.

Each crack of our blades drove the rhythm of the echoes faster as if the spirits were begging to become a part of the violence.

Boda mirrored my footwork, maintaining his guard and his one-eyed stare. Whenever I pushed him back, he lashed out with his wooden knife to keep his spacing.

"You've gotten better," I said between breaths.

"Shut it and fight." His thrust forced me to withdraw my shoulder before he swiped at my foot with his knife.

As I stumbled back and regained my guard, Annit called for Talise to call another spirit, and The Shadow made itself known.

When I reached for the new echo, the pain set off warnings from my fingertips to the rough end of my ass, but it didn't bend me to my knees. I could manage three spirits.

As if he saw the extra weight fall on my shoulders, Boda changed tactics. He closed the gap and squared off his body, allowing him to strike with both blades in a series of thrusts and slashes.

The sound of the clacking wood clashed with the torrent of echoes screaming from within.

A smile spread over Boda's face as he matched every backstep I took toward the perimeter of the clearing.

The bastard really wanted to hurt me, and why wouldn't he? I had cost him his brother and his eye.

He aimed his sword at my neck, and I moved too late. I caught the blow with my fingers rather than my long blade. The muted crack sounded strange compared to all the others. I registered the change in pitch before the pain had time to strike.

The little fuck had broken at least one of my fingers. Pain flared then fell behind the rageful spirits within me. They had a use after all.

He continued his volley, never hesitating.

The Wind's scream cut through the glut of noise.

This was over, and I would end it.

I snatched the stray spirit from the air, then battered away Boda's weapons with a heavy swing of my long sword. He may have practiced without end for the past turn, but I still had size and strength on him.

With his weapons out of the way, I angled towards his blind side, swinging my birch knife towards his neck.

His milky white eye seemed to stare into me as I attacked.

A moment before my blade found its purchase, Boda swept his arm around mine, locked my striking arm under his armpit, and drove the thick of his forehead into my chin.

I bit my cheek as the world toppled wrong side up and the cacophony of sound stopped. The stinging taste of blood coated my tongue. The gap in the canopy above framed the brilliant blue sky and the First Daughter, as if she had visited to watch our little sparring match.

Then the clash of competing echoes returned like a new wave falling over the receding water, and my rage came with it. I was sick of the pressure everyone put on me. They blamed me. They expected more than I had to give. And when I failed, they would shun the spirit thief. I knew it.

I abandoned my blades, scrambled to my feet, and threw myself at Boda.

We landed face to face, and he smiled up at me from the ground. "Do it," he said.

Voices shouted into the noise around me, but only Boda and I existed within this bubble. A drop of blood fell from my lip and splattered on his cheek, still pulled back in a smile.

"Kaylo!" Liara's voice cut through the noise as if the echoes were whispers in her presence.

She stood at the edge of the clearing wearing what had become a familiar expression of disappointment. I knew in that instant I would remember this in the quiet moments, when the worst of my daemons came to visit.

"Oh, come on. We were just starting to have fun," Boda said as I picked myself off the ground.

The boy's goading remarks wilted into silence as I walked farther away from the encampment into the forest. The spirits slipped away one by one, and their ire fled with them, leaving me hollow.

When I carried the spirits, my fury burned away the parts of me that were still my mother's son. And I let it. Being able to hold onto the spirits wasn't enough. I had to keep my head too.

"Blessed Mother," I said, crashing to my knees in the light brush of the forest floor. "I can't do it. I can't be what they need."

"You could be," Liara said from over my shoulder. "The first thing you need to stop doing is hiding from us, trying to carry too much on your own."

"Who else can do it? If I slip up, people die. The couta fucks will continue to use our spirits against us, and nothing changes."

"Are you done?" she asked. "Because when you're finished feeling sorry for yourself and placing yourself at the center of the world, maybe we can talk."

The leaves and brush shuffled under her feet as she came up behind me and placed her hands on my shoulders. "You have a unique gift, but you aren't the only spirit thief in the world. You play a large role in the Uprising, but people die if any of us fail to do our part. If we screw up, you die too."

"But they made me the commander. They all look to me."

"Some of them do, but you are not the only one with responsibilities to these people." Her hand slid over my robes as she stepped around to get in front of me. "I want you to start understanding that you are more than your ability to borrow spirits."

A soft smile pulled her cheeks up as she cupped my face. Her touch invited me to lean into her. The warmth felt out of place but welcome.

"I don't deserve any of you. Especially you."

"Well, that is very true, and you are wise to recognize that," she said. "You have a council meeting in three fingers. And you probably shouldn't be wearing your own blood when you go. It would make Hyliane too happy."

"Thank you."

Her lips found the same spot they always did, just off-center of my forehead. Her kiss pressed against my skin, and I could breathe. "Clean yourself up and make your apologies, then do what you need to do."

As we walked back to the sparring circle, I explored the gash in my mouth with my tongue. Then I examined my hand. My ring finger stung something furious. I would have to wrap it for a few span.

That boy had made solid work of me.

"What would happen if we just ran away to a far corner of Ennea?"

"We don't have to bring Wal, do we?" Liara asked.

"No." I stopped my gait. "I'm serious. Could we escape this?"

As Liara turned to me, she tangled her fingers with my uninjured hand. "You are not a spirit that hides. Sometimes you are a fool who rushes towards the hottest parts of the fire when you should stand back. It is the scariest part about you, but it is also what makes me respect you."

The small noises of the world overcame all others as her lips touched mine. The breeze that brushed through us became a part of our small symphony of insignificant sounds.

She was right. My dreams about some far-off quiet place would only ever be dreams. Maybe before I had lost so many people I loved—maybe then I could have let the turns pass me by.

When our lips parted, the weight of every crude sound rushed in and overtook my little dream of escaping. The combined orchestra of noises was missing an instrument.

"Shit."

"Not exactly the response I was looking for," Liara said with eyebrows raised.

"One of the spirit crystals split paths from the others. The Flame."

The soft curves of her expression sharpened in an instant. "You need to talk to him."

"I know."

"Unless it has to do with fighting the Gousht, you're the only one he talks to anymore."

"I know."

"If the council finds out, Wal will find himself left behind," she said.

"He's in pain."

"I know." Her grip firmed around my hand, and she paused for a moment before speaking. "His pain is real. No one can take that from him. But if he wants to be a part of this, it cannot be about his pain any more than it can be about mine or yours. Vengeance will only take us so far."

Every word made sense to the part of me that could see beyond my own anger. However, I still dreamt of Junera's hand clutching the charred rabbit. Some nights, I woke up shaking trying to convince myself I wasn't in that stone room holding Boda's limp, bloody body, waiting to die.

"You should be the one they listen to," I said.

"'Should' has nothing to do with any of this, Kaylo. Life doesn't respect easy answers." With a melancholy in her eyes, she forced the turn of her lips. "But you're right. I probably should be in charge."

Given the choice, I would have rather spent another several hours with irate spirits tearing me apart from the inside while an angry boy lashed out at me than attend a small council meeting. So I waited outside Annit's tent as the soft murmurs of conversation buzzed within.

Whatever answers I had were guesses with a bit of spitshine. But Sokan had fallen below the meeting mark, which meant I had to step through the threshold or run off into the night.

Fuck it, I thought, and pushed my way inside.

The council members sat around a small fire. Annit, Talise, and Yelan filled the intimate setting with conversation, but Hylĩane ignored them to focus her judgmental glare on me.

Gatherings were too large and unwieldy to discuss specific tactics and strategies. Instead, this small council guided the Uprising. The speed we gained in the process also removed the buffers between Hylĩane and me.

She saw past the stories people told about me and my gifts. In many ways, she and I were the only two people who knew I had no business leading anyone.

"Did cha start 'nother war on the way over ere?" Hylíane asked, breaking the flow of conversation.

"What are you talking about?"

"Kaylo, wipe your lip." Annit swiped his thumb on the corner of his mouth.

As I mimicked the gesture, my thumb came away smeared red. "Training incident. Thank you for the concern, Hylíane."

After losing my temper earlier, the anger I needed to push my way through this meeting fell flat.

"Before this breaks down into a passive-aggressive battle between the two of you, I would appreciate if we could get to the matter at hand," Yelan said, back perfectly straight as if she had been sculpted sitting next to the fire.

The Mountain sang a humble tune beneath her stoic posture, humming like a reflection of the life that walked upon her grounds—steady, knowing, and controlled with an unspoken strength.

"Under the gathering tent, you proposed freeing people, expanding our numbers. Did you have a plan, or were you speaking in the abstract?" Yelan was never one to mince her words.

"Talise." I nodded in her direction. "It was your idea."

For a moment, Talise glared at me, which was becoming a far-too-familiar occurrence. The glare didn't last long, but whenever I caught her eyes, they were aimed at me like a weapon. She never said anything, and I worried what I would find if I asked.

"As you know, our scouts have been all over the northern stretch of Tomak." She angled towards the map secured to the tent wall behind her. "There is an outpost here at the port on the Strait of Talmo, and there's a stronghold here at Lake Gancea. Both of these are too well equipped for an assault."

"Cha have annae new information?" Hylíane asked.

"I hold my tongue once. I hold my fists twice," Talise said without making the slightest adjustment in her expression. "That is the extent of my self-control."

"Cha can't speak like tha ta me."

"Why don't you let this one go, Hylīane?" Annit asked. "The young woman was quite clear on her boundaries."

As Hylīane's face contorted, trying to find an expression to settle on, I found myself enjoying the meeting a little more.

"As I was saying, these two targets are beyond us at this point. However, there is a small farming village here called Ferin Seit. The greens kept it and dozens of others going to help supply their soldiers, and of course they have Enneans working the land. There shouldn't be a heavy Gousht presence."

"There wasn't before we torched the last outpost," Yelan said. "Things change."

"That's why we have to scout, and take our time. This is the most vulnerable target," I said.

"Thas all well and good, but have cha made annae progress with cha training? If cha can't destroy spirit crystals like cha did at the mines, people are going to die."

With that, I found the anger that I needed at the beginning of the meeting. The fact that Hylīane was right only solidified my resentment.

"Did you come to shit on everyone here? We are trying to do some good, and you just want to tear us down. Do you care that the Gousht enslaved those farmers? They are being forced to work this land just like you were in the mines. Does any of that matter to you?"

"Don't cha dare talk about what cha don know!" Hylīane stood up with more size than her body could give her and looked down with a rage to match my own.

"Stop it, the both of you!" Annit's voice boomed with an intensity he saved for the battlefield. "Hylīane, I'm sick of you using your turns like a weapon against these young people. If it weren't for them, you would be lumbering in and out of that mine right now.

"And you. Stop drawing lines like everyone who disagrees with you doesn't care about Ennea. You're past your swearing day. Wear your turns better than that."

As he spoke, Annit leaned closer to the flames. They illuminated every wrinkle, scar, and feature of his fuming expression.

"Before we write off this whole meeting, we need to vote with regard to scouting Ferin Seit."

"All for moving forward with the scouting missions?" Yelan asked.

One by one, everyone, even Hylīane, tapped their heart with their right hand to affirm their support.

"Good, now leave my tent if you would," Annit said.

Hylīane left before any of the rest of us had a chance to stand, her walking stick thudding against the ground with every step.

"I'm sorry, Annit," I said.

"We'll talk tomorrow," he said, his chest rising and falling with heavy, practiced breaths.

The evening air stung with the touch of an ever-deepening autumn.

"Can you believe her?" I asked as Talise walked by.

"Just because I'm on your side, doesn't mean I'm on your side, Kaylo," she said without slowing her gait.

"What the fuck is that supposed to mean?" I mumbled.

In the course of one day, I had managed to ostracize myself from the people around me even more.

Beyond the forest-covered netting, a whole world waited for me to escape into. I could find The Priest on my own. Of course, I would die, but at least I wouldn't be responsible for any more blood.

The echo of The Flame cut through my self-pity like a battleaxe.

That's it! I screamed inside my head alongside the blaring echo, and rushed towards the sound.

One too many people had told me who I needed to become for one day.

The Flame crested and receded much like The River but with a harsher edge, as if consuming and dying were immediate consequences of the other.

Flashes of light illuminated the forest beyond our camouflaged netting.

If anyone in the encampment saw this prick's little display, the whole of the Uprising would be either reaching for weapons or running.

Even as sarcastic and bitter as he had become, I was supposed to be able to rely on Wal.

A plume of flames leaped into the air before swallowing itself and yielding to the darkness.

"What the fuck are you doing?!" I grabbed the translucent thread from the air and pulled The Flame into myself.

"Kaylo?" Wal twisted around in the dark, looking for my voice before finding me. "I was training."

"You were putting everything at risk," I said. "Can you imagine what would have happened if someone saw spontaneous flames bursting out of the forest just outside the encampment?"

"No one saw."

"People would panic. The council would leave you behind."

"So you get to train however you see fit, and the rest of us have to obey. Is that it?"

"The council decided not to use spirit crystals to fight the Goushr, Wal. What are you training for?"

His posture slumped, and he shrank in the shadows of the forest "Do you know what it's like to feel powerless? Unnecessary?"

"Did you forget that I was taken? The bastard tortured me, then beat Boda half blind in front of me. I was ready to die."

"Instead, he died." A crack broke his voice in two. He always avoided saying Adēan's name.

"I'm sorry, Wal."

"This isn't about you, you asshole! I sent them in there. My plan. And I couldn't do a damn thing to save him."

"You need to know it wasn't your fault." I let each word linger. They needed time to rest in the air so he could hear them.

"We need these crystals. You won't be able to stop every spirit."

I held out my hand. "If the council finds out, I can't protect you."

All of the words we didn't dare say—the shame we refused to show each other—filled the silence.

"You won't be able to protect us all. Some of us will die." He placed the spiritless crystal in my hand and walked away.

The brush crunched under his footfalls as he strode back to the encampment, leaving me with my thoughts and an angry spirit for company.

This has to end, I thought, stalking back to my tent to speak with the one who could end it.

The bleak darkness of The Thief's corner of The Mist held less foreboding when I visited with purpose and anger.

"Little thief, your thoughts are so very loud." Her voice crept out of the dark, sourceless.

"You need to do something. How can you stand by while Enneans are suffering?"

Her shadow-wrapped visage appeared as if the darkness uncoiled around her. "You reminded me this is all about balance, right? Well, your precious Enneans have taken from me. I gave others the opportunity to take from them."

"Check the weights on your scale, you old, bitter daemon. This isn't balance. This is genocide."

A dark fog flowed over the floor and fed her cloak as she grew into a looming figure. "Do you know what your Enneans did only days ago? When a village discovered a girl who bore a sliver of my spirit, only eleven turns to her, they formed a mob. It wasn't the Gousht. No, the soldiers stood by and watched as the crowd pushed her and shouted at her. It only took one rock even though several were thrown. Her spirit found The Mist before her body dropped.

"Nothing will make them forget their hatred. Look at what you and I did. We destroyed a mountain full of crystals, and still they killed your spirit sister for the crime of existing."

"You can't condemn them all. This isn't the way to change their minds."

"Jonac taught you medicine. Sometimes you have to cut the body to drain the infection."

"What are you talking about?"

Her massive figure shrunk to my height. "If your people want to get rid of the spirit crystals so badly, they have only to look to my descendants."

"You would shed all this blood to save your marked?"

"What would you do to save your people? I have died again and again along with those carrying my spirit. They won't stop until they have a new story, and we will give them one."

The anger I had brought with me withered away to something akin to disbelief. "You became so much worse than any of the stories they made up about you."

"Go, little thief. Give them a new story. Maybe then they will be worth saving."

Chapter Eight
Kaylo's Story

"This is a stupid plan, you know that, right?" Tomi sat cross-legged atop of a sack of dried grain, snacking on a handful of seeds.

"You think everything I do is stupid," I said.

"True, but most of that is regular stupid. This is like running barefoot in the forest at night with your eyes closed. You know, the furthest thing from bright."

When Tomi decided to take the time to pick at me, all I could do was ignore her. I continued to pack my travel sack as she continued to berate me.

"I've known you about two turns at this point, and in that short time, you've almost died a lot," she said. "Far too often to be making reckless decisions like this. I'm just saying, you could try doing the opposite of what you think is best and see if that works out better."

The Wind echoed from Tomi like a whistle whirling in and out of pitch. It made the pit in my chest feel all the emptier as I packed some vegetables and healing herbs for the journey.

Some days, The Seed's quiet didn't scream as loudly as others. Some days, hours passed by without a thought of the missing melodies. The absence would fade into the background and join the rest of those I mourned, waiting to be called forth. But today, the void sounded like the smile in The Priest's voice when he stole The Seed from me.

"If you are aiming for efficiency, there are quicker paths to The Mist."

"Enough!" I yelled, instantly regretting my overreaction.

"What's your problem?" Tomi unfolded her legs and pushed herself off the grain.

I wanted to tell her the sack in my hands felt too light. My mother's book burned when The Priest raided the Missing's camp, and all her wisdom went with it. I knew I was doing everything wrong, but I didn't know another way because I lost the last bit I had of the smartest person I knew.

But that would have been too vulnerable, so I gave her the truth beside the truth.

"I don't have good options," I said. "Do you get that? I have options that put myself at risk, and I have options that put others at risk. While I would rather not trek through the fucking woods to watch our people being forced to work the fields that used to feed their families, no one else can do what I can.

"If I don't go, who's going to count the spirit crystals they have on them? How are they going to avoid the soldiers walking around with spirits swinging from their necks? Huh? Tell me. Who should I send?"

"Why do you keep any of us around if you don't trust us?" Tomi asked, the edge falling from her voice.

For as different as they were, Tomi and Liara carried a slice of the same heart. Liara liked to say they got it from their mother, but Tomi couldn't even remember their mother. And their father had been too in the bottle and grief-stricken to do much raising. That piece in Tomi's chest came straight from Liara.

"It's not that I don't trust you. I just don't know if I will be able to hold on to any semblance of myself if any of you died when I could have prevented it."

"You're stupid."

"Tomi..."

"No, really. You think the rest of us don't feel responsible when someone else dies," Tomi said. "And forget all that. Why on The Blessed Mother are you taking Boda with you? He didn't show you his feelings clearly enough when he gave you that."

She flicked the cut on my chin, sending a small flare of pain creeping up my jaw.

I grimaced through the pain. "I'll have Acta with me too. Besides, Boda needs someone to hate right now, and if that has to be me, I'll take it. I owe him that much for Niven."

"You're no fun to tease," Tomi said. "You get too dark and regretful. It's depressing."

Between her words and her single raised eyebrow as she said them, I couldn't help the belly laugh that forced its way out. My travel sack fell to the ground as I clutched my stomach.

"Did I break you?"

"Yes," I blurted out between laughs. "Tomi, I don't know what the fuck I'm doing. All I know is I have to take the next step forward or else I'll stop moving altogether. So I need you to let me take the next ridiculous step and the one after that."

"As long as you don't get Liara and me killed, I can deal with that. Or Talise. I like her."

"Of course you do."

Her hand dove into the sack next to her, and she pulled out a red apple. "If you're going to die, at least take something with some flavor with you."

As soon as she tossed the apple, she turned and headed out of the tent.

"I wouldn't have survived a sibling," I said, as I stuffed the apple into my travel sack. It was still too light.

Boda firmly committed to silence on the journey to Ferin Seit. When he found the need to speak, he spoke to Acta. When I asked direct questions, he responded only when he deemed it necessary.

Fair to say, it was a less-than-pleasant expedition.

Acta and I chatted sporadically, but the tension between Boda and I soured any conversation to be had.

There were moments that neared absolute soundlessness. After turns of echoes occupying every moment, I usually craved the silence, but this unnerved me. It turned the quiet into a fragile thing, which I both needed to break and feared breaking in equal measures.

I felt bad for Acta.

Of all the reasons to regret my past, the pettiest one was how complicated it made my disdain for Boda. We never liked each other. From the first moment we met, the little prick had been arrogant and stubborn, looking to prove himself at someone else's expense. But I owed him, and I owed Niven.

"Sokan will be gone in a few fingers." I stared up as treetops obscured the lower third of The First Daughter. "We better get settled in while we have the twilight."

Boda looked between me and the sun several times before shrugging his pack from his shoulder.

"Sure, that seems like a good spot," I said, though, as I walked towards him, exposed roots and rough underbrush proved me immediately wrong.

"We could find something a bit more level," Acta said. However, he dropped his travel sack when he met my gaze.

If Boda was going to draw me into a fight, I refused to let it be over a few exposed roots.

Over the course of the next hour, we built a small fire and cleared the site to sleep under the stars. I set a couple of yams and ears of corn to cook in the firepit coals, then chewed on a bit of saltmeat as I waited.

Tomorrow, the three of us would have to rely on each other, and Acta couldn't continue to be our translator.

A gentle scraping noise cut through my thoughts. I looked up and found Boda working his sword over a whetstone.

Zusa always used to sharpen and clean his blade while we waited for dinner.

There had been some good days back then. Boda busied his idle hands by brushing his hair. Adéan and Chêta spoke at an indecipherable pace, like they could take themselves home in a conversation. Even Wal occasionally smiled without the bitterness that pulled on his cheeks now.

As I looked up at Boda, his scars and clouded eye facing towards me, the lightness of the memory soured. The sound of his sword against his whetstone became a symbol of how much had fallen apart.

"Acta, that was your cousin who saw you off this morning, right?" I asked.

He nodded. "Kristee."

"Did I do something to offend her?" I asked, recalling the scowl on her face when we parted ways.

"I wouldn't be surprised," Boda mumbled.

"She's scared is all. I'm all she's got left," Acta said.

"She hates you," Boda added, rewetting his whetstone.

"Just because you hate me doesn't mean everyone else does."

"No, he's right." Acta chuckled. "She hates you. She and Hylíane talk about it all the time."

"Told you."

Part of me wanted to throw dirt in Boda's face. The other part was happy that he had finally broken his silence, even if it was only to commiserate in a shared loathing for me.

"Now that you've decided to start talking, I've got a question I've been wanting to ask," I said.

"Am I supposed to guess?"

"No." I held the curse behind my teeth and took a breath. "I was just thinking back to our fight the other day."

"The one where I gave you that cut on your chin?" he asked, not bothering to look up from his task.

"Is that where you got that?" Acta asked.

I let out a sigh instead of falling for the bait. "When I attacked your blind side, you blocked the strike without a problem. How?"

The rhythmic scraping stopped, and Boda looked at me. A smile slowly bloomed across his face. "You thought you had me, didn't you? That was some underhanded shit going for my weak side."

"I'm sorry, I shouldn't have."

"What are you talking about? It made me come close to respecting you a little."

"That's very gracious of you," I said. "So, how?"

"I see shadows. It's mostly shades of gray, but when something moves on that side, I see shadows pass through the field of gray," he said. "It's not much, but it helps when people underestimate you."

"Smart," Acta said.

Boda snapped his attention to Acta as if annoyed that he had interrupted our conversation.

"No, he's right. That's clever."

For a moment, Boda's smile lost the challenge it held. He became a kid basking in the compliments of two warriors slightly older than him.

The next afternoon, erratic bursts of undulating noises tore through the silence we shared. At this distance, the cadence and tone lacked definition. One echo blended into the next, creating a clash of chaotic melodies that had become familiar in a way. When echoes called from various distances and locations, their bastardized songs blended into something truly awful, and I was the only one forced to hear it.

My connection to The Thief is truly a gift, I thought bitterly.

At least Boda acquiesced when I told him to slow down. Full of anger or not, he hadn't clung to life to die by being taken unawares.

Acta looked concerned, but I waved him away. The pain was manageable.

The cloud cover grayed out the sky beyond the forest canopy, transforming the afternoon into something timeless. Rain threatened to find us before we finished our sweep of the outer perimeter of the former farming community.

I knelt, as had become my habit before entering dangerous situations. "To the first—The Shadow, may your wisdom guide us to choices that keep us on this side of The Mist," I said with a small voice.

"What are you doing?" Boda whispered at me. "You want wisdom? Don't speak when spying on an enemy."

Acta knelt beside me as I continued.

"To the second and third—The River and The Flame, stay our hands with patience until we need to draw upon our strength."

Boda stopped walking and found a tree to lean against as I finished.

My prayers worked their way through each of The Mother's Great Spirits, reaching for something of the belief I once had. What may have looked like devotion to Boda was me grasping in the darkness to believe light was possible. The spirits had left us to fend for ourselves. They had allowed their little sister to turn The Song into a marker in her game.

"To the seventh—ancestor spirit, I'm trying to find a path beyond my anger. Try the same." I kissed three fingers and pressed them to the soil.

Acta copied the gesture.

"Are you finished?"

"That's typically what kissing your fingers indicates," I said before continuing towards the farming village.

In some ways, being consumed with anger like Boda would be easier. Rage felt powerful. This questioning and fighting with my anger put me at odds with myself. Instead of only one battle, I had to fight a second.

"Blessed Mother, let this be worth the pain."

Gray light from the overcast sky began to filter in more and more as the trees thinned out. The awful orchestra of echoes focused into something more reminiscent of The Song. Then the first field stretched out in tall stalks of corn reaching for the promised rain in the clouds above.

A watchtower broke the serenity of the landscape, jutting out from the crop with a pair of soldiers—little more than silhouettes in the gray-painted sky.

The village where I was born had been surrounded by farmland. From the few memories I could piece together, it had been beautiful. Ferin Seit had likely been the same before the Gousht marred the countryside with perches to kill anyone who stepped out of line.

We watched from the tree line, where the forest became field. Stalks of corn shifted as farmhands moved through them; Enneans, clothed in ragged robes, harvesting The Seed's gift.

These people had likely farmed this land from the moment they were old and strong enough to help till the soil. Back then, they had done so to feed their families. Communities like this formed around villages and cities where folks could barter and congregate. Their hands fed each other. They made a life of it.

But harvesting a crop they would never taste wasn't a life. And they wouldn't be forced to it much longer.

We walked the perimeter, always deep enough within the forest for its shadows to cloak our movements. One field transitioned into another as corn turned to cabbage, squash, and vined tomatoes.

With enough occupied farms, the couta bastards could keep their soldiers well fed for far longer than we could wage our lopsided war. When the people working the land died, the Gousht would replace them with more stolen Enneans. The cycle would continue unless we broke it.

An echo broke from the chorus, carried against the breeze. Sharp cuts of The Flame sang through the distorted haze of angry noise as it grew closer.

Boda nearly pounced on me when I touched his shoulder, but he restrained himself when he met my eyes. I gestured to the west and squatted behind the overgrown thicket.

Acta followed suit immediately, but Boda took several long breaths before he joined us.

Through the brush, glimpses of green and yellow moved along the tree line, a pair of voices moving with them.

"And whenever it's Terrin's rotation, he always has an excuse," the shorter of two soldiers said in Gousht. *"Not like he'd ever be caught in the fucking rain."* He lifted his chin to the sky as he continued to walk.

"Must be nice to have a commander for an uncle. If his nose were shoved any farther up that prick's asshole, he'd be smelling his supper."

The second, taller soldier came into view, a dull crimson crystal dangling from his neck. He held out his hand and caught a raindrop, then pulled his cloak tighter to his body. *"If Farley and Tulker finish what's left of the barley wine before we rotate off, I'm going to beat on them like they're one of these fucking konki."*

The moment the soldier finished enunciating his slur, the brush beside me stirred.

Boda had already slid his blade halfway out of the scabbard. Everyone who had warned me against bringing him would be saying they were right as I passed into the fucking Mist. Tomi would half enjoy saying it too.

As I grabbed Boda's wrist and strained to keep him from drawing his weapon, Acta placed his hand on his sword hilt.

The soldiers stopped. Their gazes probed the forest in our direction. My muscles tensed. My skin crawled, and I became hyperaware of the way the breeze teased the hairs on my arms. My body wanted to flee from me—to fall prone and hide in the dirt.

"You heard it too, right?"

A few droplets fell on leaves overhead, creating a soft rhythm above. *"Just the rain."*

"No, I heard something."

"Do you want to go traipsing through this forest in the middle of a storm? Get your ass moving. I'm not pulling extra hours because you heard rain fall on leaves." The taller soldier continued along, leaving his companion behind staring after the noise.

Boda showed his teeth in a snarl in my direction, no longer fighting to pull his sword free.

As the first soldier passed, I held my breath, watching his boots for any change in his gait. But the rhythm never changed.

If The Mother allowed me to escape this moment, my prayers would have to start being a bit kinder.

A handful of stifled breaths passed. Then the rain started truly falling—large, heavy drops filled with the chill of a deepening autumn. The second guard wiped his face with his sleeve, turned, and hurried after his companion.

My robes soaked up each droplet of water and clung to my skin, but I still couldn't bring myself to move. None of that seemed to restrain Boda.

The cocksure little shit rose without a care for revealing himself or stirring the bushes—his passive challenge to the soldiers who had already passed beyond earshot.

He wore his unearned confidence like a banner to call forth every would-be challenger. All the rage that I had spent my days and nights trying to stifle broke through the shoddy barriers I had constructed.

In two steps, I had Boda pinned to a tree with fists full of his wet robes. "If you don't want to see tomorrow, make that your burden, not mine."

"Three of us. Two of them. We could have killed them before they made a sound."

"Can we talk a little farther away from the Gousht outpost?" Acta asked.

I released Boda and stepped back, looking for the clever boy that I had come to know. "How dim are you? This is our first scouting mission. If two of their soldiers go missing on patrol, we will never be able to take these fields. We would be lucky if they only brought in more soldiers to bolster their ranks. More likely, they would kill the farmhands and burn the fields. They can always find more land for us to till."

"I'm sick of you acting like you know shit about the world. If you know so much, how are you so fucking bad at keeping the people you love alive? You seem to collect the dead like breaths."

"Your anger isn't going to help any of us. You think it makes you strong, but you can't see a pair of paces in front of you."

"Oh? Is there something wrong with my vision?" Boda asked, allowing his words to pick up into the air more and more. If not for the rain, we would have raised alarms. "I won't hurt anyone who doesn't deserve it, but I got plenty of anger for everyone—you especially."

As furious as he was, his wet robes hung from his body as if he were too small for the cloth. I should have never brought him here. He should have never had to carry a sword or bury his brother so young.

"Niven wouldn't want this for you."

His hand snapped to the hilt of his blade. "I said I wouldn't hurt anyone who doesn't deserve it. You say his name one more time, I might decide that you do."

He stood there, staring at me in a challenge to repeat his brother's name. Instead, I looked away in regret as the rain thickened into sheets of water falling from the sky.

Before I could find the words that someone wiser should have said to him, Boda turned his back on me and began walking back the way we came.

"So, a bit of history between you two?" Acta asked, lips stretched into a thin line of discomfort.

"This is going to be a long few days," I said as I followed Boda back to where we had left our supplies.

CHAPTER NINE

CURRENT DAY ENNEA

Kaylo stared at his father's knife clinging to the lodestone. It hadn't moved in three days. No one had come.

Beyond the lodestone, the Sanine River bent and flowed north. The water caught glimpses of the falling sun through the clouds. The view was too peaceful for the chaos in Kaylo's head.

It had been nearly eighteen turns since he sat across from Zusa beside this river. He hadn't chosen this lodestone for sentimental value, but it conjured ghosts of past decisions regardless.

If he had known his fate—the people who would die, the clash of armies to come—he still wouldn't have been able to tell Zusa no. The boy he had been was incapable of seeing past his pain and his desire to end it with blood.

He was a different man now with different reasons, chasing a different cause. Yet, he had returned to the same spot seeking another rebel army.

Tayen sat at the edge of the clearing, playing with the gnarled shadows of a contorta plant. The twists and turns of shade that mimicked its branches straightened and stretched in opposing directions. An inexperienced observer would never have known the level of concentration it took to distort shadows individually and maintain their new shape. It was far easier to move them as a collective.

The longer they waited for the Uprising, the more time she spent playing with shadows in silence. She hadn't criticized his plan or complained about the waiting. She only grew quieter, which was somehow less comforting.

In her silence, he heard all his doubts.

Maybe the Uprising no longer visited the lodestones. The old ways helped people find them, but routines and repetition created risks. Maybe they had grown more cautious.

Time never promised anything save change.

He had made promises. If the Uprising wouldn't come to them, he would have to track them down—though he had no idea how to do that. Rebel armies didn't survive sustained wars without knowing how to hide their tracks.

Tayen wouldn't wait forever. Neither would Nix and Sosun.

Days, then a span, then a moon uncoiled in his mind in a matter of moments. He could see the silence shatter, every restrained protest loosed in an instant. Tayen would crawl back into the thick of her anger. Until she left just like he had.

Kaylo could try to predict the Uprising's movements. They looked for battles they could win, people they could free. If he knew more about the state of the war, he would've had better luck.

But of course, he didn't know. He had hidden in a fucking treehouse for a dozen turns like a coward.

With every intrusive thought, Kaylo squeezed the hilt of his sword tighter until the soft ochre of his knuckles went white. Then the shadows Tayen had been bending snapped into place, and he released his grip.

Her echo went silent, and a distorted version of it sprang up on the other side of the Sanine.

"Blessed fucking Mother! Why'd you do that?" Tayen turned to him, her eyes wide in anger.

"Into the forest! Now!" Kaylo shouted, but no one heeded him. They all stood and stared at the other side of the river.

A cloud of shadows emerged from the forest's edge. The Shadow sang an echo he had never heard outside of himself. He had met several spirit dancers, but he had only ever heard them bend spirits that had been trapped in crystals.

A sword whispered against a scabbard as Nix drew her blade, and an arrow tapped against the bow as Tayen readied her aim, but Kaylo simply stood with his hand far from the hilt of his sword.

He had borrowed spirits from dancers before—felt the natural state of his cursed gift. Only imprisoned spirits fought. But he had never seen another spirit dancer take an unburdened spirit. The shadows swirled in a wide stretch of darkness large enough to contain ten warriors. The echo didn't scream. The sound moved as it would with any other dancer, if only slightly muffled by the medium of a foreign host.

"What's going on, Kaylo?" Nix asked in the loudest whisper he had ever heard.

"Do something." Tayen stared at him with concern even as she pointed her drawn arrow towards the dark cloud.

Something about her concern lightened his chest. She hadn't given up on him.

"Give me a moment." He stepped farther into the open space between his companions and the newcomers.

If the spirit dancer had wanted to, they could have taken their time and followed the echo to Tayen. They could have sprung an ambush without a second thought. Instead, they decided to make a show of themselves. It was a message.

Kaylo walked the dozen paces to the lodestone.

Somewhere within the shadow cloud, there would be arrows aiming in his direction. They could pick him off with the simple release of their fingers.

When he came to the lodestone, he slowly removed his sword and gave it to the magnetic pull. The sharp ting filled the waiting tension as he maneuvered his sword and knife into an arrow pointing to the earth.

If they understood the signals, they would know him as a friend of The Mother.

He stepped away with empty hands as the charcoal gray cloud continued to swirl. "That doesn't belong to you," he said.

The silvery thread binding Tayen's stolen spirit to The Mist wavered in front of him, and he took it.

The dark cloud dispersed into countless shadows skittering home. In its wake, a young girl stood surrounded by three archers with their bows trained on Kaylo. Each of the archers wore sand-colored robes and colorful headwraps.

Evidently, the young spirit dancer had not earned her chani cloth yet. A braid formed a circlet around her head as if to protect the tight puff of curls blooming from the top of her scalp. Her eyes narrowed as she studied Kaylo.

He held the fragment of The Shadow for a moment longer than necessary. It felt so close to touching The Song that it always reignited his longing for The Seed. Then he released it.

"Would you mind lowering those bows?" Kaylo shouted. "This is sacred ground, and I would hate to bleed all over it."

With a gesture from the girl, who was far younger than the others, the archers did as he asked.

"You know the old signs?" The spirit dancer spoke with a dispassionate cadence.

"We are looking for the Uprising. Are you with them? Can you take us to them?" Kaylo asked.

The spirit dancer waved her hand as if dismissing the question. "We don't answer questions."

"That's not going to help establish trust here, is it?" Nix drew back her shoulders. Her sword remained at her side, but nothing about her body language welcomed the strangers.

"We didn't come here to earn your trust. We didn't expect to find anyone, let alone a spirit dancer and ill-tempered warrior wearing ragged

Lost Army uniforms. What do you want?" The spirit dancer's face remained impassive.

"We escaped—" Tayen began, but Kaylo cut her off.

"We are searching for the Uprising. I realize this is a question, but I need to know. Can you help us?"

The spirit dancer paused and looked at Tayen for a moment as if to consider what she had been about to say. "Weapons first. Toss them over the river, then we can talk."

"That's not going to happen." Nix shifted her grip around the hilt of her sword as if to challenge the strangers to take it.

Between Nix and Tayen, they would be more likely to start fighting the strangers than give in to their demands. They had reasons to mistrust the world. Blessed Mother, Kaylo had plenty of reasons too. However, if they wanted to join the Uprising, they would have to bend. They would have to give up some of their power.

"This is not a negotiation. If you want to find the Uprising, you need us. We don't need you." The spirit dancer turned and her archers followed her lead.

"Wait. Are you Jani? The robes and headwraps—the Jani are supposed to help people and serve Ennea."

The spirit dancer looked back over her half-turned shoulder. "I told you. We do not answer questions. If you want our help, you will have to disarm and trust us."

What can you tell us? Sosun signed, and Nix reluctantly translated.

"She doesn't talk?" The spirit dancer pointed at Sosun.

"You got a problem with that?" Nix took a step forward.

The spirit dancer only shook her head. "If you come with me, I can take you to someone who will answer all your questions."

"Can you tell us why your friends are so quiet?" Tayen asked like the words were an accusation.

"I am a representative of my people. That is all the explanation I intend to give right now."

"A little young for a representative," Nix said with derision.

"Stop," Kaylo said with a blunt edge to his voice. He turned to Tayen. "We came here for an opportunity to meet with the Uprising. This is what we have. We either take it or not."

Tayen looked between Kaylo and the strangers with a furrow forming along her brow. She hated how many choices had been taken from her. She had told him as much several times, and still, life demanded more concessions from her.

With a huff, Tayen walked to the edge of the river and tossed her bow to the other side.

CHAPTER TEN

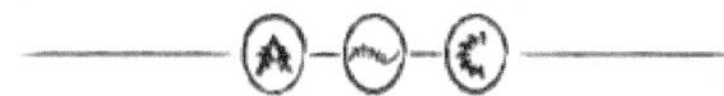

They walked for two days following the strangers. They hadn't answered any of Tayen's questions, and the time only served to exacerbate the feeling that she had been tricked.

Anytime she voiced her thoughts, Kaylo denied it. He saw the Jani robes and defaulted to trust. His nostalgia could kill them all as swift as any blade.

Not only did they not have any weapons, she couldn't use the shadows around the spirit dancer.

Tayen was done with this.

"Not the Uprising. Not answering any questions. Three grown warriors taking orders from a girl because she's a representative of their unnamed people." Tayen spoke loud enough for their new company to hear every syllable.

"Now's not the time," Kaylo said sharply.

"They're not rebels. 'Not exactly' is what they said. What are they? Seasonal rebels?"

The strangers didn't even react to her, which only made her angrier. Two armed warriors walked behind them while a third led the group alongside the spirit dancer. The fucks knew they had the upper hand.

"Tayen, I know not knowing makes you anxious, but they're wearing Jani robes."

"You're right. No one would ever put on robes to make them seem like someone they weren't. I like your purple uniform by the way."

"They didn't kill us. They didn't ambush us, which they could have. They gave us a choice, and you were the first one to throw your bow over the river.

"All in all, they are probably the friendliest people we have encountered since I met you. No offense, Nix," Kaylo said, angling his head back towards Nix.

"I'm not listening to you. As a rule, assume I'm not listening to you."

"See. Not that nice." His lips curved even though he was obviously trying to keep a straight face.

"Kaylo, I'm being serious. They haven't even given us their names," Tayen said. "This girl shows up, steals The Shadow, demands our weapons, and we're supposed to go along with it? This doesn't feel right."

"I get it. Regardless of what I have said, this doesn't feel great to me either. They threw us off balance, and I am still trying to get my feet under me," Kaylo said. "But we went to the lodestone, left our signal, and people came. I promised to get you to the Uprising. And sad as it is, this is the best I got."

She wanted to yell at him. It was just like when the Lost Army came to Dasoon. An archer marched behind her and wouldn't hesitate to kill her. Anytime she felt like she had taken a little power back from this off-kilter world, someone came along and snatched it back from her.

Kaylo stopped and the strangers behind them did as well. He looked down to meet her gaze. "Before we continue down this path, you should know there won't be freedom in a rebel army. You won't be making the decisions. They won't torment you like the Lost Army, but you will have to obey orders. Is that what you want?"

His face was earnest, eyebrows arching in a genuine question. It wasn't the type of question he liked to ask, the type that only had one answer. He wasn't leading her to his way of thinking like he always did.

Kaylo had this way of becoming a different version of himself with a single breath. He could act far younger than his turns, sarcastic and ambivalent. The next second his wrath would crack open his face into a mask of death. Or he could fade into the whisper of a man, lost in guilt and grief. However, one of the reasons Tayen trusted him was how he would occasionally drop every hint of pretense, becoming utterly honest and curious as if he wanted nothing more than to understand.

Their small convoy had all stopped and were waiting for her—not that their new guards cared about her answer. At least they didn't reach for their weapons or shout for her to move. No one would force her to follow this path. The decision belonged to her, as so few had.

After asking for power over her own life for too long, having this control struck her still. She didn't want to move a muscle.

"What if I choose wrong?"

"You'll make a new choice tomorrow. Choose your path for now, take in the world around you, and continually be open to the possibility of changing your mind."

When Tayen looked back to Sosun, the young woman joined her fists, interlaced her fingers, and shook them up and down in one motion. *"Together."*

Tayen returned the sign. "Let's go find out who these people are."

The group continued northeast through the forest for several hours until the youngest Daughters had fully taken over the sky. One of the guards collected firewood as the supposed nomads worked their way around the campsite, setting it to order. They worked as a unit, exchanging few words as they assisted each other setting a trip line around the perimeter, building a fire, and putting on a pot of water, vegetables, and saltmeat to boil.

When the soup finished cooking, they served Tayen, Kaylo, Sosun, and

Nix first, having only four bowls between them.

"No. Please, eat." Kaylo tried to push his bowl back into one of the archer's hands.

The man was younger than Kaylo, but only by a couple of turns if Tayen guessed right. The shock of red in his beard tied his heritage to the south. He smiled without showing his teeth. "As I've said before, it is our way to serve guests first."

"Do you disarm all your guests?" Tayen said with an edge to her voice. She had made the choice to follow them, but that didn't mean she had enjoyed their hospitality.

The spirit dancer tossed one of their purloined swords to the ground beside Tayen, an arm's length from where she sat. "Take it if it makes you feel better, shadow dancer."

Tayen grabbed the weapon as if calling the girl's bluff and placed it in her lap as she held her soup in the other hand. She hardly felt powerful holding broth, but she was too hungry to abandon it.

Sosun's hands danced in the firelight, and Nix translated. "How much longer until we reach your camp?"

"She doesn't answer questions," Tayen said in a mocking tone.

The spirit dancer lowered herself to sit across from Tayen. "I am confused. You came seeking help, we offered help, and yet, you want to pick a fight. Why?"

"I don't trust you."

"I understand that. I don't trust you either, but I'm not looking for a fight."

"She's had a rough go of it—" Kaylo started before the spirit dancer cut him off with a dismissive flick of her wrist.

"She can speak for herself. She doesn't need you to save her from a question, does she?"

"I'm not looking for a fight, but I'm ready for one." Tayen shifted and placed her bowl on the ground beside her. "Why did you steal my spirit back at the lodestone? Were you trying to show off, or just have some fun at my expense? You could have come out and treated our signal with respect."

"Respect? We respected your signal enough to offer you an escort back to our encampment. That doesn't mean I am willing to put my people in danger for strangers. I did what I thought was right. I make no apologies."

"You two are a lot alike," Kaylo said. "How did you become a representative for your people so young?"

The spirit dancer smiled at Tayen. "I listened. I learned. I followed my father's instructions," she said, then turned to Kaylo. "Are you really him? Ennea's Thief and all that?"

"What makes you think that?"

"My father told me the stories. The pieces fit."

"Your father? Who?"

"An elder. Any more would spoil the surprise," the spirit dancer said. "Enjoy your soup."

Tayen turned as someone tapped her on the shoulder. "Sosun wants to know why all you young people are so dramatic," Nix said.

"*I didn't say that,*" Sosun signed.

"Alright, maybe she didn't ask that, but it's still a fair question."

"We will arrive at our encampment by midday tomorrow. Get some sleep." The spirit dancer got up and returned to the other nomads.

<hr>

The strangers woke with the first glimpse of light and had the campsite set to rights before Kaylo had the chance to let out a proper yawn. Hospitable or not, truthful or not, these would-be Jani certainly played the part.

They had fed him and his companions. They knew their way through the Kenke. They hadn't tried killing him in his sleep—not that Kaylo had slept.

The more time that passed without their new friends turning on them, the more Kaylo considered trusting them. Maybe they were just overcautious Jani nomads. Maybe hope had worked in his favor for once.

The path they trod led them farther north, towards the bounds of the Kenke Forest. He noted landmarks and the time between them as had become his habit.

When the first reaching echoes began whispering to him, he signed to the others that they were nearing the encampment. It didn't keep him from nearly jumping from his skin when a high-pitched whistle burst through the morning. Three more whistles sounded in ascending pitch.

He caught glimpses of movement through the trees. They grew in clarity and frequency until the encampment came into view.

The trees rustled above the encampment entrance. Ironoak and ashburn trees in full bloom obscured the archers sitting in their perches, but they stood out clear enough for someone with the patience to look for them. They did not lower their bows when they saw the spirit dancer or her companions.

If Kaylo had expected to find the colorful, tree-lined tent city he had once known, he had been mistaken. Foliage-laced netting wrapped around the encampment in place of a tree wall. What few tents were visible over the net had been camouflaged into the surroundings with green and brown dyes.

"Home sweet home, huh?" Nix said, but no one responded.

Two guards, dressed in the familiar coverings, moved to block the entrance with their spears ready.

Jani or not, these were not the nomads of Kaylo's past. If he had the time to do so, he could find a way to blame the changes on himself. But people had to adjust to survive in wartime.

When they reached the entrance, the spear-wielding guards did not move. As different as the pair were in physical appearance—size, skin tone, and age—they wore the same heavy scowls on their faces. The shorter northerner stared at Kaylo and his companions as if to determine which one to attack first.

Beyond them, people roamed about unbothered by the scene at the entrance. A child scurried after her mother, tugging on her mother's sleeve for attention and pointing towards their small band. Her mother looked and waved her off as if they were nothing of note.

"Stay here. My father will want to greet you himself." The spirit dancer stopped beside the shorter northman and whispered into his ear before disappearing behind the camouflaged netting.

The northman adjusted his hands around his spear as his eyes landed on Kaylo. Something about this young man and his intense gaze reminded Kaylo of someone. He couldn't think of who. The feeling itched at the back of his scalp.

"Lovely weather, isn't it?" Kaylo smiled as amiably as he could.

The guard said nothing.

"Have you two been Jani your whole lives?" Kaylo asked the taller Tomakan guard with a few more turns to her. She did not answer either.

"Kaylo, would you mind shutting your breathing hole for a moment?" Nix asked. "Let's not antagonize these nice people with spears."

"The Jani aren't violent people." Kaylo gestured towards the folks walking about beyond the entrance.

"Those aren't welcoming sticks in their hands, you annoying jabbermouth," Nix said with more exasperation than anger, which always pleased him far more than it should.

"Maybe you should listen to Nix," Tayen said.

"How about we play nice and wait quietly?" Sosun signed.

"What did she say?" the northman demanded, pointing at Sosun. "That one. What did you say?!" He raised his spear towards her.

Nix immediately stepped in between the spear and Sosun. "She said we should all calm down, and I think you should take her advice."

"Don't tell me what to do." The young man took a step forward and his companion followed his lead.

Nix looked to the guards who had escorted them to the encampment. "Can you ask your friend to lower his weapon?"

The young Sonacoan man who had offered them bowls of soup

the night before stepped forward. "Jonan, there's no reason to escalate anything. Let's just wait for your father."

"You know who this is, right? He's already destroyed one Jani clan."

"Shut your mouth, piglicker." Tayen stepped forward, her echo swirling around her like the warning thunder of a storm.

Jonan swung his spear in a wild arc towards Tayen. The boy lacked self-control and a true understanding of his weapon. Kaylo lunged forward and grabbed the spear.

The blade would have sunk into Tayen's shoulder had he not intervened.

Nothing good had ever come of people telling stories about him.

Blood trickled down Kaylo's arm. The boy had attacked too wildly, and Kaylo had missed his mark. He had grabbed the bottom edge of the spear blade and it bit into his palm. It was a thoughtless mistake.

"Drop the spear before things get bad for you," Kaylo said, his voice rumbling in the back of his throat.

As Jonan tried to pull his spear from Kaylo's grip, blood began flowing more freely from the wound, but Kaylo only grasped the weapon tighter. Fear and surprise began to mix with the young man's abhorrence. He hadn't meant to injure anyone. It was clear enough on his face, but he wasn't ready to let go of his stubborn pride either.

"Jonan!" An older northman rounded the corner with the spirit dancer close behind him. "Drop the spear! And everyone, calm down."

Jonan looked from Kaylo to the approaching man, then released his grip and stepped back.

As soon as Kaylo eased his grip on the spear, the biting pain cooled slightly. He tossed the weapon to the ground in a show of good faith. Then he looked—truly looked—at the approaching northman and regretted letting go of the spear.

Kaylo darted back to the spear and leveled it at the northman. He carried more weight around his waist, and a few wrinkles had creased his forehead, but Kaylo would never forget this man's face. It had haunted too many nightmares.

Torrel waved for the nomads surrounding him to lower their weapons. "This is not how I meant to greet you," he said. "I've thought about seeing you again so many times, but I never imagined you'd be bleeding."

Kaylo took a step back as Torrel closed the gap between them, making sure to keep himself between Torrel and Tayen.

"Okay, I'll stay here," Torrel said with an attempt at a pacifying tone. "I'm sorry for my son. My children have not been the kindest of hosts, it seems."

The spirit dancer stood behind Torrel, looking on like an enthralled observer.

"Son? Daughter? You have a spirit dancer for a daughter? The Mother certainly has a sense of humor, doesn't she?" The playfulness of Kaylo's words did not pierce the harshness of his tone.

"That's fair. I deserve that. I was horrible to you. You never deserved anything I said or did to you, but that doesn't undo what has been done. I can only apologize."

Torrel's face and tone didn't hold any of the snideness or cruelty of his younger self. If Kaylo were to take this man as he was, he would have judged Torrel to be even-keeled. The Wind sang a steady hum about Torrel as if the air were meandering through the forest without aim.

Nix stood guard in front of Sosun, mirroring Kaylo's defensive stance in front of Tayen.

"We have a lot to catch up on. Won't you join me for a cup of tea?" Torrel asked.

"We have too much history for me to trust my people with you, Torrel. What guarantees can you offer me?"

"Only my promise as a father." He held out his hands in a gesture of welcome.

"Torrel!?" Tayen darted around Kaylo before he could stop her. In two quick strides, she reached Torrel and kicked him in the shin.

Guards rushed forward, but Kaylo dropped his spear and reached

Tayen first. He grabbed Tayen's raised fist before she could make things worse and dragged her backwards.

"Stop, lower your weapons!" Torrel shouted as he turned to his clan members. "No one harms them! Understood?!"

The same unsure faces Kaylo had seen time and time again on young people before battle appeared on the nomads in front of him. He stared at one Tomakan boy with shaky hands until the boy lowered his eyes.

"Shit, that really hurt." Torrel turned back to Kaylo, balancing most of his weight on one foot.

Tayen tried to wrestle from Kaylo's grip, but he held her firm. "Enough."

"Enough? After what this shit-slinger did, that's far from enough!"

"It's okay. I deserved that. However, it might be in our best interests to stop injuring each other for a moment," Torrel said, still balancing most of his weight on one leg.

Between the archers, Torrel's children, and the other guards, there were ten Jani watching Kaylo and Tayen intently. Hope had been a silly thing to allow himself. Things had gone bad, and they could go worse.

"Can you get us to the Uprising?" Kaylo asked.

Torrel offered a small grin that made him look much more like himself. "Of course."

Kaylo looked back to Nix, who remained ready to launch into a fight. "Fine," Kaylo said. "Lead the way."

Chapter Eleven

Current Day Ennea

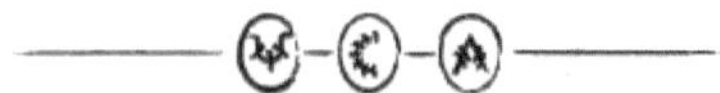

Kaylo sat in the home of the man who had cursed and beaten him as a child. He had convinced himself he deserved it. But of the many misfortunes Kaylo had earned over the course of his life, Torrel's animus hadn't been one of them.

It had taken turns in isolation to see that.

The clay tea cup warmed his hands as he waited for Torrel to speak, but Torrel moved around the tent adjusting one thing or another as if a welcomed guest had caught him unaware.

The tent itself was small. Bedrolls occupied the area opposite the entrance, a small fire blazed away in the cook pit, and a woven rug stretched out over the middle of the swept dirt floor. Kaylo and the rest of their small band sat on one side of the mat, while the spirit dancer sat on the other.

Time had a way of changing people more than it did memories. Without hesitation or difficulty, Kaylo could close his eyes and conjure the image of Torrel standing above him after beating him bloody—a looming outline in the deluge of rain like an ominous specter while the pain and mud enveloped Kaylo.

After that, Jonac had faded into clouds of smoke, which might not have been Kaylo's fault—his opinion on the matter changed on a daily basis. Either way, it had been a catalyst for far too much grief.

So many moments of Kaylo's life had grown beyond his control.

As he sat in Torrel's tent, he dug his thumbnail into the pad of his index finger. The voices of his guilt grew louder. Torrel added another log to the firepit. No one was speaking. Kaylo's chest tightened around his breath, and the heat in the tent swelled.

"Can you sit down?" Kaylo said before realizing how loudly his words came out. He paused as all the eyes in the tent snapped towards him. "You asked to speak with me, so speak."

Torrel stopped milling about and took a deep breath. "You're right. I can't delay this."

The silence might have been broken, but the tent still felt like a trap. Kaylo dug his nail in deeper to his fingertip until the skin opened. The sweet pain distracted his mind.

Torrel sat beside his daughter, crossing his legs. "I have to apologize for Jonan's actions again. I'm afraid he carries too much of his father's old rage. I hope that Nomi was more welcoming." He gestured to the spirit dancer.

"Nomi and Jonan?"

"Don't tell me she didn't introduce herself." Torrel looked at his daughter.

"It would've ruined the surprise," Nomi said with a shrug.

"What's going on here?" Nix asked. "Are you part of the Uprising or not?"

"Not exactly," Torrel said.

"What is up with this 'not exactly' shit? Your daughter said the same thing," Nix said. "You are either part of the Uprising or you aren't."

"Give me a chance to explain."

"Not another damn storyteller," Nix said, and Sosun slapped her arm, wearing a stern face.

Torrel smiled. "I was raised by a storyteller. It's my way." He took a sip of his tea. "When Kaylo left—"

"You mean, when you sent Kaylo away?" Tayen interrupted.

"Yes. I guess that is a more truthful way of saying it." Torrel looked everywhere but at Kaylo or Tayen. "What remained of the Fallen Rock Clan traveled to the mountains in the northwest of Sonacoa. We followed the signs and found another clan. Life continued as much as it could after what we had lost. Then stories found their way to us about a spirit thief who had liberated Oakheart Mountain.

"Jonac immediately knew it was you. He dove deeper into his smoke, until one day he stopped. Hearing about you fighting back against the Empire had shamed him. He had been your kana, and you were doing everything he knew he should have been.

"It took time, but he convinced the clan to do their part—to truly serve the people of Ennea. We sought out refugees, instead of waiting for them to find us. But that wasn't enough for him, not when he continued to hear stories about the Uprising and Ennea's Thief." Torrel gestured to Kaylo as if the title were a pleasant one.

"Eventually, we sent out envoys to find the Uprising and create an alliance. By then, you had left. Jonac was inconsolable for days after he missed his chance to resolve matters between you." Torrel bit his lip and paused. "It only made Jonac more determined to make you proud. We never joined the Uprising. The Jani have our own way but we don't avoid the fighting that comes our way. And we don't turn away those who need our help. Not anymore."

As Kaylo listened, one thought continued to fight for his attention. Every time Torrel said Jonac's name, he spoke of him in the past tense. *Is he dead? Did I miss my chance too?*

"So you know how to bring us to the Uprising?" Nix translated Sosun's question.

"I do."

"You have plenty of warriors, even a spirit dancer." Tayen's tone turned the statement into an accusation. "Why not join the Uprising? This war needs all of us."

"Don't talk to my father like that." Nomi's voice lacked scorn or force. She spoke as a reminder.

Torrel placed a hand on his daughter's knee to quiet her. "The war needs all of us, but it doesn't need all of us to be swords. Some of us have to take care of those who can't take care of themselves."

Even as Torrel continued to talk, he neglected to answer the one question that consumed Kaylo's every thought. It grew with each lingering moment—every word that failed to answer the question.

"Is Jonac dead?" Kaylo asked, the breath falling out of him with the question.

Torrel met Kaylo's eye for the first time. "No, he's not."

"Where is he?"

"Kaylo, there's something you need to know."

"Torrel, where is Jonac?" Kaylo's heavy voice emanated from deep in his gut with the force of his need.

Torrel sighed and nodded. "I'll take you to him. The rest of you are free to roam the grounds. You are our guests."

"I need you to stay with Nix and Sosun," Kaylo said to Tayen.

"No, I want to come with you. You need me."

Kaylo gripped Tayen's shoulder. "You may be right, but I need to see him on my own first. Too much needs to be said, and I can't have you kicking him in the shin too."

"I'm being serious."

"Tayen, please. You know some things can only be between kana and toka."

"If he does anything, I have no problem hitting old men."

Kaylo chuckled. "I know that far too well."

Torrel waited for Kaylo at the tent entrance. The fall of his shoulders gave him the look of a man about to regret what he had to do.

If he was being honest—if Jonac had truly wanted reconciliation before, why not now? Had the Uprising told him about how Kaylo left?

Had he changed his mind?

I ran away and lost my chance, Kaylo thought. *He wanted to make me proud, and I turned out to be a disappointment.*

Eyes lingered as Kaylo walked through the tent city like the first time he had come to the Fallen Rock Clan. People watched him in the way that one might stare at an animal far larger than it should be—curious and frightened. They knew exactly who he was, but that only spurred more questions.

"Is that him?" a little girl asked too loudly before her father shushed her.

Kaylo paid the girl little mind.

Over the turns, he had imagined what he would say to his old kana if he ever had the chance to meet him again. He had pled, and yelled, and cried as he spoke to the empty hallow. The Jonac in his mind had never forgiven him.

Aspects of the tent city resembled the Jani encampment Kaylo had known. Small gardens grew between clusters of tents. A larger gathering tent stood out amongst the others. However, it was all smaller, not only smaller in size but in spirit. The color had been drained from the nomadic city. It more closely resembled an Uprising encampment.

Torrel came to a tent towards the outer limit of the encampment. "Kaylo, before you go in there, he isn't the same man you knew."

Kaylo had known several Jonacs in their short time together. Whatever version awaited him, Kaylo had to face his kana before he lost his will. He pushed into the tent without a word of response.

The furs fell back over the tent's entrance, and shadows claimed the inside of Jonac's tent. A small brazier flickered beside a bedroll where a clump of blankets lay. The space lacked function. There was no table or true cookfire. The slanted walls of the leather canvas were bare. The tapestries and carvings Jonac had littered their old home with were absent. Nothing distinguished the space from any other.

A soft snore trembled through the blankets, humming in the empty space. The smell of lavender and cherry wood masked the odor of unwashed flesh.

What is this?

As Kaylo got closer, the lumps under heavy blankets took form.

Jonac wasn't wearing his headwrap. Kaylo had only seen the man's hair on a handful of occasions. To a Jani, their headwrap was a commitment to The Mother—a symbol that they would not hide their promise to Ennea no matter the danger. Everyone would know them as Jani.

Gray and white strands streaked through his fading red hair. It had been nearly two decades since Kaylo had seen Jonac, but he had aged far beyond the passing time. His cheeks had hollowed out.

The only thing that remained the same was his echo. The Seed plucked soft notes of new budding life. The texture that ran through it belonged to Jonac.

Kaylo stood at the edge of the tent, tears welling up in his eyes, as his old kana slept. He had given up on hearing that particular cadence and quality of The Seed again. If nothing else about this old man belonged to Jonac, that sound did.

Time passed with too many thoughts to count before the snoring stuttered to a stop, and the blankets shifted.

"Who's there?" Jonac asked, his voice husky with sleep.

The entrance was several paces away. Kaylo could be gone before Jonac knew he had been there. He wouldn't have to face his kana. But the shame would kill him. Kaylo stepped forward into the brazier's light, remaining silent.

"Oh, hello." Jonac sat up on his bedroll. "Who are you? Wait. No. You remind me of a boy I know. The kid is always getting himself into trouble, but he's a good one.

"You know how you can see when a person has been hurt? It's something about the way the boy carries himself—always hesitant to look people in the eyes. He hasn't told me what happened. Maybe he will someday, but I don't like to pry. We all need our secrets, especially when so little in this world belongs to us anymore."

Jonac looked every bit the man he had been when Kaylo first met him. The bitterness and anger that had grown in him after he started smoking susu root again wasn't there.

"Jonac, it's me. Kaylo."

"Stop with that. Kaylo hasn't even met his swearing day yet." The friendliness in his expression persisted even as his brow crinkled in confusion.

"You found me in Sonacoa not too far from the Tampir River. I called The Seed and a ring of razorthistle bloomed all around me. Torrel complained about the cuts on his leg for a span."

"Even longer than that." He paused. "Kaylo?"

Either sleep or smoke had left Jonac disoriented. Kaylo came closer to the light, and knelt beside the bedroll. Jonac's expression exploded into a smile Kaylo hadn't seen since he was a boy.

Jonac sat up and grabbed Kaylo by the shoulders. He pushed and pulled Kaylo as if he were trying to test his eyes with his hands. "How? Where has the time gone? You're all grown up. You really need to trim your beard."

"I can't tell you how much I've missed you. I'm so sorry."

"Sorry for what? You're here! This is a cause for celebration." Jonac stood up, and the blankets fell off him, revealing his naked chest and a pair of worn pants. His stomach sagged from the weight that had fallen from his frame, making him seem less sturdy. "Where have Nomi and the girls gone?"

A chill overtook Kaylo's lungs as if the coldest day of winter crawled down his throat.

"There's not enough light in here. Junera! Soca! They are always getting into trouble. The little things, you know. Nothing bad. Just the type of trouble that teaches kids about the world."

"The girls aren't here, Jonac."

"No matter. Let me get you some tea." He spun around the tent, head swiveling back and forth. His hands started fidgeting with one another. "Where...where are we? This isn't my tent. My cook pit should be over there. I shouldn't be here. Why is it so dark?"

Jonac grew more frantic in his searching about the tent. His foot caught beneath the bedroll, and he tumbled to the ground.

Kaylo rushed to his side, wrapping a blanket around his bare shoulders.

"Nothing's as it should be, Kaylo." Jonac burrowed himself into Kaylo, his body shaking. "What's going on?"

Jonac's echo folded one layer of The Song over another as if he were searching for something. The chaos of the sounds grew like an invasive species claiming the soil.

"It's going to be okay." Kaylo squeezed his kana tightly. "I just came by for a visit."

"But where is Nomi?"

"She's out collecting water for soup." Torrel stood at the entrance, a silhouette framed by the daylight. "Kaylo came unannounced, and Nomi wanted to make sure there would be enough to go around tonight."

Torrel walked over to the pair of them as if nothing were wrong. "We are so happy to have Kaylo back."

Jonac stopped shaking and met Torrel's gaze. "Happy? That doesn't sound like you at all, Torrel. You need to be nicer to that boy. I know you have a hard time trusting people, but you won't ever be who you can be if you look at everyone like they're an enemy first."

"My kana is as wise as ever." Torrel squatted down. "We have a celebration to look forward to tonight. Why don't you get some rest? Kaylo and I have a lot to discuss."

"You promise you'll be nice? Torrel, I know when you're lying to me."

"I know you do. I'll be nice. I have a lot to apologize for." Torrel looked at Kaylo. "I haven't been the man you or my mother raised me to be."

Jonac caressed Torrel's cheek with his thumb and gave him a playful pat. "You will find your way. I'm sure of it."

The intimacy of that moment—Kaylo holding Jonac as Jonac held Torrel's cheek—slowed the world down. Whatever was happening, Kaylo had to help his kana find peace, even if only for now.

He and Torrel smoothed out the bedroll and helped Jonac settle himself under his blanket.

As Kaylo's hands worked, he couldn't help but remember the times when he had woken up with nightmares in the early days after Jonac took him in. His kana had been a gentle man and deserved gentleness in return. He could ask his questions later.

"Kaylo?" Jonac grabbed his hand. "Do you think you could help me carve something nice for Nomi? The girls love the animals you carved them, especially Junera. If she ever lets go of that rabbit, I'll know something has gone wrong."

Kaylo's throat swelled up immediately. Junera's lifeless hand on the charred rabbit flashed across his mind. "I'd be happy to," he said, trying to keep the pain from his voice.

"That's my toka." Jonac patted Kaylo's hand and shifted to get more comfortable on the pillow.

The sounds of his sleeping filled the tent after no time at all.

Torrel tapped Kaylo's shoulder and gestured to the entrance, but Kaylo couldn't leave his kana. He should never have left. Exiled or not, he could have followed the Jani. He could have been there for the man who had saved him.

"He's not going anywhere, little brother," Torrel said.

The honorific sounded strange from Torrel. He had never called Kaylo anything of the sort, but they were brothers in a way. They shared a kana—a man who had raised them both for a time.

Kaylo relented his vigil beside Jonac's bedroll and followed Torrel out of the tent. Torrel didn't stop when they reached Sokan's light. He walked to the edge of the encampment and continued along the foliage-laced netting.

The questions fought for Kaylo's attention. His kana was the man he remembered in so many ways, yet time had fractured him.

"I need you to start talking, Torrel."

"Do you know how Jonac became addicted to susu root?"

A swell of anger fought through the questions. "Please, Torrel, tell me what happened to Jonac."

"He asked me to tell you the truth if I ever saw you again—in one of his more lucid moments." Torrel continued to walk, looking straight forward as he spoke. "He had a family before the Housht arrived. He had a son."

Kaylo stopped walking, and it took Torrel a few moments to realize it. *A son?* he thought. It made a certain sense. The fury contained within Jonac must have had a name.

Torrel faced Kaylo. The tent city hummed in the distance as people continued their lives. Unfamiliar echoes underscored the movement of the people.

"The Housht spoke of friendship at first, then their armada landed on the southern coast. Jonac's small village was one of the first they attacked. That was before they found those damned crystals, but they still had their iron and steel.

"After he lost his first family, Jonac joined the fight. From what he told me, he cut down more soldiers than he could count. It was never enough."

All the questions that had taken up residence in Kaylo's mind were displaced by infinitely more. At the same time, pieces about the man he had known started to fit themselves together.

"Two turns in, Tomak and Renēqua had joined the war. They were pushing the green bastards back to the ocean." Torrel's voice cracked with his soft rage, but he did not raise his voice. "Then they found their God Caves, and the war turned. A spirit dancer betrayed their position, Jonac was captured, and the Housht stole his spirit."

"How? That makes no sense. He still has The Seed."

"You and Jonac have even more in common than you thought. Both twice-marked." Torrel smiled as if the revelation—the hidden truth—should bring Kaylo happiness. "Without The Flame, he lost hope of escaping. They threw him in with the lot they were forcing to mine crystals in Oakheart."

An image of the mines settled in Kaylo's vision. Enneans being shuffled in and out of the dark recesses of the mines. Soldiers beating whoever they decided to. The bodies of his people emaciated and broken. He couldn't imagine Jonac amongst them.

"He worked the mines for nearly a turn before he organized his escape," Torrel said. "Of the twenty people who fought their way free, only three survived. Jonac's secret connection to The Seed saved them. Then they stumbled upon the Fallen Rock Clan."

Torrel's face grew long and his jaw stiffened. He sat on the ground, as if standing was too much to ask of him at that moment. When he couldn't force the words out of his mouth, Kaylo joined him on the dirt.

Did I ever know Jonac? he thought.

Jonac had told him a story before—three Sonacoans had escaped the mines. The Gousht tracked them down and found the clan. Torrel's mother died fighting the Gousht.

Torrel sat beside Kaylo, his eyes counting specks in the soil.

"Your mother? Jonac told me—he never said he was responsible."

"He wasn't," Torrel said. "Just like you weren't when the Gousht tracked you."

"I'm so sorry—"

"When the Gousht charged in, no one fought harder than Jonac and my mother. She took so many of those bastards from this plane with her flames." He stopped and met Kaylo's eyes. "You know, I never blamed Jonac. He did, but he couldn't wallow in it because he had to take care of me."

"Why didn't anyone tell me? Why keep it a secret?"

"It isn't easy to talk about. Jonac was the only escapee who survived," Torrel said. "I learned how to hate, and he taught me how to defend our clan if anyone ever tried to bring their violence to our home again."

When Kaylo had met Torrel, he had only been two turns past his swearing day. Of course he hadn't trusted Kaylo. Why would he? Then Kaylo had become everything Torrel was afraid of.

"Torrel, I never meant to—"

"You have nothing to apologize for. I know you won't believe that. I told Jonac the same thing, and he never believed it either. He never stopped blaming himself." He wiped his cheeks and turned to Kaylo. "The Gousht started experimenting with susu root at Oakheart. That's where they developed black tar. It was just another thing Jonac survived.

"They hadn't figured out exactly how to concentrate the drug into the paste yet, but it still left its mark. It took turns for Jonac to put susu root behind him after he escaped. Then I fucked that up. I couldn't see past my own hurt and mistrust. When I attacked you, he fell hard into his old addiction."

"It wasn't your fault," Kaylo said. "I mean the part where you beat me senseless—that was your fault—but the addiction wasn't."

A heavy silence waited between them as Torrel stared at Kaylo, then he burst out laughing and Kaylo joined in. The shape of their laughter had rough edges, cracked with pain and trauma. The breath fell out of them into their sorrowful joy.

"You are an asshole, you know that?" Torrel asked, still trying to control himself.

"And you are an absolute prick."

"I am." Torrel burst into laughter again, wiping away new tears.

For a moment, all of their trauma pooled around them and they were boys again, splashing in the mess. Their laughter petered out like a flame reaching the end of its wick.

"So, it was the susu root that did all of this to Jonac?"

"I don't know. Either the susu root or age being cruel to a man who has already faced too much cruelty," Torrel said. "He has some good days. Those days can be worse because he understands what he's lost. We look after him and love him the best we can."

"Thank you for being there for him." Kaylo clapped him on the back as they sat like brothers.

"He was there for me."

CHAPTER TWELVE

Tayen sat beside a communal garden as the nomads went about their day. The few people who looked in her direction nodded amiably before continuing on, paying no mind to how the shadows bent around the stalks of callaloo growing from the soil.

These people had built a community around avoiding the war. Sitting here, the violence felt distant. Her parents had wanted something like this for her, but they hadn't trusted anyone enough. Maybe it was for the best. With their luck, they would have ended up some place like Dasoon, being sold to the Lost Army for a sack of grain.

The little decisions—the ways life could have changed course— seemed innumerable. If her parents had sought out a community instead of going it alone; if Kaylo hadn't saved her from the soldiers who killed her family; if she had chosen to stay with the Lost Army; if she had killed Daak... So many moments and choices made her into this person. She didn't know if she liked the result.

She was selfish, rude, angry, weak, scared, lonely, and fucking needy.

What would her next choice make of her? If she wasn't going to be the rash warrior lashing out in vengeance, who was she supposed to be?

The Shadow sang a song of conflicting patches of shade, overlapping to create a richer black then fading into nothing. Shadows were as unstable as they were constant. She felt more like a shadow than a dancer.

Nomi walked into the corner of her view and sat beside the garden. Her curls were more brown than black as they fell in tight ringlets around her face. She had her father's angular nose and distinctive brow. Every other feature must have belonged to her mother.

Tayen stopped dancing with the shadows immediately.

"Scared I'll take it away again?" A sly smile crept along Nomi's face.

Did Torrel smile that way when he was younger, beating Kaylo in the rain? Tayen wondered.

"Aren't you worried what people will think about you stealing from other dancers?"

"Hmm? I hadn't thought about it much. I am what and who I am. Why should I worry about what everyone else thinks?"

"I thought this was supposed to be a community," Tayen said.

"Don't get me wrong. I care about the clan. I care deeply about what happens to them—their safety, their happiness—but I can't care about what they think of me." Nomi leaned forward and plucked a cherry tomato from a nearby plant. She ran her fingers along the shiny skin, inspecting the fruit. "Do you know how many 'no heart for a thief' stories there are? I can't carry that weight on my shoulders. They can think what they want about me as long as they treat me with respect."

"Like your father treated Kaylo?"

"My father didn't even know Kaylo was a spirit dancer. Can you imagine what he might have done if he had known?" She chuckled at the thought. Actually fucking chuckled.

"Are you defending your father? Kaylo was your age! Torrel almost killed him."

Nomi popped the cherry tomato in her mouth and shook her head as she chewed. "No. You misunderstand me. I know all too well what kind of violence people are capable of because of what and who I am. My father wasn't right. It wouldn't have been right if he had killed Kaylo, just like it wouldn't be right if anyone attacked me for my spirit ancestor. But they can hate me all they want as long as they don't act on it."

"I don't understand you at all."

"You care too much about what other people will think, especially Kaylo," Nomi said. "Warriors, kings, elders, spirits great and small—what they think about us can't be the reason why we do what we do. When my father attacked Kaylo, he was too concerned about how he lost his mother. He was too concerned about what might happen or what people would think if he didn't stop it from happening."

A drip of tomato juice ran like an orange-red tear from her lip. She wiped it away with her thumb, while maintaining far-too-intense eye contact. Tayen's instincts begged her to look away, but her stubbornness refused to break the connection.

"Why didn't you tell us who your father was before we arrived?"

"I thought that was a bit obvious. My father told me what he did to Kaylo when we found out about my connection to The Balance. Not all the gruesome details, because I was seven, but I've known for a while," Nomi said. "I assumed if he knew who I was and where I was taking you, he would walk in the opposite direction. I would have."

"And your brother? What the fuck was his problem?"

"Next spring, when we swear to The Mother, he's gone. You seem to have a lot in common with him. He is ready to run off into war, and not because he doesn't love the Jani. No, he loves this clan with all his heart. But everything looks like a threat to him. He is exactly who my father used to be." Nomi lifted her brows and smiled. "Let's just say they have had some 'conversations' about that."

"What about you? Don't you want to fight?" Tayen leaned in closer. Something about this girl drew her in. She carried herself as if she never questioned her words—like she actually understood her place in the world. Something Tayen had never grasped.

"Nomi!" a Tomakan woman called out from across the way, waving for her to come.

Nomi stood up, plucking another tomato from the plant. "I think this is the fight. People need to be out there fighting the soldiers, but people also need to be here making sure we survive. It can't all be a battle."

She popped the second tomato in her mouth and headed off towards where the Tomakan woman had been.

This is the fight? Tayen thought. That didn't make any sense. The Jani could shelter as many people and collect as many cultural touchstones as they could carry, but it wouldn't mean anything if the Gousht won the war. Probably wouldn't mean much if the Lost Army won either.

Fighting—real fighting—was the only way to keep Enneans alive.

The peak of the gathering tent above Sosun's head rose high into the forest canopy. Despite the falling sun, an odd collection of braziers and firepits illuminated the communal space in a brilliant glow. The elders had announced a celebratory feast in honor of her and her odd companions joining them. The entire community took the announcement as permission to drop the weight of their worries for a night.

Families brought large sitting rugs patterned with ornate flowers and animal renderings. They brought stews, curries, breads, roasted meats, and jugs of barley wine, setting the air spinning with greasy, spice-laden aromas that made the outside world and its problems distant. Two young women with drums played gentle rhythms that seemed to contort around one another.

When the more than forty nomads gathered in small circles around the different sitting rugs, their colorful chani headwraps turned them into a field of wildflowers. Conversations buzzed and joined the blessed aromas in the air. However, Sosun felt detached from the celebration.

She sat between Nix and Tayen, who sat beside Kaylo. Torrel, Nomi, and Etee, Torrel's wife, sat along the opposite end of the circular rug. Everyone spoke politely. They passed platters of food and made sounds of contented bellies. No one broached unpleasant topics.

Occasionally, Tayen glared at Nomi or Torrel in a manner that could have been construed as rude, but everyone else had dedicated themselves to playing their agreeable role. So no one said anything.

The group did everything they could to avoid silence. Torrel had repeated how much he enjoyed the curry goat several times when the conversation lulled.

Sosun considered faking a bellyache to escape the tension.

"Where is Jonan?" Kaylo asked.

"He brought food to Jonac," Etee said. She wore a wide smile despite the heavy atmosphere. The reds of her headwrap made the copper undertones of her dark skin dance. "That boy has never taken anything as seriously as watching over his grandfather."

Kaylo bowed his head as if it pained him to hear about Jonac connecting with the boy. "Good. It lightens the burden to know that Jonac has so many people to care for him."

The conversation sputtered to a stop. There was more to be said. Kaylo hadn't shared the details about Jonac's condition with the rest of them, and Sosun didn't dare ask.

She had seen mountain servants succumb to susu root. They lost touch with the moment after too many turns breathing smoke too deeply. The others tried to protect them—keep the warriors from noticing their condition—but they were unpredictable. One moment, they would be lucid, and the next, time would reverse for them. They would forget themselves, where they were, why their tongues refused to work.

When the warriors took them away, they never came back.

The Gousht and the Lost Nation had hurt so many in countless ways. There probably wasn't a single Ennean who hadn't felt it. Yet, they feasted and bantered like some idealized version of Ennea still existed. This little feast was a pretty lie.

Nix nudged her, and tilted her head towards the food Sosun wasn't eating. *"Is your stomach hurting you? I know it's heavy food, but you should try to eat what you can,"* Nix signed, speaking in step with her hands.

The curry goat lay atop a bed of purple yam, in Tomakan style. When she had lived in Sonacoa with her mother, they served curries with leavened bread. The air pockets in the bread sopped up the gravy so that it burst with each bite. It had taken her time, but she had come to appreciate the way the yam teased out the flavor in the curry.

It looked delicious, but it felt indulgent.

"If we win, do you think Ennea will ever be our home again?" she signed.

"Ennea is our home."

"This is an illusion." Sosun gestured over the crowded tent. *"This Ennea is dead. The Mother is scarred, and I don't know if we'll ever get her back."*

"Do you want to stay here? We can have this illusion for as long as possible."

"What?" A heat rose in Sosun's chest—the lingering feeling that she should not have trusted Nix again. Those pretty words about helping Sosun find her way to her version of freedom had been sour excrement.

"We could help. We could make a life here," Nix signed. *"You never intended to fight on the front lines."*

When Sosun first met Nix, the leader of the city guard, she had seemed like an unmoving boulder. No one—no army—could have moved her. Nix still carried herself like that for the most part, but the boulder had deep fissures left by guilt.

Sosun didn't need a Nix cracked into pieces with shame. She needed the woman who had been bold enough to sell her away in the first place, as unpleasant as that reality might be.

"Don't coddle me. I don't need you to hide me from the world. I won't be hidden away any longer." Regardless of the pain on Nix's face, Sosun needed to make her understand. *"I am no use with a sword or a bow, but that doesn't mean I don't have use. There are people fighting out there, and I am going to do whatever I can to make sure they win. We will find out what kind of Ennea we are left with afterwards."*

Nix tilted her head away, her eye still flickering back to Sosun in case she had more to say. As pathetic as Nix looked, Sosun had to make her point.

"Can you accept that?" Sosun signed, then repeated when Nix didn't respond.

"If that's what you want."

Sosun spooned the starchy yam and gamey curry into her mouth to focus on anything other than the new tension she had brought to their rug. After what the Lost Nation had done to her tongue, the different spices of the rich gravy were muddled but wonderful. It left a lingering note of sweet unctuousness.

Someone stepped up behind Etee, and Sosun jerked to attention. A young boy, maybe twelve, whispered into Etee's ear as an old woman waited behind him. The old woman's skin carried the texture of parchment, lines of age telling a story of long turns in the Waking. She cradled her hands in front of her, and her eyes found Sosun's. Her gaze held intension, which made Sosun look away.

Etee smiled, nodded to the boy, and shooed Torrel to the side to make room for the boy and the old woman on the rug.

As the woman sat, still eyeing Sosun, Nix straightened with a protectiveness that she hadn't worn since they met Nomi at the lodestone. That need to meet every conflict with brute force would never leave Nix, which in an odd way comforted Sosun. Cracks or not, Nix was still a boulder.

"Are you deaf?" The boy blurted out the question as if the words had been waiting for him to open his mouth.

"That would be a stupid question to ask someone who is deaf," Nix said.

Sosun slapped Nix's arm. There was no need to be harsh with the boy. A person's tone said far more than their words, and this boy had only meant to ask a question.

"You tell him, 'No, but I cannot speak with my voice, so I have to use

my hands,'" Sosun signed as she stared at Nix.

After making a show of flaring her nostrils in disgust for the situation, Nix turned and translated word for word.

The old woman smiled watching Sosun's hands. Then she turned to the boy, and her hands began to dance in a series of gestures. Familiar signs broke up the rapid, nonsensical motions.

"My grandma wants to know where you learned to sign. She said she's never seen signs like those before."

A buzzing filled Sosun's ears as she stared at the old woman. It hadn't occurred to her that she would meet a signing person outside of the Citadel. The servants hadn't created their language from nothing. A deaf woman taken in as a servant had taught them, and over the turns the servants had made the language their own.

This old woman spoke a completely different language. She spoke the ancestor tongue the servants had built their language from. It connected them like The Song connected spirits to dancers. This woman tied her and all the Lost Nation's servants to the rest of Ennea.

"What is your name?" Sosun signed. Nix carried her words to the boy who gave them to his grandmother.

"My grandmother's name is Linhadi, and I am Talum," the boy said, signing her name as he spoke it.

Sosun's hands mimicked Linhadi's name. She needed to get this sign right. She repeated it in a question, and Linhadi nodded. Then Sosun gave Linhadi her name sign.

The conversation moved slowly as Sosun and Linhadi worked through their translators. Sosun told Linhadi how she had learned to sign this dialect as concisely as she could, but she found her words rambling.

Linhadi's hands worked through the words effortlessly. Some signs carried the same or close enough meanings, but the fullness of Linhadi's language astounded Sosun. The servants of the Citadel had developed their language for the life they led. It had boundaries. Linhadi's hands didn't seem to have restrictions.

"My grandmother says that we should let you eat and that I need to eat."

"No. I have so many questions. The food isn't important," Sosun signed.

The exchanges took too long. Linhadi had to know how necessary this was. Sosun needed the words she didn't have. She needed to take this connection to Ennea and become part of it. How could a meal matter?

"Grandma says not to worry. There will be plenty of time to talk. She has as many if not more questions for you, but food is always important."

Linhadi's smile crinkled her face with a warmth that flames could not compete with. Sosun wanted to argue, but she couldn't in good conscience keep an old woman and a young boy from their meals.

"Thank you, Linhadi. I didn't know how much I needed to meet you," Sosun signed.

The words made their way through their channels. "We are the connections we have to each other. I am more for meeting you," Talum said.

It sounded odd coming from the voice of a young boy, but the sentiment still made Sosun smile.

After their goodbyes, the tension between the others hardly mattered. Sosun filled her stomach with rich foods without taking the time to taste them. She hadn't truly understood how disconnected she had become. The other servants had assumed the role of her family, but people died easily. She couldn't cling to any of them too tightly. But knowing Linhadi and others like her existed anchored Sosun to Ennea.

If any doubts about her path had hidden in her spirit before, they were gone now. She had to do everything she could to save what remained of Ennea.

Tayen's belly swelled by the time she decided to stop reaching for more food. It had been a long time since her body had known abundance like this. Everything had been well-seasoned, and no one cast a questioning eye her way when she reached for another serving.

By the time she finished, she didn't even bother glaring at Nomi or Torrel. She could deal with them another time. For now, she enjoyed the gentle ache of her stomach.

The meals the Lost Nation served Kaylo in the Citadel tasted different. Every bite she had resigned herself to in his quarters had felt like an act of betrayal.

The Jani came together as a community in celebration. They couldn't do it every night, and had said as much. But they had to honor Ennea and her gift of life to give survival meaning.

Survival had been the only thing that mattered for so long, even before the Gousht killed her family. Her parents had built their existence around seeing tomorrow.

Conversations throughout the gathering tent lulled. Families collected their rugs and empty pots to bring back to their homes. The few children younger than Tayen ran about the tent, picking up this and that. They teased and tittered with each other, like she used to do with her sister, Nita.

She still dreamed about Nita every so often. Most of the dreams ended with Nita vanishing in one horrific way or another, but occasionally, they would just play. Nita would pester her, and she would chase her little sister through the woods.

Even if she was only older than the children running around by a few turns, she couldn't imagine playing like they were. That version of herself had died with Nita, and once again with Vāhn.

Back then, she hadn't known much of the war. Stories and words never adequately told the truth of blades and blood.

"You are welcome to join us for the night, but Torrel suggested you might feel more comfortable in your own space." Etee directed her words towards Kaylo like everyone did, but Tayen was too focused on her plate to care. "We can bring some bedrolls and blankets here. There's plenty of firewood just outside the tent."

"Thank you." Kaylo bowed his head slightly. "We shouldn't be here too long. You have already been far too gracious."

"Stop it, Kaylo." Torrel rested a hand on Kaylo's shoulder like they were old friends, and Kaylo flinched despite his smile. "You are welcome to stay as long as you want."

"That isn't necessary—" Kaylo started.

"I know. I know. You have your path, and we have ours." Torrel's smile filled his face like he truly meant it.

Whatever had happened between the two men earlier changed the air between them. It hadn't become jovial or friendly—more trepidatious. They tested each other's boundaries with a touch on the arm or a smile. When they offered each other servings of one dish or another, they each insisted the other help themselves first. Even when they spoke to each other, their tones pulled back from their words as if they were avoiding unintended offense.

It was annoying how quickly Kaylo had forgiven Torrel.

"We should be off as soon as you can lend us a guide," Kaylo said.

"Give me a day or two, and we will have you off to the Uprising. Let me get you those bedrolls." Torrel excused himself and left.

If Torrel hadn't admitted it himself, Tayen would have had difficulty believing he had attacked Kaylo. The man had been nothing but gentle and accommodating. But if he had been anything like his son when he was younger, believing became a bit easier.

Etee and Nomi excused themselves for the evening as bedrolls were laid out and Nix fed more wood to the fire.

Kaylo yawned and stretched, rubbing his eyes as if fighting away sleep. For as much as the man could talk about his past, he still hadn't said anything about Jonac. He sat down on his bedroll like he didn't even intend to say a word before he passed out.

"Are you going to wait another twenty turns to tell me what happened with Jonac? You could add it to the end of your story," Tayen said from her bedroll.

Kaylo chuckled. "Oh, my toka. You are consistent. I'll give you that."

"Did you know that you always make a comment like that when you are trying to give yourself time to think of an answer to a question?" Tayen asked. "You could just say nothing until you're ready."

"Sometimes this kid is so annoying. Then she goes and says something like that, and I can't help but appreciate her." Nix adjusted herself on her bedroll.

Sosun slapped Nix's leg, and Nix just shrugged.

"What more can I tell you? He loses time. He expected to see his daughters running around the tent," Kaylo said, his face sinking into grief.

"But he's better sometimes, right? Why don't you go see him when he has a handle on things?" Tayen asked. "Don't forget to take me with you. I have plenty of words for that old wrinkled bag."

"I am lucky to have you, but I don't have any ill will towards Jonac." Kaylo shifted and looked into the flames. "I was ready for anything else. He could have screamed at me, begged forgiveness, refused to talk to me—but when he called out for Junera and Soca..." He looked at Sosun who was sitting up on her bedroll, watching him. "The girls would have been around your age now."

"I'm sorry, Kaylo," Sosun signed.

"No need for apologies," Kaylo said as he signed. "We all lose people, but most of us only have to lose them once. He has to lose them for the rest of his days. It's not..." His hands fumbled for the words, then he grabbed a handful of dirt and tossed it into the flames, which sputtered in response. "How the fuck do you say 'fair'?!"

"Kaylo, it's not your fault," Tayen said, her voice gliding just above a whisper.

"A piece of it is. There's enough blame to go around. I've seen enough moons to know that all this should be laid at the Empire's feet. But that gives them too much power. We still have some choices. We still have some say in what happens, don't we? I fucked up, and they're dead. And now, he calls out to them until he remembers they won't come back to him."

You were a child, Tayen thought, but stopped herself before she said it. She didn't feel like a child, and she was younger than he had been. It didn't stop her from feeling guilty about her parents, Nita, and Vāhn. She still stayed awake recalling what Pana looked like on the stone floor.

Child or not, she didn't feel any less responsible.

"We should all get some sleep," he said, lying down on his bedroll.

No one said another word as Tayen lay down too burdened by ghosts to sleep.

CHAPTER THIRTEEN
KAYLO'S STORY

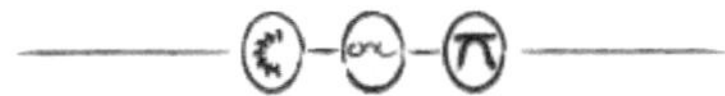

THE SMELL OF SICK hung in the tent like a bad omen. We had done our best to clean and care for what remained of Dasjoni's arm before we returned to the encampment, but the infection had worked harder than we had. The healers had cut more flesh from her arm, and still, the bad blood could take her.

By The Mother's blessing and several swigs of a medicinal tea, she had passed out. The others left to tend to less threatening wounds, but I remained at her bedside. The poultice-laden fabric over her wound had already turned a reddish-brown.

Two turns had passed since leaving Oakheart, and far too many had died. Each raid eroded our numbers. The new recruits never made up for the fallen.

I dipped a cloth into a bucket of fresh water. My mind liked to go dangerous places in moments like this, but the cool touch of the liquid helped anchor me. I could allow the guilt to consume me later.

Beads of sweat left trails running down Dasjoni's brow, which I wiped clean. Her grimace softened ever so slightly.

Dasjoni had survived the mines. She never intended to fight, but then Pem died in our first raid. One too many losses. She picked up a blade and wouldn't be refused.

I had tried to—maybe not hard enough. We needed the numbers after all. But I had tried to refuse her.

No matter what I did now, she would never get her arm or her loved ones back. Dabbing her forehead with a cloth felt insufficient. Yet, I continued.

After Oakheart, thirty-six people volunteered to fight—thirty-seven after Dasjoni changed her mind. They had placed their trust in me like fools, and now, thirteen were still alive.

Some of the people we liberated joined the cause, but far too few. Not that any number could have replaced the dead. But we needed numbers.

I had failed entirely.

Dasjoni yelped and reached for her missing arm as she slept.

There was something wrong with me. I promised the others I'd watch over her and spent my time indulging my self-loathing. Liara was right. This wasn't about me.

I reached for the mortar and pestle, taking a pinch of ground herbs and adding them to a clay cup for tea. Susu root, barberry bark, and moonlight hazel leaf made a powerful pain killer. Dasjoni needed all the help we could give her.

The liquid dribbled out over her lips as I slowly fed her some of the tea.

"I'm sorry, Das," I whispered to the unconscious woman. "You don't have to follow Pem right away. We still need you around here."

It was the truth. We needed her and many more like her if we had any hope of continuing the fight. Hylīane spent her days whispering in ears, changing minds. After this debacle of a raid, she would have the votes. They would change course and hide.

In the beginning, I hated the idea of leading anyone. I may have been right. But someone needed to lead, and the stories made me out to be a hero. People listened when I spoke. I had a chance to do good.

Hylīane would have to fight me to the edge of The Mist to take that away from me.

The furs of the tent flapped open, and the winter air rushed in to sweep away the warmth. Acta stood at the entrance, looking contrite yet insistent.

"Close the furs," I said with far too much rebuke in my tone. "She needs the warmth."

Acta did as he was told, walking over to the other side of Dasjoni's bedroll and kneeling. The air took on a heaviness as he looked down at her. They had mined Oakheart together. His jaw stiffened and death flashed over his face like he was back on the battlefield.

The young Tomakan had only made his pledge to The Mother this past spring, yet he had already survived so much. He had learned to conceal his emotions for the most part, but he wore his contempt plainly now.

"They will pay, Das," he said. "I promise you that."

The silence that followed grew more intense as the moments passed. He continued to stare down at her.

"Acta, you came here for a reason," I said.

He nodded, still looking down at Dasjoni. "There is a messenger here for you."

"Messenger?"

"Claims to be from the Missing."

"So they're lying," I said as a low growl. "What do they want?"

"They wouldn't speak to anyone except for the Hero of Anilace," Acta said, then noticed my glare. "Her words, not mine."

"Stay here." I pushed myself to my feet and through the furs without another word.

I had allowed Zusa to lie to me for over a turn. He had convinced me he had righteous reasons. But the more time passed, the clearer things became. The bastard had manipulated a bunch of kids to fight on behalf of a nation that refused to fight for the rest of us.

It didn't take long to find the messenger.

A crowd lingered around the gathering tent, murmuring with curiosity. And who could blame them? A stranger had walked into our secret encampment without an invitation.

Several heads turned my way as I strode towards the tent, watching me like an approaching storm—their faces hesitant, focused, and waiting for lightning to strike.

When I made my way into the tent, Hylīane was already yelling. "... refusin ta speak to ta elders of a community until a boy arrives?! How can you call yourselves Ennean, behaving like ta invaders?"

Annit stood between her and the stranger, playing his role as consummate peacekeeper. "All you're doing is agitating yourself, Hylīane. She is a messenger, sent to give a specific message to a specific person."

"Even messengers should follow common decency. Or ave we lost everyting of our culture to ta Gousht?"

The messenger, a tall northwoman clad in purple robes and a leather sannil, noticed me first. She faced me with a smile.

Liars always had the most amiable of smiles.

Her clothing, her manner, her posture—everything about her reminded me of Zusa.

"This must be the renowned Hero of Anilace," she said, mentioning my imposed title with all sincerity. "I appreciate you coming to collect my message."

"Now, she's ready?! He can't grow a full beard, and she wants ta speak with him?!"

"Forgive me. I mean no offense, but I have my orders. I am to speak with Kaylo, and only Kaylo."

"Ta Mother's bloody tits. He doesn't speak for us!" Hylīane yelled, cursing more furiously than she had during any of our numerous clashes.

"She's right. Anything you have to say to me, you will have to say to Hylīane and Annit. I'd be telling them directly after anyway," I said. "So, say what you came to say."

Hylīane looked at me as if I had grown as tall as the trees. All the anger drained out of her expression as her eyes narrowed at me in a twist of confusion. If I hadn't left a friend's sickbed to meet with a liar, I would have burst into laughter.

"Very well. As I told your companions here, I am an envoy from the Missing—"

"The Lost Nation, you mean? If we are going to speak, try keeping the lies off your tongue," I said, and the messenger held my gaze as I did.

"Very well. My name is Altrice, and I am from Astile," she said. "My regiment and I have been watching your encampment for a span. We noticed you had been away and wanted to give you time to settle in before approaching."

A span! I thought, resisting the urge to reach for my blade.

A full regiment of lost warriors had been watching us for a span, meaning they knew our numbers and our layout. There would likely be several scouts monitoring us right now from a distance.

"How kind of you," I said, trying to keep the animosity from my tone. "You didn't just happen upon us, did you? So, I have to assume you've been looking for us—maybe me in particular."

"It isn't for me to say. I am only a messenger sent to request you meet with my commander."

"Not interested."

"Kaylo," Annit said. "Don't be hasty. It's always wise to learn more about the world and those who operate within it."

Altrice turned and looked at Annit as if seeing him for the first time. She measured him with a subtle nod. "You keep wise friends, Kaylo."

"What's ta offer?" Hylīane's arms remained crossed, but the tone of her voice pulled back into something less combative. She squinted like she always did when she had the workings of a plan forming in her mind.

I liked it better when she hated the messenger.

Altrice pulled her lips back into a toothless smile but didn't acknowledge Hylïane's question further. "Tomorrow at midday, my commander will be at the lodestone an hour north of here. Do you know it?"

They had been paying close attention. We monitored the lodestones nearest to our encampments. Some people practiced the old ways, and we had found people in need of safe haven more than once.

I nodded.

"You may bring companions, but all must honor the ways of a lodestone," she said.

"If I choose not to meet your commander?" I asked, watching her eyes for any reaction, but she had been too well trained to reveal anything.

"The choice is yours, but you will want to hear our message. My commander is not one to stop at one attempt."

Hylïane and Annit both looked at me expectantly, though Hylïane's expression looked far more threatening.

"We will be there," I said. "But if you, your commander, or any of your companions decide to break the rules of the lodestone, you will be the first to find out how little love I have for your *Missing*. Do you hear me?"

Of all the smiles Altrice offered over the course of our conversation, this was the truest. A genuine curiosity lingered behind the acknowledgement. She understood my threat, and part of her wanted to test it.

Stories of what had happened at Oakheart had been bound to travel, and this messenger wouldn't be the first or the last to want to test the tales.

"Jolrin! Talise!" I yelled, and the furs parted immediately. I would have looked ridiculous if they hadn't, but I knew my warriors well enough to know who would be listening. "Please escort our lost envoy from the encampment."

"Until tomorrow at high sun," Altrice said.

"If we find any of your warriors lurking about in the meantime, I cannot guarantee their safety," I said. "Our watch will be on high alert, and you know how dangerous stray arrows can be."

"You don't disappoint, Ennea's Thief," Altrice said before walking out with Jolrin and Talise.

"I'm goin with cha," Hylíane said as soon as the furs closed behind them.

"So we can argue in front of the envoy?" I asked.

Hylíane started to argue—as if to prove my point—but Annit interjected. "The boy's right. Regardless of what they have to say, having you two battling each other in front of them won't help our cause. And I'm sure Kaylo will give a full report." He looked at me as if to chide any trickster thoughts lingering in my head.

"Cha betta know what cha doing. Don't turn cha back on powerful friends," Hylíane said, closing the distance between her and I.

"We can't fight the Gousht and the Lost Nation, but that doesn't mean I trust anything that woman says." I turned my attention to Annit. "While I meet with this commander, you will need to get the encampment ready. This location won't last us as long as we'd hoped."

Chapter Fourteen
Kaylo's Story

ALTRICE SAT AT THE outer edge of the clearing with three of her companions meandering about before we arrived. More than their share of blades clung to the lodestone. They all wore the same shade of purple like a proper army, abandoning any pretense about belonging to the Missing.

A basket sat beside the lodestone, buzzing with imprisoned spirits, but none of the warriors carried any stones on them.

We were outmatched. There might have been five of us compared to the three purple-clad warriors, but they were a true army. They knew more about us than we knew of them. And I was under no illusions. Their compatriots wouldn't be far. There were probably several perched in the trees with bows.

Zusa had already given away that trick. The Lost Nation would only honor the ways of the lodestone in service of their goals.

We waited far enough beyond the clearing that we wouldn't be noticed. We could still turn back.

Acta, Jolrin, and Talise were the best close-combat warriors we had amongst our ranks, and Yelan had The Mountain with her. If things went poorly, we might have a chance to escape with our lives. Not a great chance, but a chance.

"What are you waiting for?" Jolrin whispered.

"I've been lied to by 'the Missing' before, and I'm trying to decide if I'm being a fool again."

Jolrin nodded and blended back into the silence.

Their stoic nature set some people off-center. There were those who spoke far more than they acted, hiding behind words. Jolrin, on the other hand, seldom spoke. The wanton brutality that waded beneath their calm surface didn't need words to prop it up. The lost warriors would come to understand that if they played any games with this meeting.

Waiting any longer wouldn't serve any purpose.

For the final time, I counted the blades clinging to the lodestone— seven—and made sure none of the echoes emanated from the warriors— they didn't. Neither observation made much sense, but not much made sense about this meeting.

I gestured for the group to follow and made my way to the clearing.

"I was beginning to fear you wouldn't show," Altrice said, standing with open arms like we were old friends.

"I didn't get the feeling that was an option," I said, tracking the others of her party as they formed up behind her.

"Please accept my apologies for our past deceptions. We would like to start anew as friends." Altrice reached both hands towards me in a traditional greeting. I clasped her right hand between both of mine, and she did likewise. "Take a moment. Give your blades to the stone, then we can begin."

It had taken convincing to get Talise to agree to giving her axe to the lodestone, but she finally did after I promised that Wal and his loud mouth would not be accompanying us.

One by one, we each gave our weapons to the pull of the lodestone, eliciting several tings that cut through the silence.

The practice of unarmed meetings beside lodestones had begun during the Hundred Turn War. It relied on trust and a care for the culture that birthed our nations. Even still, letting go of my father's knife went against every instinct in my body.

Once we all arranged ourselves in rows, kneeling and facing one another, the talks could begin in earnest.

Altrice sat across from me. Despite being the smallest of her companions and on the younger side of the spectrum, she seemed to be leading the proceedings.

"From the little I know of you, drawing these talks out with any pageantry or unnecessary words would only waste our time. So, let me be blunt," Altrice said with an impassive expression. "You are getting in the way of our plans."

"Is that so?" I asked. The honesty threw me off balance, but the idea of disrupting the Lost Nation's plans made me smile.

"The Missing served as our network outside of Astile. We strategically planted rumors over the turns, creating a threat for the Gousht and hope for Enneans. We escorted refugees through the Lost Forest to safety. Everything the Missing did furthered our plans."

"And what are those exactly?" Yelan asked, her expression unfazed by the tension between our two parties.

"To liberate Ennea from the Gousht, of course."

"I think we all heard her say 'exactly,'" Talise said.

"You will watch your tone," the largest of the lost warriors said.

Talise smiled as if she were marking the man.

"Now, now," Altrice chided. "There is no need for any of that. We didn't come here to tell you the details of our plans, and you knew we didn't. Let's not get distracted."

"Then tell us what you can, because from our vantage point, the Lost Nation hasn't done anything to free Enneans," I said, keeping as much of my animosity from my words as I could. "And after our first experience with the Missing, we aren't interested in taking your story on faith."

"Very well," Altrice said. "Over the turns, the King of Astile has been growing an army and infrastructure large enough and sufficiently trained to rival the Gousht. Our timing and strategies are our own, but we do have the protection of Ennea at heart."

"Vague as that is, I'm assuming more questions wouldn't lead to any specifics." I studied the faces of her companions. The large man on the end of their row glared back at me. "What do you want from us?"

"Join us."

"Fuck that," Talise said.

Altrice held her hand up to preempt her fellow warriors. "Be what the Missing were rumored to be. We could provide you with weapons, help you strategize, bolster your ranks."

"And you would do this out of an innate desire for liberation?" I asked, unable to keep the sarcasm from my tone.

"The Uprising would be our eyes and ears. You would help us prepare for the war to come and get refugees safely out of the way."

"You mean you would like to control us and use us to further your ends," I said.

"How can you not see this is in your best interests?" The veneer of Altrice's pleasant messenger facade began to crack. "I saw your encampment. What do you have, two dozen warriors?"

"Forgive me if I don't trust the nation who hid from the Invasion War then sent spies out to fake a rebel resistance."

"Believe us or not, our army will force the Gousht from our shores. You can be a part of that, or you can get the rest of your rebellion killed." The look of disgust on Altrice's face was now fully complete.

"I think Talise expressed our feelings on your offer perfectly," I said, turning to Talise. "What was it again? 'Fuck that'?"

Altrice's fist bunched around the hem of her purple robes. "You little thief. Just because you've managed to spread some stories about yourself doesn't mean you have earned your place. Enjoy burying the rest of—"

The older woman to Altrice's left held up a hand to cut Altrice off. She gave a pleasant smile without a look towards Altrice. "I apologize for my fellows. We hadn't expected your response. We had hoped to work together towards our common cause, but it seems that we may have assumed too much."

Altrice shifted on her knees as if she were a child caught stealing a sweet before dinner.

This older warrior had the bearing of a true commander. She could have led the proceedings from the start, but the lost bastards liked to play games. At least they were consistent.

"I agree," I said. "You have assumed too much."

"In apology, please take the extra weapons we brought for you. It would be a waste for you not to put them to use."

The arrogance of their assumptions dug through my skin to the core of me. They most likely thought we had done exactly what they had—used rumors and stories to inflate ourselves with the people.

Our warriors hadn't died to be viewed as props in a war of rumors.

I stood up and strolled over to the sack of crystals lying beside the lodestone. The large lost warrior rose, assuming I meant to harm them. Instead, I turned the sack over and let the crystals tumble to the ground.

Now, each of the lost warriors looked confused, mouths in various stages of slacked jaws.

"The Uprising isn't a rumor." I bent down to the crystals, gathered the translucent threads of The Thief hiding within, and pulled.

I couldn't keep the smile from my face as the stones withered to sand in front of them.

The unnamed leader of their group stood up and strode toward the lodestone. "No, Kaylo. You are not a rumor. I wish the best for your Uprising. I'm sure we'll speak again."

One by one they removed their weapons from the lodestone and walked off into the surrounding forest, leaving three well-made short swords behind.

Once we got close enough to the encampment entrance, I saw Rêlan on guard duty. The skin below her eyes was irritated. She wasn't crying, but she had been. She couldn't meet my gaze.

It only took a moment to realize what had happened. I ran through the encampment to find a somber group of people milling about outside of Dasjoni's tent.

The infection had taken her about an hour before we returned.

We didn't even have the luxury of time to grieve. The Lost Nation knew where we were, and the parley hadn't ended on the best of terms.

While Annit oversaw breaking down what remained of the encampment, I arranged yet another burial. Those close to her paused their work to stand beside her hastily dug grave and say goodbye. The tears and words weren't enough. They never were.

As if to honor the proceedings, Sokan fell as we placed her body in The Mother's embrace.

Once again, I had failed to protect the people who relied on me.

I let myself into Dasjoni's tent after the last pile of dirt settled over her body. The bitter earth smell of her sickness lingered. With any hope, the herbs had taken the pain away before she walked off into The Mist to be with Pem.

The mortar and pestle lay upended beside her bedroll. I gathered them up along with the teacup, several waterskins, and her sweat-soaked blanket.

Over the turns, I had felt like a thief for many reasons, but this moment rivaled the worst of them. Someone had to pack her things. They would be redistributed. Nothing could go to waste. Yet, the idea of rummaging through the pieces of her didn't sit well in my spirit.

I sat beside a small bundle of flax at the edge of the tent farthest from the entrance. Dasjoni made thread. We never had enough to mend half of the robes that needed mending, but she had and a few others made the effort. Even if all the problems that needed fixing couldn't be fixed at once, she hadn't given up.

A line of the drawn-out flax fibers was tied to a twig at one end. I had seen her turn bundles of dried stalks into strong lengths of thread, breaking them down, combing them out, and twisting the fine fibers until they became something useful.

The hem of my robes had been sewn back together several times over. I didn't know if the thread had been hers. The beige of the stitch didn't match the soft green of my robes, but it had done the job.

This was her gift. She understood how to mend things—how to bring them back together. And I had sent her out there with a sword.

The furs parted and Talise stood at the entrance. She paused, as if she hadn't expected to find me here.

"Do you need something?" I asked.

"Hyliane's looking for you, and she isn't being quiet about it."

"She's not happy about how I treated our visitors, is she?" I tried to smile, but it felt false on my cheeks.

"You should have gone to her yourself," Talise said. "What are you even doing here?"

"Someone has to pack up her things."

"Surely, there are more commander-y things you could be doing with your time," Talise said, still not fully entering the tent.

"Most of the people who charge into battle at my orders don't belong. You understand how to be a warrior. Most of the others are just playing at it. Pem was overeager, and had horrible footwork. Dasjoni thought of fighting like a dance, always expecting her opponent to follow the right steps. Neither of them should be dead."

Talise stepped in, biting her lip like she might pierce skin. "I don't get it, Kaylo. You understand the consequences. Time after time, you go out onto the battlefield, you fight, then you go off and hide somewhere after war happens. People die. Then you blame yourself for it."

"I know. Liara's always telling me I can't blame—"

"Fuck that. You earned the blame. That's not the issue. If you make a mistake and people die, it should burden you until you breathe your last. But at least make different choices." She stepped closer and closer in keeping with the increasing volume of her voice.

"What are you talking about?" I asked, too off guard to find my defenses.

"How did Zusa die? Why were you captured? Why was Sionia alone?" she asked. "There was a plan that night. You were supposed to go with her."

I stared at her. Somehow, she managed to knock the grief out of me.

"I didn't ask for you all to break into a Gousht stronghold."

"Why weren't you with her?!" Talise yelled at the top of her lungs.

For nearly three turns, curt or not, Talise had always been in control. In battle, during an argument, over a meal—it never mattered. This was different.

"I get it. You didn't ask to be rescued. If you had stayed alongside Sionia, you may have never cracked the fucking mountain. But you were supposed to be by her side. You chose to go your own way like you always do. And she died...alone."

The furs flew open behind Talise, but neither of us turned to look. "Is everything okay in here?" Acta asked.

"Kaylo, I believe you care. I believe you feel the guilt and you want to do better. Great bastard-loving spirits, I know you are the reason so many of us are walking this side of The Mist. But I also know that you will make the selfish decision again."

"Talise, I'm sorry."

"Then prove me wrong." She turned and pushed her way past Acta on her way out of the tent.

My head must have been buried deep in my colon for the last two turns. Talise had been distant since Oakheart. Every so often, I caught her glaring or mumbling something cryptic, but I never knew why. I never expected her to tell me either.

I had prayed for Sionia's spirit every night for two turns, and I had never thought that anyone else might be doing the same.

"For what it's worth…" My spirit nearly jumped from my skin when Acta spoke. "I don't think you're making selfish decisions. I trust you."

"Thank you, Acta," I said. *You shouldn't,* I added in my head.

Chapter Fifteen

Current Day Ennea

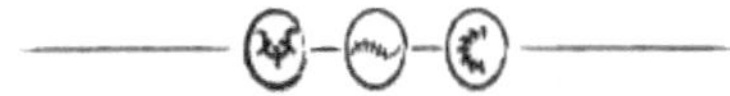

A grid of lines drawn in the dirt lay between Kaylo and Jonac, returning to a time before the Fallen Rock Clan fell. When Jonac failed to recognize Kaylo, he offered to teach Kaylo how to play, and Kaylo accepted.

"The important part is to pay attention to what you know." Jonac wore the same smile he had the first time he taught Kaylo so many turns prior. "What markers have you placed on the crosspoints? What markers have you forced me to reveal?"

There was a strange, bitter flavor to the joy Kaylo felt watching Jonac reteach him this old game. This version of Jonac had been the one he first met—the man who took him in and called him family without question. The broken man within hid behind a smile. As a child, it hadn't been apparent to Kaylo. Jonac wore his smile as the most genuine of masks.

He clapped his hands. "Don't drift away, my boy. This won't be as much fun if I beat you too easily."

"What do these symbols mean?" Kaylo held up a marker with the rune of The Seed.

"The way you can ask that question without any shame at your age is sad." His overexaggerated headshake fed into the playful tone of his scolding. "Boy, you need to learn your history. I am tempted to sweep these lines away and give you a lecture."

One by one, he laid the markers on the ground, being careful to arrange them in the correct order. When he revealed the rune for The Balance, the muscles in Kaylo's neck stiffened. But Jonac never interrupted his smile.

"There was a time when dancers used to tattoo the symbols of their spirit ancestors on their flesh, but that ran out of style." Jonac picked up The Shadow's marker. "One line with one interrupting mark for the first—The Shadow. Two for The River. Three for The Flame and so on."

Jonac looked at the final rune in the line and titled his head. He blinked as if his thoughts were fighting each other in his mind, then he picked up the wooden marker. "Sorry, what was your name again? You'll have to forgive an old man. I'm getting so forgetful."

A flash of the first time Jonac asked Kaylo for his name sprang to mind. Jonac's face had been fuller, his skin more vibrant, but his eyes held the same offer of kindness.

"My name is Kaylo."

"Kaylo? Hmm, I knew a boy named Kaylo once. That boy had secrets. People wear their pain like a blanket—not a heavy weight, but it brings their shoulders down. You can't force people to unburden themselves. I've learned that much in my time."

Every time he thought he was telling an anecdote about his young toka, he had described Kaylo with similar words—a broken boy with a hidden pain. That was how Jonac remembered him.

It was better than being the boy who had killed his family, but it was tragic in its own way. Kaylo had been so caught up in his pain and secret that he had kept Jonac at a distance. So much so that Jonac always recalled him by the distance first.

"What happened to him?" Kaylo nearly choked on the words as he spoke.

"Are you okay, boy?"

Something about the way Jonac called Kaylo 'boy' even though he was well into adulthood made him smile. "Just a bit of a cough. What happened to him?"

"Kaylo?" Jonac scratched the nape of his neck as he looked around the tent like he would find an answer lying about. Then his gaze returned to Kaylo. He squinted. "Kaylo? Is that you?"

Jonac had gone somewhere and become another version of himself. He held himself differently—older, more brittle.

If Kaylo answered, who would he be answering? The man he had left behind after Nomi and the girls died? The man who could barely look him in the eye?

The words refused to come, so Kaylo nodded instead.

"Oh, my little brother." His smile carried the weight of sadness within it. "How'd you get so old?"

"Time seems to have that effect."

He looked down at the marker in his hand as if he just realized he was holding it. As he turned it over in his hands, he grew more solemn. "I owe you an apology."

"No, please don't."

"Don't take this chance away from me." He raised a scolding finger. "I've needed to apologize for a long time now. I placed blame on you because it was easier than blaming myself or the Gousht. You were just a scared boy trying to exist in a scary world, and I was supposed to protect you."

"Jonac, you did the best you could. You gave me a home when I needed it the most."

"No. I should've done better. I convinced myself that you needed space, but I didn't do what a kana must. The pain was beating you down, and I didn't intervene. Instead, I made it all about me. Those last few moons—I missed the little time I had with my daughters, with Nomi, with you. I was weak."

"My father used to say people overestimated stormwood. Sure, it's durable, but it doesn't bend worth shit. Ashburn bends and recoils. It finds its shape again," Kaylo said. "You aren't weak, Jonac. You needed time to find your shape again. I'm still trying to rediscover mine."

"You never used to speak about your father."

"He was a craftsman. Lots of analogies about wood." Kaylo chuckled to himself.

"The turns haven't been to kind to you, have they?"

Kaylo looked at himself. He needed to let Tayen retouch his braids. Maybe it was time to finally shave away his beard. "I haven't been kind to myself. But I think I have a reason to change that now."

The expression on Jonac's face opened wide. "You're not going to fight, are you? Kaylo, you need to be safe."

"There's a kid who I have to take care of. She has almost as much anger in her spirit as I did. She needs me."

"Daughter?" Jonac's smile fought through pain.

"Toka."

"Then be the kana she needs," Jonac said. "You hear me? You be the guide and protector she needs. Nothing less."

"Yes, my great and all-knowing kana." Kaylo tried for sarcasm, but hit closer to earnestness.

Jonac struggled to his feet, and Kaylo rushed forward to keep him from falling. As Jonac found his balance, he wrapped his arms around Kaylo. If felt odd to be taller than Jonac. His head rested on Kaylo's shoulder.

They had lost too many turns. Kaylo could have known this man like a father.

When Jonac pulled away, he cradled Kaylo's cheek in his hand and smiled. "My boy, it's so good to see you. Have you seen Junera? That girl is always running off somewhere. It's not safe, but then, what can you do? There's no stifling that spirit."

Kaylo forced his smile. "I'll go look for her."

"Little brother, if you ever decide to talk about whatever's hanging on that smile, I'm here."

"Thank you, Jonac," Kaylo said. "Thank you for everything."

"No need for all the sentimentality. Go find that girl and get back here before Nomi has supper ready. She hates waiting on you all."

Kaylo nodded, then walked to the threshold. Before he left, he turned one more time. "Goodbye, Jonac."

The encampment buzzed with the movement of everyday life. No one gave Kaylo a second glance. They walked by without acknowledging Jonac was inside his tent losing time to his illness.

It was cruel how life continued to move on and left so many spirits behind.

Kaylo walked through the tent city, passing by strangers in sand-colored robes. He had made a promise to Tayen and again to Jonac. It was time to get Tayen where she needed to go.

The back of Tayen's eyelids sprouted purple and yellow streams of color. No matter how many times she tried, how long she waited, or how tightly she closed her eyes, she couldn't find her way back into The Mist. She pulled The Song closer until the shadows became a tumult of clashing noises. The distinct shadows lost shape as she pulled them closer.

"I need you," she said, but The Shadow kept her silence.

If Kaylo was right about this spirit ancestor stuff, The Shadow was here with her. She knew how lost Tayen was. "You're supposed to be wise. Well, I could use some wisdom!"

The clamoring shadows thrashed in The Song, but she wasn't any closer to walking into The Mist.

"What is going on here?" Kaylo burst through the furs, and Tayen let go of the shadows.

A fury of small ribbons of shade raced from the tent in every direction.

"You have half the shadows in town rushing into our tent. Your echo sounds like an army of drunkards playing drums. The Jani might be welcoming of dancers, but it still unnerves people when their shadows run away from them without warning."

"Are you okay?"

"Don't change the subject. What's going on in here?"

"Your eyes get puffy when you cry, and your face gets redder. Why were you crying?"

His demeanor changed in an instant. The false threat in his overacted anger slipped out from under him and took his balance with him. He adjusted himself and stood up straighter.

"I went to see Jonac again. He was there—he was himself, then he wasn't."

They had been with the Jani for three days. Each day Kaylo would go over and tend to Jonac, and each time he came back changed, wearing some extreme version of one emotion or another. And she had done nothing as he continued to touch his fingers to the burning coals. Left to his own devices, he would burn himself to death in Jonac's failing memories.

"You have to stop this."

"Do you know how many days I agonized over whether Jonac was still alive? I wondered if he had found something that resembled contentment. I prayed for The Great Spirits to hold him close after everything I had done to him," Kaylo said. "This is the fate he's been given."

"Maybe it's a kindness. He doesn't have to live with the guilt and the pain like you do. Sure, he struggles in other ways, but he thinks his daughters are out exploring the forest, not dead."

Kaylo looked at her, his brows knitted into a half-hearted scowl as if he couldn't decide whether or not to be upset with what she had said.

"The dead don't suffer. The living bear that burden," Tayen said. "You're proof of that, all guilt-ridden and hollowed out. You make me feel emotionally balanced." Tayen smiled, but her chest went cold while she waited for his response.

Several breaths passed, and Kaylo wore the same expression of dueling emotions. Then a sound ripped through his throat that belonged to a wild boar. He folded at the waist and began laughing. The laughter forced its way through him, mixed with coughing and strained breaths.

"You are a little daemon child," he said between laughs. "Emotionally balanced?"

"Hey! It wasn't that funny!"

"You nearly beat a boy to death with a rock last season." He stood up, trying to control himself. "The same day I left behind one of my oldest friends, bleeding from several stab wounds I gave him." A restrained laugh broke through. "We are fucked."

Now it was Tayen's turn to glare. Talking about Daak was too much. She had confided in Kaylo, and he was joking about it. But when she reached for her anger, she could only join Kaylo's laughter.

"You're supposed to give your toka hope, aren't you?"

He wiped his tears as he gathered his wits. "That's right. Kaylo, the hopeful one."

"The sad thing is, this is the happiest I've seen you since I met you."

"Yes. Yes, very sad. Now, can you tell me why you were collecting shadows from all over the encampment?"

He would either understand or not, but there wasn't a single possibility in all of existence he would let this go. The laughing had to stop for now. Maybe they could chuckle over the people they had nearly killed later, or some other morbid shit.

"You told me you would help me mistwalk, but you've been avoiding it. I did it once. Why can't I do it again?"

"Avoiding it?! If you aren't aware, there's a bloody war going on out there..." He paused and sighed. "Sorry. I asked a question, and you answered it. I shouldn't...it's just that you...that was foolish. You know how dangerous that is."

"It never stopped you."

"It should have!" Kaylo put his hand up and signed the word 'stop' as if he were speaking to himself. "Why? How about we start there?"

"I don't know about you, but I feel lost. We may be getting closer to finding the Uprising, but I don't know what I'm supposed to be doing. I'm fifteen, searching out a rebel group to fight a war against the Empire who killed my family," she said. "I've never wavered on any of that. But how am I supposed to do it? Will this get the last few people who know my name killed? Will I survive it?"

"And you think The Shadow can tell you what to do next? The Great Spirits aren't that helpful in my experience."

"I need to try."

Eyes closed and fists balled, Kaylo's body lifted up with an exaggerated breath. "Okay. Tonight, we will try."

He extended his arms towards her, waiting to clasp her arms to solidify the promise between them.

Tayen allowed herself a smile, before she took his right hand between hers. "By the spirits great and small, old and new."

CHAPTER SIXTEEN
CURRENT DAY ENNEA

Sosun studied Linhadi's hands even closer than she listened to Talum, Linhadi's grandson, translating her story. The old woman's hands flowed from one gesture to another as if she had practiced this specific pattern of movements before. When each phrase reached its final flourish, Talum gave voice to her words, and Sosun pieced together the gaps in her understanding.

The boy had a knack for storytelling, his voice traveling along the words as if they were his. But he, much like Nix, was only here to facilitate this conversation. Everything, save his voice, disappeared from the tent until only Sosun and Linhadi existed.

"When I handed my friend's letter to the family hiding his niece, they helped me wrap her up to face the rain. But the little girl needed more convincing to step out into the cold," Linhadi signed. *"She had just lost her parents to the Gousht, and if the soldiers found her, she would suffer the same fate. They had their ways of quashing talks of rebellion.*

"I took her hands and knelt to her level. Being deaf has taught me to say what I need with what I have, and when I looked into that girl's eyes, she understood. We were going someplace safe.

"Rain streamed off the steep rooves and ran down the sloped roads like a river towards the quarry north of the city. It didn't take long for the

*water to saturate our robes. I tucked her under my arm to keep most of
the rain off her, but the girl still shivered—either from the cold or her
fear.*

"*The usual busyness of carts and people running their errands had
abandoned the streets. We may have seemed an oddity, but the few
soldiers forced to patrol hardly cared about a poor old woman and child
sloshing uphill in the middle of a downpour.*"

It took time to find the right words. Sosun's signs felt like cousins
to this older version of the language. However, signing wasn't an art of
memorizing words but knowing how they fit into one another.

"*Why would her uncle send you?*"

"*Why not me?*" Linhadi signed. "*I may not know how to wield a
sword or dance with The Flame, but I know Renéqua. I know how to
appear meek and unassuming. When you have spent enough of your life
in silence, you understand how to make yourself known or fade into the
background. You aren't any less useful than that walking scowl and her
sword back there.*"

Talum finished speaking the translation aloud, then looked up at Nix
with a bit of fear in his eyes as if he only just realized what he had said.
"Sorry, just translating."

Of course, Nix only deepened her scowl. Sosun had called Nix far
worse herself, but Nix enjoyed playing the role of intimidating specter.

Linhadi elbowed her grandson's shoulder, and began signing once
again. "*Resistance requires more than swords. It needs all of us to bring
ourselves to the battle. I passed messages and snuck children from
occupied cities. I gave what I could do best. What will you do?*"

Everyone seemed to have the same question for her, but it felt
different when Linhadi asked it. When other people asked, they meant,
"What could the Uprising do with a little broken girl?" When Linhadi
asked, there were no implied barriers, which made the question all the
more frightening.

Sosun had imagined she would serve the Uprising like she had served the Citadel. Even if that was all she had to offer, she would still be of use. But she neither loved nor was especially skilled in cooking or cleaning. What if there were other ways to serve?

Far too much time passed for a question she should have had an answer for. *"I don't know. I just have to do something."*

Linhadi smiled. She was right. She knew how to convey her meaning with little. The way her cheeks propped up the curve of her lips and her eyes crinkled in the corners affirmed Sosun more than words could.

"Your voice may be in your hands, but your hands can still become fists. You can fight in any number of ways. Don't count yourself short, young one."

"How did you convince people to listen to you?" Sosun asked.

"They started listening when I made them." Linhadi's eyes darted over Sosun's shoulder towards Nix. *"When they decide to protect you, remind them that you will not be a bystander in your own story."*

———

Kaylo allowed himself a moment to feel warm. As people took their places around the sitting mat, the emptiness of the tent faded. The tawny weave of the mat transitioned from a deep hickory into a glowing amber at the center where a large wooden platter of stingfish sat on wilted cabbage. Murmurs filled the tiny gaps between people. It had taken days, but this felt like a Jani encampment.

"Eat. Eat," Torrel said with a smile in his voice.

Tayen didn't hesitate. She filled her bowl with cabbage and fish before grabbing flatbread from the top of a steaming stack.

Tonight would turn into a distant memory as soon as they found the fighting. No one needed to give the truth voice for it to loiter over their meal. There were never enough soft moments—warm moments to last the cold nights.

Everyone served themselves, the spices filling the air with anticipation. Everyone except Jonan. The boy sat back as if on watch, glaring at Kaylo.

His eyebrows pinched towards his nose as if considering how best to strike. He looked much like his father had when Kaylo first knew him.

Strangely, it settled Kaylo's nerves. Tranquility had grown into a warning sign over the turns.

Kaylo ripped off a piece of the flatbread and pinched a messy mound of stingfish and cabbage. Good stingfish carried enough bite from the curing to challenge the heat in the peppers while the cabbage, carrots, and onions tempered the flavors. It was the type of meal to make anyone think twice about traveling too far.

The sting and heat tweaked the spot in the back of Kaylo's jaw just right. Torrel knew his way around a pot.

Rapping his knuckles against his wooden bowl, Kaylo nodded to Torrel and Etee. "I haven't had anything this good in decades. You all have been too gracious to host us like this."

"He's right," Jonan said. "We *have* been too gracious."

The warmth in the tent faltered as people stopped shoveling food into their mouths—apart from Nix. She continued on as if no one had said a thing.

"Jonan, shush," Etee said, her voice melodic even as it bit. "Kaylo, you have given us a gift. There are many reasons we crossed paths, and all of them a kindness."

"Tell that to granda. He hasn't been sleeping right since they got here." Jonan's gaze didn't leave Kaylo.

"It's time for you to relieve the entrance guard." A shadow of Torrel's past anger overlaid his voice.

The young man looked from his father to Kaylo before grabbing his bowl of stingfish and a fresh circle of bread.

"I hope it's cold out there," Tayen said in a whisper loud enough for everyone to hear. Kaylo nudged her ribs with his elbow, and no one said another word until Jonan left.

"What did he mean about Jonac?" Kaylo asked.

"It's nothing," Torrel said. Then he met Kaylo's eyes, and sighed.

"We've found that routine helps keep Jonac comfortable. Too many things change, and he has rough nights. But don't think for a second he would want it any other way. In the lucid moments, he talks about the family he lost. He includes you amongst them."

"Tell that to your kid."

"Tayen," Kaylo chided. "That's enough. I don't need you to defend me."

"Why? You're too polite to do it yourself."

Kaylo squared his shoulders to Tayen. This may be the last time he would see Torrel, the last time he would be able to share stories with someone who knew Jonac when he was well, and she had to turn it into a fight.

A knocking noise stopped Kaylo from releasing the torrent of words he had caught behind his teeth. Sosun sat there knocking her knuckles against the wooden bowl as he had earlier.

"Tayen, it's laughable how much you and Jonan are alike." She nudged Nix to translate. *"He's trying to defend his family, just like you."*

"Defend his family? By being an asshole?" Tayen signed.

"I didn't say either of you were good at it," she signed. *"I get it. You don't know what you're doing. You've either followed someone telling you what to do or chased your anger all your life. Well, no one's here to tell you what to do, and your anger isn't getting us anywhere."*

"You all have to work on your dinner talk," Nix said, signing as she did. "Really, whatever happened to complimenting the food and talking about the boring days we've all had? Silence works too."

"Like you wouldn't have said anything if Jonan said those things to Sosun," Tayen said.

"No, I would have punched him in the throat. No offense," she said as an aside to Torrel and Etee. "But I am not someone you should aspire to be."

"I'm going to miss these dinners when you're gone," Nomi said from beside her mother. Her relaxed posture in the middle of the raised tensions made her all the more curious. "You all keep things entertaining."

"No, you won't," Torrel said. "Your mother and I have talked it over, and you are going to guide them to the Uprising."

"No, you need me here."

"We have been waiting to hear news from the front for too long," Etee said. "You know the land, and you can avoid danger better than most, even without The Balance. We trust you. Do this for us."

"Okay, but seriously, can we talk about how good this meal is?" Nix asked.

Sosun hit her in the shoulder, but the tension eased a little.

Torrel snickered at the comment. "I'm glad you like it."

"You have cared for us too well, old friend," Kaylo said.

"Only as well as you deserved." Torrel cleared his throat. "I wish we had more time, but I'm afraid we cannot continue to delay. I have a favor to ask though. Please take care of my daughter."

There was no transaction in the statement, only a request. After so many turns feeling like he had killed Jonac's daughters, Torrel trusting Kaylo with Nomi unbroke something in Kaylo. He nodded and continued on with the meal.

Breathe in. Breathe out. This is the air Ennea gave us; it is a gift. Kaylo hadn't used Munnie's mantra in far too many turns. *Life continues.* He would need something to anchor him if he was about to do this ridiculous thing because of a promise.

The complete darkness of the night waited outside of the tent. Tayen sat a few paces away, watching him as if he would renege on his word if given the opportunity—which he might have with enough time to think it through.

The people he had respected most in his life had warned him about the dangers of mistwalking, and he had decided it would be a good time to teach a child. So much for protecting her. *Breathe in. Breathe out.*

So many ideas he had accepted for truth were unraveling—Torrel had called him a brother, Jonac had asked for his forgiveness, Tayen loved him and he hadn't gotten her killed yet. Maybe teaching her to mistwalk wasn't the worst plan. Who was he to withhold knowledge?

"Do you want to talk about what happened at dinner?" Tayen asked.

The question interrupted his internal mantra. She wasn't an unkind person. Stubborn, yes. Forceful, yes. Rude, of course. But she cared for those she loved with the fierceness of a mother bear. She just didn't typically show it through such thoughtful questions.

"No," Kaylo said. "We don't need to talk about that."

"Okay, then what's holding us back?"

There she is, he thought, unable to keep the smile from his face.

"No one ever taught me how to mistwalk. I'm going to be making this up as I go, so please have some patience. Okay?"

Tayen nodded, but the tight-lipped smile spoke of many things, none of them patience.

"The first few times, I mistwalked to escape trauma. I would have sworn I was dreaming. All my fears and guilt made me want to escape, then I let my guard down and reached for the thing that felt the most powerful—the fragment of The Balance living within me. It was right there at the other end of the echoes. My guess is that's exactly what you did in the Citadel."

Tayen leaned away and looked off to the blank canvas of the tent at the mention of her experience in the Citadel. No matter how many times he asked, she never wanted to talk about what happened to Pana.

"Odd as it seems, any time a dancer is learning to listen to The Song, they are learning the first steps to mistwalk. When you listen to The Song and you hear the subtle differences in the shapes and density of the shadows, you are developing the exact sense you need. There is a fragment of The Shadow in you, and you have to be able to find it in The Song. Once you do that, you can reach into The Mist through your connection."

"It's that easy?" Tayen asked.

"I never said it was easy. Most dancers never learn how to mistwalk. Whether that's because they never try or their connection to their spirit ancestor isn't strong enough, I don't know. But it's hard to understand the difference between the sound of the shadows around you and the spirit in your own body. It takes concentration—or, you know—extreme emotional trauma." He chuckled.

She did not.

"It's okay. I'll laugh at my own jokes," he said. "Lie down and focus on The Song. Don't reach for any of the shadows, just size them up. Weigh the various shades against each other. Understand the sound of each of them and their place in The Song. Then follow them back to the source within you—the part of you that can hear and sort through the shadows as if they were a collection of stones. That part knows even if the shadows are made of the same thing, they are all unique notes in The Song."

Before Tayen lay on her back, she rolled her eyes.

At least she was listening. She always rolled her eyes when she listened just to let him know he was using too many words to express his thoughts. On a few occasions, she had told him as much, but the eye roll acted as a shorthand—her way of practicing what she preached.

"Now, give yourself the time to search. There's no rush," Kaylo said, but stopped himself before indulging too much in pushing her patience.

Her echo bloomed. The Song bent through Tayen like a lens, and the various strands of light flickered as she focused on different shadows. The way she combed through The Song was methodical. Few dancers, even those with far more experience, had this level of control.

The games she played with the shadows, making them dance in clashing movements, had taught her how to tease out The Song as if it were an instrument. She plucked each note, and the shape of it formed in her echo.

He didn't deserve the pride that he felt. He wasn't her father. It hadn't been a full turn since they met, and she had hated him for at least a season in that time. But all the rationale in The Waking couldn't snuff out the pride brimming within him.

Only fifteen, he thought. *Imagine what she could become.*

She squeezed her eyelids, and her echo lost its pace. Shadows in the tent fought against the firelight. She balled her fists.

"Calm down, little shade. Breathe in. Breathe out."

Tayen spun and pushed herself from the ground in a fluid movement. "Calm down? I can't do it. You were right. You don't know how to teach me this. 'Search for the fragment of The Shadow in you.'" Her voice twisted into mockery. "That's the best you have? Any more cliche lessons?"

"You don't have to fall back on anger because it's difficult."

"Difficult? You don't know anything. You lived most of your adult life in a treehouse." She turned and walked out into the night, the shadows flaring as she left.

"Seed and fucking Balance. Why do people keep on expecting me to be able to teach?" Kaylo ran his hands through his braids.

If Jonac had his time in order, he would have known how to lead her to The Mist.

Chapter Seventeen

As Kaylo ground the pestle against the various herbs and roots he had purloined from the Jani's supplies, the scent of the ginger mixed with ashburn bark to create a nutty, spicy smell. It had the most pleasant aroma of any balm he had made over the turns.

The moment lay still like the surface of a placid lake. His days in the hallow never settled like this. Routines could busy a mind, but being here gentled something deeper within. The peace of it was unnerving in its own right. A single pebble could trouble the surface of this lake.

He added a stream of oil to the clumpy mush he had ground down.

In an hour, he would be walking towards war. As ubiquitous as the fighting was, it would be different once they found the Uprising. They would be searching out blood. They would be beholden to the group rather than themselves.

The elation of freeing people had always fallen silent beneath the noise of losing companions.

Once the balm congealed into a paste, he stopped grinding the pestle. If he had continued any longer, he would have needed a second balm for his elbow.

The furs over the tent's entrance parted, and Torrel strode through the opening. "You're hard to find."

"No. I'm a creature of habit." Kaylo used two fingers to apply the balm to his knee. The slick chill of it stung in a pleasant way. "Just an old man easing the pain."

"You're not old. Because if you're old, then I am too."

"This body hurts in more ways every day." Kaylo's hands slipped over his skin as he massaged the balm into the old injury.

"It's my back more than my knees."

"Arrows have a way of aging joints."

The dull ache in his knee cooled with the balm. It never went away, but that had stopped being the goal several turns back.

"You've had a hard life, my friend," Torrel said.

"We all have." Kaylo began to wrap his balm-covered knee in a loose bit of old fabric. "You were looking for me. Is it time?"

"Yes, and I have something to ask of you." Torrel pulled a small stump over to sit beside Kaylo. "Something is happening. I don't know exactly what, but our scouts have reported less movement from the Lost Army. They are pulling back behind their stormwoods. We haven't heard word from the Uprising in almost four moons.

"Whatever it is, keep Nomi safe. Send her back with enough information to warn us or call for our help. Brother, I need to protect my family, and I need your help."

Torrel's gaze burned with the intensity of his plea.

It was Kaylo's own damn fault. He had spent his life getting into trouble, especially when he tried to avoid it. He had made himself into a story. Everyone had this idea that he knew what they didn't—that he could fight back the daemons.

He wasn't as reliable as the stories.

"I can't make any promises, Torrel. If you need to keep your daughter close, I understand. Tell us the way, and we'll be gone."

"You can promise you'll try. That's all I'm asking."

Against his better judgement, Kaylo reached out his hands to clasp Torrel's right hand between his. "I will do what I can to send your daughter home safely."

"Make sure to tell the Uprising not to forget about us. Our role may be to protect those who need protecting, but we promised them what blades we can offer if it comes to it. The Jani will not make the same mistake again. We will fight for The Mother with whatever means necessary."

Kaylo could only nod. Part of him hated the idea of Jani running towards a battle, even if it was necessary. Blood on sand-colored robes conjured memories better left in the past.

———

Nix edged the tip of her new knife along the inside of her fingernail, scraping away the grime that had collected there. Her patch of ground in the nook of two tents gave her the perfect vantage point to watch everyone's sentimental parting words without being subjected to them.

She had never been one for goodbyes or making connections worthy of goodbyes. The whole performance of it was unnecessary. People came. People left. Sometimes familiar faces found their way back, but that rarely had anything to do with her.

Sosun busied herself with her farewells to Linhadi and her walking translator of a grandson.

If that girl had any sense of her own wellbeing, she would be saying goodbye to Nix, the brat, and the tortured spirit dancer. Sosun had no business involving herself in a revolution when the Jani could keep her safe.

She deserved a bit of safety in this life.

In Nix's experience, people almost never did the smart thing, herself included. Getting herself conscripted by the Lost Nation, worrying after Sosun, walking towards death—maybe she was more sentimental than she gave herself credit for.

"Why are you doing that with your brand-new knife?" Tayen said, making herself comfortable on Nix's secluded patch of dirt.

"A knife is a tool. Nothing more, nothing less. I take care of it. I use it. I don't worry over the honor of a tool, only that it will last me as long as I need it," Nix said. "For now, I need it to pry the dirt from beneath my fingernails."

"Kaylo would—"

"If I ever bothered myself about what that man would or wouldn't do when I made my decisions, I would have to end my mortal existence right then and there."

Tayen chuckled. "I'm trying to imagine who you were when you were young and hopeful."

"I spawned at the ripe age of twenty-three—fully developed and completely aware of what a shitty world The Waking is."

The blade scratched the underside of her thumb as she cleaned out another span's worth of gunk. What a satisfying feeling.

"Do you think the Uprising's camp will be anything like this?"

"What's with all the wonder, kid? You'll find out soon enough."

"You're usually an ass, but this is something special. What's got you on edge?"

The straightforwardness of Tayen's personality, which Nix had come to enjoy, got annoying whenever the girl aimed it in her direction. She wiped the knife clean—or clean enough—along her pant leg and sheathed the blade.

"We should get going if we're going to take the sun with us."

Nix didn't wait for the inquisitive, sarcastic response. She got up and walked towards the encampment exit, which just so happened to take her past Kaylo and Torrel.

"Oh, Asshole of Anilace, we should get going."

"Good morning, Nix," Kaylo said, breaking away from his conversation. "I too am excited to head out into the forest with you and your glowing personality."

"Our supplies are packed. Our guide is sitting on a crate by the entrance, looking more bored than I am. If we are going to go, we need to walk with Sokan as long as we can. I have no desire to be caught unaware in the middle of the night in Gousht territory."

"A few minutes won't make a lick of difference. You know that," Kaylo said as Torrel stood beside him looking anywhere but directly at Nix.

A quick movement over Torrel's shoulder made Nix smile. "Here comes someone to prove you wrong."

"You do this every time!" Jonan yelled.

Torrel rolled his eyes before turning to meet his son.

"I can read the land just as well as Nomi. I can hunt. I'm better with a blade." Jonan gestured more than Sosun as he spoke, only with less purpose. "Why do you send her every time?"

"Because I know she'll come back." Torrel reached for his son's shoulder, but the boy brushed away his father's hand. "She isn't looking to prove herself in blood. Someday, you'll learn you're more than your sword arm."

"She also hasn't tried to kill any of us. But that's just my opinion, for what it's worth," Nix said. If she had to be here for this inane conversation, she could at least enjoy herself.

"Shut your mouth. This is between my father and me."

"I didn't say I blamed you. Trying to kill Kaylo speaks highly of your decision-making, but it does make you untrustworthy."

The boy bared his teeth like a mountain cat.

"Stop helping, Nix," Kaylo said.

"Who said I was helping?"

"Enough!" Torrel bellowed, calling even more eyes and ears towards them. He lowered his voice and closed the short distance between him and his son. "Your temper is why you don't belong out there. The same temper that is flashing up right now in the middle of the encampment like you are a child without a bit of sense to your name. Your swearing day is half a turn away, and you are showing how far you have to travel before you are worthy of pledging yourself to the Jani."

Jonan stepped back on his heels, his eyes widening with the injury of his father's words.

"Walk away now," Torrel said.

The boy stood there for a moment, fists clinched and brow furrowed, a body of a young man wrapped around a growing seed of anger. There may have been a time when their people weren't like this. Nix had never known it—not that she could remember. The Gousht arrived not long after her fourth birthday.

"You will have your time, Jonan." Torrel pulled the harshness from his tone until only the finest edge of it remained. "Son, please do what I ask."

Jonan glared one final time at Nix before walking away.

"Why me? I was on his side."

"Nix," Kaylo said, exasperated. "Why do you insist upon treating people like entertainment?"

"I know you think you're noble by tolerating the boy, but you are only setting him up for the time he meets a warrior who won't. He'll find more than sarcasm." She turned to Torrel. "And you. What made you change your attitude when you were that age? Was it an overabundance of kindness or did you finally meet the problems you were so angry with? Words won't fix what he's feeling."

Torrel looked at her as if the mirage of his expectations had been dashed away from her image. His cocked eyebrow turned from confusion to incredulous appreciation. "I don't usually take parenting advice from foul-mouthed strangers."

"Maybe you should start."

He chuckled. "Maybe I should. You know, I hadn't thought about the changes I had gone through—"

Nix waved her hand to cut him off. "This wasn't an invitation for a heart-to-heart. I came over here to say that we need to go."

"She's right. We should go," Kaylo said, clapping his hand on Torrel's shoulder. "Plus, if we don't, she'll stop being so nice."

"Blessed Mother guide your feet, my friend," Torrel said. "Take care of my daughter."

"I will. We will see each other again. I am sure of it."

Kaylo finally detached from Torrel, and a lingering melancholy moved with him—although it was difficult to distinguish from his typical affect.

For some reason, they were all ready to leave the safety and security of this place to track down a war. But if they were going to make stupid decisions, they could at least make them quickly.

"At the end of this, we will be dead. You know that, right?" Kaylo asked as he collected his travel sack.

"I tried to convince Sosun to stay, but she won't change her path. If that means I die, I die."

"I'm glad we both understand the situation."

Nix stopped the slow walk towards the encampment exit and turned towards Kaylo. "I've never been one to hope. I expected to die long before now. So if we're going to charge into war, I'm planning to do as much damage as I can. I suggest you do the same."

They had already said enough on the matter. Death didn't require words. People died every moment of every day. Words wouldn't change that. If Nix died today or tomorrow or two decades from now, it wouldn't matter. She could only control this moment. And in this moment, they needed to start their fucking trek before she lost her patience.

Chapter Eighteen
Current Day Ennea

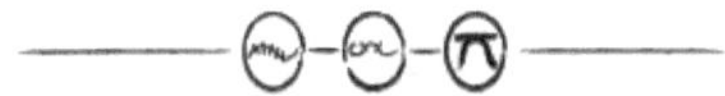

Previous prisoners had carved tally marks into the stone cell. Wal hadn't bothered. It didn't matter how many days had passed. He would die here. They would drag his filthy body to a hastily dug hole. The nameless would probably piss on him before piling dirt on his corpse.

He sat with his back against the wall staring at the words that some now-dead prisoner had carved into the stone. *May The Mother embrace me.*

Prayers wouldn't do Wal any good. He didn't need guidance or forgiveness or any of that sour shit. The spirits couldn't guide him out of his cell.

He picked up a loose stone and tossed it against the opposite wall, hitting just left of his target. The stone clacked as it rolled over the rough floor. His aim was getting better. The next stone met the mark perfectly. It was the most satisfaction he found outside of his dreams these days.

"The solitude of a mind can be an escape or a prison, my friend," the poet called out from their connected cell.

Wal picked up another stone and threw it harder, missing his mark by a wide margin.

"Wanti said she traveled the world in her prison. She found truths in her cell that had eluded her for the first half of her life," Lanigan said as if

Wal hadn't been ignoring them.

"Wanti's dead," Wal groaned.

"I should hope so. She would be nearly three hundred turns if she wasn't."

The next rock struck the top edge of the mark before rebounding and hitting Wal in the arm. "Fuck!"

"It seems that you have lots to contemplate, my friend," they said. "I will leave you to it."

As if to keep Wal from the sweet welcome of silence, footsteps echoed down the rocky corridor. This may have been better received if he didn't have to scoop saliva out of the majority of his meals. Whatever they did to the meals they didn't spit in only unnerved him if he thought about it—which he unfortunately did.

A bowl slid through the opening at the base of the cell door and puttered to a stop. Rice, a hard-boiled egg with a bite missing, and a helping of yellowish mucus. At least it was towards the edge of the bowl and easy enough to scoop out into his shit bucket.

The nameless moved on to Lanigan's cell, and the sound of the bowl scraping the floor followed. However, footsteps didn't immediately start moving back into the corridor.

Wal left his bowl of most-of-an egg and the remainer of his rice on the floor, then walked to the door. The barred window in his cell door didn't allow him to see much of the nameless man, but he seemed to be gesturing outside of the poet's cell.

Warriors talked about the nameless. Of course they did—the infrastructure of the Citadel relied on them. Even the major campaigns beyond the Lost Forest required dozens of servants to support the troops. He had heard rumors that they spoke in some form of sign language, even if they weren't permitted to, but he had never seen it.

The man's fingers tapped the side of his face, then he made a large rotating gesture at shoulder-level.

Lanigan couldn't understand this language, could they? They had been restricted to the Citadel for longer than Wal had served the army, but that didn't mean they knew everything happening within the mountain, did it?

With another series of gestures and a nod, the nameless man stepped away from the cell door. He glared at Wal as he made his way back into the darkened corridor.

Before Kaylo, the servant wouldn't have dared to look him in the eyes. He would have fallen to his knees for forgiveness if Wal had caught him signing this unsanctioned language. Now, this trained rat spat in his food.

"What did he say?" Wal asked.

"Were you eavesdropping, Commander?"

"You can't eavesdrop when no one says a damn word," Wal said. "Now, tell me what he said."

"You do see the irony in your statement, yes?" Lanigan asked with a smirk in their voice. "Never mind that. We simply exchanged pleasantries. Whatever else may have passed between us was not meant for you."

If he had the opportunity, he would have loved to run the poet through the throat. They had been prisoner for over twenty turns and had the gall to act like they were better than Wal. He had been a commander.

"Pleasantries, huh? You could at least ask them to stop spitting in my food."

"From what I'm told, you have a reputation for cruelty amongst the servants of the Citadel. Why would they offer you dignity when you gave them none?"

"They earned their place."

"Oh, come now Commander. The same people who decided the servants earned their place decided you deserved a cell at the bottom of a mountain. Maybe you could skip your rock-throwing practice for a few hours and think about how fair you believe the structures are that put both you and the servants in your current predicaments."

"Fair isn't worth the stench rising from my shit bucket. Not in this world."

Lanigan laughed. "Oh, you do have a way with words. I admire you for that. And you are right. Fair is a concept people twisted into meaninglessness. Instead, how worthwhile are those structures? Who do they serve and at what cost? There are many fine questions to ponder with your time."

Wal arranged himself back on the smoothest patch of floor he had, picked up his bowl, and ate what remained of his meal.

Many questions to ponder, he thought. Did the poet think he hadn't considered these things before?

Ever since the Gousht conquered Ennea, the number of options Wal had in his life had dwindled to nothing. The King made horrible decisions and left countless people bearing the burden. Wal doing what he had to didn't mean he approved.

He scooped up rice with his fingers and made sure not to lose a single grain to the floor.

His opinion on the matter wouldn't change anything.

CHAPTER NINETEEN

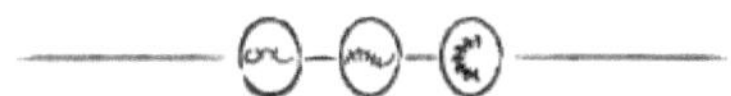

THE LIGHT FROM THE brazier flickered over the map, and Wal breathed far too heavily over my shoulder. According to his sketch, the forge sat on the edge of Gancea Lake with five other buildings scattered over the grounds.

His hot breath sent a shiver down my back. "Do you mind giving me some space?"

"Sorry, I didn't mean to—but it's perfect, right?"

In less than an hour, the Uprising would convene under the gathering tent in an open meeting. If I couldn't convince them to move forward with our next target, we might not be able to search for another. Not without the Lost Nation's approval at least.

There wasn't a single member of this little rebellion, warrior or not, who hadn't suffered our losses dearly. Passions were fading with each spirit sent off into The Mist. And when fighting an uphill battle, passion had to be the wind driving a rebellion forward.

"How many Gousht?"

"That's the best part. Twenty couta." Wal wore his pride plainly, though he had never been one for modesty.

"That doesn't make any sense. Five buildings and the forge. What else are they storing there?"

"The bastards decided to incentivize the metal workers by holding their families hostage." He jabbed his finger at the building furthest from the forge. "During the day, their families work around the grounds, organize the weapons lockers, then the soldiers bar them inside this shack of a building at night."

"I know we didn't need more proof, but they are fucking evil."

"The forge fires never stop burning," Wal said. "Say nothing else about the green bastards, they know how to motivate people."

I spun around on Wal. "This isn't funny. Those are families. I'd be doing whatever they asked of me too if they had my parents."

"I didn't mean...I meant...well fuck, Kaylo, if I don't laugh at something, I'll put my blade through my own eye." The pride had vanished from his expression.

It wasn't his fault. I knew who Wal was, but sometimes his humor turned my stomach. Imagining those families stealing glances of each other, no more than forty paces between them, praying for another day in The Waking. And not being able to do a damn thing but survive.

"This is good," I said, restraining my fury. "We need to scout more—get a good count of the Enneans on the grounds."

"Forty-two," he said with a seriousness that he rarely allowed anyone to see. "I learned all of their faces as best as I could so I didn't mess up the count."

Sometimes I let Wal's clever mouth distract me and forgot that he cared. "You did great, Wal. Truly."

His smile returned, but his eyes still held onto his seriousness. "If we are willing to fight ugly, I have an idea about how we can—"

Acta nearly threw himself through the furs as he burst into the tent. Both Wal and I had hands on our blades before he had uttered a word.

"Mist on fire! What the fuck are you doing? Are we under attack?" Wal demanded.

Acta held up a finger as he caught his breath.

"Really? He wants us to wait?"

"Wal," I chastised.

"Maybe he should slowly walk into the tent next time. Then he would be able to speak right away."

"Yes, but then how would we make time for your witty commentary?" I stood and placed a hand on Acta's back. "Breathe, then tell us whatever you have to say."

"I was doing my rounds." He took another deep breath. "And I overheard Hylïane talking to some people. She's calling a vote. The numbers are on their side. They're going to force us to treat with the Lost Nation."

She had done it, and the only thing that surprised me was how unfazed I felt.

Every chance she had, Hylïane had brought up making a deal with the Lost Nation. She even met with them behind the small council's back, not that she had been able to keep the secret.

To hear her tell it, their army would protect us and keep the fight alive. Those of us determined to kill ourselves on Gousht blades could continue to strive for our goals.

And after the last raid, there were more non-combatants than warriors in the Uprising.

Pretty pathetic uprising, I thought.

"We can't let that happen." For some reason, his tone had settled after hearing the news.

"People are afraid. Every time we leave the encampment we bring home more bodies—break more hearts. Why wouldn't people choose protection? Even if it is a lie." I looked down at Wal's map. The forge was a day and a half out. "If they hand control over to those assholes, we'll be done for good. They'll have us harassing small convoys of crystals for their stockpile."

"We need Annit. He will know exactly who we need to convince before the vote," Wal said.

"No!" I said with more certainty than I had felt in a long while. "No, we can't involve Annit. He may believe in what we are doing, but he believes in doing it the right way. If the people want something, he won't go against them."

"What are you thinking?" Acta asked.

"I'm thinking your cousin is going to kill me if I survive." Just remembering Kristee's death stare made me shiver.

Acta smiled. "Not just you."

"Who do you think would leave tonight?" Neither of them looked confused by the question, as if they'd had the same thought.

"I could speak to Jolrin, Shalani, and Rēlan," Acta said.

"Wal, you speak to Boda and Talise." I counted up our numbers in my head. "Talise might need some convincing, but she may hate the Lost Nation even more than we do. And Boda will come at the mention of blood."

"Do you think you can convince Liara and Tomi?" Wal asked.

"I'll have to, but first, tell me your plan. The one where we fight ugly. Can we do it with ten?"

———

Any minute, the call would rise, and the entire Uprising would make their way to the gathering tent. It wouldn't be long before they noticed I wasn't there.

I couldn't do this without Liara. I wouldn't. The last time I went off on my own hadn't ended too well.

With a final heavy breath, I pushed my way into her and Tomi's tent. Both sisters whipped their heads around ready to tear into whoever had intruded. Liara's face softened when she saw me. Tomi's did not.

"We didn't hear the call," Tomi said, her tone flat. "We can find the gathering tent on our own."

"You'll be pledging yourself to The Mother this turn, Tomi. Eventually, you'll have to grow out of being an ass to everyone." Liara got up to greet me, then stopped when she took me in. "What's wrong?"

"Do you believe in what we are doing? Do you believe in the Uprising? Truly believe?"

"What are you talking about, Kaylo? Of course I do," Liara said.

"He's finally cracked. I told you he was strung tighter than a good bow." Tomi went back to fiddling with the fletching on an arrow, evidently pulling her insults from her immediate task.

"We don't have time for this. We need to leave now."

Liara grabbed my hand and brought me farther into the tent where they had been sitting together. "Slow down, and tell me what is happening."

"Hyliane has the votes," I said as calmly as I could. "As soon as we walk into the gathering tent, the Uprising will become a part of the Lost Nation. We'll be at the beck and call of some king we've never met. We won't be liberating anyone."

The bitterness I felt towards the Lost Nation and their lies laced my words. I hated how entirely I had let myself be duped. They couldn't be trusted. I couldn't give them the chance to break everything we had fought so hard to build for ourselves.

"We just have to convince the people she's wrong," Liara said. "If that takes time, it takes time."

"Fuck that," Tomi said, putting her arrow to the side. "Your cracked lover is right."

"Seriously, Tomi. Now isn't the time to be insulting him."

"There's always time for that," Tomi said, without smiling at the continued insult. "When people get comfortable, they stay comfortable. The Lost Nation will make whatever promises they need to, and people will get complacent. How many misfit camps did we latch onto? Every one of those sad bastards settled into surviving like it was the only thing that mattered. Do you think they started that way?"

"There's a forge." I knelt down and pulled the map from my sack, laying it on their swept dirt floor. "Here. There are minimal soldiers guarding a large group of metal workers and their families. We need to bolster our ranks. We need to show the people we can do what we intended—grow into a real resistance."

"So what? You expect us to run off and raid this forge without a vote? Is that who you want to become? Do you even have enough warriors?"

Outside the tent, a muffled voice rose into the air, too distant to hear clearly, but it could only be one thing. The gathering call had begun.

"We don't have the time. If you and Tomi join us, we will have enough. Wal has a plan."

"Oh, does he?" Liara rolled her eyes. "How much fire is involved?"

"Enough. You won't like the plan, but it will work."

"Clan meeting," the caller cried out, much closer now. "Gathering tent. All welcome."

"You said you trusted me. You said that I need to be a leader—not just someone searching for blood, but a leader," I said, holding Liara's gaze. "This is how I can do that. This is the only way I know."

"That was good. Well played," Tomi said.

Both of us glared at her before the announcement rang out again.

"We aren't running towards our death, right? Tomi will be safe?"

"If you're willing to fight ugly, we won't lose a single warrior."

Liara narrowed her eyes. "How ugly?"

When Liara, Tomi, and I reached the meeting place, the others had already arrived. I rushed forward. Something about escaping off into the night for an unapproved mission had stirred me in a way going to battle never had. A nervousness shot through my joints, demanding that I move.

I only counted six warriors as we approached the others.

Ten warriors had barely been enough to carry out the mission. It would have demanded perfection from each of us. With nine, The Mother would have to pick up a spear alongside us.

Acta grimaced a bit as I searched the ranks looking for the missing warrior. "Shalani said she couldn't leave her mother behind. She won't say anything, but she won't join us either."

"Did you tell her to bring her mother?" Tomi asked. No one broke a smile.

"Be honest. Can we do this with nine?" Liara asked, and eight sets of eyes folded in on me like walls of a prison. "If we can't, there's no point in dying just to die."

"If every single one of us plays our part perfectly," I said. "Wal, this is your plan. What do you think?"

Wal stepped back from the redirected focus. For as often as he reached out for people's attention with his overabundance of sarcasm, he withdrew when people looked at him like a leader. He had been that way before Oakheart, but it had only gotten worse.

"Wal?" Talise urged.

"I'm thinking," he said, and let another few moments pass. "Yes, we can do it. I will have to rearrange some things, but yes. I believe we can do it."

Chapter Twenty
Kaylo's Story

WE ARRIVED AT THE forge two days later with plenty of daylight to study our conquest. From the high branches of the surrounding forest, we watched.

Nothing obscene happened. Metal workers came and went from the forge. They delivered blades to the storeroom—no traps to avoid. The guards escorted them without obvious violence. A trio of older children washed clothing at the lakeshore.

The degradation came in the things we didn't witness. When metal workers walked the grounds, they never stopped to speak to the other Enneans. These people were family or family to their fellow captives. Yet, they ignored each other. They had become spirits passing on separate planes.

Somehow, these soldiers had trained their captives to ignore their kin.

It always amazed me how different the imagining of horrors compared to the reality of them. The violations of our bodies and our people had been made commonplace like a daily chore. The violence had spawned a culture of its own.

Once I marked the captives' casual avoidance of each other, I hated the sun for not falling faster. Yet, we waited and watched.

Wal employed the help of Jolrin, Rélan, and Tomi in making

preparations. Boda refused, demanding to be as close to the final planning as possible. I was too weary to bother forcing the issue.

We mapped out our routes, watched, and waited until Sokan finally set.

If we didn't act tonight, we couldn't count on the rest of the Uprising being there when we got back. Especially without the nine of us, it would take time to pack the camp and plan a route, but that wouldn't delay them long. If Hylíane's voice had become as trusted as it seemed, there would be no promises of finding the encampment even if we started back tonight.

As far as we knew, they could have been off to see their new puppeteers in the Lost Nation even as we prepared for the raid. But we could only control the battle in front of us.

From the tree line, the forge looked like any other village.

I usually felt anxious before a raid. Not now. Something about Hylíane forcing my hand emboldened me.

Blood owed blood. The truth of the saying never wavered. We would take payment from the Gousht tonight.

Liara approached, and her echo held the waiting energy of a tide yet to come in. "If you are having second thoughts, tell me now."

"Actually, I'm surer than ever."

"I never got that about you," she said with the hint of a laugh in her voice. "When things seem their worst, you leave all your doubts behind. It's like when you decided to help me break out Tomi. You made a decision, and it settled as a fact in your mind."

I chuckled. "I was pretty sure we were both going to die. I had just accepted it."

The lightness abandoned her expression. "That's not what's happening here, is it? This isn't some suicidal quest. Because if Tomi gets hurt—"

I held up a hand to cut off the threat I had heard so many times before. "I can't explain it. For the past two turns, I have been trying to figure out my role in this resistance. I couldn't figure out how to be the leader everyone else wanted me to be. Looking out there, right now, I know what to do."

"Are you sure you're comfortable with Wal's plan?" she asked. "There's no honor in this."

I pushed off the tree I was leaning on and stepped closer to her so she could see me as clearly as possible as I said this. "I disagree. When a snake attacks your family, the honorable thing to do is save them, even if you have to grow fangs yourself."

Wal cleared his throat from behind us as if he were interrupting a tender moment. "Talise, Acta, Jolrin, and Boda are ready," he said. "Are you sure Boda's the right person for this? He literally can't see out of one eye, and he's about as even-keeled as a rabid bear."

"He's the one that's not even-keeled?" I inclined my head towards Wal to make my insinuation understood. "Yes, Wal. I'm sure. He's the only one. He's the fastest, and he knows what's at stake. We have to trust him eventually."

"Fine. But when he fucks it all up by charging into the middle of a barracks to fight the soldiers with his fists, don't blame me or my plan."

"Make sure they are in place and wait for the signal," I said.

I allowed him time to leave before turning back to Liara. "You keep on insisting that I need to find out how to be the leader our people deserve. So I thought about the leader I imagine you would be. You would make the decisions you thought were right, and you would own them. I've seen it."

"Kaylo, I believe in you. You know that, right?"

"I'm trying to be the person who doesn't need to be believed in." I pulled her close with a hand on the nape of her neck and touched my brow to hers.

She smelled of sweat and the sunflower oil she used in her locs. I knew her by that scent. "We need to get in place," I said.

"Don't die." She forced a smile.

"You either."

"This is the air Ennea gave us; it is a gift." I took a breath, reciting Munnie's teachings, and ran my hands through the grass. "Life continues."

The Ennean prisoners had all been locked away in their respective quarters. The soldiers had gone into their barracks to do whatever soldiers liked to do to pass their time between oppressing my people. Four guards remained: two archers on a perch and two patrolling the grounds. Everything had played out exactly as Wal had said.

He had become an excellent scout.

Dark clouds slowly overtook the sky, stealing away the moonlight. It was such a simple thing for Liara, and yet, it marked the first step towards blood.

I pulled a pair of reeds from my robes. When Wal scouted the forge the span prior, he had laid the groundwork. Every night he blew into the reeds, eliciting a high-pitched cry that resembled a nighthawk. If the guards had found the sound alarming before, it wouldn't be as unfamiliar tonight.

If Wal's brilliant ideas hadn't been so encumbered by everything else that came out of his mouth, people would understand how smart he actually was.

Once I sounded the signal call, there would be no turning back.

Talise, Boda, and Tomi waited beside me, Boda looking far too eager for my liking. Better eager than hesitant, but neither would have been better still.

I placed the reeds between my lips and blew three quick notes followed by a fourth sustained note. Boda almost rushed forward at the sound, but Talise caught the back of his robes.

Heavy moments passed, and I brought the reeds back to my lips. Before I could sound the call again, the pattern repeated from the north. Talise and Boda darted into the clearing.

Whatever happened now would become my burden to own.

The two shadowed figures raced through the darkness, hunkered low and moving fast. The grass around the clearing had grown to knee-length, further cloaking their approach to any who may have been watching.

A part of me hated not being the one out there, risking my life. It happened every time. Annit had always reminded me that I had a role to serve. My sword couldn't cut down every obstacle. The words never made the feeling dissipate.

I tapped Tomi on the shoulder. "Time to move."

As the two pairs of shadows crept towards the guards on watch, Tomi and I headed towards the storeroom and the echoes of stolen spirits.

When the plan included twenty warriors, each component allowed more room for error. If one of twenty fell or failed, there would be others to step into their place. With nine, no one could fail or we all would.

I had to trust the others would do what needed doing. Still, I expected a bell to break apart the whispers of crickets in the night.

When we reached the wall of the storeroom, I took a deep breath. "This is the air Ennea gave us," I whispered to myself.

Two sharp notes cut through the air, and time stopped.

If another signal didn't sound off soon, the plan would be over. Every other time we had gone on a raid, I'd had a better vantage point. Even when mistakes were made and warriors fell, I knew. In this moment, I had no way of knowing if anyone was alive apart from whoever had called out the signal and Tomi.

They haven't rung the alarm, I told myself. *Move forward.*

The small but undeniable sound of a scuffle filtered through the quiet night then fell silent. My lungs swelled with a breath as if I could stop the world from spinning by refusing to exhale. Then two more high-pitched notes sounded off.

Have faith, I thought before waving to Tomi. She nocked an arrow.

We made our way into the storeroom, following one particular echo. When I found the tawny crystal waiting for me, I picked it up and knelt.

"To the fourth, The Mountain, forgive me."

Outside the storeroom, everyone stood beside their assigned buildings. Both barracks and the commander's quarters had been barred from the outside.

Everything that happened next had to happen at once. If any of the soldiers reacted too soon, the prisoners' lives would be at risk.

Wal and Jolrin sparked their flint stones and ignited the wicks of their respective canisters of firestarter. The ugliness that was to come had been earned.

I called on The Mountain spirit using the stone—no reason to take the spirit into myself for this—and I placed my hand against the wall of the building where the metal workers' families slept. I allowed myself to think about how they had crammed thirty people in a hut this small and still managed to post a guard inside. It stoked the undying hatred within me.

All at once, I turned a section of the wall to dust and debris as Wal and Jolrin tossed their lit canisters of firestarter into their respective barracks.

The night erupted into screams of shock, horror, and agony.

The guard watching over the hostages looked up from where he sat on his chair beside the door. If he were younger than fifty turns, I would have been more surprised than the old man looked. He stood awkwardly, and Tomi loosed an arrow into his chest.

The hostages were quickly backing away from the chaos towards the walls of their prison. I stepped through the mess of bodies, and drove my father's knife through the underbelly of the guard's chin and into his soft palate to finish him off.

How little did they think of our people? Sending this old man to jail Enneans was insulting.

When I removed my knife from his head, he slumped off the chair with his eyes rolling back into his skull. Blood leaked from him like a torn waterskin.

"Stay here," I said to the freed hostages, but I hardly needed to say a word. The lot of them tucked into a mob of wide-eyed and horrified faces.

Outside of the shack, screams emanated from both barracks. The wooden doors clattered against the heavy timber bars blocking their exit. Flames illuminated the grounds, and a dark, acrid smoke caught the scant moonlight breaking through the cloud cover.

The soldiers who had thrown themselves through the windows of their fiery coffins found themselves skewered by the warriors waiting outside.

Everything was going perfectly until one of the barracks doors fell from its hinges. A burning man tumbled from the building, followed by four soldiers with their weapons drawn.

One tried to call The Wind with an azure crystal, but I snatched it from the air. Its anthem of rage quelled all other sounds as I watched Acta, Jolrin, and Talise engage the bastards.

We had caught the soldiers off guard. Even as they fought, they coughed on smoke filled with the ashes of their dead brethren. Steel clanged. Flames flickered over the battle, distorting everyone's movements.

All the fighters had fallen before I could reach the skirmish.

One too many bodies lay on the ground.

As I stepped closer, I refused to look at the two warriors left standing. If I looked at their faces, I would know. Someone who I had fought beside—someone who had believed in this cause and me enough to run towards blood in the middle of the night—had fallen.

No one on the ground moved, not even a twitch. Limbs and gore covered the faces of the dead. Then I saw him. Acta's eyes peered through an opening in the pile of corpses, as if he were trying to see through to the moonlight.

The Wind's anthem grew louder and quicker like a hurricane making landfall.

He lay at the bottom of the collection of bodies. This young man who had survived the mines, who had warned me about Hyliane's plans, who had been a warrior of circumstance and learned the blade better than most, had passed through The Mist.

My debt of blood only deepened the more I fought to repay those I had lost.

The moment he broke through the tree line, he had understood the risk. They all had. But none of that quieted the anger thrashing about in my bones as I looked down at his still-open eyes.

A hectic slamming noise broke into The Wind's chorus.

We hadn't set the commander's quarters aflame. I had questions for him. So we had barricaded him in as we slaughtered his soldiers.

"He will feel this," I promised Acta. I pointed at Jolrin and Talise who stood back silently. "With me."

My fury, shame, and grief walked beside me as I strode towards the commander's quarters. At the edge of my awareness, I sensed the others watching me. But it didn't matter.

As soon as Jolrin and Talise lifted the bar from the commander's door, the man charged at me like a wild animal. Then he crashed to the ground as Talise cracked the heavy timber over his back.

Lying at my feet, he looked small. He had his undergarments on, a gray stretch of fabric covering his soft form. He turned from side to side taking in the soldiers who had died for him.

I hoped he loved them. I hoped he knew what made them laugh and the names of their parents. For whatever would make the pain of seeing their bodies broken and burning worse, I hoped.

I unsheathed my sword and brought it to his neck. *"Up,"* I said in Gousht. When he didn't move, I poked the tip of my blade into his shoulder and repeated myself.

He rose, not to his knees like I had expected, but the man had the gall to stand and face me. Surrounded by his slaughtered men, wearing his underclothes, he looked at me as if he were my better.

"What do you know of Kyernan Janome?" I asked, my distaste for the

commander coloring the guttural syllables.

He smiled. Not something brash. He didn't show his teeth. But he curved his lips enough to let me know I didn't have power over him. If he didn't want to speak to me, he wouldn't.

I returned the smile.

His bones barely resisted my blade when I lopped off his hand. His smug expression broke into unbridled pain as he squealed into the night, clutching at the wound with his uninjured arm.

I looked over my shoulder and found Wal watching intently. "Tourniquet."

Wal obeyed, taking a belt off a dead soldier and drawing it tightly around the commander's now-shorter limb. If Wal's smile were any indication, he drew the belt tighter than necessary. It elicited the cry of pain he was looking for.

"There's more I can do before you die," I said. *"Now, tell me what you know of Kyernan Janome."*

Even as he leaned to one side, clutching his missing hand, he bared his teeth at the demand.

I grabbed his ear and drew my blade from lobe to arch until it came free from his head. I let it fall next to his lifeless hand on the dirt.

Murmurs of the onlookers underscored his screams.

"Where is The Priest?!" I ignored his screams. *"Where is Kyernan Janome?"*

The air of high standing abandoned him as he bled, unable to cover the new wound with either hand. *"I don't know. I've never met him. All I know are the rumors."*

"Then tell them to me."

"People say he's ambitious. He takes whatever placement takes him a step up the ladder. Last I heard, he was hunting down nomads."

"Jani?"

"I don't know what you fucking call them."

My blade slid through his throat easy as roast boar, and he collapsed amongst the other pieces of himself.

When I looked up, my warriors were watching me—my friends, the people I had trained, none of them wearing the same expression. Some of them were aghast, others angry. Boda looked like he might have come to respect me for the first time.

I found Liara standing next to her sister. Her features were stretched long and her eyes carried something akin to pity.

"Get the metal workers," I called out. "Wal, Talise, take some warriors and burn whatever is left standing. If the Gousht want this land back, make them rebuild on ashes. We are out of here within the hour."

Everyone set to their tasks save Liara, who hadn't stopped looking at me as if I were somehow in need of fixing.

I followed the clattering of echoes and went to work breaking down crystals without another look to spare for Liara and her pity.

CHAPTER TWENTY-ONE
KAYLO'S STORY

ANNIT HAD BEEN ON watch day and night with a rotating string of warriors since we left. Even in the cool evening light, the exhaustion weighed clearly on his face. An underlying rage stirred through his echo like the coals remaining after a fire, refusing to go out, yearning to be the flames they had been.

He didn't say anything as the line of forty-two newly liberated Enneans filed into the encampment through the gap in the camouflaged netting. And before I could explain myself, he left.

"You'll have to give him time," Liara said.

I nodded as the people we left behind greeted the metal workers and their families.

In all of my handwringing about absconding into the night and raiding a forge without the clan's permission, I hadn't truly considered what would happen when we came back. I had been far too focused on surviving the raid. Now, I would have to answer for my choices.

"What in Ta Mother's bloody asshole did cha think cha were doing?!" Hylïane dug her walking stick into the earth with every step towards me. Everyone, new and old, turned to see the commotion, but it didn't slow her down. "Cha think cha can risk alla our lives and jus come back like nothin happened?"

"Can we talk somewhere a bit more private?" I asked.

"Private?! Oh, cha don't like all ta eyes, do cha? No. You left alla us. Now, cha can explain it to alla us."

"Do you see those people behind you, Hylĩane?" I asked, keeping my tone as neutral as I could. "You were about to hand the Uprising over to the Lost Nation. Where would they be if you had your way? You care about your own safety so much. What about theirs?"

"Ta Gousht are burning villages. Consolidating tere forces." Hylĩane drove her walking stick into the ground to emphasize her words. "Tese little raids are jus makin tem angry. Cha can't take down an empire with a handful of swords. We need a real army. We need a real general."

Hylĩane was beyond any convincing. Her fears controlled her. I turned to face those I had left behind and saw unsure expressions. They needed direction.

"I get it. You're scared. But we saved these people, whether we did it the right way or not," I said. "The Lost Nation won't protect you. They will only use you. This started as a battle for freedom—to liberate ourselves and our people from Gousht chains. You have every right to be afraid. We have lost so many who began this journey with us."

Acta's eyes peered through the pile of bloody Gousht corpses, and I blinked the image away.

"They died fighting for a cause bigger than all of us. That doesn't make the pain less. I loved them all. I grieve them all." I turned back to Hylĩane. "But I won't let you tarnish their memory by making us beholden to the cowards who hid behind their little forest. So we went out and continued the fight."

"Where's Acta?!" The cry sang over the commotion in a piercing tone.

Kristee moved through the crowd, turning shoulders and studying faces, then stopped and turned her glaring eyes at me.

Hylĩane looked me over as I stood staring back at Kristee. "She asked a quession, young man. Where's her cousin?"

She didn't smile or anything so obvious, but her tone was gloating as if

Acta's death served as her vindication. I had never hated her—truly hated
her—until that moment.

"He was a good warrior, and he believed in what we are doing," I said
in my gentlest voice to Kristee.

Her wail as she fell to her knees broke my anger.

Acta had been her last living kin. He had carried her through the turns
they spent in the mines. Plenty of us would mourn him, but she would
never be whole again.

A couple of people close by tried to comfort her as she wept.

Yelan stepped up to Hylïane's side. "We should discuss this somewhere
quieter. The boy is right about that much." She turned to me, face
impassive as always. "Get these people settled. The council will gather at
first light."

"Thank you," I said.

"Don't thank me, boy. You may have killed the rebellion you were
trying to save," she said before ushering Hylïane away.

———————

The hours passed as we set to work making what shelter we could for
the new residents of our camp. In four days, our numbers had doubled.
We ran our food stores down to the barest necessities in a single evening.
However, there would be more hands to share the labor as we rebuilt
our stocks.

None of the Uprising appeared to resent the metal workers and their
families. Too many of them had been through similar journeys to get
here. Unfortunately, their grace did not extend so far as to include me.

Whatever they felt about me, we needed more wood cut down to
size to keep the additional fires going. The fact that the wood waiting to
be cut had been tucked away at the far edge of the encampment made it
an easy escape.

As I set to the task, sweat streamed down my back like a water
dancer's most unimpressive trick. Stray glances angled toward me as

people passed by.

The people who had demanded my leadership had come to resent my decisions. And their ire didn't wander. Nine of us had left, eight of us returned, and their judgement fell solely upon me.

It was almost funny. After turns of worrying that I would be shunned for being a spirit thief, my ostracization had nothing to do with The Thief or any stories.

The axe's heft felt good. I set a new piece of ironoak on the tree stump and hacked away. The blade cracked the wood. Each blow vibrated through the axe's handle into my bones, a subtle pain that grounded me.

No matter how much I tried to focus on everyone's newfound contempt for me, I couldn't make myself care—not in this moment.

Acta had insisted on leaving before the people could vote. He had helped hatch the plan to escape the encampment. He had even insisted on being one of the first into the fray.

Hadn't he?

The crack in the ironoak log finally snapped open, and two pieces of wood jumped apart with the force of the blow. I collected one and began cutting it down.

Acta had survived the God Caves for five turns. It was almost impossible to picture him at twelve, covered in soot and debris from the mines.

I hacked into the new piece of wood.

The Gousht had stolen The River from him. It was easy to forget Acta had been a dancer. I had never seen him dance, but we had spoken about it. It always sounded like he was talking about a place he used to love to visit—some place too far away now.

Even in The Mist, he will be missing a piece of himself.

A sharp pain cut through my palms as I brought the axe down again. I was gripping the handle too tightly, but I welcomed the pain. Blisters could be tended to.

Acta had been a good warrior, even if he hadn't had a choice in the matter. He couldn't have gone home after Oakheart. The Gousht had burned his village to the ground.

Where could he have gone? He had to take care of Kristee.

I gripped the axe handle until the pain screamed and blood trickled down my wrist from a broken blister.

Here I was recounting the handful of facts I knew about my fallen friend, and I couldn't remember the name of the song he liked to sing. The few notes I could remember bounced around in my skull, repeating again and again.

How much did I know him? I thought. I knew the things that happened to him, but those traumas weren't him.

"Ahhh!" I yelled as I brought the axe down on a piece of wood already smaller than a firepit's need. The pieces jumped apart, tumbling in different directions.

"Kaylo?" Liara said from over my shoulder. I hadn't even heard her echo approach.

"Not now, Liara," I said, letting my anger elongate her name into its distinct syllables.

"Yes, now," she said, matching my energy.

I turned around and glared at her, but she didn't react. She stood there as if waiting for me to acquiesce. Even as so many people despised me for exercising my command, I had no power in this moment.

Liara turned and began walking away, presuming I would follow like some trained pet. The arrogance—if The Song still sang to me, it would have been bellowing through the ground. As it was, I stormed after her in silence.

All the people who had envisioned me as a leader had an unending list of opinions about how I was supposed to lead. None of them actually wanted to step up and take on the responsibility, the guilt, and the blame that came with leadership. No, they wanted a say without the weight of obligation.

She led us away from the encampment. When she finally stopped and turned to face me, I had to hold all the unsavory words I had ready in the back of my throat.

"Are you okay?" she asked, pouting her lips and arching her brow like I was some broken thing to pity.

Three old ironoak trees surrounded us like a barrier to block out the rest of the world, but the barrier was only an illusion. The world and its problems wouldn't respect it.

"What is it, Liara?" I asked. "We have forty-two new people to shelter. We don't have time for a heart-to-heart."

"I'm sorry about Acta."

"Don't do this, Liara. It wasn't my fault. One. We lost one and freed forty-two people. I won't apologize for that." Grief mixed with the anger in my voice, but I fought it back down. "Acta charged into battle knowing the danger. He died a warrior's death."

"You cannot control who passes into The Mist. You can't carry each death like you wielded the blade."

"Stop it. Please, stop it."

"I'm just telling you a truth you already know. You cannot keep everyone from dying. You can't protect Wal, or me, or even yourself from the end. When we find the point of the blade, there is nothing you will be able to do." She stepped closer to me. "And that's okay."

"I don't need this from you." I stepped away and found my back pressing against bark.

"It's going to have to come from someone. You tortured a man. He might have been a Gousht commander, but he was a person."

"You've killed plenty of couta yourself."

"We are fighting a war. Violence is a tool, but we can never become it. We would only turn into another version of the Gousht."

I clenched my jaw so I wouldn't curse her for comparing me to the green bastards.

"Grief doesn't have to be anger," she said. "Acta wasn't just a warrior. He was your friend."

The strain and stretch I felt in my muscles vanished as if my body would drop if not for the tree propping me up.

Tomorrow's Promise, I thought. That was the name of the song he liked to sing.

I should have sung it beside his grave. The words I had said had been far too generic. He deserved better than platitudes.

"This can't be about revenge," Liara said. "That's just giving the power back to the Gousht—reacting and fighting on their terms."

There was her pity again. Right there in her green eyes and downturned mouth.

I wasn't the helpless orphan I had been. I hadn't been that boy in a long time.

"What then? Blood owes blood. The saying exists for a reason. It is part of us. If not vengeance, what would you have? Mercy?"

Her brow folded in at the word as if it made her ill. "No, they don't deserve mercy. They haven't earned it. But they also haven't earned the right to dictate our actions. We should be fighting for freedom. The Gousht are an obstacle, not the aim."

"Blessed fucking Mother! What do you want from me?!" My voice grew with each syllable. "I didn't choose this, Liara. You and everyone else told me I needed to lead. Now, everyone has an opinion about how."

"You used to care about my opinions." She did not match my volume. Instead, her words wore an injury as they left her lips.

How many times am I going to hurt her? I thought. A part of me wanted to pull her close, soothe the pain. Beneath that part, a bitter voice refused. She had started this. She should have known better.

"I can't deal with this right now," I said. "There's a council meeting in the morning. I have to get some sleep before Hylïane berates me."

Without an apology or a word of care, I slipped from the ironoaks surrounding us and left. The phantom hum of Acta singing *Tomorrow's Promise* followed me the rest of the night.

Chapter Twenty-Two
Kaylo's Story

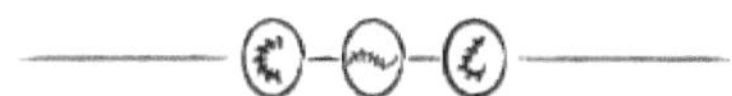

I HADN'T FINISHED HALF my report before Hylíane demanded answers to her questions—though calling them questions was generous. She spat accusations that rose in pitch at the end.

On top of Acta's death, she lay the doomed fate of the Uprising at my feet as if she hadn't been trying to kill it since before it began. But I didn't interrupt her ranting. Any attempt to defend myself would only further prove my guilt.

She knew her word games well, and I had no desire to play them.

In the past, Annit or Yelan would have put a stop to her tirade, but neither of them seemed bothered by her words. Annit barely looked in my direction, and Yelan wore her forever impassive expression as if this were no different than any other meeting.

Their betrayal hurt far worse than anything Hylíane could say. How many times had we sat around a fire to discuss our path forward? The Uprising had been born out of a need to fight. And to fight, we needed more warriors. We couldn't hand our freedom over to the Lost Nation for a false promise of safety. If they couldn't see that, I had no use for them either.

"If tose warriors out tere are so expendable tat cha can weigh tere deaths against tose cha freed, cha will end this wit too much blocd on cha hands. Tose scales will neva balance," Hylïane said.

In a way, I agreed. Acta couldn't be replaced. Even if we managed to drive the Gousht from our shores by some miracle of The Mother, how many Enneans would survive? Every life—every breath—had to mean something.

What she didn't understand was we didn't have to fight to die out.

Every turn under occupation weathered away more of our culture. They enforced their ideals, taught their history, and reworked our cities into facsimiles of their own. They didn't even have to be subtle, just consistent for long enough. In a few generations, my people would forget their heritage. They would become more Gousht than Ennean.

Warriors like Acta knew who we were. Which meant we hadn't only lost him; we lost another anchor line to our past.

"And cha left tha boy behind in ta soil," Hylïane said, coming to the end of yet another rant.

Talise gave me a familiar glare. Even though she had liberated the forge with us, apparently every dead friend would only remind her of how I had failed Sionia.

The entire clan wanted me to make decisions they didn't have the stomach for, then condemn me when life didn't turn out perfectly.

"You would have us serve the Lost Nation instead?" I'd had enough of her patronizing lectures. "More than two turns have come and gone since Oakheart, and you have done nothing but complain about the paths we have taken. The only solution you have is to let the nation who let Ennea fall—who manipulated people through the Missing—order us about. For what? Some false protection?"

"Ta Lost Nation has an army. We don't need ta send folks who don't know anyting about warfare ta die. Let tem fight. Help in what ways cha can. We can survive tis, all of us," Hylïane said.

The Lost Nation had promised they would never be far away. It may have been the only thing they hadn't lied about. We caught glimpses of scouts in purple robes. Messengers continued to visit despite our refusals.

And, in the end, they had swayed a champion to their cause.

Hylïane had done their work for them. She wanted safety so badly she ignored the snare set around their promises.

"We talked about this," Yelan said. "Freedom is unpredictable and dangerous, but at least we have a say. You want to give that up?"

"Tey offerin protection. Tis boy is offerin a romantic death." Hylïane focused her attention on Yelan and Annit as if they were the closest to falling for her false hope. "At least some of us would survive wit tem."

"Coward." As usual, when Talise opened her mouth in a council meeting, she never held back. Hylïane looked aghast, but it didn't deter Talise. "Every time we risk our lives, we have to justify ourselves to you. Why? Because it's so scary this far from the fighting?"

"How dare cha?" Hylïane looked to Annit and Yelan like they might speak up for her. "Jus because I don want ta charge inta war, doesn't mean I don want ta liberate our people. Cha risk us all."

"I get why you're upset," Yelan said. "These fools ran off and broke every tradition we abided by. But the Lost Nation? You think they would care what our people said? You think you could call a vote and listen to debate?"

We had all pushed back against Hylïane before. Talise had called her horrible names and told her to keep her cowardice to herself, but no one ever held her to account like this—forced her to defend her words with more than fears. And she looked crestfallen for it.

She had been fighting from the high ground a moment ago. She hadn't even been able to mask her glee. Then she mentioned the Lost Nation and found the battle turn against her.

"Tas not fair, Yelan. Tis isn't about ta Lost Nation. Tis is about how these children keep puttin our lives in danger. Tey can't run off and do what tey like regardless of what ta rest of us want. We ave to be more strategic ta keep our warriors and ta Uprisin safe."

"Do you want to see our people free?" I asked.

"Of course, I do," she spat back.

"Oh, you do? So much that you would sell us out to the Lost Nation? What did they promise you? Are they going to give you a nice, safe homestead on the other side of the Lost Forest while the rest of us do their spying?"

"Kaylo, don't do this," Annit said with exhaustion in his voice. "We need to calm down."

"Forty-two people are free today because of what we did—what Acta sacrificed. Do you want to go out there and tell them it wasn't worth it? That you would rather sell them to the Lost Nation than be scared another day?" The volume of my voice crept up as I leaned into the conversation. "You don't get to shout, 'I told you so,' and claim credit for the free people out there."

"Kaylo, that's enough." Annit's voice took on more weight.

"You are weak, Hylïane. I don't know how you survived all those turns under Oakheart Mountain. Maybe this isn't the first time you tried to sell your people out. Did you make friends with the couta for a few extra rations along the way?"

"Enough!" Annit bellowed.

Hylïane couldn't meet my eye, but I continued to stare at her. Her posture curled into itself like a turtle retreating into its shell. Her cowardice paraded itself around like injury.

How many spiteful words had she tossed in my direction? She could handle a few of mine.

"We are supposed to be leading this community." Yelan stood, looking between Talise, Hylïane, and me. "Lost Nation or not, you two ran off like you don't have to answer to the people. You can't berate them like their lives aren't at risk too."

Yelan rolled her eyes and sighed before finding her neutral expression. "I think we are done for now," she said, offering Hylïane a hand up from the swept dirt floor.

The old northwoman had never seemed as old or frail. She took Yelan's arm and struggled to balance herself.

"Annit, you need to have a conversation with your boy here." Yelan gestured towards me and walked out with her arm around Hylīane.

"Give us some space if you would," Annit said to Talise.

Talise met my eyes as she rose. "Hylīane's wrong, but that doesn't make you right, Kaylo."

"What does that mean?"

She walked after Hylīane and Yelan without answering.

"Talise, I can't bring her back," I shouted as she pushed her way through the fur-covered threshold.

"Kaylo, leave it be." Annit sat beside me. Without his usual smile, the burn on his face became more pronounced. His echo receded into the softest flicker in the night as if even the spirit stepped away to leave us to our words.

"That woman hasn't had a kind thing to say to me in two turns. Why do I have to keep my tongue? She's lived long enough to learn manners."

"A leader has to wade through the waters of everyone's criticism. You can't unload it on an old woman who's scared about people dying."

"A leader should do this. A leader should do that. Would you have gone to the forge in my place?" I asked. "You always have so much to say about leading. You do it. Everyone knows it should be you."

"I'm not having this conversation again," he said, his voice reaching deep into his lower register like a warning.

"What conversation?!" If The Seed were still with me, The Song would be shaking the leaves of the forest to the Sanine River and back. 'You say 'no' or 'I've had my time,' but you never say why. Tell me. Why are you putting this weight on someone half your turns?"

He looked into the firepit, and his echo returned. It ranged like a fire trying to catch and spread through the forest. "You don't want to know. I shouldn't be anyone's leader."

"Not good enough. Not when you are constantly telling me about what kind of leader I should be."

"I have too much blood on my hands!" His head whipped back to me as he yelled, The Flame a drum thundering through the air. "You don't think I've led people before? I've done what you did. Only when I did it, more people died."

Annit stood and walked over to the firepit, his anger and guilt stalking beside him in The Song. The fire sputtered and flared as he tossed another log on the flames.

"It wasn't long after they found those cursed fucking rocks under Oakheart," he said. "I led my warriors through the streets of Protisi. We were going to reclaim it—liberate our people. By that time, the warriors I fought beside were the only family I had left.

"Someone had tipped off the Gousht, and they surrounded the city with a much larger force. The fighting carried us through the streets. Bodies of warriors and innocent Enneans littered the ground. My family whittled to smaller and smaller numbers.

"Soldiers backed us into a dead-end alley. Screams overtook the air. I had failed. Another sister fell with an arrow in her chest, then I let The Flame loose. I fell into The Song until I didn't know where I was or who I was."

The browns of his eyes hardened to a hollow hue as he fell into his story. His fists flexed at his sides as he continued to speak louder than I had ever heard him speak.

"Everything was burning when I pulled myself from The Song. Flames crawled up my robes and scorched my flesh before I could put them out."

He stared into me like a challenge. "That's right. These burns weren't the Gousht. I did it to myself.

"The fire turned the night to day. Homes collapsed. Pain enwrapped me so entirely that it took me far too long to look for the people I called family. There was nothing the flames hadn't touched—the soldiers, my warriors, the people who had barricaded themselves in their homes to survive the fighting."

He paused, and in the silence, firelight washed over the burns on his face. "Not many of us escaped that night, but I did. It didn't matter much. A group of soldiers found me several days later, barely surviving my burns, too ashamed to return to the Ennean Resistance Army."

The tension in his stance released, and his arms hung at his sides.

"I'm sorry, Annit."

"I didn't tell you that story for your pity. I told you that story because I know the path you are heading down. You have choices to make. Your people don't need you to hack off limbs for your personal vendetta."

"Who told you?"

"It doesn't matter," he said. "Save the family you have left, Kaylo."

"What if I'm not strong enough?"

"You could be if you chose to be." He turned to the fire and stared into the heart of it.

"You shouldn't let that story define you. It happened a long time ago."

"You don't see the irony in that, do you?" A bitter laugh escaped his lips in a heavy puff of air. "The memory of that night, the lessons of that night, the consequences of that night define me. We can't separate ourselves from our mistakes, my young friend. That would only dishonor those we've hurt along the way. Don't deny it, but don't wallow in it either. I am the person who killed those people just as I am the person who is trying to be better than my anger and self-pity."

This broken man had been there all along, beneath his smile and good nature. This was the man I had seen the night the mines fell, raging against his enslavers. We had been in several battles since, but he had never let this version of himself join the battles.

The fire cracked. Wind brushed the tent. Birds sang in the forest. We sat with the slight noises and our tragedies between us.

If Annit wasn't qualified to lead our warriors because of his past, neither was I. I needed to stop this another way. The dead were piling up on my spirit.

Without another word, I rushed from the gathering tent. The sunlight stung my eyes as I pushed through the furs. A few people were milling about the grounds, and I couldn't bear meeting their eyes. It was all too much.

No one would be in the supplies tent this early, and no one would question me sneaking off to check on our inventory.

It was a small canopy to keep the weather from our supplies, but large enough for my purposes. I moved a crate of root vegetables to one side and laid out a spare fur. This would be best lying down.

She had to do something. She was the only one who could.

The tendrils of darkness reached out, as if to claim whatever light remained in my spirit as I charged into her realm. "Spirit!" I shouted. "Spirit!"

My words vanished into the void, and the noise died almost as soon as it left my lungs. Though, they weren't my lungs. They weren't my lips. It wasn't even sound. All of those concepts had no meaning here, except for the projections of ideas I cast into the expanse.

I need you, I thought, hoping she might bother with an unspoken plea. *I am you and you are me, and I need you.*

No reply came. I stood in the midst of nothingness, waiting for a spirit who I knew more by her curses than her true name. She had never made me wait so long without an answer. Maybe she hid within the shadows, indulging on my need—my failed attempt to hate her.

"Please. The seventh—the Balance—the misunderstood daughter of Ennea, I need you."

If I continued down this path, I would only continue to lose more people I loved. Liara would die, and I would be left behind to think of all the ways it was my fault. I wasn't suited to lead a rebellion. I couldn't protect any of them.

"I know I told you to mind your place, little thief." Her words emanated from the thick coats of blackened fog all around me. "But this is unfortunate. I didn't think you would break so easily."

The only thing separating her shadow cloak from its surroundings was the way it maintained its form. Eventually, its static nature formed an outline creeping closer towards me.

"I'm too tired to spar with you. It doesn't matter anymore. Maybe it never did. I'm done." My voice whined through my words, and I didn't care. "Help me. Help me end this. With a snap of your fingers, every crystal prison would shatter—every stolen spirit would return to their dancer. We would have a chance to win.

"It has been thirteen turns since the Gousht started killing us. Hasn't it been long enough? Hasn't enough blood been spilt?"

"Oh, Kaylo," she said, her voice turning sweet. She peeled back her shadow cloak hood, revealing her two-toned face. "No."

"What? What do you mean, 'no'?"

"The Gousht have done horrible things to the people you claim. Has killing soldiers stopped your people's suffering? If you knew your people would never be free of the Gousht, would you stop fighting—stop the bloodshed?" Her question rang with an earnestness that felt out of place for her. "Enneans have oppressed mine for longer than the Gousht have known this land. They may never stop regardless of what I do. And if that's the case, they deserve what they get."

"You're not making any sense. Your people are dying too," I said.

"My people have always been dying!" The shout broke through her sweet facade. "Even as the Gousht burned their homes, they found time to cast my descendants away."

Wrinkles gave her black and white visage shape, as her fury settled in her brow.

"I was with them. Every time. People who claimed to love my children became monsters. I felt their confusion as those who they loved, and I loved by extension, killed me. They became every foul word you have for the Gousht," she said, her voice pulling back into a quieter anger. "The kind ones exiled us. The honest ones didn't bother."

No heart for a thief. No safe haven, I thought somberly of the old saying.

"Only a grave will do," she said, finishing my thought for me.

"If you allow the Gousht to continue, the only pieces of your spirit in The Waking will be trapped in stone beside your siblings."

"At least that will be my choice," she said with a reformed calm.

Part of me understood the defiance, even if it lacked all sense.

"Do you think your descendants would want this? Have you asked them?"

The shadows around her shuddered, then her face settled into an unmoving mask of black and white. She didn't have an answer, which was an answer of sorts.

Nothing I could say would make her see what she must do. If she felt my love for Liara and wouldn't do anything to save her, The Thief couldn't understand love.

"You've become worse than any of the stories."

I turned my back on her and left The Mist.

When I came back to The Waking, the herbs in the medical supply tent were there to greet me. Their silence still unnerved me when I noticed it. The moonlight hazel needed trimming.

"You're back." Liara sat on a stool near the tent's threshold.

"I...Liara...I had to speak with her."

"Did you convince her this time? From the look on your face, I'm guessing you fought with her again." She lowered her gaze to the dirt. "I will never understand why you tempt the spirits like that."

"Why are you here?" I arranged myself to sit in front of her.

"Avoiding the topic. Okay. Tomi said she heard Annit yelling in the gathering tent before you stormed off. I figured I should find you before you made another bad decision. Too late, I guess."

Her voice sounded thin. The day hadn't taken her spirit from her. I had. By continuously failing to meet her basic expectations. She should have left me alone.

"I'm sorry," I said.

"For what?" She met my gaze and held it like a challenge.

"For everything in general and a few things in particular," I said. "I don't know how to let go of this anger. There are moments when I think I have it under control, then it's loose. I can't keep losing people, Liara."

"You're going to. This is a war even if we aren't an army. People are going to die."

"What am I supposed to do?"

The River sang an elongated melody of unending depth, as if we were a moment surrounded by countless others until it all became one singular thing. The expanse of it was oddly calming.

"None of us have the answers, Kaylo. Not on our own anyway. We have to be a part of this together," she said. "So the first thing you can do is stop pushing everyone away."

"We had to go to the forge. You were as much a part of that decision as I was."

"Exactly. But you still act like you were the one that ran Acta through. Every one of us made a decision to be there." She shook her head as if she were explaining the sky to a fish. "Right or not, our decision hurt people. We all have to bear that and help this community heal."

"What do we do?" I said, attempting to smile.

She chuckled. "If you can stop seeing leadership like we expect you to be the tip of the spear rather than part of its grip, that would help."

"I'm sorry. I'm sorry about Acta, about last night, about so many things. You were right. I'm becoming the violence, but I don't want to be."

Her locs hung down below her earlobe. It would take turns to grow them back to what they had been. Still, she would always be the flowing fighter I had found in the forest with her red hair chasing her like a storm.

Any touch of playfulness dropped from her expression. "Then do something about it. You are the only one who can."

"So an apology isn't going to be enough." I smiled at my own attempt to lighten her spirit. She didn't.

"It never is." She stood up. "I love you, Kaylo. But I can't love what you're becoming. Make a change."

Before I could respond, she walked through the furs, her echo lingering like her scent.

I unsheathed my father's knife. I was far more like my mother. He had been stoic even as the soldiers beat down their door. How had he contained that rage? The Gousht made him forge their weapons, cast their symbols, take his talents and trade them for some figment of safety.

My mother had been ready to let Nomar burn to the ground to save me. That I understood.

CHAPTER TWENTY-THREE

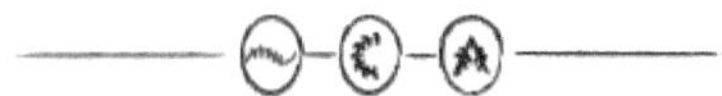

THE DAY HAD JUST broken through the darkness. Several people milled about. A slight wind moved through the encampment carrying the first signs of a coming winter. This wasn't something I wanted to do, but it was necessary if the Uprising had any chance of remaining intact.

If I waited any longer, more people would break their fast, see me standing outside of Hylíane's tent, and the rumors would begin to flurry.

"Hylíane," I called through the furs covering her tent's entrance. It felt odd speaking her name without adding a taste of bitterness to it. "Hylíane, we need to speak."

The furs hastily parted, and the northwoman stood there with a scowl. The past two turns had taken a toll on all of us, but Hylíane even more so. Her age settled deeper into her wrinkles, and she leaned more heavily on her walking stick than she once had.

"Whatis it cha want, boy?"

"To apologize and have a word," I said. "Would you give me a moment?"

She didn't react immediately. Her scowl continued on as if I hadn't spoken—probably reliving the last words I had said to her the night before. I had gone too far. There were many justifications for what I had said, but justifications couldn't make a thing right.

Eventually, Hylíane stepped aside silently.

Her tent was meager, as were most of our tents. However, she hadn't left a single possession on display. A pot of water sat on a stone-lined firepit in the middle of the small space. Her bedroll leaned against the leathers of the tent wall next to her pack.

There were no immediate plans to relocate the encampment, though we would have to soon.

"They will neva catch me again," she said, her eyes landing on the bedroll along with mine. Her words had been quiet, but a fierceness underscored them. It had been the most genuine thing I ever heard her say.

I had seen my share of horrors. The Gousht resided in every nightmare. But my story had never gone past the lip of the mines. Those who had survived Oakheart had experienced this occupation in a different way than the rest of us. If I had to wake up every morning only to dig the earth out from the core of a mountain, knowing that my life could be snuffed out as easily as a candle's flame, it would have changed me down to the spirit.

Yesterday, I had accused her of collaborating with the Gousht.

"I'm sorry," I said in all sincerity. "What I said was unforgiveable. No matter how much we disagree, I know you love our people."

Again, she didn't move or show any sign she had heard me. She simply stared at me, her mouth a straight line and her eyes void of emotion.

"May I sit?" I asked.

Finally, she nodded.

"I guess I should offer cha tea." She walked over to her simple display of belongings and pulled a pouch from her travel sack.

We did not speak as she busied herself over the kettle with two clay cups. The small bundle of leaves she added to each cup smelled of cinnamon and something slightly bitter I couldn't put my finger on. She placed a steaming cup in front of me.

In two turns, we hadn't had a private conversation. What I knew of this woman could be summed up in a few sentences far more bitter than the smell from the tea.

The tea tasted earthy with the subtle line of cinnamon running through it. On a chilled morning like this, it warmed my chest and helped me forget my nerves for a moment.

"Thank you, Auntie." I had never used the honorific with Hylïane before. She had always been more of an adversary than an elder, but things had to change.

"Enough." She sipped at her drink. "I'm not in ta mood fa games. And I'm no auntie ta cha."

There was the warrior I knew, relentless and cutting with her words.

"No games. I made a mistake. Several, actually, and I am here to find a way to move forward. You and I have created a rift within the Uprising. We are supposed to be leading these people, but we have only set them at odds."

"I ave done no such ting."

"Hylïane, you've berated every plan I brought before the council. You've used the names of dead warriors to prove points. You even organized a vote to hand us over to the Lost Nation."

"Child, cha ave no sense of ta evils ta Gousht can unleash. Whatever heartaches cha think cha know are nothin of their malice. Still, cha insist on tempting tem ta do worse."

I squeezed the cup in my hand, the warmth spreading from the clay into my palm. The way she so easily dismissed those I had lost—like I were a child crying over a missing doll.

"I have no right dismissing your pain, and you have no right dismissing mine." It was a struggle not to say more on the matter, but this couldn't turn into another fight. By the end of the span, the Uprising would split in two if we didn't come to terms.

"My mother studied history. Before she and my father were murdered, she was collecting stories she believed needed to survive. Those pages are gone now, but I learned from them. No story is so clear it can't change with another telling."

"Cha always use so many words ta say so little. Wha do cha want ta say?"

"You and I have been telling ourselves stories about what each of us wants. Every time you avoid fighting, I assume you are too scared to fight. But that's not it, is it?" I asked. "You are worried we are going to bring the Empire's wrath. You don't want it to get worse for people—not just us, but the people under their watch."

Hylīane sipped her tea with both hands on her cup, looking at me over the brim.

"Barberry, right?" I asked, finally putting a name to the bitter scent in the tea.

"Helps ta ache in my joints."

"Even if they aren't killing occupied Enneans, they are killing off everything that makes us who we are. If things continue as they are, our language will die off in two generations. In three, we will be more Gousht than Ennean."

"Cha know ta Gousht started driving people east? Killed ta ones tha couldn't walk and marched ta rest ta work camps where ta Gousht position is more secure," she said. "I know we can't outlast tem. We need ta fight. But cha rush ta battle like cha can save ta world with a sword. Cha can't."

"I don't have all the answers."

"Oh, cha don't? Tha's ta first I've heard cha admit it."

"And the Lost Nation does?"

"More tan a pup like cha?"

If it wouldn't have killed her, I might have thrown the cup directly at her head. For as much as she avoided battle, she instigated a fight every time she opened her mouth.

"Can we stop it? Can you stop acting like I am your enemy?"

"Cha are. Cha ave proven how dangerous cha can be."

"What is your great plan then? Please tell me, if I'm doing such a horrible job leading our warriors. Hand our people over to the Lost Nation? You don't think I know what the Gousht are capable of. I can promise you, you don't know anything about how dangerous the Lost Nation is."

No matter how many times we sparred over plans, we returned to the same refrain.

"We retreat ta one of ta cities ta Gousht left behin in ta west. Patch our wounds and figure out where ta go from tere. Ta Lost Nation might not be such a bad option."

"Even if the Lost Nation doesn't use our people like puppets, agreeing to work with them will break us. Those of us who served 'the Missing' will leave. So will the people who refuse to be subservient to some king they've never met," I said. "Too many of us know what it's like to have our freedom taken from us. The Uprising will die under the Lost Nation. If you want that, push for the vote. There is no telling how many groups will splinter off into their own directions."

Hylīane stared at me with her dark brown eyes. I had seen what she looked like when she wanted to wring my throat. This wasn't it. She was listening.

"I'm not going to convince you of anything here and now," I said. "You'll have to decide if you object to the war we are waging enough to destroy this community."

"Cha did tha when cha ran off in ta middle of ta night."

With one final sip, I sat the tea down and rose from the ground. "I deepened the cracks. You're right about that. But the Uprising can still be saved, and you're the only one who can do it," I said. "Thank you for the tea."

The stakes of her decision were too great to enjoy the quizzical expression on her face—one brow lifted higher than the other, pursed lips, flared nostrils.

Everything I had said was true, and she knew it. I had pointed out the power that lay at her feet and the consequences of using it. Now, the fate of this tiny rebellion fell on her next choice.

Before she could say something and drag me back into another war of words, I left. I had said all I could. She knew all the points I had regurgitated a hundred times over to try to convince her we had to fight. Saying them again wouldn't help.

The sound of waves crashing against stone—harsh and rhythmic as if each crash promised another—carried me to Liara's tent. Sokan hadn't fully broken over the horizon. Something unpleasant was haunting Liara's dreams.

I couldn't control what would happen with the Uprising, but I could help Liara. That would have to be enough for now.

Without announcing myself, I slipped into her tent. Tomi was snoring, lying at an odd angle on her bedroll, but Liara slept silently. If not for her echo, I would have confused it for a peaceful rest. Nothing apart from the slight tightness in her cheek proved otherwise.

She often had nightmares.

The sisters had a few odds and ends scattered over the dirt floor. Most would have assumed the mess belonged to Tomi, but Liara had never been one for keeping her space tidy.

I liked that I knew something about her that most people would never guess.

Kneeling beside her bedroll, I took a moment. She had tied her locs up with a bit of azure fabric. The tiny stream of light sneaking through the furs landed across her neck, setting her skin aglow.

Her echo crashed louder than before.

When the first shake didn't wake her, I tried again more forcefully. Her eyes sprang open, and she jerked away from me. The fear and her movement—Shay recoiling from me with her dying breaths flashed in front of my eyes. I fell back on my ass.

Shay and Liara were nothing alike. The way Liara responded to being woken up hadn't been disgust, but it startled me all the same.

"What are you doing?" Liara whispered at me with as much force as she could muster.

"Sorry. You were having a nightmare, and I...sorry."

Too many emotions wrestled for the moment. The way Liara had been so beautiful. The fear that took her when I woke her. Shay's bloody and ashen face. Liara's anger filtering into her tone. I couldn't respond to it all at once.

"I have nightmares. You know that. What are you doing here?"

"I heard your echo. It sounded like it does when you're in danger. I wanted to make sure you were okay. Are you?"

The roundness of her cheeks returned, and her shoulders dropped as she took a deep breath. "I'm fine. It wasn't anything."

"If you want to talk about—"

"I don't," she said with finality. "Is there something else you need?"

"I spoke with Hylíane."

The challenge in her expression broke. "You what? What did you say? What did you do?"

This short morning had already carried too much weight that the tone of accusation in her questions made me laugh.

"Can you both shut it?! I'm trying to sleep." Tomi threw an empty water skin in our general direction, but missed by a great deal.

"Don't assume the worst. I apologized."

"You what?" Liara asked.

"Seriously!" This time an empty scabbard flew into my shoulder. "The next one will be sharper."

"I have to get ready for the clan gathering," I said, keeping an eye out for a dagger. "We'll talk later."

Looking at Tomi covering her head with her blanket, I couldn't help myself. I called out my goodbyes far louder than necessary before scurrying out of the tent.

Something hit the furs after they settled back into place. I could only hope it wasn't a blade.

While I sat waiting for the gathering to begin, my thoughts lingered on Acta. As the swelling crowd stared in my direction, some hiding it better than others, I imagined him watching from The Mist. He had died to continue this fight. With a singular vote, it might end.

No one remembered the fallen of a failed movement.

The whole of the clan, including the newly welcomed metal workers and their families, settled in under the large leather canopy. And still, Hylïane hadn't arrived. It wasn't like her.

"What will we do if they vote to give up on the war, or worse, join the Lost Nation?" Wal asked, far too close to my ear.

"I don't know."

"Blood is owed, Kaylo. We cannot sit by as these cowards abandon the dead."

"It might be better if you don't talk during the meeting," I said. Before he could retort, I continued. "Calling the people you need on your side 'cowards' doesn't go over well."

Wal sucked his teeth. "I'm much more diplomatic than that."

"Wal, I have seen you call a baby ugly in front of his mother. You used to get beaten on a regular basis by Ms. Hanack because you couldn't keep your wit to yourself."

The affect drained from his face, and Wal transformed into a different person. Any glint of a smile or fiery anger snuffed out, leaving a straight-lipped, committed expression. "When I have reason to, I know how to control myself. And I have blood to collect for Adēan."

Long stretches of time would pass in which Wal didn't mention Adēan by name. He went about his days as someone eerily similar to the boy he had been, maybe more diligent and focused in his goals, but still the Wal I had known.

In moments like this, the performance failed. He showed me how much Adēan's death had changed him.

"So, if it doesn't go our way, what are we going to do?" he asked.

"It will be a mess. It won't be just two factions. There will be those who want to fight, but can't leave behind their families or friends who can't join the battle. There will be those who don't trust me after what I did, even if they want to keep fighting. Unless Hylīane decides to choose to work with us, the Uprising will splinter into smaller and smaller pieces."

"Hylīane has never chosen a battle in her miserable lifetime. She'll run and hide under the Lost Nation. We might as well start planning what to call the next rebellion." Wal stared ahead into the crowd, wearing the same faraway look as he wore before charging into a skirmish.

"I think—no, maybe I hope—we were wrong about her. When I spoke with her earlier, I saw a bit of fight in her. She isn't a coward; she just believes differently than we do."

"Now's the time to find out, I guess." His gaze shifted with many others towards Hylīane as she walked into the tent.

The crowd made room for her and her walking stick. The tent was far too small to accommodate everyone in a large circle as the Jani had. Instead, we sat in concentric circles, with those on the small council sitting closer to the middle.

The scattered conversations converged into silence as Hylīane settled in next to Annit. Between the two of them, I would have to work my way to forgiveness. Hopefully, they would give me the opportunity.

Yelan stood, but most of the crowd's attention remained on Hylīane and me.

"To begin, I want to welcome our new brethren. Each and every one of us under this canopy have known Gousht cruelty. Our stories are as similar as they are unique, yet whatever the details, they brought us here. The Mother gave us each other. For that, I am thankful. Jolrin, if you would please."

The young Tomakan warrior rose, standing as a part of the third circle radiating from the center of the tent. Apart from Acta's cousin, Jolrin had been Acta's closest friend and confidant. Their eyes wore the signs of recent tears, and a fine layer of gray stubble had begun to grow from their usually clean-shaven scalp.

"To the first—The Shadow, our wisdom when the darkness seems..." Jolrin continued their prayer as I looked around the gathering tent.

Everyone had their particularities when it came to praying. Some looked up and watched sunlight fight through the leather canopy of the tent. Others murmured their own prayers in soft voices. Unlike the Gousht, we did not dictate the way a person had to engage with prayer. People closed their eyes or didn't. Some sat, others knelt, and the few at the outer edge of the tent stood.

Their relationships with The Mother and The Great Spirits were their own.

Eandrine, a metal worker past her middle turns, met my eyes. There was a question in the upturn of her brow.

Of course the newest members of our small community had felt the tension. They'd had to spend turns of their lives hyperaware of the emotions around them. A bad day for a guard could mean violence in any number of ways.

Freeing them from the forge had been the right thing to do. I had no doubts about that. However, they never should have been subjected to our infighting. It was a poor welcome.

"To the seventh—The Thief...I never know how to pray to you," Jolrin said, looking towards me. "Your descendant freed me. So many of us are here because of your gift. But your gift has taken far too much. Please choose our people over theirs.

"And The Blessed Mother..." They paused and brough a hand to their forehead. Their voice grew thick with grief. "Protect those spirits that we are not able to save. Hold them tight, and tell them of our love."

As Jolrin finished, Kristee sobbed. Her cries reinforced the quiet everyone else kept, as if the act of not speaking allowed her more space to grieve. She buried her face in her hands as she knelt, and those near her tried to comfort her with small touches.

I had lost people before—people who I had been closer to, loved even. With each one, I blamed myself. However, for some reason, Acta's death felt different.

Kristee continued to cry for him, though her sobs lessened.

I stood up, drawing the full attention of the gathered encampment. "Acta was my friend. I led him into battle at the forge, and he died."

Kristee stared daggers at me, a quiver shaking her lips. She had lost the last of her family. It was exactly what she had always feared. I had finally earned the ire in her stare.

I should have remained quiet and let others have their say first, but some words had to be said. Even if it meant people would never look to me as a leader again, I had to speak.

"I'm sorry. Not for what Acta, I, and many others around this tent did. There are forty-two Enneans sitting with us who hadn't been before, and I am not sorry for that," I said, nodding to Eandrine as I spoke.

"My father was a crafter, mostly wood, but he worked with metal when called to it. He liked to say that a piece wasn't finished until it fit. He could make wood into art, but it didn't matter how pretty it looked until it could serve its purpose.

"What we did—raiding the forge—was a good thing. How we did it, was not. It was a pretty piece of wood that didn't fit. I am sorry for doing what I did the wrong way," I said, turning to look to Hyliane.

"I have never known exactly how to refer to our mismatched group of survivors. Even as small as we are, it would be easier to call us an army—warriors fighting for a common cause. There would be less to lose. Warriors die in battle, and the army must move on. A clan carries the memory of the dead with them because those who died were more than their role. They were family. It's time to admit what we are. This clan is too important. We cannot break it. Let's make something that fits, for Acta and everyone we lost along the way."

It hadn't been what I intended to say. I had stayed awake most of the night trying to think of the right defense for our actions. All the justifications made sense when I practiced saying them aloud, but I couldn't bring myself to make any excuses.

I sat and the weight of the crowd's attention shifted towards Hylīane. Our disagreements had never been hidden. Even the newest members of our fragile clan seemed to know where to redirect their focus.

Her walking stick made a dull thud when she planted it into the dirt to heft herself off the ground. She scanned the gathered faces, pausing for a moment on mine before continuing. Whatever she decided to say, when she finished, we would either be a clan or a shattered rebellion.

"Before tese young people decided ta sneak off into ta night, I had arranged a vote on joinin ta Lost Nation. We had been fightin for two turns, and our numbers continued ta whittle down wit each encounter. Our people followed an angry child inta battle and died.

"Everyone around tat angry child seemed ta ignore reality. Our small band of raiders was an annoyance ta the empire. One tey would eventually kill off," she said, and paused as if looking for her words. Maybe she hadn't quite made up her mind. "When I questioned ta latest raid, people dismissed me as a coward. Tey insinuated tat I cared for my own safety more than ta good of our occupied brethren."

She turned to find me and leveled her piercing gaze at me. "I am no coward. It is not cowardice ta side against half-cocked plans tat get people killed. If cha want ta call this a clan, the legacy of tese past two turns is death."

Murmurs stirred in the crowd. I had to clench my jaw to keep myself from shouting at her. People had died, but people had also been saved. There were Enneans both under this tent and scattered across the countryside who no longer woke under the Gousht's brutality.

"Maybe tat is not fair. Maybe I ave focused too much on our losses because I ave become so used ta loss in my life," she said. "What Kaylo says is true. We are fragile. If I continue ta insist we choose safety over war, we won't last. However, if we continue ta choose war and count our dead, we will eke along in our grief.

"How do we become a clan and continue our uprisin? We can't, not like this. Kaylo and I are tearing this community inta factions," she said. "We formed a council ta lead our little group before we knew each other. Ta council is outta balance and headstrong. Our losses will continue on if we don't change who we follow."

I stared at the clever old northwoman. She was trying to cut me out. She meant to remake the clan one way or another.

"Remove Kaylo and me from the council," she said.

The murmurs buzzed through the crowd, but she hushed them with a wave of her arms.

"I will not dismiss what Kaylo has done for many under tis tent. Let him lead ta warriors inta battle, but he will have ta convince a council he doesn't sit on first."

The words of defiance that I had strung together in my head unraveled. I had been ready to fight Hylïane for my position. But why? I had never wanted the power I had been given. Yet, it felt as though something had been stolen from me.

Before I could say a word, I saw Liara sitting amongst the crowd. If I fought this, the Uprising would fall. Factions would split off in different directions. I had to keep us together.

In the midst of so many voices clashing, no one noticed me as I rose to my feet again, save Hylïane. The look she gave me was somewhere between a challenge and an offering. Her suggestion hadn't been an attack necessarily. It was something more akin to a test. Could I put the clan ahead of my personal needs?

Conversation dimmed as people began to realize I had stood. I rose my hand to calm the debates. "The direction of our clan moving forward isn't up to Hylïane or myself. We have always raised decisions this large to a vote. I will abide by your decision."

The meeting under the gathering tent continued for hours. People debated the merits of appointing a new council. Leaders were nominated. Votes were cast.

It had not been what I expected, what I feared, nor what I hoped. But we left the gathering tent as a clan.

CHAPTER TWENTY-FOUR

Sleep eluded Kaylo. For thirteen turns, he had thought about returning to the Uprising. Even in his dreams, it never went well. He had abandoned them—left them to fight a war he had started.

It had come so easy, calling a bunch of misfit spirits a rebellion. He hadn't even considered the words before he said them. Everything after had been far more difficult.

As much as the Uprising had changed and grown, that part had probably stayed the same. The doing always cost more. And what had they accomplished? The Empire still had free reign over the countryside. As much as the Uprising pestered the Lost Nation and Gousht armies, they hadn't been able to build enough of a force to challenge either.

It was folly. He was rejoining the losing side of a war.

The campfire wavered beside Tayen as she slept. During the daylight, it was difficult to remember how young she was, what with all her talking. But as she lay asleep, her features settled into a child's.

If she died because of this foolishness—when he could have driven her away instead of towards the madness—he would never forgive himself.

So why was he still going through with it? Because of a promise?

He grabbed a stick and tossed it into the fire. The wood shifted slightly and sparks jumped into the air.

"Do you need me to take watch?" Nomi asked from her bedroll.

"No. I won't be sleeping anyway."

Nomi untangled herself from her blanket and scooted over to him. "Good. I have something I wanted to talk to you about."

"It really wasn't an invitation—"

"Your story—it wasn't bullshit, was it? You've really spoken with The Balance?" she asked while staring at him with an intensity that unnerved him. She blinked, but the rest of her remained as still as if time had stopped flowing.

"Yes, I have."

"Is it true about her and the God Caves? There are so many stories about the evil Thief. It gets hard to piece together who she actually is."

Kaylo sighed. It wasn't as if her questions weren't fair or she didn't deserve the answers. A fragment of The Balance lived within her the same as within him. But he had given too much of his life up thinking about—agonizing over—The Balance. She wasn't worth the energy.

Still, Nomi was Torrel's daughter, and if Kaylo'd had the opportunity to ask his questions to another spirit dancer at her age, it would have changed his life.

"It's true. From what I can tell, most of the old stories are bent versions of history. People never liked the idea of a dancer being able to take the gift of another, which shaded stories and how they were told. But The Balance definitely created the spirit crystals and showed the Gousht how to use them."

The trees moved more than Nomi. The effect was strangely disarming.

"It's why you can break the crystals and free spirits if you know what to listen for. There is a piece of The Balance singing underneath the trapped echoes within crystals."

"Why?"

"Because she imbued the crystals with a fragment of herself, just like us," he said. "Remove it and the crystals shatter."

"No. Why did she do it?"

Nomi's focused stare ceased being a challenge. This girl, who was named after one of Kaylo's motherly figures who frequently told stories about thieves, hadn't condemned The Balance after he confirmed what she had done. Instead, Nomi wanted to know what led The Balance to her choice.

For all he knew of Nomi, she was a mystery. He found himself wondering after her thoughts—the ones she left unspoken.

"The Balance said she's tired of watching people abuse her descendants. She wants to make Enneans rely on us—force them to see who we are. Her bitterness consumes her. No matter how many people die, she feels justified because of how people curse her name and her people."

"Sounds like what Jonac did."

"What?" The comparison came wildly out of the abyss. Her words caught Kaylo too off balance to be angry or hurt. "They are nothing alike."

"He blamed you for what the Gousht did to his family. He and my father cast you out like you were worthless because of the lie they told themselves about protecting the rest of the Jani.

"The Balance blames Enneans for believing false stories and acting on them. She didn't focus her wrath on the storytellers or even those who hurt her descendants. Everyone is responsible in her eyes, and they all must be held to account to protect her people. Even if her people are also killed in the process.

"I admit, it's not perfectly analogous. But you forgave Jonac. You never even blamed him. Why can't you at least empathize with The Balance?"

Kaylo searched the firepit, the dark edges of the forest meeting the light, and the sky above. The Balance and her shadow cloak were nowhere to be found. This wasn't some trick of perception. He hadn't fallen into The Mist or a dream.

"You're far too grown for your size."

"Lots of people say things like that. My father likes to say I have learned to view the world from outside myself. He calls it wisdom, but maybe I'm just weird."

"I'm starting to think your father is right," Kaylo said, shaking his head. "I don't know if she deserves forgiveness, but I know I haven't tried."

"How do you know where to go?" Tayen asked as she fell in step beside Nomi.

"There's not much of a secret to it. Last time I made the trek, they told me where to find their next encampment site. If they have to change plans, they mark the trees. No markings yet."

"That's it?"

"What did you expect me to say? The Balance guides me in all things. I am merely a conduit for her works on this plane." Nomi's tone didn't reflect the clear sarcasm, which made her endearing in a way. No matter what anyone said, she never adjusted who she was.

"That would be nice wouldn't it. Wish The Shadow would guide me."

Nomi bent down and collected a fallen tree limb from the ground. "How do you know she isn't? I'm guessing The Great Spirits affect more than we know. They probably only announce themselves when they want the credit."

She dug in her travel sack and pulled out a length of soiled fabric.

"What are you doing?"

Instead of answering, Nomi wrapped the fabric around one end of the tree limb, sprinkled it with firestarter, then rolled it in fallen leaves. The leaves created a small crown around the top of the torch.

"Hold this," Nomi said before thrusting the tree limb into Tayen's hands.

"Why the leaves?"

Nomi brought out a flint stone and unsheathed her knife. "Hold it lower," she said as she started scraping her flint against the blade of her knife. "Damp leaves create a lighter color smoke."

Everyone had come to a stop around the two of them, but Nomi didn't react. She continued sparking her flint with a rhythmic motion.

When the torch caught a spark, the firestarter-soaked fabric burst into flames. The heat forced Tayen to lean back as far as she could. The leaves sizzled in the heat, and wafts of white-gray smoke rose into the air.

"Hold it high," Nomi said as she repacked her flint rock, laced up her travel sack, and sat on the ground with her legs crossed.

Even as Tayen did what she had been told, she stared down at the strange spirit dancer. Nomi was equal parts frustrating and fascinating.

"Could be a while," Nomi said. "Switch arms if you have to."

"Why in the name of The Blessed Mother do I have to stand here while you take it easy?"

"I'm a guide. I guided."

Sosun chuckled, and Tayen whipped around to find her friend hiding her smile with her hand.

"Why don't you hold this thing?"

"How would I speak?" Sosun settled her lips into an exaggerated pout. *"You wouldn't want to take away my voice?"*

"That's low." Tayen turned to Nix and Kaylo who had both followed Nomi's lead and sat down.

"Respect your elders and let us rest," Nix said without a hint of playfulness.

"I hate you all," Tayen said, shifting the torch into her other hand.

It took far longer than Tayen would have liked. She switched the torch back and forth between her hands a half dozen times before a group of warriors strode through the trees into view.

Each of the four warriors carried a spear and had either a small axe or short sword hanging from their waist. None of them looked pleased to see Tayen holding the torch aloft, but when Nomi stood up, one of the warriors dropped her spear and ran to embrace Nomi.

"It's been too long," the warrior said, squeezing Nomi close.

"My father's been waiting for word."

"It would be polite to say you missed me." The warrior disengaged from the embrace. "Speaking of polite, who are these people?"

"Wen, meet Tayen, Sosun, Nix, and Kaylo," Nomi said, pointing as she made introductions.

Wen's eyes went wide when she heard Kaylo's name. Her expression didn't betray joy, anger, or excitement, just plain shock.

Every time, Tayen thought. Kaylo's notoriety continued to get more annoying. He hated it, and said as much. But it also made Tayen feel small.

The other warriors wore similar expressions as they stared at Kaylo like a Great Spirit come to The Waking.

"Can we get moving?" Tayen asked. "I'd like to put this thing down."

Wen's expression snapped back to neutral. "Of course. Please follow us." She turned to her companions. "Two rear, one up front with me."

None of them exchanged words or looked for clarification. They simply formed up in front or behind Tayen and her traveling party. The efficiency of it was far more reminiscent of the Lost Army than Kaylo's stories would have indicated.

The small rebellion had grown organized.

Maybe Tayen hadn't made a ridiculous decision. If these rebels had steady hands, she would happily be their blade to wield.

The forest grew denser the farther they walked. The trees and foliage became more tightly compacted apart from the cleared path they followed. Eventually, the trees grew into a wall, completely unlike any tree wall Tayen had seen before.

Where others felt in conflict with the land, this wall settled into the soil and became a part of it. Moss and foliage climbed along the line of ironoaks. Colorful bushes grew along the wall. Somehow, they had made a barrier feel organic.

The guards at the entrance nodded to Wen and her companions as they led them through.

Rows of uniform tents filled the interior of the encampment, only interrupted by a large tent in the middle of the grounds. Tents of various sizes and long stretches of gardens skirted along the tree wall. People milled about, but no one seemed aimless.

Wen made a harsh turn towards a wooden shack near the entrance, and escorted Tayen and her companions through.

The space was empty. Wen walked over to one corner and lit a brazier. "We ask new guests to wait here. Someone will be by shortly."

"Is this necessary?" Nomi asked. "You know who he is. I brought them here myself. They aren't dangerous."

"If any of the stories I've heard are true, he is very dangerous. Whether or not you brought them, I am responsible for what happens next. There are people who will want to speak with your new friends."

"If I can clear things up a bit," Nix said, "I don't really care for Kaylo. We aren't friends. We just have similar destinations."

"Thank you for clarifying," Wen said dryly. "I will let my superiors know you don't have a close relationship with Ennea's Thief. Wait here, and they will let you know how helpful your information has been."

"For someone who hates talking, you can't shut your mouth," Sosun signed.

Wen and the other warriors left, and the sound of a wooden latch dropping into place followed.

"How badly is this going to go?" Nix asked Kaylo. "Between your friend Wal and this little welcome, I'm getting the impression you didn't leave on the best of terms."

"I've never hidden that." Kaylo sat at the edge of the room and leaned against the wall. "A lot can change in thirteen turns. Blessed Mother, things were never this organized when I fought with the Uprising"

"The surprises keep coming. Are you saying you weren't an organized leader?" Nix raised the back of her hand to her forehead. "I may need to sit down to recover from the shock."

"Can you stop talking?" Tayen said, allowing her frustration to darken her tone. "We are finally here. This is the Uprising, and I don't want you jeopardizing this chance because you need to be quippy."

"You think they'll turn you away because of sarcasm?" Nix asked.

Sosun smacked her shoulder.

"You're going to have to stop doing that," Nix said as she signed.

"You're going to have to stop being an asshole and battling the whole world," Sosun signed. *"Maybe this moment doesn't need your cleverness."*

"How did you all survive each other for over a moon in the forest?" Nomi asked.

The latch on the door scraped against the frame as someone lifted it out of place. An expectant silence followed.

A diminutive figure stood in silhouette as light flooded the dark room. Slowly, the intensity of the light faded as Tayen's eyes adjusted.

A Sonacoan woman with tight red locs tied into a braid stood in the doorway. Her face angled into her straight-lined lips. Regardless of her height, her stance gave her the bearing of command.

"It's true," she said, staring at Kaylo. "Why are you here?"

"I want to help."

"How long before you leave again? It would be nice to have some warning."

"It's nice to know some things haven't changed." Kaylo forced a smile. "I'm glad to see you safe."

"No. This isn't a lovely reunion with hugs and stories." She stepped farther into the room. "Things are going well here, and we don't need you mucking it up."

"Tomi, please listen."

She looked around the room as if finally noticing her audience. "Just like the old Kaylo, collecting people and leading them into danger."

"Lambast him all you like. Truly, I'm enjoying it, but please don't imply I'm following his lead," Nix said.

"You must be the one with the smart mouth Wen told me about," Tomi said. "This conversation isn't for you."

"We came to fight the Gousht, not you," Tayen said.

"Don't tell me you've filled this kid's head with war stories."

"Stop talking to him like that." Tayen stood up, fists clenched beside her.

"Tayen, sit down. I earned far worse than a few less-than-kind words," Kaylo said, redirecting his attention to Tomi. "I deserve your anger and your suspicion, but I need you to hear me out. If you want to send me away afterwards, fine."

"Sadly, it's not my call," Tomi said. "I think it's a bad idea, but she wants to see you."

Kaylo paused and his mouth opened as if he had a question, but he stayed silent and stood.

Tayen made to join him, but he waved her off.

"I have to face this alone, little shade."

Tomi walked out the door and Kaylo followed. The unmistakable sound of a latch falling back into place rang into the room.

Once again, he had shut Tayen out. Left her behind. They wouldn't be here if it weren't for her, and now she got locked in a shack while he visited with his past.

Kaylo had to take full advantage of his longer gait to keep up with Tomi as she charged through the encampment. Row after row of tents flew by.

Assuming two warriors slept in each, as had been standard, at least three hundred warriors lived within the tree wall. Few tents were occupied. Warriors would be busy training or maintaining the encampment itself.

Running these small communities, especially a community as organized as this, required constant maintenance. People required food, water, medicine. Training weapons broke. Real weapons aged and rusted.

A paddock of goats bleated away in the distance.

Tomi stopped beside a larger tent towards the center of the

encampment. The tanned leather didn't rise quite so high as the gathering tent, but it swept out to make room for several people to meet within.

"You shouldn't have come back," Tomi said before stepping away from the entrance.

The words to heal the past didn't exist, so Kaylo pushed through the furs without any.

Inside, a woman leaned over a long table, facing away from him. Her red locs had been braided into a single coil falling below her shoulder blades. It would have taken lifetimes for him to forget the shape of her.

He opened his mouth, but stopped himself. If he started with an apology, it would never be enough.

Every muscle in his body begged to embrace her. Forget the turns apart, and clutch her like the memories he had replayed every day since he left. She had fit the crook of his arm perfectly in those mornings before the world made demands of them.

Until right now, he hadn't known she was alive. Seeing her upright would have to do. He owed her the chance to lead the moment.

"Liara?" His voice came out as a whispered prayer.

She turned slowly. Her throat bobbed within her graceful neck. Age had only made her more beautiful. Her cheeks still sat high and plump on her face, but the first touch of gray faded the red hair over her left ear.

Kaylo should have asked Tayen to help him retwist his braids. He should have bathed or washed his robes. The best he could do was flatten the wrinkles in his robes with the blade of his hand.

"I'm surprised Tomi didn't bruise you up a bit before you got here." Her voice had settled and smoothed in the turns apart, but it was distinctly hers.

"You know Tomi and me. We have an old rapport. It only seems like she can't stand me."

"What are you doing here, Kaylo?" she asked. "I should have you bound for what you did before abandoning the clan."

He closed the distance between them, but when he got within two paces, she stepped back. "I know. I have a lot to make amends for, but I took in a girl about a turn back. She had a lot of anger."

"You know a bit about that."

He chuckled, but the sound pitched into something more painful. "I've been trying to keep her from making the same mistakes I did, but then I realized, I had been taking her choices from her. She deserves to make her own stupid choices. She chose to join the Uprising, if you'll have her."

"And that would be a stupid choice?"

"No...I meant...you don't—" He stopped his tongue from stumbling over itself. "Are you having fun?"

"It's been over a decade, Kaylo. I don't know what I'm supposed to do here."

"Me either," he said. "I should have started with apologizing, but I don't know how to say sorry and make it adequate."

"When you left, life moved on. I was angry for a long time, but there was too much to do. People started looking to me more. The pressure made me make some bad calls, and I thought I could understand a bit of what you felt."

When Kaylo had decided to search for the Uprising, there was a question he knew he would have to ask. The hardest part of it had been answered, but the question still scared him.

"What happened to the others? Annit, Talise, Jolrin, Rēlan?"

"Jolrin and Rēlan took off with Wal after you left. And Talise is leading a small Uprising clan in Renēqua."

Wal hadn't mentioned a word about leaving the clan with anyone because of course he hadn't. However, that wasn't the part of Liara's response that stuck out.

"Liara, what happened to Annit? Where is he?"

She shook her head. "I'm sorry, Kaylo. Infection a few turns back. An arrow wound that shouldn't have been much of anything ended up being everything."

Of course Annit had died. People died in war all the time. Kaylo couldn't expect everyone he loved to have survived in his absence.

Still, his abdomen refused to take a deep breath. Kaylo walked to the table and leaned against it. A map sprawled over the entire surface, detailed with notes and small carvings to represent different army movements. He scanned the details to avoid thinking about Annit.

"So you're the one making decisions now? Honestly, you should have been the one doing it back then."

"Are you really back? You aren't going to run away again?"

The sound of hope cutting through her pitch filled his lungs with life. She wanted him here.

Kaylo faced her and brought his hand to her cheek, but she backed away.

"I'm happy to see you. Truly, I am, but I have a wife and children. My life moved on," she said. "If you're here to fight, we could use you."

"Children, huh?" He hated the sound of bitterness in his voice. "That's great. How old?"

Liara straightened. "This isn't the time for all that. Right now, I need to know if you're here to help us. Are you back?"

When he first agreed to help Tayen find the Uprising, he hadn't expected to see any of his old friends. People died in war. He hadn't planned on picking up a blade again. Of course, he would have helped Tayen. He wouldn't have abandoned her, but that was different from charging into battle.

"I follow the girl," he said. "She wants to be here. So I am here."

"Somehow, in all this, you became something of a father."

The word struck him as peculiar. He was nothing like his father—nothing like what a father should be.

"She's young, but good in a fight. She'll be a lot of help in a raid."

"The time for raids is over, Kaylo." She moved to another side of the table, grabbed a baton lying on the map, and pointed to a figure beside the Lost Forest. "The Lost Nation is on the move. The Gousht are shoring up their ranks. The war is coming to an end one way or another."

"And what are you supposed to do about it?" He regretted his tone immediately.

"We have plans," she said, a wall forming in her stance.

"Plans? I've seen the Citadel. They have thousands of warriors ready to fight. The Gousht have even more," Kaylo said. "It's impressive how organized this encampment is. I'm sure you have a few more like it, but what can you do against either of these armies?"

"You've been to the Citadel?"

"Wal captured me and my toka—tried to make us fight for the Lost Army. We only escaped a moon past."

Liara's left eyebrow tweaked upwards. "Wal? He's alive?" She shook her head. "That doesn't matter. If either of these armies are allowed to win, Ennea will be lost. There won't be anything we can do to stop it."

"Tell me what you need me to do."

"Start by telling me everything you know about the Lost Army."

CHAPTER TWENTY-FIVE

Tayen sat on her bedroll in the tent she and Kaylo had been allocated. It had been a long day, what with being locked away in a shack while an angry woman from Kaylo's story led him away to decide their fates. They had only just finished eating a quick meal and laying out their things before they were supposed to get some sleep because in the morning, they would be assigned duties.

How in the burning Emperor's balls was she supposed to go to sleep after that?

Kaylo walked into the tent and sat down on his bedroll as if it were any other night. The jerk burped and excused himself like his gas was all he had to answer for.

"You too tired or should I pick up where we left off?" he asked.

Somehow, he interpreted Tayen's narrowed glare as an invitation to begin story time.

"The new council had been in place for over a turn and a half at this point," he said. "I was chasing after Wal when a northman pushing a wheeled cart almost ran me over. The man wasn't far past his middle turns, but his hairline had receded and he looked weighed down by the day. His expression widened, and he apologized profusely after he recognized me. I waved him off, and hurried to regain ground.

"There had been a time when I never could have conceived of not knowing everyone's name in the Uprising. But in the past six seasons, our numbers had grown too large to safely house in a single encampment. We had already created a second clan, and it was nearing time to break off into a third."

Kaylo continued to speak as if they weren't sitting in the Uprising encampment. As if this afternoon hadn't happened.

"'Would you slow down?' I called out, but Wal either didn't hear or didn't care." Kaylo animated his voice to highlight Wal's ridiculous behavior.

"I sidestepped a little girl running after her friend and ran to catch up with Wal. He could be unpredictable when he was angry, and it was best if I could be there to mitigate the damage."

"Kaylo, stop," Tayen said. "Are we seriously not going to speak about what happened today?"

His face quirked in genuine confusion. "I thought this was where you wanted to be?"

"We aren't going to talk about her?"

"Who? Tomi? I've told you she's a bit gruff, and it doesn't seem like time has cooled her down."

Tayen stared at her kana. This man had mentored her for nearly a turn. He had saved her life and taught her lessons that she had never thought to learn. And yet, he was still this dim.

"Liara is alive," Tayen said.

"Yes. Do you have a question?"

"With everything you've told me, I expected her to be dead. I mean, with the way your story has gone, I expected everyone to be dead. Why did you leave if she's still alive?"

Kaylo peered over her shoulder into the nothingness of the leather tent wall. His eyes went distant before he brought himself back. "That's exactly what I'm trying to tell you. Can I continue?"

What could Tayen do besides nod?

Chapter Twenty-Six
Kaylo's Story

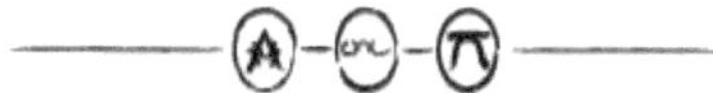

BY THE TIME I rushed into Wal's tent, he had already tossed the piecemeal map of Port Anno across the swept dirt floor. The pieces of parchment we had spent hours organizing looked like scattered leaves.

"They don't know what they are talking about!" he yelled.

"Blessed Mother! It took two moons to draw that map, Wal. If you need to throw something, grab a rock."

"Who are you telling? It wasn't like you went out there scouting for a span at a time, sketching the harbor and the docks, standing by and doing nothing as the Gousht shipped off our fucking people."

"No, I wasn't out scouting," I said, matching his tone if not his volume. "I was busy here trying to keep the clan fed and make sure our warriors knew which side of the spear to hold."

For a moment, he looked like he wanted to hit me—balled fist, furrowed brow, shoulders tensed and lowered. Then he stopped himself.

"What are we supposed to do? You heard all the reports, not just mine. You know what the shit-sippers are doing. How can we allow the Gousht to send our people off?"

He was right, of course. We all knew the Gousht had been shipping imprisoned spirits back to their Emperor since they had discovered the cursed things. The idea of them playing with stolen spirits in their faraway home was bad enough. But our people. The old me would have ordered an immediate attack after the first report.

But the Uprising had grown too large in the past six seasons to make impulsive decisions. More than two hundred fifty people relied on us. The council was right about that much.

"Not now doesn't mean not forever," I said. "We come up with a better plan to free them."

"How many will we lose before then?" Wal asked. "Does Liara even care?"

As much as I agreed with Wal about raiding the port, it took all the patience I had left not to react to him talking about Liara. He did this every time he disagreed with her and the rest of the council. He wanted to goad me into a fight.

"Liara and the other councilors are trying to keep us from getting our warriors killed in a battle we can't win."

"Of course you're on her side."

"Burning Mist, you prick of a man, we are on the same side. I don't agree with them, but they aren't out to sabotage us." I took a few steps to the edge of the tent and sat on a patch of dirt not covered in a piece of our map. "How many times have they approved of our plans? There is a reason there are so many of us now."

"It wasn't a bad plan, Kaylo."

"It wasn't a great one either," I said. "Now, stop throwing a fit and pick up the map. If you tore any of this parchment, be ready to defend yourself. You know how hard it is to get parchment."

"You'll have to stop threatening to fight me sooner or later. I'm getting better."

"If I win, great. If you win, maybe you'll put me out of my misery."

"Shit, Kaylo. I'm supposed to be the morose one here."

The anger I felt the first time Boda and Jolrin reported that the Gousht were forcing chained Enneans onto ships hadn't faded. It had hardened into resolve. With every setback, the green bastards sent more of our people away. "Let me look at the map some more. There has to be a better way to raid the port."

Wal collected the map, and together, we laid out the pieces of parchment until the drawing formed Port Anno beside a harbor with the same name.

We talked and plotted, poking holes in every plan we could conceive. The Gousht defended their ports too well. They had the numbers and well-secured positions. Any large-scale destruction would kill more Enneans than Gousht.

The ink on the page became a series of blotches on the parchment with the changing hours.

When we finally put the maps aside, I promised Wal we would come up with a plan. We would not abandon our people. And I made him promise not to cause a problem with the council. Then I left him to his thoughts.

On the other side of the tent, the day had given way to the evening. The air in the south caught the spring much more quickly than in the north. A smattering of people moved between the tents, but most people had made their way to one communal fire or another to share a meal.

Despite the pain outside this tent city, our not-so-little community found time for joy. The dancing firelight and murmurs of pleasant conversations reminded me of the Fallen Rock Clan. These small moments made the occupation feel farther away.

Part of me wanted to scold people for their smiles, their lack of vigilance. But guards watched the perimeter, and hanging our heads wouldn't save our people.

Jonac had told me once that he had felt the same way when he first joined the Jani. They held celebrations. They danced and told stories like The Mother wasn't dying beneath their feet. It had taken time for him to learn that their joy enabled them to continue on. Their celebrations kept traditions alive.

I still needed more time to accept it, but I didn't have to make that everyone else's problem.

At the edge of the encampment, a small fire glowed within the leather lining of my tent. Liara must have been waiting for me. She should have known I wouldn't have taken her decision well.

Not her decision entirely. She only held one vote of five, but it never felt that way.

After hovering over the map for several more hours, each of their objections became glaringly obvious. We would have sacrificed far too many warriors only to disrupt the port. The Gousht would have been back at it within a span or two.

When I walked in, Liara looked up from her book. She didn't say anything, just looked back down to continue reading.

It had been five turns. She had always been the water dancer staving off two soldiers in the night, twisting and turning in her white robes. Even her locs had nearly grown back to their original length. But so much had changed.

Liara had become a leader within this community. People looked up to her, not because of her connection to The Great Spirits or some fluke on the battlefield. She had earned people's respect by listening.

"I'm sorry about Wal," I said.

She glanced over her book, met my eyes, then returned to reading again.

"I'm sorry about me too." I sat beside her—not too close to be presumptuous, but not too far as to be combative. "We couldn't see anything beyond the people in chains."

"Is that you trying to admit we were right?"

"Do you need me to say it?"

After marking her place with a leaf, she put the book down and sat up. "Kaylo, you stormed off while Annit was halfway through what he had to say. The minute you heard no, you stopped being interested. The people chose us for the council for a reason. We don't have to be at odds."

"You're right. You were right earlier today, and you're right now."

Her face turned up in a gentle smile. Nothing about the expression gloated. It empathized.

"There are horrific crimes happening to our people wherever we look, but we can't help them if we die first. As sickening as it is, we need to be patient," she said. "Your little army went from twenty to two hundred, but you're still fighting like they are twenty.

"If you want this to work, you need to learn how to be a commander instead of a brash boy with a small group of friends."

"Well, fuck. Don't hold back how you feel."

"How I feel is I love you. I also know how committed you are to making yourself responsible for the world." She rose a hand to stop me from responding. "That's not a bad thing, but it makes you rash. It makes you forget about your responsibilities to the people immediately around you."

"All that makes sense, but you realize what you've done, don't you?" I asked. "Every time the council votes against one of my plans, Hylĭane stops by to gloat with her condolences. She can't help herself."

"No, she can't, but you can thank her and move on." Liara brushed a hand along the nape of my neck. "Somehow you have managed not to kill each other in the past three turns. I've been impressed by your restraint."

"Can we talk about something other than Hylĭane and Port Anno?"

"Of course we can." Liara picked her book back up. "After you go out there and bring back some dinner from one of the fires."

"Yes, Councilor."

I started to get up, but she grabbed my sleeve and pulled me into a quick kiss. It had become her habit to grab my robes before I left and kiss me. The small joy of it hadn't dulled. With her grip on my clothing, she told me she didn't want me to leave. She wanted me close.

We fought, we laughed, we waged literal war, but we always had this.

She released her grip on my sleeve. "Now, go. I'm hungry."

CHAPTER TWENTY-SEVEN
KAYLO'S STORY

A RABBIT DANGLED FROM the snare, its limbs still scrambling for the ground beneath it. I rushed forward to end its life as quickly as I could. The pop its neck made ran down my spine, and it was over. A quick cut turned its blood into a stream that slowed to a trickle as it hung there lifelessly.

I dropped to my knees, kissed three fingers, and touched them to the earth near where the blood pooled. "The Mother welcome your spirit," I said.

"What does The Mother care?" Boda asked. "Look at the world. If The Mother is real, she has a twisted sense of humor."

"I'm not here to argue beliefs with you. We check the snares and see if we can't bring some larger game back to the clan. Simple as that."

We'd had versions of this conversation before. It was a game he played. He would poke at me with his words and test my resolve. If my patience broke, he won. He had proven that I—like everyone else this side of The Mist—didn't truly care about him. Our kindnesses were lies.

If I kept my tongue still, the game would go on. He would find another way to challenge me.

His stubbornness was endearing in a way. He cared enough to push. He could have gone silent or left. Instead, he stayed and played his games.

Once the rabbit's blood stopped flowing, I began to dress the kill as my father had taught me. Large as it was, its meat would never spread quite far enough as more and more people continued to join the clan.

"Why do you always insist I hunt with you?" he asked.

My father's knife caught in the fur halfway through a cut. It needed sharpening. "The same reason I always give, Boda. You have more to learn about the land if you are ever going to lead people in battle."

"And for the hundredth time, there are plenty of people to teach me. Why you?"

"Because you're such pleasant company." I continued removing the rabbit's organs, careful not to damage the meat.

"These little hunting trips aren't going to make me forget how much I hate you."

"I've got plenty of people who hate me," I said without looking up from my task. "What I need is more hands that know what they are doing. Go check on the next snare."

His presence loomed over me for a moment as if he were deciding whether to argue further. If I looked up, he probably would have chosen to dig his heels in for yet another battle of wills. Instead, I kept my focus on the rabbit, and he eventually trudged off.

Blood covered my hands and made it more difficult to hold my knife as I worked, but I had grown up understanding how to adjust the tension in my grip to keep control. I focused on the way the leather-wrapped hilt scraped my palm ever so gently.

The scent of the rabbit's death mixed with the damp earth around me, and the metallic gaminess turned into a memory.

One of the few times my mother had taken me out hunting, she corrected the way my father had taught me to dress a rabbit. He had always had too light of a touch, as if he hadn't already killed the creature. So when he skinned an animal, he went too slow—didn't use enough force. It inevitably damaged the pelt or the meat, and in his eyes, the damage only became further proof that he needed to be gentler.

Instead, it wasted part of the animal that had died so we could live.

That day, she taught me when not to be gentle, how gentleness could cause more damage at times. Once the rabbit dried a bit, I would make my cuts and skin the catch with enough force to make a clean separation.

I had my father's heart, and my mother tried to teach me when to use it.

Once I tied the rabbit to my belt, I went off looking for Boda. He wasn't hard to find, crouching beside a squirrel, working his knife to dress the kill.

His impaired eye faced me as I approached. I had failed him, which was part of the reason I had been gentle. But he wasn't broken, and me treating him as if he were only left us both worse off.

"I'm not bringing you out here to teach you to hunt. You know the forest well enough, though you could be a bit quieter in the brush," I said, then shook my head as I started traveling down the wrong conversation. "I've been bringing you out here to measure you."

"Measure me?" He whipped his head around to stare at me with his healthy eye. "What right do you have to measure me?"

"Like it or not, I command the warriors, and you serve at my pleasure." I stole the gentleness, the apologetic politeness from my voice. "You can dislike me. You can hate me. Hylïane gets under my skin every chance she can, but we work together for the sake of the Uprising. If you want to be a part of this rebellion, you will have to learn to respect my position."

The defiance in his expression faded as his features loosened.

"I have been taking measure to see if you can work alongside me," I said. "You are one turn from your swearing day. All the grace you get for being a child will be gone."

The fight and rage I expected to rush towards me never came. He sunk to the ground from where he crouched and could no longer meet my eye.

"Your hate and anger have driven you for three turns. You can wield a sword better than most. You understand your position on the battlefield and how to move as a part of the unit. But hate will only get you so far." I sat, keeping enough distance not to push at his boundaries. "Continue as is, and you'll never be more than a warrior taking orders. That would be a waste."

"What do you want from me?"

"I want you to finish checking the snares on your own. You need time to think. Figure out if you can fight for the Uprising or if you're only ever going to fight for yourself." I held his gaze for a moment before getting back up and patting the dirt from my backside. "Let me know when you decide."

As I turned to walk away, my little speech replayed in my mind. Something about it felt familiar. It wasn't how my parents, Jonac, or Zusa would have gone about dealing with Boda. But Munnie—she had always been straightforward but never forceful. Maybe I had learned something of what she tried to teach me.

"You're just going to leave me out here on my own?"

"We both know you're capable, Boda. And the encampment's never quiet anymore. Take advantage of the space and let yourself think." I spoke louder as I got farther away. "Just let me know when you get back."

The sun barely fell two fingers before I saw the encampment through the trees. If nothing else, I had been right about the quiet. The more Enneans who joined our cause, the louder the days became. Echoes and clanging tools. Kids laughing and boisterous campfires. Training drills and speeches. All the noise made me regret coming back early.

Out here, in the forest, there wasn't a war raging on. I had no responsibilities other than keeping myself upright, and even that wasn't essential.

The rabbit bounced against my hip, which meant more food to add to the stores. Sunlight filtered through the trees, creating patterns over the forest floor. It had been a good day.

Whispering echoes interrupted my peace. Natural echoes and the echoes of the few trapped spirits we kept for training mingled in the air. Their clashing melodies fought their way into something resembling The Song. Eventually, the noise would work its way back to feeling normal.

Through the trees, I spotted a crowd forming around the entrance. Any lingering peace broke. I picked up my pace while fighting my instinct to sprint back.

Arriving a few moments earlier and out of breath wouldn't help the situation.

Instead, I studied the scene as I approached. Tomi stood at the entrance with an arrow nocked but not drawn. Voices overtook the haphazard echoes, but no one screamed in distress. Something was amiss but nothing immediately life-threatening.

The Lost Nation sent another messenger? I thought. It had been a while, but they never strayed too far.

The crowd parted as I approached, revealing two Tomakan men at the center. Strangers encircled by a swath of warriors. No purple robes or any other sign that they belonged to the Lost Nation. They had their arms stretched to either side, empty palms showing they weren't carrying any weapons.

Talise and Annit stood between the men and the warriors, while Hylíane waved her walking stick at them from the growing crowd.

We had taken in strangers before but only on our terms. We watched the lodestones. We patrolled the nearby forest. This was the first time someone apart from the Lost Nation had stumbled into our encampment uninvited.

If they found us, who else might have? I whipped around, scanning the forest for any sign of green and yellow amongst the trees. Nothing stood out. Not that I could see.

"Back the fuck off!" Talise yelled. "Tomi, put the bow away. What are they going to do, spit really hard?"

"Blood banners fa sure," Hylíane said as loud as her lungs would allow. "No chances."

"Please. No, we ain't blood banners. Promise. Blessed Mother, I promise." The larger of the two men had stepped in front of the other to speak, but his voice trembled as he did.

The noise of the scene made walls that tightened around us. A single mistake, and blood would find the air.

I searched for the eyes of my warriors in the crowd—Jolrin, Rélan, Ame. I made sure they saw me and felt my stare in return. The tension in their stances eased.

Moments ago, I'd had no responsibilities.

A fair number of hands still rested on sheathed weapons. Liara had pulled Tomi to the side, but one fewer bow wouldn't matter much. Spears and swords would do the work just fine.

"Jolrin, take the warriors and get people packing," I said, hoping that my voice hadn't betrayed the fear swimming in my throat. "Two men, no matter what their intentions, are not the threat. But if anyone is following them, we need to be ready to move immediately."

Jolrin hesitated, looking from me to the two strange men.

"Now," I said, holding their stare. "There are plenty of us who know what to do with a blade if need be. You are needed elsewhere. Take these warriors and show me you have a clearer head than this foolishness."

The rumble of the crowd had settled since I joined in the commotion, which worked in my favor. Loud voices rarely helped anyone focus their thoughts.

"Okay." Jolrin nodded as if still convincing themself. They pulled their shoulders back and stood up straight. "You heard the Commander. Two hours to pack. Make ready the stores and your personal supplies. You know what to do. Move!"

A wave spread out from Jolrin, and one by one the crowd followed suit. Each person responded in a similar fashion—swallowing their adrenaline and forcing themselves to disperse. Warriors began leading everyone away to start the process of dismantling the tent city.

"No, wait! Wha are cha doin?" Hylīane yelled at the thinning crowd.

Before she could infect people with more fear than necessary, I intercepted her. But she cut me off before I could start speaking. "Tis is not how we do tings aroun ere, Kaylo. We can't just ave strangers walk into ta encampment. Cha know, as well as I, tha tere are more and more blood banners every day. I barely trust ta ones cha bring back from cha raids for three moons."

"No one is talking about trust, but we don't need a mob to make decisions right now. We need to be ready to move, and we need to figure out what is going on. You're welcome to be a part of that, but we are going to do this calmly."

Hylīane's eyes thinned as if she were confused. "Cha won't let them outta cha sight?"

"Not for a breath."

"Cha ave changed, aven't cha?" She allowed herself to loosen. "Handle tis. We will get movin by midday."

With the crowd dispersed, I found Wal waiting, wearing the same contemplative look he wore when he stared at a battle map. He was weighing the strangers, the scales tipping back and forth.

He could look as hard as he liked as long as he stayed quiet.

Annit and Talise stood to either end of the pair of newcomers. I could count on them, regardless of how the situation played out.

"We are going to take a little walk," I said to the Tomakan men. "I have questions, and I expect answers."

The larger of the two stood a head taller than me, his shoulders wide as the oldest ironoak. He looked beyond me as the tent city began to move. "You're running because of us?"

"I think a tent would be a better place for this conversation." I gestured for them to follow and set out for Annit's tent.

Annit was fastidious. He liked to live on the perimeter of any encampment we set up. His tent would be a quiet, controlled environment.

I parted the furs and gestured for the newcomers to enter, followed by Annit, Talise, and Wal. We sat them to the far edge of the tent before starting a fire. Annit set a pot of water on the flames, and the rest of us settled in—save Talise, who blocked the way out with her arms folded and a knife in one hand. It wasn't her best weapon, but she didn't need an axe to bleed out two unarmed men, even when one was bigger than any of us by weight and height.

"Let's start with your names," Annit said with far more cheer than suited the situation.

"I'm Taku, and this is my brother, Intalik," the larger one said.

"Brother? Your mother didn't feed him?" Wal said.

"My father died in the Invasion War. Intalik's father died this past turn."

"My apologies for Wal's rudeness. Unfortunately, it is the whole of his personality," I said. "I hope you understand why your arrival has stirred some emotions around our little encampment. Do you know who we are?"

"Are you Ennea's Thief?" Intalik asked with a reverence that felt strange.

Some people we liberated in our raids had heard of me. The stories they told made me sound invincible. Between Ennea's Thief and Hero of Anilace, I didn't know which moniker I disliked more.

Before I could answer, Taku spoke up. "You're not Jani. You don't have the robes, and you have far too many weapons. Which makes you the Uprising. The way your people reacted to you, it's not hard to guess who you are."

"I prefer Kaylo."

"Were you looking for us? How did you find us?" Talise's tone was neutral, but the knife in her hand lent its edge to the questions.

"Five days ago, the Gousht killed our little sister," Taku said. "She and some others got it in their heads that if the people of Colian fought back, we could force the greens from our city. People started to listen—too many people. They made an example of her. So yeah, we get why you're a little jumpy when strangers show up."

"You didn't answer the question," Wal said. "How did you find us?"

"Luck," Intalik said with an enthusiasm that didn't fit the setting.

"We didn't set out looking for anyone. You know what would have happened if we stayed," Taku said. "When we found a few tracks nearby, I thought we would find the Jani."

I hadn't encountered many blood banners. The ones I had were fervent in their hatred of rebels, as if it would make the Gousht see them as less Ennean. They weren't crafty, but then again, they didn't have to be in a sword fight.

These brothers didn't seem the sort.

"How did you escape the city?" I asked.

"My brother worked with these smugglers—" Intalik started before his brother's elbow cut him short.

"I did what I had to do in the city. Some of the people I did some work for had ways of getting past the wall," Taku said.

Everything about them fit a certain story—an oddly jovial man and his overprotective brother. Neither fit the mold of a spy in my mind. Nor did they seem like they were working against the idea intentionally. They simply seemed out of place in the most natural way possible.

"Taku, let's start over with proper introductions. We will tell you how things will work, then you can decide if you want to stay with us or be left behind," I said. "If you decide to stay, it won't be easy. You'll have to earn trust."

Taku gave his brother a long glance as Intalik grinned like an eager child, then he nodded.

After introductions, I charged Annit with their care and oversight. They needed new clothing and something to fill their bellies, though I didn't know if we had enough fabric to cover Taku. Most of all, they needed to be watched at all hours. I wouldn't lose another clan.

Regardless of whether they were blood banners, we needed to leave as soon as we could.

I dragged Wal along with me as I left the tent. Talise stayed behind,
which served us well enough. She wouldn't have taken her eyes off them
even if I had made it an issue, so I decided not to.

"A smuggler," Wal hissed.

I couldn't keep the smile from my face. "There is an opportunity here."

"You want to sneak into Colian!" Wal ran his hands through his
braids like he might pull them out if I continued speaking. "The council
just nixed a plan to raid a small port. Now you want to infiltrate the
biggest city and port in all Tomak? While they are actively searching for
dissidents? I'm starting to see why Hyliane never takes your side."

"Can you lower your voice?" None of the others who shared Wal's
tent were around, but the leather and furs only muffled voices so much.

"Oh, are you afraid of someone overhearing that you not only want
to trust the strangers who happened upon our encampment, but you
want to have them lead us into the heart of one of the largest Gousht
strongholds in Ennea? Do you think they might look at you a little
different?" Wal closed the gap, placed a hand on the side of my head,
and peered into my eyes as if he were looking for something. "I'm not an
expert, but you don't seem to be concussed."

I pushed him back. "Fuck off, Wal. I'm not saying we go raid Colian
today. You and the other scouts were able to sneak in and out of Port
Anno just fine."

"Kaylo, the council will never go for this. This conversation is
pointless. We might as well talk about taking a stroll through Stone City
or stealing a Gousht ship to go assassinate the Emperor." He pursed his lips
and looked up at an angle as if contemplating it. "Actually, let's do that. If
we are going to get ourselves killed, why not make a statement?"

Every word I could think of to twist his name into a curse bubbled
up from the pit of my stomach. Wal, the revenge-obsessed, short-sighted

                JAMES LLOYD DULIN

prick who had suggested plans riskier by tenfold, thought he could mock me like this. The fucking gall.

But berating him had never done either of us any good. We had been through some version of this conversation too many times. I would curse him and pick at old wounds. He would return insult for insult and walk off in a fury. Then, once I found my senses again, I would apologize.

The routine had grown boring.

Instead, I sat down near Wal's bedroll and took a breath. "Can we light a brazier and talk about this? If this idea is as ridiculous after we talk as you think it is now, we drop it."

"Look at you being all diplomatic," Wal said. "It looks good on you."

He took a moment to bring over a brazier, fill it with ironoak coals, and serve two cups with water from a bucket in the corner before he sat down. Neither of us spoke while he moved through his tasks.

"Let me start by saying I know this is risky..."

"And the sky is big," Wal said.

"Instead of ruining my attempt at behaving like an adult by being you, why don't you listen before you speak?"

Wal opened his mouth with raised eyebrows, ready to sling insults at me. Then he stopped, leaned back, and gestured widely with his hands as if offering me a stage.

"This idea is risky, the council will hate it—at least most of them—and it may be a trap. For the time being, I'm going to set that aside," I said.

Wal didn't speak. Somehow, the boy who always had bloody knuckles because he couldn't help but make sarcastic comments during our lessons back in Nomar had learned to hold his tongue. I almost said as much, but it would have unwoven the moment.

"Colian has always been the goal. Grow the Uprising large enough to take Colian, take one of the Gousht's biggest ports, and cut off their supply lines between Renéqua and Sonacoa, right?" I asked rhetorically, I hoped. "It's been three turns, and we have two hundred warriors. It will be decades before we have enough warriors to take the city by force—by ourselves.

"If there is truly a rebellion growing in the city, letting it die may be killing our only chance. The Gousht aren't going to give us ten turns of raiding and growing before they start sending their forces out en masse to search for our encampments. Am I wrong?"

Wal waved his hands in a noncommittal agreement. "They've already started to increase their numbers in smaller communities. And the ones they can't afford to secure, they burn to the ground. So no, you aren't wrong."

"At least we agree on something," I said before catching my snide tone from coming out. "What if we could use our newfound friends to introduce us to some likeminded people in Colian? What if we help them grow within the city before we strike? What if we get the couta fucks to focus on us, only for an attack from within the city to take them unaware?"

The placating look that Wal had given me at the start of my little plan shifted. He leaned forward instead of back. His eyes narrowed like they did when his brain ran wild with ideas.

"If we could get the people weapons... Fuck! If you could destroy their stash of crystals before the rebels launch their attack, the green bastards wouldn't know what to do with themselves. We would flank them from within the city." Wal scratched at the stubble growing on his chin.

"Doesn't seem so ridiculous now, does it?"

"The council will never go for it," he said.

"Maybe."

"A man whose sister was in the rebellion and who has a way into the city—it's probably a trap. Those two buffoons out there could be blood banners."

"Could be," I said. "But they don't seem the crafty sort."

"Which could mean they're really fucking good."

"This is worth it, Wal. I don't see another way to really make a difference. We are never going to have the reach of the Lost Nation, and there's only so many places we can hide from the Gousht."

"And you were getting along so well with Hylïane. She is going to hate you with the strength of a thousand spirits."

I couldn't help but smile at that. "Nothing outlasts time. Certainly not Hylïane's patience with me," I said with a shrug.

For all my speeches and plans, I never had hope. I had rage and desire, but hope felt like a fool's endeavor. The thought of taking Colian and freeing an entire city of our people at once sparked a flicker of the hope I had avoided so dearly.

Chapter Twenty-Eight
Kaylo's Story

Sunlight dappled the floor beneath the gathering tent as I sat across from the council. No one spoke. Each council member wore a different look of anticipation as they waited for me to begin.

I swallowed and my throat felt like it would trap my next breath. The words refused to come.

Wal and I had planned for this with every stolen moment as the clan traveled east and resettled. We plotted and schemed for ways to convince at least three council members to agree with our ridiculous plan.

Kristee would never. Her nose crinkled as she stared at me with quiet contempt. Even before Acta died, Hyliane had swayed her. She believed in survival over risk.

Which left Annit, Meta, Eandrine, and Liara, all pragmatists in their own right. I couldn't count on relationships or our histories. They needed to see the truth. Eventually, the Gousht would stop seeing us as a nuisance. If they organized their forces against us, they would destroy us.

Tomorrow always seemed like a given until today turned bloody.

"In the past three seasons, the Uprising has grown far more quickly than any of us were prepared for," I said. "Some might see this as the time to slow down and rethink our next moves—our priorities. We have neither the speed of a raiding party nor the strength of an army.

Reassessing would seem like wisdom if it weren't for our context."

The council had been right about our plans for Port Anno. Liara had been right. We were no longer fifty warriors descending on a farm. Two hundred blades moved differently. Information channels ran slower. Coordinating movement throughout the battlefield grew more complex. More bodies didn't always equate to easier battles.

I looked into Liara's eyes. She would never endanger anyone just because she cared for me, especially if Tomi was one of those people. I needed her to believe. Her vote would be the wind that either carried us forward or drew us to a halt.

"We don't have the luxury of waiting any longer. We are too big to ignore. Our raids have been too successful, and the Gousht will not suffer us much longer. They have tolerated us because the Lost Nation would take advantage if they sought us out in numbers. But that equation will start to break against us soon. Our growing numbers may feel comforting, but they are a target painted across our chests. We either prepare to defend ourselves against an army we are incapable of defeating in combat, or we strike before they do."

Eandrine scrunched her face into a visage of doubt. I needed them to see what I saw. Our success and our future teetered along a knife's edge. If they couldn't see that, they would choose patience, and the Uprising would fall.

"We have scouting teams constantly searching for our next encampment sites in case we have to leave at a moment's notice. It is already becoming more difficult to find safe haven on our land. And our numbers don't help," I said. "Patience is wisdom when time is an ally. It is folly when the enemy is closing in."

"I think we get it, Kaylo," Kristee said. "No more dramatics. Tell us your plan."

In a way, Kristee reminded me very much of her cousin. Of the many things that could be said of Acta, he was a sure heart. Once he believed, his sights never shifted. I could have spoken through to my dying day and never convinced Kristee of my point of view.

"If the brothers, Taku and Intalik, can be believed, there is an underground movement in Colian to fight back against their overseers. They don't have the resources to fight the Gousht on their own—neither do we. But together, we could take the city back."

Kristee scoffed, and although the others had kept their mouths closed, they looked as unconvinced as she sounded.

"'If the brothers can be believed?'" Kristee said incredulously. "The big one is an admitted smuggler. How can we believe a word he says?'

I had been ready for this question. "That's one of his greatest assets. Smugglers existed before the Gousht, and they'll exist after. They have ways in and out of most large cities. Taku will be our guide."

"You want us to take the biggest city in Tomak with two hundred warriors and a hypothetical rebellion, with pitchforks and kitchen knives, with the help of a few smugglers?" Elder Meta asked with the full weight of his judgement falling on his tone.

He was a hard man. It hadn't been his physical strength that carried him through the laborious farming camp we liberated him from. His will would outlast the lot of us if his body would allow it.

"Of course not. I want to arm the hypothetical rebellion, then take back the biggest city in Tomak," I said, as if his question hadn't been disingenuous.

"Kaylo, please don't let this conversation devolve into hollow jabs at one another," Annit said, his face painted with the disappointment that I had grown more used to seeing since we raided the forge.

Their disbelief made sense. What I had proposed sounded more than foolish, but I needed them to dig below the surface. They couldn't see that now was the time for rash plans. If we didn't do something to drastically grow our numbers and solidify our position, we would die. A foolish move with a hope of succeeding was far preferable to a promised failure.

"An uprising can never be isolated," I said. "If we believe in the

Uprising, we need the people to join us. Not just the handful of people we liberate from a raid or those who happen upon a lodestone seeking sanctuary, but the entirety of Ennea. We need our people to understand that we are stronger than the Empire—not because of The Song or the size of our army. We are stronger because this is our home, and when we fight for it, it isn't because of an order. It is because life without our connection to each other and Ennea herself isn't life.

"I may be wrong. The Gousht might not come looking right away. We may have time to grow our forces little by little before we have to make our move." I paused to scan the council. It didn't matter if I could read their leanings. I wanted them to see my conviction.

I stopped at Liara's eyes and took a breath to settle myself. She didn't have to offer encouragement or understanding. She just had to be her. Mine. "However, if we wait and there is a growing rebellion in Colian, it will not survive without us."

"Their rebellion is not our responsibility," Kristee said.

"I disagree. Their fight is ours. They are our people," I said. "We cannot attack tomorrow, but we can scout the city, seek out the rebels. This could be a chance to align our fight with theirs. Please don't let our caution kill more of our people. Allow us to see if there is a chance to earn our self-proclaimed title."

Elder Meta smiled, and his sandy brown skin wrinkled with his age. "There are moments when I think you may be as big as the rumors, young man. Tell us what you have planned."

While we traveled to our latest encampment, Wal and I had assaulted Taku and Intalik with questions until they had nothing left to say. We analyzed outdated maps of the city and dreamed of the possibilities.

"Permit me to take Taku and Intalik along with a small contingent to Colian. It is a big enough city to get lost in. The brothers have ways of reaching out to the rebellion. We need to speak with them. We need to weigh them. I won't add our blood to theirs only to kill both rebellions.

But if they have the means to unite their people, we could change the course of this war."

Most of the encampment had fallen asleep hours ago. Liara lay beside me, her breath marking the passing seconds, but I couldn't find sleep.

I had never been so terrified of getting what I wanted before. Kristee had voiced every objection and doubt that lingered in my mind.

In the beginning, the idea of taking Colian had been a dream. We spoke about it over campfires after training to keep us hopeful. No one ever expected it to happen. At least, I hadn't. I had expected to die long before we could make such foolish decisions.

If we did this, it would be firestarter on a steady flame. The quiet war of raids with the Lost Nation army looming in the background would be over. There would be no more small battlegrounds.

I had barely been able to carry the weight of the warriors who died under my command. With this decision, I had chosen the deaths of thousands for the small chance of freedom.

But they were already dying. The very idea of what it meant to be Ennean died more every day. Every time an enslaved Ennean died, another took their place in the mines, the fields, and the forges.

At least they would die fighting, I thought, not completely convinced.

Liara groaned beside me.

As I fought the daemons within my waking thoughts, she was fighting something in her dreams, again. She turned and her blanket came off her shoulder. I repositioned it, but she jerked away when I touched her.

"Liara," I said. "Wake up."

She whined, and her face tensed. Still asleep.

When I shook her shoulder to wake her, she lashed out with her fist. I tasted blood from my lip.

"Liara, it's a dream." I grabbed her wrists.

She whimpered and shook her head, then her eyes jolted open. She looked around as if searching for an escape. When she found me, she stopped, her chest heaving.

"You're okay. It's going to be fine."

She narrowed her eyes. "You're bleeding." She reached out to wipe the blood from my lip, but stopped. "Did I do that?"

"No one can control what they do in their sleep."

"I'm sorry." She shifted back, putting distance between us. "I would never. That wasn't okay."

"I've lived through worse. Bloody Mists, you've done worse to me in training."

"This is different," she said, with a finality in her voice.

"Are you ever going to tell me what you dream about that gets you so upset?"

She buried her face in her hands, and her locs fell like a curtain, shielding her from view. "My father. I told you he drank after my mother died. He loved her like the soil loves rain."

With her face still hidden behind her red locs, her arms began to shiver. I reached out to place a hand on her shoulder, but she recoiled.

"Please don't. Not right now. Not during this story," she said. "Tomi looks a lot like my mother. It used to be a point of pride for my father. After she died, he barely looked at Tomi. When he drank, he got mean. He hated seeing my mother in his daughter's face. I tried to get in the way, but it didn't help.

"He always apologized in the morning. Swore off barley wine—until the next time." She lifted her chin, and her hair parted, revealing her tear-lined face. Snot collected above her top lip. "We had to leave him. He would've killed her."

"I'm so sorry, Liara."

"I don't like to talk about it. The dreams get worse when I'm worried about something," she said. "I know how I voted, but you know you're only supposed to be scouting, right? Don't get yourself in trouble. You need to promise me."

Even when I wasn't putting her directly in harm's way, I forced nightmares on her.

"Kaylo, I need you to promise me. Tell me you won't make a reckless decision. Tell me that even if The Priest himself shows up, you'll make the right decision and keep yourself safe." She swallowed hard and coughed. "You matter too much to some of us."

"I promise to come home to you." I lifted my hand slowly, and raised my eyebrows in a question. When she nodded, I held her cheek and wiped a tear away with my thumb.

———————

The light had broken into the morning and begun to filter through the tent. It warmed and played with the red undertones of Liara's umber skin. She hadn't slept well.

I leaned in and kissed her where her cheekbone gave the curve to her face. She had fought enough battles in her sleep. There was no reason to wake her from the peace she had found. Goodbyes always fell short of the right words, and we had said enough last night.

"Thank you for being mine," I whispered before I put on a clean set of robes and left with my travel sack.

Outside, a small gathering formed near the encampment entrance.

There had always been tearful goodbyes when raiding parties set off. Regardless of the danger, we didn't always return home fully intact. No one named the fear directly, but we all understood some people may not return.

It had never been that way for scouting expeditions. And that was all this was. However, it didn't feel the same—not to me and not to the rest of the clan.

Apparently, Hyliane didn't feel the same either. She stalked over to me with heavy falls of her walking stick before I could come near the other scouts.

"Tis is cha idea of protectin ta clan, goin off wit two strangers who might be blood banners? If I knew cha were tis stupid, I woulda never said no ta those envoys from ta Lost Nation. I just turned one away ta other day."

"Did you now? I didn't hear about any envoys coming around the encampment."

"Don't change ta subject!" Hylīane shook with her anger.

"I don't trust them. My eyes will be open the whole time," I said. "Who knows, this might be how you get rid of me."

"I gave cha a chance," Hylīane said before storming away.

After so long, her outbursts had become almost endearing, but I had no time to give her any mind. I joined Wal, who waited separate from the crowd while the others said their farewells.

"What was that about?" he asked.

"Hylīane wanted to wish us luck." I clapped him on the arm. "Don't look so glum. This was your idea."

"No, this was your idea. It was only my idea if it goes well," he said, but his smile failed to reach his eyes. "Do you ever think about him? Every time there's a big goodbye before a mission, I think about Adēan."

"I remember the first time you two *said* goodbye," I said. "Couldn't tell if we were going to be able to separate you in time to leave."

This smile was real. "Do you think I'll know when I've claimed enough blood for what I owe? Will it still hurt this much?"

"There will never be enough. The couta have taken too much to balance. But we can make them hurt for it. We can help the people on this side of The Mist."

Eventually, Boda, Talise, Yelan, and Annit finished their goodbyes and joined us. Boda wore a pleased-with-himself smile I had never seen on him before. Over his shoulder, a young northern girl carried a matching expression.

"Are you sure you want to go?" I asked. "She looks like she misses you already."

His smile soured. "We should get a move on, Commander."

"Oh good, I was worried you might be overly pleasant on this trip," I said, before turning to address the full party. "We are three days out from Colian. There's no need to push ourselves too hard. We get there safe and rested. Understood?"

Even after three turns, addressing my elders like Annit and Yelan like this took effort. But neither wanted to lead, and we needed to move with one mind. So, ill-fitting or not, I had to wear the burden.

"Do we really have to take Intalik?" Taku asked, his trepidation clashing with his intimidating build. "I can make all the introductions you need on my own."

"For the last time, this isn't up for discussion. Two teams. Two guides. And if I suspect you haven't been fully honest with us, you won't have to worry about your brother. You'll find each other on the other side of The Mist." I couldn't match his stature, but I had no problem matching his size with my tone.

Taku looked between me and his brother while taking a step back.

"Kaylo, do you mind if I have a moment?" Annit asked.

"First, I need Taku to tell me he understands," I said.

"I just...I don't want..." Taku paused and looked to the others in the party, but no one moved. No one spoke. "I understand If this is how we prove ourselves, we will do it."

"What's the worry, big brother?" Intalik asked. "We've walked the streets of Colian our whole lives. This time we just walk with new friends. Right?"

Taku nodded, his expression still sullen.

The energy of the group had transformed. There had been banter and animosity, fear and excitement, comradery and anticipation. Then everything had muted.

It wasn't the ideal way to begin a scouting mission, but Taku needed to understand his position. I would do everything I could to get him and his brother back safely, but not at the expense of our mission or my people.

"Kaylo, please?" Annit said before walking a stretch along the camouflaged netting surrounding the encampment.

I followed, ready for a fight, but when he stopped, he smiled gently.

"Things changed after you raided the forge," he said without accusation or anger. "We drifted apart. Part of that is because you remind me too much of myself, ready to run into any battle if it takes you closer to your goal."

"And what goal is that?"

"Blood. You may question every last enemy about your priest—you could even kill the man, but it wouldn't stop the need for blood," he said. "Right now, that aligns with what the clan needs. Don't let yourself get distracted by it."

"What is this? You voted for this mission."

"I did. I think this is the right move. You were right about us being at the precipice of either disaster or greatness. We need to find a way to bolster our numbers and fortify our position quickly before the Gousht know what kind of threat we are."

"Exactly."

"Which is why you need clear eyes," he said. "When we get to Colian, you need to be able to walk away if this turns out to be the wrong move. You think you have guilt now. It's nothing compared to what you will carry if you lead the Uprising to its downfall."

"Is that why you're here? You're ready for us to fail?" I stared into Annit's pleading eyes. The Flame simmered like a low hum around him.

"Someday—and I hope someday soon—you will learn that there is a wide gulf between agreeing with you and being your enemy. I am your friend, Kaylo." He pointed toward the rest of the party. "They are your friends. Trust them enough to disagree."

The constant push and pull of being thrust into leadership meant I hadn't stood on solid earth in turns. Everyone had their own opinions about what I should do and how I should do it. That had never been Annit before. He had always supported me without pushing. I had broken something between us when I led the raid on the forge, and I had felt the loss these past seasons.

Instead of being his second chance to balance the blood, I had become his second chance to avoid failure.

"We need to get moving to make the most of the light," I said.

"Okay." He nodded with a slight smile. "I've always wanted to visit Colian."

He positioned himself at the back of the party and I at the front.

"Blessed Mother." I bent down, kissed three fingers, and placed them on the dirt. "If you can help us in any way, now would be the time."

CHAPTER TWENTY-NINE
KAYLO'S STORY

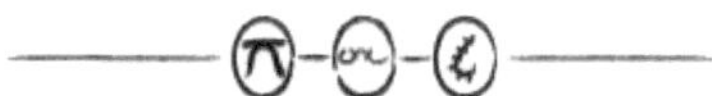

MUCH LIKE PORT ANNO, the tree wall surrounding Colian towered unnaturally high into the air. Occasional gates flanked by archer towers interrupted the long stretch of ironoaks.

When I was a little boy, I had begged my parents to see the big city. Its fabled markets supposedly held trinkets and treats that didn't exist anywhere else. The trade between Renéqua and Colian turned the city into a sprawling cosmopolitan bastion for art and education.

I never imagined seeing it for the first time like this—on my belly, hiding on the crest of a hill. Still, even trapped within walls, it was a beast of a city.

Sokan started to roll down the west side of the sky, casting shadows from the tree wall and marvelous towers that had survived the turns. Sunlight and shadows transformed the structures into a labyrinth running out to the northern coastline.

Whoever called the tree wall from earth hadn't understood The Seed. Even at this distance, gaps in the wood broke the illusion of an impenetrable wall. Imperfections were to be expected from a Gousht soldier with a crystal. Even still, this was shoddy craftwork.

The absence of The Song tingled like a missing limb as I studied how poorly they had put The Seed to work.

No matter what happened within the city, I wouldn't find my piece of The Seed. If rumors from dying soldiers were to be trusted, The Priest had climbed his way to the top of the Gousht hierarchy in Ennea, firmly locked away within the Stone City.

At least with him in control, any slight against the Gousht rolled through their command structure until it landed at his feet.

"The passageways," I whispered over my shoulder, at Taku more than to him. "You're sure they're safe, right? I'm not interested in any surprises."

The big man stared at me like he wanted to test the stories people told about me. "Unless something's changed in the last span, it's the safest way in and out of the city. Smugglers don't give up their secrets easily," he said. "You have the payment?"

We didn't have much use for Gousht coin, but we had pilfered plenty from dead bodies over the turns. Resources were resources despite the markings etched into the iron.

"Why do I get the feeling relying on people willing to steal and cheat to get by isn't the greatest plan?" Wal asked in typical Wal fashion.

"Shouldn't you have discussed this before we trekked three fucking days?" Boda asked with his annoyance dancing freely in his voice.

"Agreeing with the kid doesn't feel good," Talise said.

"Shut it, all of you," I said. "Taku, you'll lead us through the passage after dusk. Intalik will stay in the back with Annit."

"No, my brother's with me," Taku said.

"You're not making demands." His deep brown eyes met mine, and he held them for far too long before looking away. I could almost see his imagination throttling me. "If either of you die, my plans have gone to shit. I'm not putting either of you in danger, but I'm also not making it easy on you if you're lying."

"Trust would go a long way here, Ennea's Thief," Taku said.

"Ennea's Thief is just a story. This is reality, and in reality, we don't have time for trust."

———

Under the light of The Youngest Daughters, Taku led our party along the far side of the rolling hills, blocking any glimpse of the city. He slowed and began looking intently at the grass and clover. It didn't take much light to spot the difference between the natural flora and a small patch of graying grass two paces wide at the base of a hill.

"You wouldn't have had a change of heart, would you?" Taku asked. "You could leave someone behind with my brother. You don't need both of us to explore the city."

"If you're going, I'm going." Intalik stepped forward, bent down, and reached for something in the graying grass. "I know you want me to be safe, but this is a good thing, brother."

"We will protect him," I said.

Intalik arched backwards and strained his muscles pulling at the hidden lever in the graying grass, but nothing happened. He grunted and threw himself back again. Still nothing.

"Move." Taku pushed his brother out of the way and reached into the same patch of grass.

As he pushed off the ground with his legs, something beneath the dirt creaked. The abnormal patch of earth separated from the hill—only slightly at first—then it burst open as Taku staggered back to keep his feet below him.

A dark passageway crawled into the earth at the base of the hill. The moonlight only made it a few paces beyond the entrance before dying out. The walls of the passageway were compacted dirt, compressed firmly until it became smooth like shaped rock.

"One brown crystal and look at what smugglers can do," Taku said, still breathing hard from his exertion.

Yelan crouched at the entrance, staring into the black, and sucked her teeth. "A real dancer could do better."

"I don't think they were going for beauty," Intalik said, his tone turning the statement into an innocent observation.

"You will have to leave weapons here," Taku said. "Take knives if you can hide them, but everything else will only bring us trouble."

"Not happening," Boda said, gripping the hilt of his sword.

"Do you think the Gousht just let Enneans walk around the city with swords? Maybe you should stab a few of them on a busy street to see if they notice you." Taku towered over Boda, and still the boy glared back like he was the bigger of them.

The Song thundered from deep within the earth, ever quickening. Yelan twisted her foot and anchored it in the ground like a stake. With one swipe of her arms, the ground opened a small chasm beside our party.

"No more arguments. Everything that can't fit in the fold of a robe goes in." Yelan turned towards me. "Light the torches, and let's get through this abomination of a tunnel."

We did as she said if for no other reason than the tone in her voice wouldn't accept anything else. She covered our possessions, and Annit passed out lit torches.

Firelight stretched further into the void of the tunnel. Small notations marked the walls near the entrance, but beyond that, the walls were nondescript packed earth.

"The faster we make it through, the faster we leave," I said to Taku. "I'm not playing any games with you, I promise. You and your brother are my responsibility. I take that seriously. If you do what we discussed, you decide what you do next. You can join us. You can leave. I just need this one thing of you."

"Kind of downplaying breaking into Colian and setting up a meeting with a secret resistance, aren't you?"

Despite the gravity of the situation, I laughed. "Fair point. Still doesn't change what I need from you."

With a look back to his brother, Taku stepped into the passageway, and I followed.

After the entrance slammed shut behind the last of us, the flames shuddered for a moment as if threatening to give us to the void. Yet, they continued to flicker along the walls. Twice, the tunnel diverged, accompanied by markings along the bare wall.

This kind of infrastructure took time and planning. Taku may have been a smuggler, but he didn't strike me as the meticulous type. He was more of the take-orders-and-swing-a-big-stick type. We would need to do some talking on the other end of the tunnel.

Taku glanced at the markings as we passed them and led us through without hesitation.

A dockworker and a smuggler who understood how to move underground. His people must have had a hard time letting him go.

The journey stretched on for far longer than I would have imagined. Either that or the darkness looming at the end of our torchlight had played with my perception of time.

Once again, we reached a fork in the passageway, taking the left path. Taku slowed his pace and watched the wall.

Three vertical slashes marked the compacted dirt beside a wooden ladder running up through an opening in the ceiling.

"Let me do the talking," Taku said. "Keep your knives hidden. These people don't care much about causes. Your money will make them listen, but it won't make them agree."

The big man only needed to climb the first rung of the ladder to reach the wooden panel above. Three rapid taps followed by two more, then one final tap that rebounded off the tunnel walls.

Nothing happened right away, but Taku didn't show any signs of worry. He continued to stare at the wooden slats above him.

When the hatch flung open, I reached for the sword that was no longer at my side before I could think better of it. A new source of light filtered into the tunnel followed by a woman's voice.

"Taku? I thought we got rid of you."

"I have business. Eight coming up."

Murmurs too gentle to decipher hummed through the opening above. If Taku left on poor terms, it would make bartering for safe passage even more difficult.

It took everything in me not to call out to get a read of the situation before I climbed the ladder. As much as I resented being pushed into a leadership role, it had become familiar. Keeping my mouth shut didn't come easily.

"One at a time," the voice called down. "We won't hesitate to use violence should we feel the need. Isn't that right, Taku?"

Taku met my eyes as if to ask if he really had to climb the ladder, then pushed himself upward.

Feet shuffled on the floorboards above. "Next!" the voice shouted. "We don't have all day."

I chuckled to myself. If I died at the hands of some smugglers after everything I had survived, the spirits would greet me laughing.

The ladder creaked as I climbed. The room above was windowless. Walls of wooden panels contained the lantern lights held aloft by two figures. As soon as I could see over the lip of the hatch, two pairs of rough hands grabbed me under the armpits and lifted me into the room.

Five people. Not so many we couldn't handle ourselves, but they had every advantage.

A young woman, maybe a few turns older than me, sat in the corner aiming a crossbow at my chest. Crossbows didn't have as much utility as longbows against groups of people, but in this circumstance, it would kill me as well as any arrow.

Muffled shouts came from the tunnels. "Don't worry," I called out. "Everything's fine." Lowering my voice, I turned the woman with the crossbow. "Everything's fine, right?"

The two men holding my arms patted my robes, then one stripped my father's knife from a pocket in the fabric's lining. He tossed it into the corner where it clattered against Taku's short blade. Then he removed the coin purse from my hip and jingled it with a smile.

"Next," a woman carrying a lantern shouted.

The large men who had helped me up the ladder pushed closer to Taku and reached down to drag up Wal.

One by one, they removed any hidden weapons at the threat of a crossbow bolt. Boda yapped a bit too much for their liking and earned a smack upside his head. Otherwise, the process went smoothly, if a bit jarring.

They had done this before. Each person in the room knew their role. The large men who lifted us out had found every hidden weapon. The woman with the crossbow didn't shake as she aimed her bolt at each of us in turn. No one spoke apart from the woman with the lantern. And the man holding his own lantern in the far corner watched it all.

The way they each periodically looked back to the man in the corner made it clear who held the power.

"When we helped you and your brother escape, I assumed it was a one-way trip. Did you forget something? I promise you the guards seized anything you left behind," the man in the corner said, his face shadowed by the brim of a hat.

"Dalik, I never planned on coming back. I swear. But we ran into the Up—"

"No need for backstory," I said before Taku could say too much. We had coin to pay, but the Gousht had more, and I had no doubt they would pay it for my head. "We have business in town, and we happened upon our new friends here. They mentioned you might be of some assistance."

Dalik placed his lantern on a wooden table near where he stood and stepped forward. The light filled out more of his face, but the brim of his hat still cast shade over his eyes. His smile revealed a missing tooth and brought a dimple to his warm brown cheeks.

"Friends? Isn't that nice? We all could use more friends in this cruel world," Dalik said. "Friends of mine don't make trouble for me. Are you here to make trouble for me?"

"We're just here to have a conversation."

"Your conversation wouldn't happen to involve those?" He pointed to the pile of knives in the corner.

The way he controlled the room and his people while maintaining his charming smile spoke tales about the man. He wasn't someone to trifle with. He had at least some modicum of power in the largest port city in Ennea, despite the Gousht. Or maybe because of them.

"You wouldn't respect us if we didn't come prepared to protect ourselves," I said. "You've seen the coin we brought. We are simply looking for safe passage and an introduction. There's no need for you to be further involved."

Dalik looked at Annit and Yelan. "These young people think they can control everything, don't they?" He turned back to me when he didn't get a response. "I already have your coin. Why do I need to do anything?"

"We both can count. Eight of us. Five of you."

"The math is more complicated." Dalik tilted his head towards the woman with a crossbow trained on me.

"Annit," I said.

The subtle ticking of his echo crested into a forceful knocking, demanding its freedom. The lantern Dalik left on the table flickered out, then the flame returned once everyone had sufficient time to notice.

"A dancer?" Dalik smiled wider and swayed back and forth with a new giddiness. "Taku, you made interesting friends. Lonyea."

The crossbow shifted back Annit.

"Not so quickly," I said. The silvery thread of The Flame drifting from Annit hung in the air, and I grabbed it. With a twist of my wrist, the echo's knocking thundered in conquest. The lantern on the table flared, glass shattered, then the light snuffed out, leaving a single lantern to illuminate the room.

Dalik lifted his hand to Lonyea with the crossbow. "You broke my lantern."

I released the spirit, and its echo returned to Annit.

"I assume the coin in my purse can buy a new one."

"Confidence, I like—when it is earned. Coins," Dalik called out, and the man who had stripped me of my purse tossed it to him. "Hefty. Maybe enough to disregard you destroying my property. That all depends on who you want to meet."

"Corelina."

"Huh." Dalik's shoulders relaxed. "So you *are* here to start trouble?"

"Since when is talking trouble?"

"Oh, boy. You know better than that. Don't call me stupid to my face." He pulled open the drawstrings of the purse and sifted through it with a finger. "The purse is mine, and you forget my name. You can have your meeting."

"Half the purse is yours. You get the rest when the last of us are through that hatch on our way out."

Dalik laughed. "I have to know your name, boy."

"No, you don't."

"You will stay here until the sun rises. Then I want you out," Dalik said, emptying a pile of coins into his hand before throwing me the rest. "If Corelina decides to meet you, she will be at Tan Tila Square at high sun. Taku will know her."

Dalik stepped closer. "You bring trouble to me and mine, our next conversation will not be so pleasant."

The door to the backroom unlocked with the sun, and we stepped through the storefront of a tannery onto the streets of Colian. The air smelled of salt water and carried a chill from the ocean.

I expected the city to remind me of Nomar. After all, Nomar was home to the second largest population in Tomak. But the two cities existed in different worlds.

A horse and cart almost ran me over as I exited the tannery. The sun had just risen, and already, the streets were full of movement. Workers made their way north towards the docks. A soldier harassed a young Tomakan man who looked too young to be a dock worker and too old to be a school child. Storefronts opened their doors and set out signs advertising their goods in Gousht.

Despite being in the heart of Tomak, people of all hues and nations walked the streets. Some wore robes. Others donned pants and tunics, pretending to be something closer to Gousht. Our eclectic group would fit right in.

"This feels wrong," Wal said, stopping beside me.

"The big cities never stopped being big cities," Yelan said. "Shops and laborers continue on much like they did before. Only now, the bulk of their work and wares serve the Gousht."

"Don't gawk," Annit said. "The easiest way to seem out of place is to be a rock in the middle of a river."

"You could just say 'keep moving.' Why do old people always speak in metaphors?" Boda said.

Talise grunted and walked on while the rest of us were still talking about moving. I followed her lead.

A pair of pale-faced women walked by clothed in overly ornate dresses and carrying parasols to shield themselves from the sun. They continued their conversation as if they were at home on the streets of Colian. As if this was their land.

Every scouting mission starts with surprises, I told myself. It was true, but it didn't mean I felt more comfortable in this strange city.

Young Ennean children shuffled into a large building at the end of the block adorned with the broken circle, and a tall Gousht man closed the door behind them.

The soldiers in Nomar were known, but they stayed apart from us.

They never settled into the city like common folk. How extensive could a rebellion be? The Enneans acted as if nothing was strange about the Gousht walking up and down the streets, stopping in shops.

We made our way out of the busy street into an alleyway, and I pushed Taku against a brick wall. Despite our height difference, I stared him down. "What the fuck is going on here?"

"What are you talking about?"

"I think our young Kaylo thought the city would be a little more... controlled," Annit said, placing a gentle hand on my shoulder.

"We outnumber the Gousht three to one here," Taku said. "Yeah, if we fought back, we could overpower them, but people would die. Most of us aren't warriors. So we get by. The less we push back, the more leeway we get."

"The entire city gave up?" Talise asked, but it sounded more like a statement.

"Do you think we had given up in the mines?" Yelan asked. "These people are trying to survive. They will smile and do as they're told so long as their families are relatively safe. From what I hear, it's the same way in the Stone City and Tol Tian."

"The Gousht were never trying to kill everyone—just our culture," Intalik said, as if he were a sage of wisdom. It stood apart from everything I knew of the man's jovial innocence. "People resist in small ways, but nothing that would get them killed. Not like our sister."

Whatever rebellion lay beneath the face of the city would have to overcome more than the Gousht. Even on the farms we raided, there were people too scared to leave the routine of their servitude. It would be much worse here.

"We have five hours or so before we have to meet Corelina," I said. "We follow the plan. Annit, Wal, Talise, and Intalik, investigate the docks. Keep an eye out for any patterns or routines that can be exploited."

"I don't like it. Don't separate me and my brother." Taku used his stature to make me take a step back.

"We need guides. That's why we brought you," I said. "This is happening, whether you approve or not."

The mountain of a man stared down at me with a question in his eyes. It was the same calculation running through my head. Could he and his brother break away from us? He certainly had the strength for it, but they might not both make it unscathed. And the Gousht were looking for people connected with their sister. They could only go unrecognized on the streets as long as they didn't call attention to themselves.

"I'll be okay," Intalik said. "I grew up here and worked the docks, same as you. What's a walk by the dock?"

Taku turned his attention to Annit. "You are responsible for him."

Annit smiled the warm smile he usually carried with him. "I'll care for him like family."

CHAPTER THIRTY

KAYLO'S STORY

I LEARNED MORE ABOUT the Gousht walking around Colian for a few hours than I ever had in their schools. The buildings might have been ours. Most of the people were Enneans. But the couta had found a way to replace everything Ennean about Colian.

The sound of Gousht consonants clanged off the brick. Their fucking language marred every sign and street posting. Enneans parted for Gousht dressed in overly heavy clothing.

Most of the Enneans still wore traditional robes, but we had passed several wearing the same ridiculous fabrics as the Gousht. And they wore just as much sweat on their brows in the spring sun.

"How many of these people are blood banners?" I asked Taku.

He winced at the term. "Everyone makes adjustments or they die."

"Alright," I said, biting back several insults. I hated when people used nuance to avoid a question. He knew what I was asking. "How many believe the shit they spew?"

"It's hard to tell," he said, the tone falling lower as if he were probing a wound. "When you don't know who to trust, you don't share your doubts."

We made our way to the famed open market, partly because it would be easy to be lost amongst the crowds and partly because I needed to see what I had imagined so often in my mother's stories.

On our way to the market, I couldn't help but to marvel at the expanse of the city. Five Nomars could have fit within Colian. The Stone City had always held more people, but Colian stretched across more land.

If I had to run and find my way back to the tannery on my own, I would have lost my way eight times before losing the light.

I stared at the back of Taku's head as I followed close behind. I had gambled the lives of those I loved and moderately cared for on this stranger's word.

The large man turned onto the widest street we had encountered by double. We had finally reached the market, and I was ready to see my mother's words come to life. The rows of vendors with colorful carts of fruits, fabric, and trinkets—they were nowhere to be found.

My mother could have been exaggerating the truth for a young boy with big dreams, but it wouldn't have been like her. When she spoke about history and culture, she spoke truth. She cared too much about our people to twist them into a fantasy. Those tricks were meant for daemontales.

A handful of vendors and carts sold their wares along the streets, but everything stood evenly spaced. No more than a couple of people gathered around any given cart. The noise, the mess, the wonderful chaos my mother had told stories about, had been sanitized.

A green and yellow banners draped along the eaves of the buildings to either side of the street. Soldiers stood interspersed throughout the carts.

How could I have thought they would allow it to be anything else?

"This is what you wanted to see?" Boda said, walking beside me down the market. "The fruit doesn't even look ripe. The robes are gray, green, or yellow."

"It used to be more. That's what my mother used to say," Taku said with a genuine note of sadness.

"I came here when I was a kid," Yelan said. "You couldn't walk through sideways. Everyone was bartering this for that. I met a kamani man who could make small animals with colored glass."

A soldier glanced our way with more focus than I cared for, so I hooked my arm through Yelan's and pulled her to the nearest cart. She didn't question it for a moment.

"Spiced nuts, darling. Your father would love some," she said.

The vendor, a white-haired Tomakan woman, perked up at Yelan's comments. Her robes were worn and the smile on her face struggled with exhaustion. "Best spiced nuts in the city."

Three rows of small burlap bags lined the top of the cart, none of which were quite full.

"How much for a bag, Auntie?" I asked.

The woman looked from me to the nearest soldier with an uneasy glance. "It would be proper to call me 'ma'am.'"

"Apologies for my son," Yelan said. "His father appreciates some things that should remain in the past."

The vendor nodded. "Young people have to learn to be more thoughtful of their surroundings," she said. "Three coppers for a bag, five for two."

"We'll take two, ma'am," I said, pulling five reddish coins from the pouch promised to Dalik.

Her smile returned in full, and she passed me the bags with a pat on my hand. "Thank you, young man. Mind your mother now."

By the time we turned away from the cart, the soldier had turned his focus elsewhere. We caught up with Boda and Taku, and I pulled a nola nut from one of the bags.

The nut crunched with a satisfying pop, but the flesh turned into a flavorless mess in my mouth.

Taku chuckled when he saw my expression. "Spice means something a bit different nowadays. The Gousht prefer to taste the thing itself, or so they say. Meat should taste like meat."

"And a nola nut should taste like bark?"

He grabbed the bag from me and popped one in his mouth. "It's not bad if you aren't expecting actual spice."

For the thousandth time, I wondered how these people had conquered us. They couldn't even handle a chili flake.

———————

Tan Tila Square stood far and apart from all other city squares I had seen in my life. Where others centered around a wooden stage in the middle of a thoroughfare, Tan Tila had no stage. Instead, levels of stone had been called from the earth in a semicircle clearing amongst a cluster of buildings. The stone seating cascaded down to a focal point, from which a speaker could address the crowd.

Furthermore, Colian hosted five town squares. One would have never been adequate for the city.

"The Stone City has something similar, but the stonework is much more ornate," Yelan said as if seeing the awe in my thoughts.

"If we could do this, why doesn't every city look like this?" I asked.

"That is a question we could speak on for days," she said. "Safe to say there are many reasons, culture being one of them and isolation being another. We may be two hundred turns removed from the blood of the Hundred Turn War, but people largely kept to their nations.

"Colian was different. This port connected Renêqua to the rest of the continent. You had to have noticed this isn't a strictly Tomakan city. People from all over Ennea settled here. They brought their cultures, ideas, and most significantly, their resources with them."

A long-since-dulled pain flared. I knew so little of my people and my land. Whatever opportunity I would have had to explore it unencumbered had been stolen from me. The stories I could have learned. The memories I could have made. Gone.

"You see her?" I asked Taku.

"Not yet," he said. "Sokan hasn't reached her peak yet. Corelina still has time."

A smattering of people sat on the tiered levels of stone, while others walked through the square as if it was commonplace. A woman seated in the first row held a book in her hands, the title on the spine in Gousht.

"Spread out. We look out of place standing like this," I said. "Keep Taku in your eyeline. He'll let us know when our contact has arrived."

"How? Am I supposed to shout when the rebel leader shows up?"

"How about you make eye contact and gesture? Some things are simple." I met his eyes and gestured towards the woman with the Gousht book with two fingers. "Just remember, your brother is with our friends by the docks. Nothing tricky."

His lips curled into the beginnings of a snarl before he nodded and found a place to sit along the first level.

Sokan rose as we waited. I picked at the bag of bland roasted nuts. Every few breaths, I looked towards Taku, trying to position myself as to not make it obvious. Occasionally, he caught my gaze and subtly shook his head.

If Corelina didn't come, we could still scout the city as best as we could. Whatever knowledge we could earn would help, but the council would never allow any plan to move forward in Colian without the local rebellion.

Not that I disagreed. Our two hundred warriors would barely fill the market.

A blur of movement in my peripheral vision caught my attention. I turned to find Taku waving as openly as he dared towards one of the several streets funneling in and out of the square. A woman of her middle turns with loose black curls and a cedar-brown complexion leaned against a clay brick wall.

As she stood there, shadows draped over half her face. She returned my stare. Fear did not exist for this woman. From her posture to the straight line of her lips, she had the gaze of a warrior looking over her battlefield.

This is a leader, I thought. *This is the type of person to follow into battle.*

It took all my patience not to bound down the stone tiers and rush to Corelina. I took a moment to make eye contact with Boda and Yelan before walking towards the inlet.

A soldier walked through the square between Corelina and I as I made my way towards her. This was a horrible meeting place.

In addition to the soldiers who routinely crossed the square, at least three others posted up around the clearing.

The others filtered towards the same street; however, when I got close enough for words, Corelina turned away without saying a thing. She walked at pace with the fastest of the foot traffic—not so quickly as to attract attention, but quick enough to pass most people on the street.

"Is she running?" Boda asked at my side.

"Does it look like she's running?" I asked, trying to calm my own worries.

"We were supposed to meet her at the square," he said. "Where is she taking us? How do we know this isn't an ambush? We are relying on the word of a stranger and the honor of a smuggler, chasing after a woman who couldn't bother to say a word."

"If you're scared, leave. We can connect back at the tannery."

"Fuck you. Don't act like this isn't suspicious."

Corelina took a sharp turn down an alley.

"We are a rebel uprising scouting a potential target Everything is suspicious, and it should be. Just keep your eyes open."

One alley turned into another then another before ending at a flat stone wall. The lack of brick or stonework made it clear—a dancer had called it from the earth. Yelan gave me a look that confirmed my suspicion.

Corelina placed her hand on the wall where it met the clay brick of the next building. A hidden door folded into the flat stone, creating an opening.

"In," she said, much more as a command than an invitation. Then she was gone.

"This is definitely an ambush," Boda said.

"This is what we came for." Yelan walked to the entrance, but stopped for a moment to run her hands along the opening. "Ingenious."

"Taku, you're next," I said.

He hesitated, staring into the dark room on the other side of the hidden entrance then back to the alley as if he expected to see someone behind us.

I tried to temper my suspicions. Taku had done all we had asked of him.

"None of this is fair," he grumbled before following Yelan through the entrance.

When I got close enough to see what Yelan had seen, I couldn't help but agree. They had molded a single flat piece of stone to the frame of the door so that it created a seamless facade. Before I crossed into the dark building beyond, I turned back to Boda. "You don't have to come."

He flashed a rude gesture then stepped through the threshold.

It took a moment for my eyes to adjust to the low light of the room—a food cellar. It smelled of meat and dried fruit. Salt clung to the air. My belly grumbled as soon as I set my sight on a crate of apples amongst similar collections of root vegetables.

Many a night, I had danced in the forest beyond Nomar with Shay and reached out to the bare apple trees, helping them to bud, flower, and form a ripe red fruit. When I couldn't find the song, Shay taunted me, but only because I knew how much she enjoyed apples.

The produce looked perfect sitting in the crates. Which, in addition to the abundance of food, spoke to a certain amount of wealth.

These aren't the food stores of an underground rebellion. I gripped the hilt of my knife through my robes to feel the comfort of it.

"This way," Corelina said from another doorway leading out of the cellar.

Several armed warriors waited in the next room, but none of them had drawn their weapons. From the wood-slatted walls, to the floorboards, to the simple but well-crafted table in the middle of the room, everything about this building spoke of wealth.

Corelina sat in the chair at the far side of the table, looking at us without a word.

"Yelan?" I gestured for the two of us to sit.

"What, no hospitality for the rest of us?" Boda said without any care or restraint for the volume of his voice.

"No more. Not here," I said before taking my seat.

Corelina had brought six of her warriors with her. At least one was a shadow dancer, but they were too close together to tell which. She waited with impeccable posture and held my gaze.

"I am Kaylo, and this is Yelan. It is a pleasure to meet you." I reached across the table in a formal greeting, but she did not reach back.

"I know who you are. I know the stories, Hero of Anilace," she said, and for the first time her voice took on emotion—disdain.

"We are not here to cause any problems for you," Yelan said as I sat back trying to measure what I had done to this woman.

Is it because I am a thief? I wondered.

"We're all rebels here. All we do is cause problems," Corelina said.

"The Uprising has been growing. We have some resources. If your rebellion is as well organized as your safehouse..." I gestured to our surroundings. "We could help each other."

"I took this meeting because I knew Taku's sister. Her death was a tragedy, and I owe her kin this much. But I don't know you, and I don't make decisions based on widely exaggerated tales."

After turns of being treated as a leader by some and The Mother's chosen by others, her apathy towards the stories about me made my muscles relax.

"Thank you," I said, more boisterous than necessary. "The stories get most of the details wrong anyway. But this isn't about me. This is about what we can do for our people."

"Our people?" Her eyebrows raised in the first sign of emotion on her face. "My people are the people of this city. They are my concern."

"We can't fight the Gousht in isolation," Yelan said.

"Are you volunteering my people for slaughter so you can move your plans along?"

"Get off it, lady," Boda said. "If this house says anything about you, you haven't been one of 'the people' in quite some time. The Gousht don't let people keep wealth like this without something in return."

The warrior closest to Boda rounded on him, and Boda pulled out his knife.

"Stop it!" Corelina shouted. "Stand down, Kernac."

The warrior stepped back into position with his back pressed against the wall, but it took a moment for Boda to lower his knife.

"Is this the type of warrior you have to offer me?" Corelina asked.

"Boda is a person of many faults, but I will never question his purpose in this fight," I said. "I do, however, have some questions about you. From what I've seen of the city, this food could go a long way."

"Let's just say we have benefactors who remember the way things used to be." She leaned her elbows on the table, breaking her perfect posture. "Rebellions need resources."

"That's exactly what we came to offer—weapons. We have plenty of metal workers amongst our ranks. If we worked together, this city could be free. Isn't that what you want?" I leaned forward, matching her.

Corelina smiled. Despite the context, she had a pretty smile. "Free? Being caught in a battleground isn't freedom. Do you even have enough turns to think towards the future? This isn't a question of potential. It's a question of leadership."

A slow hum that ran in opposition to the flow of The Song echoing from Yelan grew closer. Echoes of stolen spirits occupied every corner of this sprawling city. But this particular one continued to creep closer.

"If we were to consider—" Corelina started.

I pushed myself up from the chair, and several of Corelina's guards reached for their weapons as I did. "Do you have any crystals in this house? Any warriors carrying them?"

"What are you talking about?" Corelina's strict posture and expression made way for her confusion.

"They are coming," I said to Yelan.

An echo's crescendo stopped. In its place, a rattling chaos clattered beneath our feet. I found the translucent thread binding the spirit to its crystal and took it for myself. The Mountain's rage became a tempest within my gut. My knees nearly buckled with it. I was usually better prepared for the pain.

"What is happening?" Corelina demanded. All her guards held their weapons, waiting for her orders.

"They were going to bring the building down," I said through strained teeth.

"How do you know?" Corelina turned to her warriors without waiting for answers. "Check the streets."

No one hesitated to follow her orders. Boots thudded against the floorboards as the warriors rushed out of the room. A second echo of The Mountain surged to life, and I took the second spirit as well.

"Soldiers in the front!" a warrior called out.

"More in the alley!" another warrior yelled.

"What have you brought to my door?" Corelina grabbed the shoulder of my robes roughly. "This is the help you offer?"

"I implicitly trust my warriors." I didn't dare look in Taku's direction.

It would have put us on weak ground to be at odds in front of Corelina. I stood up as straight as I could with the spirits in my belly and her grip on my robes. "Can you say the same for yours? Your benefactor? The smugglers who arranged this meeting?"

"If it weren't for this young man, you would be buried under rubble right now." Yelan stepped towards us. "You have to have some way out."

"Firestarter bombs!" came a call from the front of the house.

Glass shattered. Boots pounded against floorboards. A pop broke the world around me, and everything went quiet save the ringing in my ears.

As the force knocked me to the ground with the others, a strange thought occurred to me. I couldn't help but wonder how much firestarter they would need to do this much damage.

CHAPTER THIRTY-ONE
KAYLO'S STORY

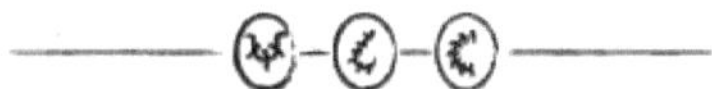

STONE CRASHED TO THE ground and broke the floorboards, revealing the dirt beneath us. Planks of burning wood fell from the ceiling, filling the destroyed room with a dozen flickering fires trying to shine through the dust and debris.

At least Liara didn't come. The thought came calm and gentle.

A layer of wreckage covered me like a rough blanket, which I lay curled beneath, coughing on the foul air. Everything hurt, but nothing specific hurt more than the whole. The sound of the explosion rang in my ears. Despite it all, I kept hold of the stolen spirits.

When I pushed my way through the wreckage, I found Corelina's dead eyes staring at me. Blood rushed from a large gash below her hairline. Whether this wound or another had killed her, I couldn't tell.

I was an observer in the middle of a battleground that bloomed around me out of nowhere. It felt separate from me. Distant. The closest thing to a tangible feeling I could name was relief.

I hadn't died.

"Kaylo," a desperate voice called from behind me.

Horror replaced my relief. Yelan lay on the jagged remains of the floor, a large chunk of the stone pinning her legs to the ground. "You have to get the survivors and move."

"I can get you out."

"There's no time! Go!"

Her echo pushed through the ringing as she slammed her fist on the ground. A rough pillar of stone rose from the ground to support the burning ceiling above us.

I hadn't noticed them before. Several pillars jutted from the dirt to anchor the pieces of the broken ceiling in place. She was the only reason the lot of us hadn't been crushed to death.

"Kaylo?" The croaking voice unmistakably belonged to Boda.

"I have a fragment of The Mountain. I can get you out of here." I stared at Yelan with desperation.

"My legs are crushed. I'm not making it out. Now, go!" She slammed her fist down again, sending another pillar up from the ground.

The fire was spreading. The smoke continued to fill the chamber.

Sweat gathered on Yelan's forehead. She had a couple of cuts and scrapes, but she looked the same. Nothing about her was dying, but her blood painted the bottom of the stone pinning her legs to the ground.

"I'm sorry," I said, turning to search for Boda.

Someone scurried towards the entrance we had come through. One of Corelina's warriors.

"Boda!"

"Here." His voice was weak.

As I worked my way to him, he pried his upper body loose. However, a beam weighed down his legs. I pulled on the anger of The Mountain fragments within me and shifted the ground beneath him to create a gap large enough for him to escape.

"Take my hand, we are getting out of here." I grabbed him before he could fight me like he always did, and pulled.

"This was a shitty plan," he said as he made his way to his feet.

"Save the commentary for later. We still have to escape the squadron of soldiers outside."

The broken floorboards and rubble created an unsteady path, but we pushed our way through the cellar. Creaks called down from the ceiling. Ash fell like snowflakes warning of a blizzard.

"Hurry!" Yelan called from her promised grave.

Sounds of clanging metal carried through the open hatch to the alley. What remained of Corelina's warriors had made their way from the crumbling building.

How did they know? With all the safety protocols Corelina went through, how did they find us?

The metal clanging ceased before we made it to the hatch. Then I caught my first view of the alley, and I had my answer. A soldier pressed Taku against a wall while the rebels lay dead on the street.

A trickle of blood ran down Taku's cheek, but he had no other injuries.

Of all the Enneans who escaped the collapsed basement, they spared Taku. For all his intimidating size, they allowed him to live.

Hylīane had been right. This giant of a traitor hadn't only sold us out—he had given up the rebels at the same time. He had turned on his blood, and it would be the last thing he did.

A crash rang out as the ceiling gave way in the meeting room and a cloud of debris plumed from the open door. Yelan's echo fell silent.

"Yelan!" Boda pushed towards the wreckage we had left behind, but I grabbed him firmly.

"Can you fight?" I asked.

He looked from me to the collapsed meeting room to the rear exit of the cellar. "There are at least twenty soldiers out there."

"I didn't ask about them. Can you fight?" After everything I had been through with this boy, I refused to lose him to the fucking Gousht.

"My shoulder's a bit messed up, but I can fight."

"Then hold on." I knelt and allowed myself to sink into the rage of the spirit fragments within me. Their fury reached through the soil and silt into the bedrock beneath the city. Millions of tiny particles fed the rhythm within the echo.

Much like Yelan had, I slammed my fists into the ground. Stone and sediment in the earth heated far beyond what would be possible without The Song. The particles solidified into rough pillars beneath my fists. I used The Mountain to shift the pressure around each pillar and lift them from the ground. They shot up and slammed into the stone ceiling of the cellar, sending debris falling down around us.

"What in The Mists?!" Boda yelled.

I didn't have Yelan's grace and experience with The Mountain, but I didn't need grace for this—just brute force.

The stone facade lining the back of the building sang within the bastardized Song.

"Be ready," I said.

The first syllable of Boda's question was cut off by a thunderous clap as I cracked the facade from the rest of the building. The rear of the structure swayed like a threat. It only took a subtle shift in the foundation. The back wall collapsed into the alleyway in a series of crashes and a monstrous thud.

Screams were broken in half. Some shrieks lingered in the air, but I paid them no mind.

A cloud of dust blotted out the world beyond the fallen wall. Any number of soldiers might have survived, waiting for us in the dust. I could only hope that Taku lay under the rubble. Getting Boda out was more important for now.

"Move!" I grabbed Boda and charged into the dust.

Stone and bodies littered the ground. I lost my footing several times, but pushed forward regardless, trying not to breathe in the blood and debris.

A shadow swayed towards me. I didn't have time to worry about who it might be. With my father's knife in hand, I rushed the figure and grabbed its clothing. The feel of padded armor between my fingers was all I needed. I plunged my knife into the soldier's gut and continued to push through the debris.

Near the edge of the dust cloud, the mouth of the alleyway took form with a street running perpendicular. If we could make it to a thoroughfare, Boda and I could blend in. We could escape this mess.

The noise of crashing stone sounded off at intermittent intervals. The structure would not last. The bodies, the stores of food, and whatever weapons the rebellion had hidden away would be buried beneath the rubble.

We should have never come. I was wrong to have pushed for this. Yelan should be back at the encampment instead of buried under some building in a strange city.

Before I had the chance to let my self-pity get the better of me, an archer in the Emperor's green dashed into the cross street. She drew her bowstring and aimed at my chest. The distance between us was too great. The arrow would rip through me before I took two steps. I dove for the ground, and bits of rock in the street cut at my robes as the arrow soared overhead.

Blood was owed. Pain be damned.

I gathered my feet below me as quickly as I could and charged the soldier. She had notched another arrow, but before she could properly draw the bow, I drove my shoulder into her torso.

She looked up at me, straining for breath. This pale, slender-faced woman didn't know me. I had no name for her. Yet, for all our anonymity, she had killed Yelan. Not with an arrow. Not with any orders. But with the colors she wore.

I lifted a nearby rock and bashed her face in. Bones broke with the first blow. They imploded with the second. By the fourth strike, she had become a mess of blood and viscera.

"Boda, stow your knife!" I shouted, still straddling the soldier. "We need to find the others and get out of here."

He didn't respond. The fool had run off without me. We needed to stick together.

"Boda!" I turned around.

The boy lay at the edge of the dust cloud. An arrow protruded from his chest. He wasn't moving.

"No," I said, even as the shock stole the air from my lungs.

That arrow had been meant for me. It didn't belong to him.

I raised the rock once again to punish his murderer, but I hadn't left enough of her to punish.

With all the strength left in my body, I threw the bloody rock against the nearest building and screamed.

Somewhere in my mind, I knew I had to move quickly, but I couldn't. I stumbled to Boda's side. "Get up," I said, yanking his lifeless arm. "You have to get up."

Blood formed a growing circle in the fabric around his wound. A layer of dust covered his face, and I began to wipe it away. Much of it caught in the crevices of his scars.

I pulled him onto my lap, his dead gaze staring into the peak of the sky.

"Say something." I shook his body. "You must have something insulting to say. Look at how badly I fucked up."

His head lilted to the side, giving me a clearer view of his uninjured eye. For a moment, he turned into Shay—a burn across the side of her face, chest bloody, dying while I couldn't do anything to stop it.

"Don't go. We can still make it out."

Several echoes of trapped spirits made their way closer as I held him.

I shook my head, muttering the word 'no' in repetition. When it mattered, The Thief's curse couldn't do anything to save Boda. None of my long-winded speeches about liberating our people could help. I couldn't do a thing.

In less than four turns, I had gotten his brother killed, destroyed his home with Zusa, and taken away one of his eyes before stealing the rest of his life.

Buzzing noises wrapped around oddly syncopated rhythms began to scream louder and louder, announcing more soldiers on their way.

I wiped a streak of blood from his lips with the sleeve of my robe, only managing to smear the blood across his cheek.

If I had any chance of escaping, I had to leave him here. But the couta couldn't have his body. It belonged to The Mother.

With a scream, I pulled on the two fragments of The Mountain within me and slammed my fists on the ground. Pressure compacted dirt below the surface, creating air pockets. The ground beneath Boda dimpled. I scrambled away as Boda fell into the new pit in the middle of the street.

"Blessed Mother." I placed three fingers on the dirt and brought them to my lips. "Hold Boda tightly."

I made a series of sweeping gestures and the pit walls fell inward, burying Boda in The Mother's embrace.

A commotion of jumbling weapons and echoes grew far too close. When I turned, they were forty paces away.

"One last time," I promised The Mountain as I called on the echoes. A slab of stone rose from the ground, blocking off the soldiers' path. It would not stop them forever, but it would give me time to get away.

"I will find a way to free you, but not today," I said, letting go of the spirits and sending them back to their crystal cages.

The streets were largely empty. The chaos of a building collapse and roaming soldiers would have been enough to send most common folk indoors. With my father's knife stowed, I rushed through the streets searching for a clothing vendor.

As I ran, I pictured Taku. He had been nervous before heading into the cellar. I had written it off. Who wouldn't have been nervous in that situation?

I had been a fool.

Yelan and Boda were gone, but I could still find the others. There was still one more blood banner amongst them.

Every street I turned down reminded me of the last, but it didn't take long to find an open store front. The man behind the counter looked at me aghast, but once he saw my coin purse, he didn't care much about why I was caked in dust and wearing bloody robes.

CHAPTER THIRTY-TWO
KAYLO'S STORY

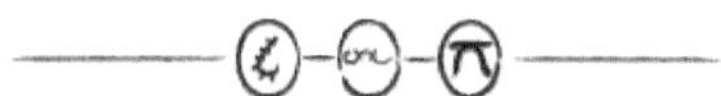

THE BLOOD NESTLED IN the wrinkles of my knuckles refused to flake away no matter how much I rubbed at it. The docks were too busy for anyone to notice or care about blood-stained hands, but I continued to rub at them regardless.

Apparently, business at the docks didn't shut down because of unpleasantness in the southern part of the city. Ennean laborers used pulleys to hoist crates on and off immense ships as soldiers stood by, watching with some variation of the same smug look.

I had to find the others. They had a blood banner amongst their ranks and didn't even know it—unless he had already turned them in.

Scores of screams emanated from the hulls of several ships loaded with caged spirits. Every fourth soldier wore a crystal around their neck or buried in their uniforms. The wailing created a torrent of noise that I would have shut out, but I needed to find Annit's echo

I had killed Boda and Yelan and the whole fucking Colian resistance movement. The least I could do was return the others back to the encampment safely.

But for the context, the docks would have been an awe-inspiring sight. Forgetting the cargo brought to and fro, the masts of these ships reached higher into the sky than I could have imagined. Waves lapped against their hulls with barely any effect.

After fifteen turns of Gousht incompetence, I finally understood how they had conquered us. They had built so much of their empire in service of war. The soldiers weren't people sailing off to battle. They were resources. They moved ships, swung blades, and carried out their orders. In some ways, they were tools of their Emperor as much as we were.

A man who looked like Wal but a dozen turns older disembarked from a ship carrying a crate.

If I didn't find them soon, forced labor at the docks would be the gentlest of their fates. I fought through the noise of spirits cursing The Waking, peering into the heavy fog of noise searching for a single droplet. The spirits' ire drilled into my skull as I let my walls down to sift through the clamor.

A soldier with deep-set wrinkles glared at me.

No matter the pain, I had to fix my face, straighten my gait, and push through it. I bent down beside a pile of crates and hoisted one into the hands of a laborer returning for another load to stock in the vessel beside us. The Tomakan man twisted his face with a raised eyebrow before taking the crate from me and returning to the ship.

When I looked back, the older soldier had focused his attention elsewhere, and I joined a throng of Enneans walking the docks before he could find me again.

Then, in the gaps between the hectic cries of trapped spirits, a singular echo sang something closer to The Song. I kept myself from breaking through the crowd and darting towards the sound. Instead, I gently peeled away from the laborers who looked far more worn than I did, even after I had walked through the rubble of a collapsed building.

Annit's echo grew clearer as I walked away from the docks into the alleyways that separated the field of warehouses.

A group of Ennean children scattered as I turned one corner. Even in a

city teeming with soldiers, they managed to find moments of freedom—
of childhood.

Boda at thirteen flashed in front of my eyes. Waves of red hair rolled
over his scalp. Back then, he had been aggressive and standoffish. But he
laughed with his brother and greedily took seconds from the pot when
there was enough. He had smiled when he practiced with his sword, not
the rageful smile of a soon-to-be-man who wanted to kill his own grief.
No, he had smiled with the thrill of the adventure he hadn't completely
understood.

"I'm sorry, Niven. I failed."

I was done losing people today. The alleyways were tight, designed
to house as much storage on as little land as possible. A single fire would
jump from one warehouse to another with ease.

If it weren't for the innocent Enneans who would suffer for it, I would
have sparked a flame and watched it all crumble.

Annit's echo started to overpower the mess of trapped spirits. One
final turn, and I found myself standing in front of a pair of chained
warehouse doors.

Intalik had done it. He had turned them in.

I had a white-knuckle grip on the hilt of my father's knife but no one
to plunge it into. Not yet.

Going in the warehouse might mean dying or being caught. It might
mean never seeing Liara again. It would definitely mean blood. Whether
it was a smart idea or not, I had to find them.

The chain had enough give to slip in. At least I had that much luck on
my side.

"Blessed Mother," I said. "Guide my friends to safety."

Pulling the door as far as the slack would allow, I pushed myself
through. The ironoak door squeezed me against the frame. The gap
hugged my shoulders then caught my hip before it relented.

When I finally wriggled through, I found myself surrounded by dimly lit crates. A row of dust-crusted windows lined the top of the outer warehouse wall. A smattering of echoes reverberated through the building, but nothing so strong or clear as Annit's.

He still had his spirit. In a city seemingly overrun with crystals, that had to mean something.

The rows of crates kept me from charging directly towards my friends, which was for the best. I wouldn't help anyone if I got myself caught as well.

With every turn, I expected to hear the murmuring of soldiers or Wal getting himself in trouble with his big mouth. Instead, I couldn't hear anything.

My pulse thumped in my neck as if the blood wanted to jump out of its own accord. All the reasons for quiet became horrible images in my head. My friends bound and gagged. Broken and bloody. All dead, save the dancer, because the Gousht didn't waste spirits.

Annit's echo grew until its familiar cadence became as clear as a cloudless sky.

Around the corner, they all stood in a circle, leaning against crates. No Gousht. No weapons drawn.

"What in the name of The Blessed fucking Mother?" I asked.

Their heads jumped in my direction. Wal nearly tumbled over himself pulling his knife from his robe.

Intalik threw his arms wide. "Friend! Where are the others?"

The gall of this blood banner bastard. With three long strides, I threw my shoulder into him. His back and shoulders cracked into a crate behind him, and we both hit the swept dirt floor below. I pulled my father's knife back to plunge it into the soft parts of this traitor, but several hands caught me and dragged me backwards.

"He's a blood banner just like his brother!" I screamed.

Annit wrapped his heavy arms around me from behind. We were of a similar height, but he had turns of muscle on his frame. "Calm down. Your shouts will make this worse for all of us."

"Where are the others?" Wal asked.

"Where's my brother?" Intalik still lay on the ground with a ridiculous, confused look painted on his face.

"Dead. They're all dead. Especially that blood banner brother of yours." I spat on the ground, unable to do much more from Annit's grip.

"Dead?! Blood banner?!" Intalik's voice quivered. "Fuck you. Where is my brother?"

"Wal, take Intalik away," Talise said, the only one not in some level of heightened emotion. "Watch him. Keep him safe."

"Where am I supposed to take him? If Kaylo says he's a blood banner, might as well bury him here."

"We don't know anything right now," Annit said, his voice loud in my ear.

"I know exactly what he is." I strained to get free, to no avail.

"You know nothing!" Intalik yelled, beginning to cry.

"We can't have them screaming," Talise said. "Now go. And he better be safe with you."

Wal stowed his blade and helped Intalik up roughly before guiding him around a set of crates.

"If I let you go, will you calm down long enough to tell us what's going on?"

At a simple nod, Annit released me.

"The soldiers around the docks doubled in force about an hour ago." Talise sat down as an invitation for me to do the same. I reluctantly did. "We thought it might be a good idea to hunker down. Looks like we were right."

"It was a trap," I said. "We made it to the safehouse only for the couta to bring it down on our heads. Taku was the only one who made it out. The soldiers had him waiting outside without a scratch on him before I brought a ton of rock crashing down on them."

"The resistance?" Annit asked.

"Everyone there died. Whoever their benefactor was is as good as dead too," I said, recalling how blood welled up in one of Corelina's eyes as she stared lifelessly at me. "Boda and I made it through, but..."

"They captured him?" Talise asked.

I shook my head, and that would have been enough for them to understand that Boda had died, but it wouldn't have been the truth of it. "Exactly like you said, Talise. I keep getting other people killed. My family, the Jani, Zusa, Sionia, Acta, and now Boda."

"That's not what I said—"

"No, you were right," I said. "I'm a fucking curse."

"Enough." Annit's voice held far more command than volume. "Self-pity and blame won't get us out of this. We need to get back to the encampment and regroup. Intalik too."

"But—"

"All you have is a guess, and that isn't proof." The battle in Annit's eyes that appeared in certain moments roared to life. "We'll keep a watch on him, but no one is killing that boy. Not yet."

As we walked south towards the tannery, people meandered the streets much as they had before a building collapsed on a group of rebels and a regiment of Gousht soldiers. I had thought there was something special about the docks that kept that part of the city running after the incident. But watching people's faces as they went about their day, I would have been surprised if they knew anything had happened.

An errand boy with a satchel strapped over his shoulder raced past us.

The couta had such control over this city, they could kill the resistance and people would tend to their daily chores. The shopkeepers, the dock workers, the hired help, all had too much to contend with in their lives to think about rebellion. Sure, most still spoke in common tongue and wore their hair in traditional styles, but that was lacquer on the surface. This wasn't Colian anymore. It belonged to the Emperor.

I already had several reasons to want to open Intalik's neck, but this sham of a city only infuriated me more.

Wal placed a hand on my back. "Don't worry. We can figure out how to make them pay after we get back. They will bleed for what they did."

I nodded. Behind the thin veneer of smiles and sarcasm, Wal was as bloodthirsty as any of us. Occasionally, I would catch him speaking to Adéan when he thought he was alone.

Maybe we were wrong to hide our rage away instead of unleashing it. We lived in the relative safety of our encampment. We bashed our heads against their infinite numbers and buried our dead afterwards.

Maybe I should have burned it all down when I'd had the chance. Let the spark crawl from warehouse to warehouse and consume. Damn the consequences.

Enneans would have died, but so what? They were already ghosts of themselves. This was all about resources for the Gousht anyway. If we destroyed what they were after, maybe they would finally fuck off

The sign for the tannery swayed slightly with the wind.

When we got back to the encampment, the council and Hylíane would urge caution. That would be the wrong reaction. We needed to become bolder, not more hesitant.

We pushed our way through the front door of the tannery and three blades were unsheathed, not to mention the crossbow pointed between my eyes.

Talise grabbed the one nearest to her and threw him against the wall with enough violence to jolt the sword from his hand.

A throwing axe crashed into the wood next to her head. "Let him go," Dalik said with force, not volume.

She released the gangly man, who picked up his sword and stepped back. The glare he mustered looked less intimidating given his shaky breathing.

"I told you not to make trouble for me, didn't I?" Dalik asked.

"I heard it," the woman with the crossbow said.

"When you go around knocking buildings down, the Gousht get

anxious. Anxious soldiers look a little harder at missing shipments and folks lingering outside the city limits." Dalik drew another throwing axe from behind his back. He ran a finger over its edge. "That gets in the way of my business."

"Fuck your business. Our friends died," Wal said.

"And while you do have my condolences, I don't care. You were cargo. I got you into the city. That was my job. Your job was to not get noticed and not die. You fucked up, not me."

"They're saying Taku was a blood banner. Tell them he wasn't," Intalik blurted out after keeping quiet for most of the walk.

"You people keep telling me irrelevant things like I am supposed to care. Why?" Dalik threw his hands back in an exaggerated gesture.

"Open the passage, and we'll be out of your city—far, far away," I said.

"That wasn't the deal."

"The way I see it, you have three options," Annit said. "You can turn us in. Maybe the Gousht will give you a pat on the back, but that won't last when we tell them of your involvement in the Uprising. Collaborators don't last."

"We ain't collaborators," the gangly man said.

"You could try to kill us. You have the blades and the numbers, but we have The Song. Chances are you won't get out of that clean— definitely won't get out of that quiet. Soldiers won't miss a fire and sword fight after everything that went down today."

"Let me guess. My last option is to let you go, right?" Dalik smiled. "You don't think I have soldiers on my payroll? I can sell them any story I need to."

"You can try," I said. "Did you know a full regiment of soldiers died today? Do you think you'll be able to sell your stories, or will the commanders be looking to clean house? You're an annoyance at the moment. When a unit of Gousht go dark and you were involved, will the right people be willing to look the other way?"

Dalik pointed his axe in my direction. "You think you're smart, but you still don't understand. Neither did the rebels you got killed. The Gousht have won. I'm willing to make some coin off your losing game as long as I stay clean, but that doesn't mean I can't see you have no hope."

"Fuck you!" Wal shouted.

"Shh." Dalik signaled for Wal to be quiet. "You'll take away my options if you draw attention."

"What is it going to be?" Talise asked, prying his axe from the wall with a simple motion.

"Sadly, I think you're right. I don't have any great choices, but I know when to cut my losses and move on. Give me the coin and get out of here. Don't ever contact me again. My tunnels are cut off to you."

I tossed the coin purse to Dalik.

He waved his hand, and his compatriots lowered their weapons. "If you decide to test my forgiveness and make your way into my tunnels again, I won't have as many options. I will send every last spirit you travel with into The Mist."

"I appreciate your honesty," I said, gesturing for Annit to head towards the back room that concealed the tunnel's entrance.

Wal followed close behind. "This city sucks anyway."

"He's much more pleasant usually," I said.

"No, he isn't." Talise grabbed Intalik's collar and ushered him through the doorway.

"If you keep playing the savior, more will die," Dalik said. "The Gousht have dealt with your ilk with every conquest."

"You don't think they've dealt with smugglers before? This doesn't end well for either of us if they get their way. It won't matter how many coins you hoard." I walked into the back room and continued into the tunnel after the others.

CHAPTER THIRTY-THREE
CURRENT DAY ENNEA

Tayen gripped the arrow shaft and wiggled it from side to side, opening the gash in the tree a little wider. The wood reluctantly released the arrow as she jerked back one last time. She inspected the metal arrowhead before dropping the bolt onto a pile of arrows she had collected.

When she said she was willing to do anything for the rebellion, she thought she had signed herself up for battle, not clearing arrows from the practice range.

She moved to the next arrow, and the shaft cracked as soon as she put the slightest pressure on it. The fissure ran the full length of the wood. She ripped the broken shaft from the tree and threw it to the pile.

Over the last turn, she had killed, fought, bled, and trained every day. For what? To clean up after rebels?

She snatched a fallen branch from the ground and swung it with all her might at the nearest ironoak. The impact crawled up the branch and traversed through Tayen's arms. The wood splintered, and a chunk flew off into the foliage.

"I remember that anger," a voice called out from behind Tayen.

She spun around to find Liara several paces away with her arms crossed. They had been briefly introduced, before Tayen's group had been rushed off to find their quarters. Tayen hadn't had the opportunity to truly size Liara up.

The commander was more petite than the fierce warrior Kaylo had described. Tayen always imagined her features would be harsher. His stories painted her as direct, someone who never avoided confrontation. But this woman had a roundness to her cheeks that made her seem pleasant.

"Tayen, right?" Liara closed the gap with a few steps. "I wanted to get to know the girl who brought Kaylo out of hiding."

"Kaylo makes his own choices."

"I didn't mean any offense," Liara said. "Being the commander means I have to be curious. I have to know my warriors—their skillsets, temperaments, motives. The battlefield can be a hard thing to predict, especially without knowing all the factors."

"Is that the best you could come up with?"

One of Liara's eyebrows arched just as Kaylo had described in his stories. "Excuse me? If you plan to serve the Uprising, you need to learn how to speak to your commander."

"You don't sneak up on all your new recruits in the middle of grunt work to ask them what their favorite color is. The only reason you are here is because of Kaylo. Otherwise, you wouldn't have remembered my name."

"Are you sure you aren't his daughter?"

Tayen felt her muscles seize in unison. The Song wailed like the promise of a thousand tiny shadows. "I am my parents' daughter through and through, Commander. What is it I can help you with?"

In all her imaginings of what the Uprising would be, she hadn't pictured an interrogation by the commander about her kana. People always made everything about Kaylo. It wasn't his fault, but it was irritating.

"You're right. I'm sorry, Tayen. I approached this conversation poorly," Liara said, and the stiffness abandoned her posture. "I've spent thirteen turns wondering if Kaylo had survived, then he showed up with you, acting like a protective parent. Curiosity won?"

"He told me about you. Did you really threaten to tell everyone he was a spirit thief if he didn't help you rescue Tomi?"

Liara smiled a tight, high smile, holding tension in the narrowness of her eyes. "Not my proudest moment."

"And you broke into Oakheart for him?"

"He's told you quite a bit, hasn't he?"

"So he's been telling the truth. Everything that he went through. It's true?"

Liara walked over to the nearest arrow protruding from an ironoak and began to unwedge it from the wood. "His truth, to be sure. Most of his stories are probably dark and brooding, aren't they? But there were good times too. In between the blood, we built a family."

"Is that what the Uprising is for you? Family?" Tayen asked. "I'm not looking for a family. I am looking to fight for my home. Are you going to help me?"

"How old are you?"

"Old enough to do more than collect practice arrows?"

Liara chuckled. "Everyone does grunt work. It doesn't mean you won't fight. Don't be too eager to die, though. You have too much living in front of you."

There had been a time Tayen would have raged against the idea that her future still had meaning beyond the blood she owed. But that anger didn't bubble up in her gut like she expected.

"I'm not looking to die. I'm looking to make Ennea a place worth living in."

A smile spread across Liara's face—one that didn't have a second meaning. It was just a smile. She tossed the arrow she'd taken from the tree into the pile Tayen had started. "Me too. Report to Tomi tomorrow morning. I want to see what you can do with the shadows."

With that, she turned and headed back towards the encampment.

"Does that mean I can stop collecting arrows?" Tayen shouted after her.

"No," Liara called back, without turning around.

Kaylo led Nomi into the forest until the echoes from the encampment faded into nothingness. The superfluous noise would only be a distraction, and they had work to do.

"Set the crystals over there," Kaylo said.

As much and as often as he had protested people insisting he teach others, he had asked Nomi to accompany him. He knew things no one else could impart, things he hadn't been allowed to share with the spirit dancers in the Lost Nation.

"Losing a spirit—having it stolen away—isn't like being disarmed. A spirit isn't just some tool or weapon; it is a piece of you," Kaylo said. "You can walk through your clan's encampment and know exactly where to find your father. You have a sense of your surroundings that only The Balance can give you. Losing that would be like having your sight stripped from you. You could get by. You would go on. But your relationship with the world would be changed forever. You would be changed forever."

Even as he heard himself speaking, the ache of The Seed's absence throbbed. The forest—he had loved the forest once. He yearned for the feeling of being enveloped by the fullness of life, lingering in The Song. It had taken turns for the forest to not feel like a graveyard after it went silent.

"I am not the person I was before The Seed was stolen from me." Kaylo held up his hand to stave off Nomi's comments. "This is not about pity. This is about understanding the truth of what spirit crystals have done to our people. We didn't lose the war because we were outnumbered, nor because they had found a way to wield our spirits. We lost the war because too many of us were stripped of our senses. Our people didn't know how to walk the world without their spirits, much less fight an empire.

"I say that to make it perfectly clear. When we break a crystal and return a spirit back to its rightful place, we aren't only returning a weapon or a tool. We are returning someone's ability to sense the world around them fully. We are giving them hope."

Nomi inclined her head as if to ask permission to finally speak. "What does that have to do with me? I'm not charging into battle or raiding caravans for crystals anytime soon."

"I think you underestimate the hour. Your father and the rest of the elders have committed their swords when the Uprising calls. That call is going to come soon, and you will have a choice. You don't have to choose now, but you should be ready when the question comes."

"So what is it you want from me now?" Nomi asked without affect.

Kaylo had to stop himself and listen to the girl. Too many people in his life had turned trauma into sarcasm and dark humor that a direct question felt like an attack.

"For now, I want you to learn how to free a spirit."

Nomi removed five crystals from the sack while Kaylo explained how to search for The Balance's echo hidden beneath the trapped spirit. As he explained, she searched. It trailed behind the trapped spirits' cries. Subtle faults in the mimicry gave it away.

"Do you hear it?"

It took time, but once Nomi knew what to look for, she found it.

Whether or not she intended to use her gift to fight, she attacked the new skill like a puzzle to unravel. She picked up the dull crimson crystal to the far end of the line and closed her eyes.

The Balance didn't sing with anger like The Flame did. It hadn't been stolen. This fragment of The Balance had been placed here with purpose.

Nomi opened her eyes and grinned with the left side of her lips. "I hear it."

The crystal shattered inward as if it were made of hollow glass. Sand poured through her hands to the ground, and a slight red aura escaped like dust in the wind.

"That was easy."

"Good, now try it again."

Nomi worked her way through three more, gaining speed and certainty with each new crystal.

As she reached for the fifth, a stone with a soft blue shifting beneath the surface, Kaylo stopped her. "Leave that one."

"Why? I need more practice."

"You seem to have it," he said. "I'll let Liara know that you are ready to head back with whatever messages she might have for your father."

Nomi twisted her gaze on Kaylo, making the same expression as when she encountered the first crystal. She was trying to solve him.

Oddly enough, of all the people who had tried to figure him out, Nomi might be able to. Those eyes saw deeper than they ought to.

"Go on. I'll follow right behind," Kaylo said.

She did as she was told, and when the trees cut her off from his view, Kaylo returned his attention to the lone crystal on the forest floor. The River sang like rapids thrashing against stone, and The Balance tracked behind.

The crystal was only five paces away. He could sense The Balance—hear her. He reached out to pull her from the stone. The mines had been much farther than five paces. There had been thousands of crystals beneath the surface.

He closed his eyes and pictured the translucent thread linking The Balance to The Mist. The more he grasped for it, the more elusive it felt.

Even five paces away, he couldn't do it.

There were other spirit dancers. The Uprising didn't need him.

He rushed forward and snatched the crystal, shattering it to dust immediately.

Back in the solitude of his tent, Kaylo listened to the echoes clamoring about the encampment. Most echoes sang through dancers, interlocking and creating an abstraction of The Song in its fullness. Some few echoes raged into the composition from their cages.

Spirit dancers needed to train, and some sacrifices would always be deemed necessary—even if those who sacrificed were never consulted.

Each refracted melody led to a singular presence within him. The Balance would always be there. He followed the broken Song into The Mist.

The same multitude of darkness welcomed him as it had a little more than a span past. He could get lost in the layers of it, but he hadn't the time to pick apart the scenery.

"Spirit! Spirit, you know I am here!" Kaylo's voice whined even through its volume. "I need your help. Balance, please."

A rush of shifting darkness swirled as if a non-existent wind scattered the overlapping clouds of black, and she appeared. Cloaked within her shadows, she loomed over him, waiting.

"I do not know how your connection to us works. If you're constantly with us and see all we see, then you know what I'm here to say," Kaylo said. "One of your other descendants helped me see you—understand what you tried to tell me all those turns ago.

"For every person the Gousht stole from me, Enneans have stolen countless more from you. You felt each loss. Every unkind word. Every banishment. Every last breath. The pain of it compounded by each new trespass.

"When the Gousht killed those I loved, I started a war." He took a deep breath, hearing his own words. "You aren't just a part of me. We are the same. We made the same mistakes."

Cloaked in shadows as she was, something about her stance shifted and softened.

"I'm not asking you to repent. All I am asking for is help. Help me destroy the crystals like I did at Oakheart." He straightened his back and focused on the shadows hiding her face from him. "I forgive you."

Time stretched as the silence layered amongst the shadows. The outline of The Balance's shoulders rose and fell as if she were breathing. The softness stiffened.

"Insolence." The words came as a series of rumbling syllables. "Forgive me? As if you have the right? As if you could understand?"

She threw her arms to either side and the darkness swirled about him, a tornado of pitch. "You place yourself too high, little thief. Assume too much. I do not need forgiveness, especially from you."

Kaylo searched for an escape, finding nothing but swirling darkness rising like a cage. If she kept him trapped, Tayen would be alone. He would've abandoned Liara once again.

"How many times have I saved your life? You come begging for power, as if I were not the one who aided you in the first place." Her visage grew larger and the blackness swirled faster. "You did not break Oakheart Mountain, you arrogant fool. I did. I reached through you in your moment of need and ripped the crystals from the earth. It did nothing! It changed nothing!"

The fear stopped. Every potential disaster and folly he constructed in his mind collapsed. She had never lied to him before, even in her obfuscation. If she had broken the mountain's crystals, she had the power to do everything he had asked of her. It was no longer a guess or a hope. She had the power, and chose to abandon her people—her descendants—to the Gousht.

More than anything, a feeling of pity settled in Kaylo's gut. Her anger had consumed her. The help she had given him hadn't changed a thing. She could do more, but the anger was too comfortable. If nothing else, he understood that feeling.

He turned from her and plunged into the swirling black. It was endless, and yet, he continued his march.

"You turn your back on me?!"

"I won't cross The Mist for you again. Release me and be done with me," Kaylo said with a sadness.

───────────

When Kaylo pushed through the furs to the command tent, Liara, Tomi, and three strangers were huddling over the table. They turned to see who had interrupted them in unison.

"Get out of here," Tomi said with utter exasperation.

It still threw Kaylo off to see Tomi fully grown. Muscle had added to her small frame, giving her presence more weight, but the bratty girl he had known still shined through. Maybe he had that effect on people.

"I need to speak with Liara."

"Kaylo, later. We are in the middle of a discussion," Liara said, shaking her head.

"Please," Kaylo said. "It's important."

"Commander, we have everything we need to move forward," one of the strangers said, a heavyset northman with a broadaxe latched to his back. "If you need the room—"

"No," Tomi said with her full attention on her sister. "I told you this would happen. He is not in charge here. He isn't a part of the Uprising anymore."

Liara sighed with her whole body. "Tomi, I need you and the regiment leaders to give me the room."

No one pushed back against Liara's decision once it was made. They nodded their understanding, collected their things, and left.

Between the organization of the encampment and the respect of her reports, it became immediately clear who should have been leading them all those turns past.

Kaylo stepped to the side to allow the regiment leaders to pass. Tomi stopped, glared at him, then left without a word.

"She still hates me, huh?"

"She didn't hate you before. No one defended your decisions to me more than she did before you left. But then you left."

The past had a color to it that changed with the passage of time. Tomi had always been antagonistic, or maybe she had just been a kid.

"You didn't come here to talk about Tomi," Liara said, spreading her arms wide. "Everyone is gone. What was so important that you needed to interrupt my meeting?"

Put in context, Kaylo hesitated. It was important, but would Liara see that?

"You have spirit crystals in the stores."

"That's it? You wanted to confront me about our stores of crystals?"

"You've got a lot. You're trying to train your spirit dancers, and none of them have been able to do what I did at Oakheart, right? They can't break crystals without touching them. If that's part of the plan, you're fucked. They won't be able to no matter how much they train."

Liara walked back from the table, sat herself down in a chair, and pinched the bridge of her nose like she was trying to fight off a headache. "Do you think I'm reckless enough to rely on a twist of fate? Yes, we are training the spirit dancers, but they are not the crux of our plan."

"They'll never be able to do it. I never did it. It cannot be done."

"What are you talking about, Kaylo?"

"It was The Balance. She was the one who reached through me and broke Oakheart. She thought it would change the way people saw spirit dancers, but it didn't work. People turned me into the story. It didn't change what people thought about spirit dancers or her."

"Okay," she said. "Thank you for telling me. I'll have the spirit dancers focus on other skillsets."

She acted so casually, as if he hadn't just told her that the myth that propped him up as a leader had been a lie. Was she that much more confident? Settled?

"What is the plan?" Kaylo walked towards the map. "You said that the Lost Nation is on the move, and it's forcing your hand. What's the target?"

"Kaylo, you aren't a part of this anymore. I'm happy to have your help, but you are not here to make decisions. I have that under control."

Notations on the map detailed troop estimates, Uprising encampments, Jani encampments. Small carvings of nondescript people rested on different cities. It would take days to make sense of the swell of information.

"You did what I could never do. You made the Uprising into a rebellion rather than a vendetta," Kaylo said, inspecting the poor craftwork of the carvings. "I don't know if it counts for anything, but I am proud of you."

She smiled and her shoulders slackened. "It means a lot, actually."

"I want to help you. I have no interest in command or challenging your decisions. But Tayen is my responsibility. So I will be here until the tragic ending."

"Tragic?"

Kaylo brushed his thumb over the number beside the Citadel. Translating people into numbers made them feel small. There were people who cared for each one of those numbers.

"Whatever happens, Enneans will die. Even if we win, that's tragedy enough."

"The Stone City," Liara said. "We are going to take Stone City."

"You're joking, right? Stone City? The impenetrable city?"

"It was always going to end there. The city that fell has to rise again," she said, walking towards the map. She plucked the figurine from atop the Citadel. "The Lost Nation knows it. The Gousht know it. Whoever controls the Stone City will be victorious."

"How are you going to take it?"

"Sometimes a smaller militia can do far more than a larger force. The Gousht will be focused on the Lost Army. We have already cultivated a resistance within the city like what you tried to do in Colian. Once we give their dancers back their spirits, the Gousht won't be able to stop us."

"So you *were* relying on the spirit dancers."

"We will sneak dancers into the city and they will disrupt the crystal stores." She flipped a corner of the map to reveal a more detailed rendering of the Stone City. "Here, here, and here are where the Gousht keep their stores."

It wouldn't be that simple. The Gousht would be guarding each store. They had built up guards to protect their collection of spirits more and more, even back when Kaylo led the Uprising forces.

"Once the stores are destroyed, the city's resistance will join in, and our forces will swarm the city through the gates. It would have been easier if the dancers could have eliminated the caches from afar, but we will make do."

"This plan is reckless, and you were never reckless."

Liara leaned back and met Kaylo's eyes. "You're right. But it will be our last chance. Without the Lost Nation, the empire would destroy us in an instant. If the Lost Nation somehow banishes the Gousht, half our forces would return to their lives. They wouldn't stand up against the Lost Army, and that damn King Shonar would take everything.

"If we don't do this now, Ennea will die to one knife or another."

"What can I do?" Kaylo asked.

"The Priest isn't going to be a problem, right?"

"Liara, what do you need me to do?"

She pointed to a store in the Stone City keep. "This will be the hardest store to break."

"Done."

"And find Nomi for me," she said. "We need to call all arms if we have a chance of making this work."

CHAPTER THIRTY-FOUR
CURRENT DAY ENNEA

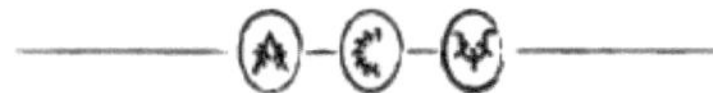

To complicate his game, Wal marked the wall with a third target before returning to his patch of stone floor. It hadn't taken long to perfect his aim with the first two targets. He collected three stones, took a breath, and tossed each stone at a different mark on the opposite wall in rapid succession.

The first stone met its mark, the second deviated from course, and the third missed by more than a hand's length. He smiled at the challenge.

"The game continues?" Lanigan called out from their cell. "It might be more satisfying to occupy your mind rather than your body. There will never be enough stones to fill the hours."

"You amble towards death your way, and I'll do it mine."

"Why so morose?"

"Have you noticed the walls? I don't know what you have over there, but the walls in here are pretty big. The general of the last Ennean army personally burned my face and then told me she would keep me in here until my hope rotted away. I'm not feeling too optimistic."

"Was it better when you had free reign to treat Citadel servants like work animals and snatch up children from beyond the Lost Forest?"

Wal collected his stones. There were reasons he focused his mind on a child's game. He had no desire to think about what he had done and how completely he had failed.

"Commander, you will have to face the questions eventually. Not because I asked them, but because you will ask yourself." Lanigan's voice reached out like an open palm. "You're a decent man under that vileness."

"What would you know—"

Footsteps rushed down the corridor. Hurried breaths followed.

Wal readied himself and his stones. If they meant to take him, he would make one of them blink funny for the rest of their days.

A servant ran into view, the lantern light bathing over her ashen bronze skin and short red curls. No food in hand. No fresh piss bucket. She didn't even stop at Wal's door to glare at him.

"You forgot the food," Wal said through his barred window, but the servant continued to Lanigan's cell.

Her hand flashed in rapid gestures, flickering in front of her like she was trying to bat away a fly.

"Slow. Slow," Lanigan said, their voice soft and calming.

The servant paused and then continued. She settled into a steady pace, but did not stop for several minutes. Lanigan did not interrupt her again.

Servants didn't have the autonomy to run through the Citadel without orders. If she had been caught, she would have been whipped or beaten or both. Whatever she had to share must have been important. At least important enough to silence Lanigan, which was a task in and of itself.

Her hands stopped.

"Thank you," Lanigan said. "Go. There's no need for you to get caught. It will do no good."

Before she left, she walked to Wal's door, close enough to touch him through the bars. Her rich brown eyes stared at him. They contained disappointment, anger, and a silent accusation. Then she turned and snuck back into the dim corridor.

"What was that?" Wal said.

Lanigan did not answer. They had never not answered before.

"Poet, speak," Wal said, pressing his face to the bars in a meaningless attempt to get closer to his one companion. The metal touched his cheeks with a chill. "You're frightening me."

"When you were commander, what did you want? Did you want free people or dead Gousht? The Gousht might be dead and gone in either scenario, but the state of our people would be very different."

"What are you on about? Lanigan, what did the servant say? What was so important?"

"Tell me!" they shouted, and a rage born of twenty-one turns in captivity leaped out from their voice. "What were you after?"

"Dead Gousht," Wal said, and felt his shoulders slump with the admission. "If I cared about our people, I would have never fought for King Shonar. I just wanted the Gousht to die."

"And now?"

A quiver ran through Wal's arms, setting his hands shaking as they rested against the stormwood door. "I don't know. Every reason I had is still there. My dead haven't gone away. But the wrongness of this place is hard to ignore from this vantage point."

"Honest. I'll give you that," Lanigan said. "Tanis has left the city. She is leading the war party to the Last Wall."

"That's fucking daft. The Stone City won't fall."

"When have you ever known Tanis to make rash decisions?" Lanigan asked. "The end is near."

CHAPTER THIRTY-FIVE
KAYLO'S STORY

THEY KEPT ME SEPARATE from Intalik as we walked westward towards the encampment. I watched him all the same. The Gousht had followed me back to an unsuspecting home before, and I refused to let it happen again.

If he deviated from the path we walked, I moved to keep him in my sights. When he slowed, so did I. He took a piss, and I relieved myself a handful of strides away.

He hadn't made an overt attempt to signal anyone or leave a trail from what I could tell. For the most part, he walked and cried over his blood banner brother. The others had their sympathies, but I had none to spare.

Blood banners were human. I could admit that much. They experienced loss and pain like anyone else, but they had betrayed the rest of us to save themselves. For that, I would keep my sympathies for those who would mourn Boda and Yelan alongside me.

As we came to rest after the first day of hard travel, we settled amongst a naturally thick cluster of ironoaks. It wouldn't make sleeping easy, but it would obscure us from any prying eyes as much as possible.

We ate in silence. Everyone had lost someone. We had all lost our slim dreams of turning the tide of the occupation. The firelight danced across gloomy faces, and we organized ourselves for a restless sleep.

I kept the first watch, promising not to slit the traitor's throat in the night. They all had some plan to bring him before the council and weigh his innocence—except for Wal. But I couldn't have been sure if he agreed with me out of principle or bloodlust.

Before the cellar collapsed on Yelan, I would have shared their ideals. I had seen Zusa execute Enneans because he doubted their loyalty. It disgusted me. But something in me broke with the floorboards of that building.

Volunteering for the first watch had been a poor decision. I wouldn't have been able to sleep, but I could have tried. Instead, I left myself alone with my thoughts and the looming trees.

My mind kept escaping to memories of Niven. Not Boda. I had far more memories of Boda than of his brother, but they didn't rise to the surface.

After one particularly rough training session, Niven had pulled Boda to the side. Zusa and Boda had gone after each other, and as usual, Boda left the exchange worse off—lip bloodied from Zusa's open hand.

Niven made no attempt to whisper and his words carried. He sat his brother down and told him that today wasn't the battle. His anger treated every moment like a competition for blood, but their parents hadn't crossed into The Mist so their sons could fight endlessly. They were meant to live.

He had said, "Yes, we have to train for the battles to come, but we must live the days we have. It is the only thing that makes our battles worth fighting."

Ever since his brother died, Boda treated every day like the battle. The boy hadn't lived in over three turns, and now, he never would again.

I had thought he needed an outlet for his anger. If he could aim it at the couta, it would give him direction. It might allow him to find something beyond the anger for the people he spent his days with. But it hadn't. All I did was steal the few days the boy had left.

The archer who killed Boda hadn't stolen his life. I had.

Wal stirred from his bedroll and took a seat beside the fire next to me. He dropped a sack of runes in the dirt. "Need a distraction?"

"Not now. No games."

"What's the plan?" Wal asked as if he hadn't heard the warning in my voice.

"I don't know."

"Come on. Planning is what we do. We can come up with something," he said. "We have to. If we go back to the council empty-handed, they're going to turtle up and hide away. They might reconsider the Lost Nation's offer. What about Port Anno?"

"I don't have any plans, Wal," I said, allowing my bitterness to saturate my tone. "Look at what happens when I make plans. How many Enneans have I killed? It has to be more than the average Gousht foot soldier. My numbers probably rival their commanders'."

"That's not fair. You have to give yourself some grace."

"Do I? Why? All I do is promise frightened people revenge. And all they do is die. I'm done."

Wal tilted his head to the side, and the firelight caught him at a different angle—shadows drawing more attention to the fierceness in his eyes. "Done? What does that mean?"

"That means stop following me around like you're my kid brother or something. I don't have answers. No more telling people what to do. No more speeches. I'm not a commander. I'm a thief, and you all would be better off keeping your distance."

"We're all sorry about Boda, but that wasn't your fault. Taku—"

"What? Taku was a blood banner? Who decided to trust him?" Tears welled in my eyes, and I hated myself for them. "What do you care? You hated the boy."

"That's not fair."

"No? Tell me you didn't hate Boda," I said. "You hate all of them. I think you even hate me a bit for my part in what happened to Adéan. Tell me I'm wrong."

"If you need to stew in your self-pity, go ahead, but don't bring him into this."

"Like you don't bring him into every conversation we have. Adéan is your only reason for getting up anymore. Do you have enough blood yet to make it right?"

"Fuck off, Kaylo."

I grabbed the sack of runes Wal had sat beside me. "That's exactly what I mean to do. When I said I was done, I meant I was done."

These ridiculous runes. This waste of time Jonac drilled into me. How many hours had I lost carving them, twiddling them in my fingers, placing them on lines drawn in the dirt? I threw the sack into the firepit. Flits of sparks jumped and a log cracked with the impact.

The leather pouch landed at the edge of the pit and started to smoke.

Wal rushed to the pit and kicked the bag from the coals before too much damage could be done. "You're always looking to sacrifice yourself, aren't you? Do you think if you push everyone away, you won't be responsible for us anymore? What about Liara? Going to set what you have with her on fire too?"

Hunched over the burnt pouch of runes, he looked at me, clenching his jaw and squinting. He was still the same boy who couldn't keep his smart words to himself when Ms. Hanack had him read aloud in the Nomar church. Only more bitter and angry. Still trying to lash out at the world.

I stood up and walked away from the firelight. *When will they get it?* I thought. *How many times do I have to tell them? I'm not the hero.*

I found a crook of an ironoak to nestle in for the night. The fire flickered between the trees until my eyelids got heavier than my stubbornness.

The next two days of traveling passed as I waded through a stream of memories both real and fabricated of all the friends and family I had lost.

When Annit tried to break through to me, I didn't engage. I responded with as few words as possible until he gave up just like he had after I led the raid on the forge.

Everything he had done to keep me from falling down the same self-destructive path had failed. And he knew it. The kindness he offered me. The condemnation after I placed myself above the council. The pity. None of it could reach me now. We were too similar.

Even Talise tried her best to be cordial, but we both knew she had been right. I got Boda and Yelan killed, just like Sionia. Their bodies stayed behind as I ran away.

I had gotten good at escaping the dead.

Yet for some reason we still brought this blood banner, this piece of rotten excrement, back to our encampment. Intalik talked to the others as we walked, telling stories about him and his brother like he might endear himself enough to avoid death.

As Sokan hung low in the sky on the third night after our flight from Colian, we found our way back to the encampment. A dark pink reached overhead until it could reach no farther, shifting into a blue so close to black that it had lost itself.

"I will call to gather the clan in the morning," Annit said, still a hundred paces from the encampment.

"Tonight," I said.

"This can wait. We don't have to deliberate over everything tonight. Take some time with Liara."

"Time won't change what needs to be said. Or done. I let you all hold me back for three days too many." I sped towards the encampment before he could continue his plea.

The warriors guarding the entrance welcomed me home, but I offered them no mind. I stalked towards the gathering tent to await the rest of the clan. Pleasantries—holding Liara—it would only get it in the way. Some fires needed to be tempered, but not this one.

Eventually, the ramblings of a crowd outside the tent began to grow.

The first person to enter was a Sonacoan woman I didn't quite know. I recognized her face but didn't have a name to attach to it.

She paused when she saw me sitting alone, turned back as if to leave, then resigned herself to the awkwardness of sitting in this oversized tent, just the two of us. I returned her nod of acknowledgement, but I couldn't find a smile to offer her.

A moment later, the tent filled with people speculating about the meeting. Eight left. Five returned. I couldn't blame them for creating reasons before reasons were given.

"Where is he?!" Hylíane's voice bellowed as she entered the tent, each word distinct and clear without any flourish of her accent.

The crowd turned towards the entrance as she burst into the tent, her walking stick digging into the ground with each stride forward.

She saw me—not that I was hiding. "Where are tey? Tis was suppose ta be a scoutin mission? What happened?"

Annit came rushing into the tent followed by Liara, whose eyebrows were knit with worry.

"Give us a moment to explain, Hylíane," Annit called over the seated crowd.

"Explain now," she said. "Explain why Yelan isn't ere."

I stood up and the focus of the clan found me as it so often had. "She's dead. So is Boda, and it's my fault."

"Cha damn right tis is cha fault," she said with more venom than she ever had. "Cha never shoulda gone tere."

"You're right." Her expression lost its edge with my words. "I made the wrong decision for the last time. We followed a pair of blood banners with an enticing story, and Yelan and Boda paid the price for it."

Intalik stood between Talise and Wal towards the outside of the tent. "My brother was no blood banner."

Wal smacked him upside the head for speaking up.

"No, Wal. Let him speak. Let him tell us all how the Gousht knew where to find us," I said, taking several steps towards them.

"How am I supposed to know?" Intalik asked, looking around the room as if someone might save him. "The greens killed my sister, and now, they got my brother. What about that means we are blood banners?"

Some of the faces in the crowd softened at that. This shitwit's sad words would save his life. Give him enough time to betray us again. How many would die next time?

"Out of all the rebels the soldiers killed, they kept your brother alive. Why?" I continued forward, and the crowd made a path as I did.

"How am I supposed to speak for the Gousht? None of that is proof."

"No one else knew about our mission. There's no way the Gousht could have known."

Of course, he was right. I had no proof, even if I knew what I knew.

Zusa hadn't needed proof. His executions hadn't been the act of barbarism I thought they were at the time. It was pragmatism. Those two strangers we pulled from the caravan could have been telling the truth. It hadn't mattered then, and it couldn't matter now.

They claimed they had been enslaved. They had no love for the Gousht. And we begged for their lives as they knelt in front of Zusa.

The memory hadn't stopped flickering through my mind since leaving Colian. Zusa had known—believing a lie was more dangerous than not believing the truth.

He slit one of their throats and speared the other through the belly before any sad stories could get in the way of a good decision.

Several paces still separated the blood banner and I. Wal and Talise each carried a tension in their stance as they held Intalik in place.

I slipped my father's knife from my belt, ready to do what needed to be done.

"Others knew," Hylïane said from over my shoulder. The vulnerability in her voice stopped me more than her words.

"What are you talking about?" I turned to find Hylïane unable to meet my eyes.

"I told tem. I told tem," she mumbled to herself. "I never stopped speakin with ta Lost Nation. Tey said tey would take care of it. If tings went wrong, tey promised ta be tere."

"What did you do?!" I yelled.

"I told ta Lost Nation where cha were goin. What cha plan was. Tey agreed it would be bad if cha tried ta fight cha way through Colian. Tey have plans for a free Ennea. Tat's what we all want, right? I neva thought tey would do anyting ta interfere."

This hunched woman leaning on her walking stick had fought me from the first moment we spoke. She had played contrarian. She had held the deaths of those I cared for over me to prove her points. Even after we made our attempts to cooperate, she had gone behind the council's back to conspire with the Lost Nation.

Her wrinkles had never seemed more pronounced than in this moment. To see her was to look upon a woman incapable of harm. Too fragile. Too weak to raise a weapon. Whatever strength she had carried in her bones had been stolen by the mines and the turns.

And yet, that image was a lie. Hylīane was the most dangerous person under this tent.

Her duplicity had killed Yelan. Killed Boda. Killed the Colian resistance. I almost gutted Intalik. All because she assumed she knew better.

My anger broke into a field of clarity. Her mouth continued to move, but the sound faded into the meaningless whine of the world.

I raised my knife. The blade cut through Hylīane's throat like taut fabric. Her eyes widened, but she shouldn't have been surprised after what she had done.

Blood washed over my knife hand. Her walking stick fell first. Then she crumpled with a pitiful, open-mouthed expression.

When the sound returned, it erupted louder than the chaos of a thousand echoes. Hands latched on to me at all angles, dragging me away from her unmoving body.

Intalik stood slack-jawed, the one stationary person in a crowd rushing every which way. I couldn't tell if he was surprised to be alive, shocked by what I had done, or simply calculating how best to escape.

She saved him from me. She saved me from killing an innocent man. For that much, I was grateful.

I didn't fight the people trying to restrain me. I had done what needed to be done. They didn't need to understand or agree.

Amongst the people rushing for the exit, Liara stood next to Tomi. Her cheeks stretched wide in pain. She would never see me the same. I had joined the line of violent men she had known, starting with her father.

It had to be done.

Eventually, the crowd dispersed, leaving me with the council. They grouped together in a tight circle at one end of the tent as I sat at the other. I hadn't said a word in my defense or offered any resistance. I simply waited.

Someone had taken Hylīane's body away, but the almost apologetic look on her dying face lingered in my mind. She owed Boda and Yelan far more than an apology. She had broken the Colian rebellion and our Uprising with one decision.

"Talk to him then!" Liara shouted at the councilors.

Their mumbled response did nothing to alleviate her agitation. She broke from the group and stomped in my direction. The anger in her brow did little to cover the hurt in her eyes.

"Why?!" she demanded.

"I'm sorry, Liara."

"Tell me why," Liara said, her voice losing force.

Annit fell in beside her and placed a hand on her shoulder. "Whatever Hylīane did, she did for the Uprising. Misguided or not."

"That's exactly what people would have said." I spoke only out of respect for them, not out of any need to convince. "She knew how to bring people in. They would have listened and empathized. Boda and Yelan are gone because of what she did. Blood owes blood."

"You don't have the right to execute one of us!" Eandrine had never yelled at me or even in my presence before. She had always been level in all things. "Who will you kill next?"

"We are supposed to be fighting for Ennea—for the cause. Not for blood or vengeance or retribution," Annit said, and I saw the disappointment in his eyes.

"If Hyliane's to blame, so are you," Kristee said, wearing the same puffy-eyed anger she had when Acta hadn't come home. "You brought them on that fool's mission. Should we execute you now?"

I almost laughed. After the countless times we had disagreed, I had never agreed with Kristee more. I was responsible.

Elder Meta's lips tilted upwards in pity. "Kaylo, what would you have us do? We cannot allow this. Justice and vengeance must walk different paths."

The clan had chosen their council wisely. Each had the strength to bear the weight of their own opinions without hindering their understanding of one another. The clan would be fine.

"I did what needed to be done. You might not see it, but that doesn't change the truth of it." I stood and strode towards the exit.

None of them blocked my path, but several called after me. Only Liara followed, her echo carrying a sorrowful swell. The moaning current of the ocean pulled against a raging rhythm underneath.

I had only made it a few steps beyond the tent before she reached me.

"Where are you going?"

When I turned, her nose flared even as tears began to fall. She deserved this least of all, but I had made up my mind.

"You don't need me. Everything I've done has only made your life worse. If I stick around, you or Tomi will end up buried in a hasty grave beside a battlefield," I said. "Tell me I'm wrong."

"So that's it? You're going to run away and leave us behind? Are you that much of a coward?"

"Yes!" I shouted loud enough to unsettle myself. "I am afraid every day, but I push on pretending to be someone I'm not. I'm not a leader or a hero. My curse doesn't make me valuable. It makes me a liability."

"This? Still? After five turns of knowing you, you really haven't changed. Are you that insecure? Be better than The Thief. Stay and fix what you broke."

I started to turn, but she grabbed my shoulder and spun me back to face her. "How dare you, Kaylo? I never knew you were so weak."

"Then you weren't listening," I said. "I cannot do this anymore. Too many dead lie at my feet. I won't watch you die!"

"Blessed Mother, you are so self-important. This isn't about you. The Uprising is bigger than that."

I grabbed the back of her neck and drew her into a kiss. She met my lips for a moment before pushing me away.

"Goodbye," I said.

She didn't stop me from turning away a second time.

A part of me still wished I could be the person she needed me to be. That part wanted to be the hero from the stories that dispelled the crystals under Oakheart Mountain with my will alone. But that part was a fucking fool.

Boda could have attested to that if he were still alive.

Once I made it to the tent I shared with Liara, I grabbed my belongings. Most of what I needed hadn't been unpacked from our scouting mission.

The last time I lay in this tent, Liara had unburdened herself. Dreams of her father plagued her, and now, I had become another man who failed her. Her father hadn't been able to escape the death of their mother and took it out on his daughters. I couldn't escape all my dead either, and she deserved better.

The furs covering the entrance flew open, and Wal stepped in. He looked from me to the travel sack in my hands.

"Where are we going?" he asked.

"I need my father's knife."

He held out the blade. He had cleaned Hylïane's blood from the steel, but a new patch of reddish-brown had settled into the leather wrapped around the hilt.

"There are at least a dozen of us that will follow you," he said. "They can't exile you. Hylïane betrayed us. What in the bloody fucking Mist was Liara thinking?"

"Watch your mouth," I said, gripping the hilt of my knife hard enough to feel the woven leather digging into my palm.

"Fine." He waved his comment away. "Give me a moment. I will get the others."

"I'm going alone."

"What are you talking about? Think of everything we could accomplish without those fools holding us back."

"Those fools are the only reason you are still alive, you ridiculous shit." I sheathed my blade. "Your mouth has always had a sharper edge than your blade. It's time you shut it and listen to someone. If you want blood, follow orders."

"I'm not the one who executed an unarmed elderly woman."

"This is where our paths diverge." I hefted my travel sack over my shoulder. "Don't follow me. I don't need anyone following me ever again."

"You need to calm down and think for a moment."

I rushed Wal and grabbed him by the throat, driving him back to the edge of the tent. "No more talking. I'm done with hangers-on."

The look on his face as he pawed at my arm confirmed everything I knew I was: a fraud, a failure, a thief. I pushed him through the furs, and he fell hard on the other side of the tent.

"Don't follow me."

A small crowd gathered around the commotion. I felt the weight of their expectant eyes one final time. Talise pushed her way forward to help Wal off the dirt. She didn't say anything, but her glare did.

"I get it. You were right about me," I said before charging towards the encampment exit.

Chapter Thirty-Six

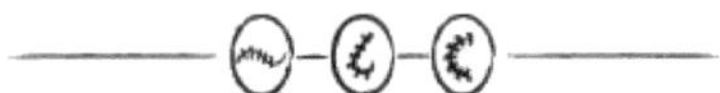

Kaylo sat in their meager quarters amongst the rows of Uprising tents, retelling a moment that could have broken the rebellion. He had killed an elder and recounted it as honestly as he could to a girl he had promised to protect.

He didn't dare look at Tayen. The horror that must have been plastered across her face—he couldn't bear it.

In his dreams, Hylíane's lips trembled as she fell to the dirt. He couldn't recall if they had when he killed her. The difference between a haunted memory and the truth might have stood days apart.

"Where did you go?" Tayen asked with a care she only used in moments like these, after he revealed part of his story that made him hesitate to continue.

"I'm not a good person," he said. "I killed an elder. I almost killed an innocent man."

"She betrayed you. You thought he betrayed you. Boda and Yelan died."

"She did what she thought she had to. After surviving the mines, who wouldn't have done it? She searched out what seemed like the safest path for her and those she cared about."

"Do you want to hate yourself?" There was no sarcasm in Tayen's voice, just a soft question. "Do you want me to hate you? Is that the point you're trying to make?"

The easiest answer would have been 'yes.' At the beginning of all this, he had wanted her to look at him with disgust and walk away from the violence. He had wanted her to see what he saw in himself for so many turns. But things had changed.

He had found someone to love again—a new love for someone who would never be his blood but felt like his child all the same. If she hated him, it would break the fragments of his spirit that remained intact.

Stronger people would have said as much, but Kaylc simply shook his head.

"What happened next?" Tayen asked like an invitation.

CHAPTER THIRTY-SEVEN
KAYLO'S STORY

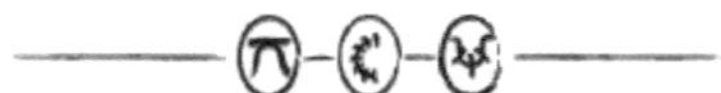

THE CHILL OF THE water lapping against my feet eased the pain. At some point in the last three days of walking, I had twisted my ankle. I hadn't stopped to take care of it. I had barely done anything to take care of myself at all, including changing my clothing. Hylīane's dried blood still coated the front of my robes.

Sunlight refracted through the gentle rapids of the river. It bent and distorted the rocks beneath the surface.

During the easy turns of my life, I hadn't needed a purpose. I moved through the days with my parents and Shay. Eventually, Shay and I happened upon Munnie, and we filled our nights with The Song. That had been enough for me.

I hadn't understood the nature of our existence. As much as my mother would lecture me, the fact of our occupation never settled in my head. I hated the soldiers and Ms. Hanack as a child would. They made rules I didn't like and treated us unfairly. But I never saw my home as a prison. My home was where my father cooked oats with berries.

After I abandoned my family, I attached myself to Jonac, then Liara, then Zusa. I walked in the shape of their footsteps. My anger drove me, but I never understood what I was doing.

There was a moment, about a turn past, when I thought I had grasped it. Our scouts came across a small paper mill. Four Enneans kept it going while an equally small number of soldiers watched over them.

Even the Gousht needed paper, I guess.

At first, it seemed like a waste of our time to save four people. Then it hit me. An Uprising couldn't be about killing the Gousht. It had to be about freeing our people—all of them.

I had said nice words about liberation before, but it had always been a means for blood. After the mill, I had tried to make it about life first and foremost.

But that was the thing about malitu in the stories. They were always after blood, even if they convinced themselves otherwise.

When I thought I finally understood my place and my purpose, I had lost hold of the truth. I fucked it all up because I had dreams of freedom. I was a prisoner fighting my jailor, and blood was the best I was going to get.

I grabbed a rock from the riverbank and threw it into the water, breaking the rays of sunlight filtering into the river.

"Where now?" I asked, despite being alone.

No one responded.

It had been six turns since I left Nomar, and I still didn't know where to go. Suddenly, I was sixteen again, lost in the forest. But this time, Jonac wasn't going to happen upon me, and The Song wouldn't be there to comfort me.

I couldn't go back to the Uprising. Even if they would take me back, it wouldn't be long before I got Liara killed. And the way she looked at me after Hyliane... I had done what needed doing, and she could only judge me for it.

None of them understood the burden. None of them had to wear it—had to be better than the cursed fucking spirit living inside them.

If I had to carry one more body, one more debt of blood, I would shatter completely.

Liara would have said that was my self-importance and self-pity talking.

"Self-pity is a distraction," Munnie had told me once. "It makes you focus on yourself instead of the problem."

"I am the problem!" I screamed, scattering birds from a nearby tree.

I felt for my father's knife at my side and drew it from its sheath. Even though he had been dead six turns, it still felt like the knife belonged to him.

Every turn or so, I rewrapped the stormwood hilt with a new stretch of leather. This latest wrap bore several signs of wear, even beyond the blood stains. His knife deserved better treatment.

He had carried this knife for nearly two decades before he died. He hunted with it and whittled with it—though he had better knives for detailed work. It had never killed anyone before I took it from him.

I rubbed at the wrapped hilt. There was too much blood soaked into the leather to know if this particular stain had belonged to Hylíane. I placed the tip of his knife below my ribcage. Turns of killing had taught me exactly how to find the right angle to puncture the heart.

"Blessed Mother," I cried. "I can't do this anymore. Don't make me do this anymore."

My hand shook as I held the knife. I could feel its point dimpling my skin through my robes.

If The Mother took me, I would have to face everyone who crossed before me. They had to understand this. All I did was hurt the people I cared about. No one on this side of The Mist needed me anymore.

The sting of the metal tip piercing my skin was quiet. I pushed enough to make myself bleed, then stopped. My muscles seized up.

I was so close to an ending. All I had to do was pull. The blade would do the work. I only had to guide it.

Shay's face flashed in front of me. She would be there on the other side. Everyone would be there, and I would have to explain myself.

I screamed, trying to force myself to leave this place.

"Coward!" I threw the knife to the ground and curled up beside the river. "You're such a coward."

———————————

When I picked myself off the ground beside the riverbank, I needed to focus on something besides the torrent of ugly thoughts inside my head. I took off my clothing and bathed in the river. The cold seeped through my skin into my bones, but the way the gentle pain enveloped me felt comforting.

Still naked, I pulled myself from the river. I didn't allow myself time to think about why the tip of my father's knife was caked with dried blood. It took effort to scrape it away. Then I pulled the skin of my cheek taught as I shaved the growth of several days from my face.

The robes I had in my travel sack had accompanied me to Colian, but they were far cleaner than the ones I had been wearing for the past three days.

Once I finished dressing, I started removing the braids from my hair. I had done a poor job of tending to my hair as of late. It needed time to be free before it became brittle. With the tips of my fingers coated in sunflower oil, I slowly uncoiled each braid until the loose strands created a frizzy mess encircling my head.

If I had a chani cloth to wrap my hair, I would have done so. Instead, I allowed it to be what it was—curly gray hair in need of time to heal.

For hours, I tended to my small needs until I had nothing left to distract my hands.

After a moment of searching for my next task, I chuckled to myself. It was the loudest noise I had made in hours.

All my busy thoughts about where I should go next distracted me. I hadn't paid any mind to where I had ended up. This wasn't just any riverbank. I found myself sitting next to Sand River.

It would take some investigation, maybe even waiting for the stars to come out, to discover exactly where I was, but I knew this river. Depending on how far west I had walked, I would only be a day or so from Nomar.

The thought of being so close to my childhood home made me feel like a child, which was exactly what I wanted to be. I didn't want to be responsible for anyone anymore. I needed someone to tell me what to do. I needed a kana.

Munnie might not have even been alive, but I had to check. She had been my only kana not to turn on me or demand anything unsavory of me. I could trust her with my choices, even if only for a little while.

———

It took less than a day to reach the jagged rock formation an hour's trek north of Nomar. It would have taken even less time if I hadn't given my old home such a wide berth. Soldiers were the least of my reasons. The city held memories.

Then again, so did Munnie's hallow.

The break in the rock had seemed bigger the last time I saw it. It still looked like the work of time and circumstance, which only spoke to Munnie's control of her spirit.

If I had been honest with her all those turns ago—told her about the echoes—everything might have turned out differently. Even if she cursed me and turned me away, Shay might have survived. My parents might have been heartbroken by the truth, but they might still have had hearts to break.

"Regret is the promise of stubborn people," my mother's voice said inside my head.

I had been stubborn. And she had been right.

I walked up to the stone and traced the opening with my fingers. Rough edges bit at my touch.

After so long, this place had become more dream than memory. Only here and now, under the pads of my fingers, did it become real again.

The sound of my footsteps kicked off the stone, creating a lovely pattern as I made my way through the stone gap and descended into the hallow. Tight walls constrained my movements. Then, all of a sudden, they expanded into the chamber below the stone.

Only the small rays of sunlight streaking in through the entrance illuminated the space. They caught the dust I had kicked up from the ground. I gave my eyes time to adjust, and slowly, the chamber came into view.

At the far end, a small garden of overgrown plants bathed in a stream of light. Munnie must have created a series of cracks to let light shine through.

The closer I got, the more neglected the garden looked. Each plant fought the others for space, reaching towards the light. She hadn't tended to them in some time.

It could mean several things. It didn't necessarily mean she had died. Though nothing in the space looked cared for.

She had been old. Time hadn't stopped because I left.

One of the plants at the center of the tangle caught my eye. A shabby excuse for a blackberry hung from a branch. The bush hadn't gotten enough light or water to produce much.

The last time I met with Shay and Munnie, I had pulled lush blackberry bushes from the soil. It was the first time I came close to falling into The Song. I had almost been able to hear The Seed screaming in colors as I called the thicket of bushes to life around me.

Maybe it didn't mean anything. Munnie planted a barberry bush directly next to it. People liked blackberries. Some things weren't about me. Wasn't that what Liara was always trying to get me to understand?

Odds were, I would never find out anyway. Munnie wasn't here.

I kicked the dirt and a small cloud of dust burst to life in the little light available.

After an adjustment period, the small streams of sunlight filled the space far better than I had originally assumed. I peered into the darkness and found a figure staring back. I smiled.

Munnie's carving of The Mountain looked every bit as breathtaking as I remembered it. As I stepped closer, more of the fine details of the likeness took shape. What she had been able to carve from the stone humbled me and my shoddy whittling skills.

"Incredible, isn't she?"

The voice sounded like a memory. I didn't turn around. If I did, and it was only my mind playing with me, I wouldn't have survived it. Hope felt like something I could only shatter if I reached for it.

"I taught you better than to ignore your elders."

Slowly, I turned, waiting to be undone when I found myself alone. Then, Munnie was there, smiling.

Her hair was finer. She bent forward like her back couldn't handle the weight of her shoulders. But it was my kana. Wrinkles moved along with her smile.

I had seen her—imagined her—so often over the past six turns, and here she stood.

The strength in my legs nearly gave way. "Munnie?"

She lifted her hand to my cheek. The soft leather of her thumb swept one of my tears away. "Welcome home, Kaylo."

With that, my knees forgot themselves, and I fell to the ground in front of her, weeping. "I'm sorry, Munnie. I'm so sorry."

She placed a hand on the back of my head as I cried. It may have been minutes, but it felt like hours to let go of all the tears I had collected.

Once my well ran dry, I looked up to find her still there.

"There's a little wood in the corner." Her finger led the way. "I can't carry much these days, so there's not much waiting for us. Do your best and make us some light. I think you have some stories I need to hear."

Words would only bring more tears. So, I set to the task.

She hadn't lied. Two logs and a handful of twigs lay in a pile near one edge of the chamber. I would have to remedy that.

It took no time to start the fire. Light filled the room with gentle flickers as Munnie sat in her old rocking chair. It leaned slightly to one side and creaked louder than I remembered.

"Before you welcome me into your home, you should know something." I gripped the hem of my robes to keep my hand from shaking. "I'm a thief."

"Ennea's Thief from what I hear."

The shaking stopped. I raised my gaze to meet Munnie's eyes. She hadn't stopped smiling. "You know?"

"That my toka is one of the most infamous freedom fighters on the continent? Yes. I'm not so old that I forgot to pay attention to the world," she said. "Only question I have is, what are you doing here, and why are you alone? I guess those are two questions."

"I fucked it all up, Munnie."

The wrinkles of her smile snapped back into place as her face went flat. "That neither answers my questions, nor shows respect. Does it?"

I couldn't help but let go of a chuckle with a puff of air.

"Funny, now?" she asked in her still-chiding voice.

"I missed you, Munnie."

"Oh, my boy. I missed you too. Now, how about you tell me a story and keep the cussing to yourself?"

Before I could begin, I had to figure out where to start. My mother always said it was the most important decision about a story. I should have begun with Shay in the forest, but I couldn't. Not with Munnie. Instead, I began with waking up in Sonacoa before Jonac found me.

When the fire receded, I stopped to collect more wood. When our bellies rumbled, I used what little Munnie and I had between us to make a stew.

Munnie was the perfect audience. She never interrupted, never questioned. She simply listened as I rushed through the events of my past six turns.

CHAPTER THIRTY-EIGHT
KAYLO'S STORY

As I entered her domain, the layers of absence shifted across one another, almost like fabric tangled on a clothing line. These moving pieces of darkness had once scared me—even back when I thought I had stepped into a dream. Nothing so void of light should have been so alive. Yet, as I stood amongst it now, the wavering dark felt familiar.

After all, The Thief had concocted this landscape herself. She took her torment and made it manifest. If I were to do the same, I couldn't say it would appear much different.

"I know you're there. You know I'm here," I said, and the void swallowed my voice almost immediately after the words left my mouth. "Let's forget the game, shall we?"

Two overlapping shades of black parted and The Thief stepped out from an even darker absence. Her shadow cloak appeared light and wispy—purplish in comparison to its surroundings.

"How come you tend to visit me after tragedies? Do I cheer you up?"

"Is your plan working? Are there others in The Waking using your gift to free spirits? Have they turned centuries of stories around yet? Or are you still just killing in retribution?"

"Sarcasm? I thought you said you didn't want to play games." She sat, and the void sustained her weight as if taking an unseen form. "You want me to undo what I have done, right? What makes you think that I can?"

"Beyond your original interference? You reached out to the crystals in the first place," I said, more unsure of myself than I cared to admit.

All these past turns, I assumed she could undo what she had done—remove the pieces of herself from each crystal like dismantling a trinket. But what if it were more like a carving? The wood that had been shaved away couldn't be forced back into a solid block.

She touched The Waking before. The memory struck me. I had stood here in front of her as she twisted a carved bauble in her onyx hands—the rune I had whittled with her symbol. She had stolen it from The Waking only to return it to me in The Mist.

"Oh, clever boy. You do remember the times we've shared."

"You can touch The Waking. Your gift can break the crystals. There's nothing holding you back from saving our people besides your pride."

"Pride?" Her voice wavered with a bit of grit in it. "You want to know pride? Pride is knowing spirit dancers could save you and refusing to ask for their help because your stories curse them. Because you grew up with a silly little saying. Because relying on my gifts would mean admitting you were wrong. That you had ostracized and killed for superstition."

"You want every Ennean to change everything they know to be true? You've only proven them right by giving the crystals to the Gousht." The patience I had promised myself to keep began to slip. "I was the closest thing you had to getting your way. They told stories about me using your gift, and I failed. There's no winning the game you set up. You were made to be The Balance, and you don't know the meaning."

"Be careful, little thief. You come and go by my good graces, and I have had enough of your insolence." She lifted the hood of shadows from her two-toned face. Her eyes turned to narrow slits of alabaster in a mask of onyx flesh. "Maybe you would like to stay. I can imagine an unending corridor of absence for you while your body wastes away in The Waking."

"Great strategy. Trap Ennea's Thief away in The Mist. I hope my so-called spirit siblings fare better," I said, but the bravado in my words meant nothing, not when she could see the fear in my thoughts.

Her nose flared in what would have been a sneer if she had lips to complete the picture. "You're no longer welcome here, little thief. I won't warn you again."

"No warning necessary. I've given up on you. There's no reason to come back."

The Thief flicked her wrist as she sat on her throne of nothingness, and a force threw me backwards. It dragged me into a far thicker darkness. The layers blended into one. The movement stopped. It became only dark, and I continued to fly through it as if pulled by an invisible string latched to my waist.

Is this it? I thought. *Did she change her mind?*

I tried to call out to her, but no sound came. Apparently, even my speech had been by her allowance.

Rules of distance—beginnings and endings—didn't apply in the void. My fall into the darkness could last forever. Munnie would wake to find my body breathing but otherwise lifeless, until the breathing ran its course.

What would I have then? Would this darkness remain my prison even after I withered away in The Waking?

Nothing moved around me. Without a reference point, the difference between falling and remaining still vanished. For all I knew, I could be frozen in place within the dark.

Then I crashed into solid onyx.

***

The moment my eyelids popped open, I jerked upright. A high-pitched, distant buzz rang in my ears. My jaw ached like I had been clenching and grinding my teeth. I could feel my pulse leaping out of my neck.

The darkness of the hallow couldn't compete with what I had just experienced. Even underground, surrounded by stone, the tendrils of moonlight reaching into the chamber from the entrance and the vents above the plants gave the hallow more dimension than the utter nothingness in The Thief's void.

She let me go, I thought between heavy breaths, then paused as if someone would hear my thoughts.

It took several minutes of focusing on the rise and fall of my diaphragm to settle my nerves. If I tried, I wouldn't have been able to count the number of times I had escaped into The Mist. People kept warning me about how dangerous it was, but I never understood what that danger could be like. They probably didn't even comprehend their own warnings.

It hadn't been longer than a handful of moments, but in that time, I knew the darkness had become my entire existence. I would have been trapped there with my thoughts in unending absence. And I could barely coexist with my thoughts now.

She just had to do it—show me how powerless I was compared to her.

I had cursed The Thief before because of her stories, because she created the spirit crystals, because she refused to do anything to save our people, but the hatred I had previously felt hid beneath the shadow of the distain I felt for her now. Not even the Gousht had made me feel so powerless.

"She is worse than the stories," I whispered to myself. "She's earned every one."

The idea of trying to sleep after what I had experienced made my breath catch in my chest. Even blinking made me a little uncomfortable.

The subtle threads of moonlight creeping into the hallow above the tangle of plants Munnie called a garden beamed at me like a new day. I picked up my father's knife and walked over to my new distraction.

I hadn't sat down to trim a plant since I lived with the Jani. Not really. With the Uprising, I had always been too busy. I cut away what I needed and kept moving through the day. That, and tending to plants had reminded me of Jonac, which I desperately avoided.

The thoughts on the other side of my eyelids at the moment scared me far more than my old kana. I grabbed a wayward branch of the barberry bush and ran my knife along the joint. A nice clean cut. It would grow. It would be better off for the help.

With each cut, I walked further away from the memory of what The Thief had done to me. Instead, I allowed myself to think of Jonac.

In the early days, before I tried to run away, before he smelled of susu root, we would venture into the forest. He would teach me the names of plants I hadn't known and how to use them.

"Touch. Touch," he would say. "Get a feel for it in The Waking. How else will you find it in The Song?"

One time, he bent next to an innocuous-looking plant with small buds of white sprigs sitting on a field of green leaves. "Do you know what this is?" he asked. "Smell. Touch."

It wasn't an odd request, so I did. There wasn't much distinctive about the plant.

"Rub the leaves and release the oils to get a good smell."

As soon as I lowered my nose to the leaf, I jumped back from the foul odor. "What is that?"

"Snakeroot," he said. "The stem and the leaves can be poisonous. Eat an animal who grazed on snakeroot, and even its meat will sour your insides."

"Blessed Mother, why'd you have me stick my nose in it?"

"You'll be fine, and now, you know what to look out for," he said. "Ennea was dangerous long before the Gousht arrived. You need to know those dangers too."

The man had even spoken about poison with a smile back then.

A stem of the blackberry bush prickled against the pads of my fingers as I searched for a good place to cut. I slipped my knife through the branch when I found it.

A hand clapped down on my shoulder, and the whole of my body flinched.

"I'm working with a knife, Munnie! Say something if you want my attention."

"There is far too much demanding in your voice for my liking, and I have been calling your name."

It took a moment for me to register the sunlight beaming in through the cracks in the stone above and the heavy collection of clippings surrounding me.

"Sorry, Auntie," I said. "I lost myself for a moment."

"Why don't you go find yourself and some firewood while you're at it? I have some potatoes and peppers I rustled up from the forest some days back, but I'll need a fire to make anything out of them.'

After being depended on to lead a small rebel army for the past few turns, taking care of some plants and firewood sounded nice. I gathered myself and collected firewood from the forest surrounding the hallow. Munnie had the dregs of a garden not far from the entrance. It had faired only slightly better than the patch of plants inside. I plucked a couple of tomatoes from a plant that needed some care.

When I returned to the hallow with a satchel full of wood, Munnie was kneeling in front of seven crystal prisms protruding from the earth.

As of late, my prayers marked occasions more than any formal routine. I said the words before running towards danger or after a tragedy. But Munnie prayed in earnest just as she had when I was younger.

The nostalgia of seeing her at her old practice soured the more I thought about it. Since I left, I learned the truth about the power they wielded. And how they refused to use any of it to protect the people who prayed to them.

"Come," Munnie said, still facing the crystals. The Song radiated through her like a beacon in the night, a steady heartbeat under the earth calling me home.

"I'm done with prayer," I said, carrying my load of firewood to lay on the scraps of what we burned the previous evening.

"After all the gifts The Mother bestowed upon you?"

"Gifts?!" I rounded to face Munnie. "I never told my parents what I was. The Mother tied me to The Thief, and people hated me for it. I thought it was ignorance that made them hate me, but she earned every curse. And The Seed—my only solace—was taken from me with The Thief's power. Fuck these gifts."

"After all this time, you still call her The Thief?"

"Yes!" My resentment flooded into my tone. "The cursed bitch stole from all of us. She stole our spirits, our land, our lives, and handed them to the couta. There are no grievances worth her genocide."

"You lower yourself with insults."

"I lower myself? Munnie, I am lower than the bedrock. The Mist is full of my mistakes. Insulting that traitor is a drop in a sea of blood I owe."

She hadn't moved from where she knelt. For all my curses, she hadn't raised her voice or narrowed her eyes. "Did I ever tell you about my daughter?"

The question caught me off guard. Shay and I had been endlessly curious about Munnie when we met her, but she never entertained our questions. She never held back affection or knowledge, save the answers that we craved the most. We wanted to know her.

"Her name was Verice, but I called her Veri." The tone of her voice shifted down in pitch. "She loved colors—the brighter the better. She sewed her robes from wonderfully dyed thread. Her paintings were more striking than a sunset.

"She died young." Munnie hadn't lost her smile, but tears had joined it. "The healers tried every concoction they could mix—herbs, oils, rare flowers. Nothing helped. She coughed blood until she died in her sleep. Beneath a pretty quilt she had woven."

"I'm sorry."

"I'm not looking for your condolences." She stopped and collected herself as if her curt tone had shaken her too. Her shoulders rose and fell with her heavy breaths as she searched for her fragile calm.

"I apologize. This story isn't for your pity, Kaylo. It is for your understanding," she said. "I cursed The Great Spirits, The Mother, even her Daughters in the sky. None of it made the pain go away. It just made me bitter and angry."

"This isn't the same. The Thief didn't make your daughter sick."

"Does it make you happier? Do your curses take away your pain? You are burying yourself in a grave you dug for others. The Great Spirits and the Gousht don't care what words you call them. It won't change them, but it will change you."

"You want me to speak kind words about the Gousht?!"

"I want you to stop dirtying our language by giving them our words. I want you to stop reducing their trespasses to an insult. They have earned our vitriol. We don't need to call them 'couta' to prove it."

"What does it matter?"

"Maybe if you can stop making it your responsibility to punish The Balance and the Gousht, you can stop punishing yourself."

I crushed the tomato I had brought in from the garden, its pulp oozing through my fingers. "After everything I told you last night? You know I'm not innocent."

"Kaylo—"

"If I deserve such sympathy, where is Shay?! Where are my parents?!" The stone walls trapped my screams, and they reverberated through the chamber. "Do you know what happened that night?"

The two images that would forever be engrained in my head from that night flickered in my vision: Shay jerking from my touch and my parents standing side by side, waiting to die.

"Shay was scared and still breathing when I left her. My parents faced soldiers with a kitchen knife and a hammer as I escaped through the back window. I abandoned them!"

"Kaylo, you were a child. You didn't do anything wrong."

"I don't even know what happened to them. They were all still breathing the last time I saw them. Tell me how they died. I know you know. The Gousht are never quiet about their punishments."

"I don't think it's helpful—"

"Tell me!" My scream shook through my body and left me breathless.

"Your father died fighting the soldiers that night. They executed your mother on the caller's stage. Then they hanged all three bodies above the square as a message. They didn't remove them until the birds had made them unrecognizable. Is that what you wanted to hear?"

As she said the words, I saw them. The Gousht had hanged bodies over the square before. I could remember how the stink made it harder to ignore them as the days rotted their bodies.

"What did they say happened to me?"

"Until the stories spread, I thought you had been sent to the mines," she said. "It wasn't your fault."

I puffed out a throaty chuckle. "No, it was Rena's. Did you know that? Shay insulted a little blood banner girl named Rena, and she sicked the soldiers after us like a good little traitor. At least I was able to kill the person who got Boda killed. Rena got away with it."

Munnie's soft expression hardened, her nose flaring and her upper lip curling for a brief moment before it settled back into concern.

"What was that look?" I said with an inherent demand.

"The past is the past, Kaylo. Let the spirits move on."

"Munnie, if you know something about my parents, I need to know."

"I didn't know Rena played a role that night, but I know the name." She closed her eyes and shook her head. "Violence won't bring them back."

"How do you know the name?"

"Things are changing. The Gousht want to prop up Enneans who have assimilated—give the people examples of 'good' Enneans to look up to. They named Rena as regent of Nomar. She still reports to the priest like the babe she is, sucking on mother's milk. But she is responsible for managing the concerns of common folk—who gets supplies for their trade, mediating domestic disagreements, granting the construction of new dwellings."

Munnie stopped speaking. Her lips stopped moving, but I continued to stare at them as if they would part to make sense of what she had just said.

"No," I whispered to myself. "That doesn't make sense. She's no more than a couple turns past twenty. Who is she to make any decisions for anyone?"

"There are rumors about what she's done for the Gousht. People who had hid their gifts for turns on end were suddenly discovered. Those who whispered about stories of rebellion went missing."

"That was Rena?" Five turns later, and the blood banner still made her trade uncovering secrets.

I should have felt rage. The most aware part of me wondered where my anger had gone. Instead, everything slowed. My mother's fears—our people forgetting our stories and becoming darker-skinned versions of the Gousht—were coming true.

The Gousht's promise couldn't be mistaken. Fight and die. Join and thrive. Sure, thriving might mean spitting on the ideals your people had valued for centuries, but it would be so much more comfortable than an arrow in the gut.

Before the violence erupted in Colian, the streets had been peaceful. They had returned to the status quo immediately afterwards. I had seen the Gousht sit by and watch Enneans labor away. Those workers had probably gone home to families that night. Some of the Enneans even lived in opulent homes, profiting off the broken-back dock workers same as the Gousht.

What was left to rage over? The Gousht had defeated us entirely.

"Don't go off and get yourself killed now," Munnie said, apparently unaware of how dead I already was. "You are welcome to stay here, but I won't have you rush out to bloody your hands only to return to this hallow."

I nodded and walked over to the patch of plants on the far side of the hallow. They still needed more tending. A single night hadn't been enough.

"Kaylo, I need you to hear me."

With my father's knife in hand, I sat in front of an overgrown sage bush, which had killed the herbs beneath by hoarding all the light.

"I heard you." I sliced into the plant.

CHAPTER THIRTY-NINE

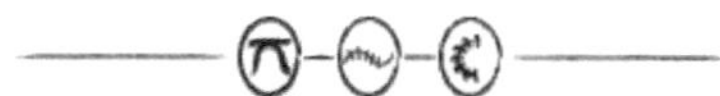

Admitting it might have killed Wal, literally knocked his spirit from his body into The Mist, but Lanigan had been right. He could only exercise or throw his little stones so much before the hours beat him into submission.

It could have been a moon or a turn. The days stretched long and thin. Empty, meaningless hours lingered on until he could force himself to sleep again.

He tossed another stone and hit the target for the thousandth time.

"Poet, you're too quiet," he shouted. "Say something before I assume you've gone and died on me."

"Commander? Are you really asking for conversation? Why the sudden reversal?"

"Never mind. A moment of lapsed judgment."

"Oh, that's no fun," Lanigan said. "How about a game? Something simple. No quoting sonnets or twisting words about. A question for a question."

"Fine. I go first. What is it you're planning with the servants? I see them come in here and sign away with every shitty meal."

Every time he had asked something similar in the past, the poet had obfuscated. They had broken into cryptic poems, told stories, and never come close to answering the question.

"Flawed question, my friend. I'm not planning anything. I am but a wheel on the cart."

"No. You suggested this game. Answer the question."

"Then ask the right one. I answered the question you asked."

"In that case, what are the servants plotting?"

"Sorry, Commander. It is my turn to ask the question; make sure you don't forget yours."

Wal threw a stone wildly at the opposite wall. The stone ricochetted and hit him in the ear. "Fuck!" Pain splintered through his skull, only adding to his frustration.

"May I pause the game to ask if you're alright?"

"Just ask your fucking question."

"Do you hate Kaylo?"

A chuckle burst from Wal's throat, bitter and lifeless. The poet hadn't pulled this game from the ether. Why did he constantly bring up the traitor? Why did he insist on picking at old wounds?

"Yes. If it weren't for Kaylo, I wouldn't be here. Even before he left me to bleed out into the sand, he abandoned me," Wal said. "When I found him and his girl out there, I thought The Mother had given us a second chance. I convinced myself he might follow through on his promise. We both owed blood, but still he ran. He abandoned me again.

"Is that what you want to hear, poet? Do you enjoy my pain?"

"Is that your question?"

"Fuck you and your childish games. Tell me what the servants are plotting or be done with it."

Manipulations. The world ran on manipulations. From the servant, to the poet, to the bloody king, everyone had their aims. Wal had always been more honest about it than most, and people scorned him for it. Lanigan played games and played with words to hide their true goals. That didn't make them better—only a better liar.

"I don't know," Lanigan said.

"You might think I am a petty man for my anger, but you will know it firsthand if you don't give me more."

"They haven't told me much of their machinations, but they are working towards an end. They have asked me to play a role, and I have agreed," they said. "The servants, more than anyone else, have earned their secrets. I would not pry. My guess is they are chasing their freedom, and I find it to be a worthy cause."

"Will you tell me when they share more?"

"If I believe I can trust you with the truth."

It was an honest answer, but what would it matter? If a prisoner trapped in a cage under a mountain couldn't be trusted to keep a secret, no one could. Wal could tell the servants he knew. He could tell the rodents. He could shout it through the cavernous expanse with abandon.

"My turn," Lanigan said in a sing-song phrase. "How did you become a part of the Lost Army? You said without Kaylo, you wouldn't be here. What happened?"

A number of sarcastic responses flittered over Wal's tongue before he thought better of it. If the poet wanted honesty, they could have it.

"After Kaylo left, covered in the blood of an old woman who deserved it—did your friend tell you that?" Wal waved off the question as if Lanigan could see him. "The council took charge of the Uprising. They shut down raids. They refused to fight. After everyone we had lost, they wanted to take a step back and reevaluate.

"They didn't care about how many people continued to suffer and die under occupation. They wanted to save themselves. A turn went by. We set up a freecity called Aerolyne along the Strait of Talmo, while the Gousht continued to kill our people. The council decided to make themselves safer instead of fighting."

The anger and the helplessness Wal had felt at the time leached out of the memory. He relived it all.

"A few of us refused to stand by and watch the Gousht grow stronger. The council had made us powerless. They abandoned the cause. Five of us left in the night for an outpost we'd scouted back when we were a true rebellion."

Wal's jaw clenched as he recalled the night. They had been so confident. Before anyone sounded the alarm, they had killed seven soldiers. He could still feel the friction in his hand from when he yanked his bloody blade free from a soldier's gut. Then the alarm rang.

"The Gousht had neglected the outpost for several turns, but recent activity near the Astilean border changed things. The soldiers swarmed us." His throat caught on the words. "Two of us died before they had us on our knees, their commander pacing in front of us."

The commander's metal armor had reflected the moonlight. For some reason, that shiny, unmarred armor appeared as clearly to Wal in his cell as it had that night.

"This isn't my first cell," Wal said. "They only fed us enough to sustain one person, so the three of us thinned like dead trees decaying in the forest. When they were bored, they would pick one of us to beat. Every time they opened the doors to our makeshift shack of a prison, I prayed it wasn't my turn.

"Eventually, they put us to work, mending this or that. The beatings never stopped. Even after they killed Jolrin. I worked and bled in that cell of mine for two seasons before the Astilean Army raided the outpost. They saved me. They gave me a way to fight back. To spill the blood I owed."

The day of the raid, it had been Wal's turn for a beating. He had cowered when the doors opened. Those bastards made him cower.

"When I had the chance, I earned as many honor markings as I could. Not for ambition." Wal's voice lowered to a growl. "I killed to take myself back from them."

"I'm sorry that happened to you, my friend," Lanigan said.

"I don't need your apologies," he said. "I need a way to finish what I started."

"What happened to the other prisoner?"

"Rēlan died in battle." Wal smacked the stone with the flat of his palm. "The Gousht never stop taking."

He plucked a stone from the ground and tossed it at one of the targets he had made. There were reasons he didn't delve into the past. It didn't accomplish anything.

CHAPTER FORTY
CURRENT DAY ENNEA

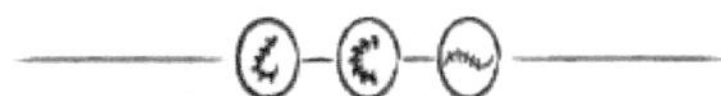

Nearly three hundred Enneans crammed into the gathering tent and the surrounding grounds waiting to hear what Tayen already knew: in seven days, they would be infiltrating Stone City.

When she decided to join the Uprising, she imagined being a part of Kaylo's stories—ambushing caravans, liberating small towns on the coastline, charging into battle with level odds. People liked to say when the Stone City fell, Ennea fell, because Stone City was considered to be impenetrable. It withstood a Gousht siege for two turns before falling, and only then because traitors opened the wall from within.

Liara stood at the center of the gathering tent, and the crowd swallowed its noise.

The water dancer from Kaylo's stories had become a true power. Nothing about her resisted the weight of leadership. No stories swept the countryside telling tales of her deeds, yet every eye under the canopy looked to her. Warriors gray from age to orphans who had picked up their first blade a moon past gave her their respect.

Kaylo looked at her like a fool turning wise to his mistakes. Even now, as he waited for her to lay out what would be the decisive battle for Ennea, he wore a melancholy smile with a stare lost in time.

Liara turned to face the circle of curious faces before speaking. "In a span, twelve days at the most, the Lost Army will descend upon the Stone City. They will fight for the right to crown Ennea's ruler. We cannot allow that to happen. The Mother needs no ruler. Her people need the freedom to determine their own future. Anything else would be the end of Ennea.

"As we speak, the Jani and every clan sworn to the Uprising are on their way here. In seven days, we will take Stone City ourselves."

No amount of respect could have quelled the buzz that erupted throughout the tent. Liara had just told people they were likely to die. Whether or not she said the words, no clear-headed person would have heard anything different.

"We are not alone. There is a growing resistance in the city, waiting for us. We will give them their power back by relying on those we have too often ostracized. Three teams will accompany spirit dancers to free spirits from the largest caches of crystals in Ennea. We will not allow the Gousht to turn our spirits on us.

"That is when the resistance will throw open the gates for our forces. Your regiment leaders have your orders."

Liara paused and slowly looked to the warriors kneeling all around her. She lowered her voice, and the crowd leaned forward. "Make no mistake. We have two options: we fight, we take the city, and return Ennea to her people; or we become subject to a King or an Emperor."

A chant started from the other side of the gathering tent. "Fight. Fight. Fight." The repetition carried through the crowd until everyone had begun chanting.

Tayen had assumed people like Liara only existed in stories—warriors who could captivate people to their cause. She had just announced their plan to attack the most fortified city in all of Ennea with an army far too small, and the crowd swelled to meet the challenge.

A balding Tomakan man in his later turns rose up in the midst of the chanting. His expression had not been swept into the fervor.

With a wave of her hand, Liara hushed the chanting clan.

"I understand your reasons, but we have survived this long because we are slow and careful. This is too much too quickly. I will not send my sons to die in a fool's last attempt at freedom."

A mixture of groans and grunts clashing in affirmation and disagreement rang out through the tent.

"This is not an army. It never has been and never will be," Liara said. "Those who choose to stay behind will not be faulted. This battle will be bloody. It will come sooner than I'd like, but it is necessary."

"We need more time," a voice called out from the crowd.

"There is no time to be had," Liara said. "If we could delay the Lost Army, we would, but we cannot split our forces."

"We could deal with whoever loses their battle," another voice called out. "Let them weaken each other."

"We should strike Colian while the Gousht are distracted."

Liara sliced her arm through the air, and the shouting ceased. "Under this gathering tent, we have our traditions. We work and move as a clan. You have leaders and orders, but each warrior is a free Ennean.

"There is a difference tonight. We are not here to debate strategy or targets. I have come to ask you to join me. Your voices are welcome, but the clans are on the move. This battle is going to happen."

Even the ardent supporters in the crowd shied away from the break from their traditions. Faces soured. People searched the crowd for the next voice to speak up.

Sosun stood, and all eyes followed her. Her hands flowed from one sign to the next.

"No," Nix said from beside Sosun.

Sosun smacked Nix's shoulder and pointed over the crowd to Liara.

An air of confusion filtered through the gathering tent, until Nix rose.

"This is Sosun. She escaped from servitude to the Lost Nation, but it left her unable to share her words," Nix said. "So I will translate, even if I think she's fucking stupid."

Sosun repeated her words.

"If you need more time, I will give it to you. No war party travels from the Lost Nation without servants," Nix translated. "They call us Nameless. They have discarded us even though they rely on us. The servants of the Citadel will give you time. We will show the Lost Nation they cannot take our freedom, no matter how hard they try."

Tayen knelt in silence as a roar welled up from the warriors around the tent. Sosun had always said she hadn't planned on picking up a sword, which Tayen assumed to mean that she would help care for those who remained in the encampment, the elderly and injured.

Her friend had volunteered to walk back into captivity, and it enraged Tayen as much as it made her proud.

Sosun continued to stand, staring at Liara as the crowd sounded their approval.

"You're asking us to place the fate of this siege wholly on your ability to delay a caravan of thousands," Liara said.

Sosun's hands flashed from one gesture to another as Nix translated. "No, I'm telling you to depend on a forgotten community whose strength has been underestimated at every turn. The Lost Nation will not make it to the Last Wall before at least fourteen days have passed."

The tide of sentiment had turned. Sosun had humbled three hundred warriors with her bravery. Liara and her advisors may have come up with the plan, but Sosun made the Uprising believe.

When Sosun knelt, her hands shook at her sides. She had promised to delay the warpath of the only remaining Ennean army on behalf of all Citadel servants.

If she allowed herself to think about the gravity of what she had taken on, the shaking would consume her. Instead, she stared at Liara as the rest of the briefing continued.

Several people spoke up and asked questions, but no one dared to back away from their obligations after what Sosun had said. In a way, there was an insult buried in the compliment. If a girl who had been enslaved and abused was brave enough to face an army on her own, how could a warrior do anything but charge into battle?

People always treated her as helpless. They would find out how wrong they were.

Her hands stopped shaking. Linnard had used people's assumptions—their underestimations. She saved lives because people overlooked her. And Sosun would do the same.

When the gathering tent began to clear, several warriors nodded in her direction and wished her luck. She returned each nod and smile, but she did not stand to join the exodus.

Strangely, the prospect of walking out with the crowd seemed more daunting than infiltrating an Astilean war march.

"That was stupid, you know that right?" Nix said once the crowd had dissipated. "If anyone recognizes you, they'll execute you and continue marching after wiping the blood from their blades."

"No one recognizes the Nameless."

"I hope you know you're not going alone," Nix said, signing at the same time.

"I have to," Sosun signed. *"They'll recognize you."*

"Maybe they will. Maybe they won't. There will be thousands of people to get lost amongst." Nix stood up and started walking out. "Before you try to think of something clever to say, I am going to pack my things. We'll march towards our death tomorrow morning."

Sosun flashed a rude gesture at Nix, but Tayen stood where Sosun had expected to find Nix. The girl looked frightened. The only other time she had been frightened was after she had run Pana through with a spear.

"Tayen, this is something I have to do."

"Don't leave," Tayen said. "I know it's selfish, but you can't leave. Everyone I love leaves me, and I cannot watch you go without saying something."

Sosun rushed to her feet and pulled Tayen into an embrace. It was easy to forget Tayen's age. She had lost too many people over the last turn.

She let Tayen go to speak. *"I am not leaving you. I am walking my own path. You have to go to the Stone City, and I have to face the Lost Army."*

"It's too dangerous."

"What do you think separates Astileans from the Gousht? They may be Ennean, but they are the ones who enslaved me. They took my tongue and forced me to breathe poison. It took me turns to pull away from susu root. I still crave it.

"It won't stop if they win. They'll still need their servants." Sosun slapped the back of her hand down firmly in the palm of her other hand before curling her fingers inward to emphasize 'servants.' *"They cannot win. If I can do anything to stop them from taking more people, stealing more tongues and futures, I will."*

"I just don't want to lose you."

"I told you that I would find my own way to fight this war. It was never going to be with a sword. This is it," Sosun signed. *"I need to make this decision for me, and it has nothing to do with you. But I am not planning on dying. I still have a lot of words to teach you."*

"How do you say 'swear to it'?"

Sosun joined her fingers into a point, brought them to her lips, then touched them to her forehead.

———

As soon as Tayen passed the threshold of the gathering tent, she ran. Her body needed to ache to make sense of this pain.

Sosun had her own journey, which had nothing to do with Tayen. Paths diverged. Life was never some promised, stagnant thing. She wasn't owed anything.

But she wanted a family.

The encampment swelled with activity. Much needed doing if they meant to set siege to the Stone City. But not even the fear of their foolish plan touched Tayen's heart.

A soft sting crawled up her thigh. Her lungs felt the labor of her speed. It wasn't enough.

She raced past the guarded entrance to shouts of confused warriors. The rough forest floor forced her to focus on each next footfall. The trees diverted her this way and that. All manner of plants in the tangled undergrowth reached for her feet. Nothing stopped her.

The danger didn't settle in her mind.

She had spent countless hours with Sosun over the last several span, learning a language, confessing her thoughts, coming to rely on her in a way she could never rely on Kaylo.

She miscalculated her next step, and an exposed root snagged her foot. If she had been moving slower, she could have caught herself. Instead, her speed drove her tumbling into the harsh undergrowth.

The rough edge of a shrub dragged along her cheek, and the pain burned like it should. Her body came to a rest, sprawled across a patch of leaves, weeds, and broken plants. Dirt clung to her face as she rose.

She slammed her fist into the earth, which sent the force recoiling up her arm.

The Song reached for her with sweeping cries, singing far louder than the haunting sound of a shadow forced into the light.

Her mother had told her that The Song and The Shadow would always be there for her no matter what happened. But it wasn't true. The Shadow ran from her grasp every time she reached for it.

"Not anymore," Tayen said.

Whether or not the shade below the forest canopy blended into a single pitch of darkness, each shadow had its own place within The Song. Thousands of infinitesimal shadows hummed in concert.

There was a reason only dancers could hear The Song. The noise was a door to The Mist, but it didn't exist within any of the countless shadows. The pathway sang from the fragment of a Great Spirit within each dancer.

Tayen listened, following the symphony of noises to their origin. An indescribable piece of her that existed beyond the physical. Like a feeling, it carried weight without taking up space.

She had been expecting to find a piece of her—like an organ, like a heart—to pinpoint the beating. Instead, she followed the intangible sense of a familiar stranger within. The Shadow.

Clouds draped over the ground with subtle hints of pinks and yellows like a sunrise caught in the lining of each effervescent formation. They carried on as far as Tayen could see.

Each shift in color stuck out from the shadows, which offered dimension to the clouds. The contrast felt important in the same way that a thought can flitter off when one gets too close to it.

"You're there, aren't you?" Tayen called out, her voice carrying into the open horizon.

Slowly, the purple shadow of a cloud billowed into a puff of smoke before reforming into a tall, slender body. As if encased within glass, the purple-black smoke churned beneath the surface.

Her round face swelled at her cheeks and dissipated into a halo of dark, swirling clouds above her brow. She had no mouth but was no less striking for the absence, if it could be called an absence.

"Why have you kept me at a distance? I've needed you so many times, and you always refused me. You're supposed to be a guide, the wise spirit."

"Child, wisdom is neither an oracle nor a commander."

"What does that mean?!" Tayen yelled. "Everyone I love is either dead or walking towards death. I need to keep them safe. I need you to keep them safe."

"Your demands are not welcome here," The Shadow said, her voice shifting into a firmer, more solid tenor. "My descendants and I are called wise because we search for answers, not because we have them."

"What am I supposed to do?"

"Search, child. The future is unwritten. What would you make of it?"

"I want the people I love to live!"

"Then stop them. Hide and survive, but even that has its risks," she said. "You want guarantees. There are none. Sometimes I forget how little time my descendants have had to search The Waking."

"So, what? I'm supposed to forget the people I care about? This is all so much bigger than me or anyone else in my life. Am I supposed to think past them? Is that it?"

The Shadow walked towards Tayen, and with each movement, her limbs lost form only to settle into place when they stopped. She reached down in a cloud of purple vapor, then her hand solidified on Tayen's cheek.

"Love and attachments are not your enemies. They are not distractions. They are guides by other names." Her charcoal eyes teemed with movement. "Would you steal their choices from them to keep them safe? What lives would you wish for them? What risks are you willing to take for them?"

The spirit's cheeks pulled into a mouthless smile. "Find the question that leads you searching for the right answers."

"And if they die?"

"The morning light is not promised to any mortal. Ask yourself, if they live, what would you like them to see when they wake?"

CHAPTER FORTY-ONE
CURRENT DAY ENNEA

The morning light had only begun to break over the trees. Nix walked the encampment, enjoying the last moments before she marched to her inevitable death.

Even a turn ago, she would have been smarter—sadder and lonelier maybe—but she definitely wouldn't be following Sosun to fight an army by themselves.

If she never objected to Wal conscripting Tayen; if she hadn't gone searching after Sosun because of her guilty conscience; if she had done what Wal asked and given Kaylo up; if she had left the three of them to fend for themselves in the forest, she could have lived out the rest of her days as far away from the fighting as possible.

I'm too nice, she thought.

Several warriors milled about making preparations for their own ridiculous plans. They had to know death would wash over them and their compatriots like a torrential storm. Most of them probably thought they would be the ones to survive. Desperate people made stupid decisions and followed them up with delusional thinking.

Nix had no time for the delusional thinking bit.

When she reached the tent, she drew the furs aside. Kaylo stirred as the light streamed in and fell across his face. He sat up and the blanket fell from his bare chest, revealing the map of scars and burns he had earned.

Before he could open his mouth to say something unnecessary, Nix pointed to the girl and shushed him. To his credit and forever saving grace, he closed his mouth and let the child sleep.

"I need your help with something," Nix signed.

"What is it?"

Nix released the furs and let them settle back into place. Time had run short for everyone within this tree wall, and she had no desire to waste it explaining things to Kaylo.

The man took his time dressing and coming out from his tent—time she didn't have. If she and Sosun were going to delay the war march, they needed to leave as soon as possible.

She walked off without a word, waving for him to follow.

"Good morning to you as well," Kaylo called from several steps behind. "When you ask for a favor, typically you actually ask."

Something about annoying him helped stave off the thoughts of impending doom.

Nix strode into a tent towards the perimeter of the tree wall where the rebels kept their medical supplies.

"Are you hurt? Do you need a poultice? What is going on, Nix?"

"Look at me," Nix said. "I am about to infiltrate the Lost Nation war party. I can't make it by as a servant, so I need your help."

She looked towards a pot of ink and several long spines from a succulent she had found by the river. It had taken her hours to mix the soot, water, and sap in the right proportions.

"That's not necessary. There will be plenty of recruits on the war march. You don't have to mar your face permanently."

"I'll still be plenty pretty."

"Nix—"

"Kaylo, I need you to do this. I need to be believed the moment they see me. It is the only way I will be able to protect Sosun," Nix said. "You would do it for Tayen."

"Lie down over there." He pointed at a bedroll laid out for sick and injured people. "How many turns have you served?' How many battles? How many kills?"

"I should be relatively new. They won't recognize me, but I'll need enough battles and kills to quiet their questions."

As Nix settled herself on the bedroll, Kaylo collected the ink pot and spines. "I have no idea what I'm doing. You know that, right? I've stitched wounds, but I've never inked a tattoo before."

"Don't worry about it. If you fuck up, it will only get Sosun and I killed."

"I really hate you sometimes, Nix."

He dipped a spine into the ink pot. Its hollow center would hold the ink as he punched it into her cheek. She had asked enough questions during her Lost Army training to understand the basics.

She grabbed his wrist before he began. "Thank you for helping me keep her alive."

He smiled. "Just think, if you hadn't talked me into searching for the Uprising, we could be getting on each other's nerves far, far away from here."

With the gentlest of touches, Kaylo positioned the needle against her left cheek. The spine pricked her skin, making her want to scratch it away.

"Every tattoo starts with the first battle," Kaylo said before unsheathing his knife and tapping the other end of the spine with the flat of his blade.

She flinched away from the pain. It stung like a hornet, but without the lingering tingle.

"Don't move," he said. "This is going to take time."

Each time he repositioned the spine, she held her breath. With each tap, she exhaled. The more he worked, the hotter her cheek became. A small fire burned a trail behind his needle.

"The things we do to keep these kids alive. If they could stop running towards death, that would be nice," Kaylo said as he reset the spine.

"I'm just thinking about how boring things were before I met you."

"I blame the kid. Before her, I spent most of my time tending my garden."

Nix put up her hand to stop him. "You did a good thing. You didn't have to take her in."

He dipped a rag in a bucket of water and wiped her cheek. The cool touch of the wet cloth tempered the sting. "Yes, I did."

"When you charge off into the Stone City, don't die."

As he reset a new spine on her cheek, he smiled. "That is perhaps the most pleasant thing you've ever said to me."

"Kaylo—"

"Stop talking, or I won't be able to finish this."

"I'll say this once," she said. "You aren't a complete asshole. You have something of value to offer. Not saying you aren't an annoying tit most of the time, but I think you're a far better person than you think you are."

"Nix, you are a shockingly kind person."

"No, we're done," she said, relaxing her head on the bedroll and closing her eyes. "Finish stabbing me with the needle now."

"As you wish." Kaylo tapped the spine and a new pinprick of flames sparked on her cheek.

***

When Kaylo peeled back the furs to his tent, Tayen was sitting on her bedroll.

"Is it time?" she asked.

The small pitch up in the middle of her question hit him in the bridge of his nose. Her pain settled into him. Every day between today and their foolhardy siege, he would consider taking her and running.

He wouldn't—partly because she would hate him for it, partly because they couldn't hide from the blood forever. But the thoughts would come regardless.

"It's time," he said, holding the furs aside for her.

When she stepped out, her face contorted. One eyebrow shifted up without the other. Her mouth fell agape.

"Did I do a good job?"

"Blessed fucking Mother, what did you do?" Tayen stepped in closer, oblivious to Nix being a person rather than a thing to inspect. "They're red and puffy."

"The swelling will go down," Kaylo said.

"The lines are wobbly."

"They're mostly straight," he said, feeling far more defensive than he had a right to.

Nix grabbed Tayen by the shoulders and pushed her back an arm's length. "Most of the warriors don't have straight tattoos. It's not like they have artisans mark their kills. Kaylo's mediocre work will fit right in."

"Last time I do you a favor," Kaylo said.

"Probably," Nix said with a morose smile.

Sosun pushed Nix for the comment before turning to Tayen. *"Don't put yourself in more danger than necessary. Listen to him. He'll do his best to keep you safe. Don't die."*

"Those are supposed to be my words. You're the one sneaking into a war march without a weapon or anyone but this tattooed jerk."

Watching their goodbye felt wrong. Tayen and Sosun had only known each other for five or six span, but there were circumstances that sped intimacy along. The same circumstances that made Kaylo willing to die for Tayen far too soon.

When time ran short and hope stretched thin, people grabbed onto those around them with a fierceness that defied reason.

Tayen buried her face in Sosun's shoulder as they hugged for what might have been the last time.

Earlier, Kaylo had joked about the hardships he could have avoided if he hadn't taken Tayen in. He hadn't been wrong. The slow dullness he had been living in hadn't been nearly as painful as the fear and worry he had felt since she came along. However, the pride he felt made a fine balm.

Once Tayen let go of Sosun, Kaylo stepped forward. *"You are a far braver warrior than any prick in the Lost Army. Make them see what power the servants hold."*

She clutched onto him and he returned her embrace. He let out a heavy breath. This young woman deserved infinitely more care than life had given her.

"Remember," he said still holding her. "Their weakness is they don't know your strength."

She let go of him and stepped back. *"Give them another story."*

"Nix, see you around." Kaylo offered a smile and his hands.

"Be smarter than you look, hero." Nix clasped hands with Kaylo and returned his smile. "Now, we better get going. If we wait too long, we might think of a less dangerous plan. Where would the glory be in that?"

Nix and Sosun collected their belongings and walked down the line of tents towards the encampment entrance. They shrank into the distance and passed through the gap in the tree wall.

"Blessed Mother, watch them, guide them, protect them." Kaylo turned and walked back towards their tent.

"Where are you going?" Tayen asked.

"If we are going to lay siege on the Stone City, I want to finish my story. You coming?" Kaylo said before stepping through the furs into their tent.

Chapter Forty-Two
Kaylo's Story

I THRASHED AWAKE AND stabbed at the air in front of me with an empty fist.

The soldiers from my dream were gone. They'd had me surrounded on an empty market street in Nomar. Rena, still impossibly young, had ordered the soldiers to attack, smiling all the while.

No matter how many times I had dreamed some version of the same encounter over the last two moons, I never found a way to avoid the trap. I followed the blood banner through alleyways and thoroughfares, then turned a corner. The soldiers were always there, holding their blades as Rena used them like her weapon.

I hadn't gotten a full night's rest since Munnie told me about the new regent of Nomar.

These dreams would kill me if I didn't do anything, but then what could I do? Charge into the city and kill her? Burn her house down around her?

Despite what happened in my dreams, I had never run into Rena on one of my supply trips to Nomar. I walked in and out with whatever supplies Munnie had sent me after. The city was far too big to bump into the regent in the market. Not that Rena went to the market with the common folk.

There would be runners to do that sort of thing for powerful blood banners.

All that didn't mean I hadn't asked after her. I knew where she lived—the old house by the western barracks. It had belonged to an elder councilor and her family before the Gousht arrived. It made me want to spit, thinking of Rena sleeping in their home.

People's tongues had been quite free on the subject as soon as I convinced them I had no love for the regent.

She lived alone. The lantern light from her window rarely expired. Apparently, the young woman had been working herself to the quick ever since her blood banner parents had died.

That was the best of the news I had gotten. Everything else had seemed to go perfectly for life's little shit stain. Power. Wealth. Protection.

In idle moments, I daydreamed about creeping into her stolen home and taking the blood owed. But Munnie had been clear. If I took my vengeance, I would have to leave, and Munnie needed me. The way she had been struggling on her own—she deserved better.

I owed her for what she had done for Shay and me. Even more for being my last refuge.

She had finally started to put some of her weight back on, resembling the kana I had left behind. If I left now, I would be killing her slowly.

I unsheathed my father's knife and looked at it. The leather wrap still bore the stains of Hylíane's blood.

When I thought about how she had betrayed us, I could convince myself I had done the right thing. It became harder when I remembered what the Gousht had done to her.

I had no such qualms about Rena. And yet, she continued to breathe less than an hour to the south.

Munnie's gentle snores hummed through the chamber.

I sheathed the knife once more.

The stores of firewood would last Munnie at least three seasons, and if I tended the gardens any more closely, the plants would die from

not being left the fuck alone. But we could always use more salt. I had
drained our supply on the last rabbits I preserved.

Nomar would be waking by the time I reached the tree wall. No use
in wasting time lying down not sleeping. Not when we needed salt.

The tree wall surrounding Nomar brought me a perverse sense of joy.
It hadn't existed when I lived in the city. The greens thought the city was
too big and well equipped for any rebel group to threaten their hold.
Then came the Uprising.

These tightly knit trees had the same effect they did anywhere else.
They restricted movement. It was unnatural. Ennean spirits belonged to
the very land we lived on. Penning us in was a crime.

But the wall did something else. It told a story: the Gousht were
scared of a bunch of kids and wandering folk who picked up whatever
blades they could to fight back.

The story made me proud in spite of the damage I had done to so
many.

I found the section of the wall Munnie had shown me and grabbed
hold of a slightly discolored tree trunk—a duplicate of the others to
either side of it in every other way. It took several jerking movements to
wriggle the section of tree from its place.

The segment created a gap big enough for one person to squeeze
through sideways. Given my recent experience with the smugglers
in Colian, I wondered how many small entrances and exits existed
throughout the city. Then I wondered how Munnie had found this
particular one.

Once I slipped through the gap, I wedged the segment of ironoak
back into position.

The orange glow of morning light draped over Nomar. Shadows
stretched in blues and purples, capturing the city in two tones. Every
time I saw it, the sight brought me back to the city I had grown up in.

On the southern side of the city, the morning market would be getting underway.

Even as the Gousht built barriers to our freedom, they made room for commerce. It distracted the people, but it also made them active participants in this new world being created around them. They had reason to work for imperial coin.

It didn't bother the Gousht to pass out their small trinkets and circulate them throughout the city, only to collect them on the other end.

The more I studied the Gousht, the more I grew to understand that the key to their success lay in systems. They created complicated rules to bind their soldiers into service, to maintain power within a single family, to disrupt natural communities, to extract labor from people. The rules of the intertwining systems contradicted one another. Some were written, while others had to be culturally understood.

When I was young, my father traded woodwork for grain—a simple exchange. Far too simple for the Gousht to interject themselves.

Their systems were an ugly mess of perfection. Say one thing for the green bastards, they understood how to turn a situation to their advantage.

I passed under the wooden sign of what had been my father's workshop as it swayed with the wind. The same words lay embedded within the wood—*Craft and Forge*. Even the cracks in the facade my father had often spoken about fixing remained just as they had.

It felt strangely offensive that Nomar hadn't changed in the past six turns. Like they hadn't felt the absence of my parents or Shay. They had continued on like they had after the Gousht murdered so many others. They had survived and mourned in silence.

The first time Munnie had sent me through the tree wall to purchase spices, I thought people would recognize me immediately. After all, I had lived in Nomar for most of my adolescence. I ducked my head as I walked. But people were too busy with their own concerns to pay me any mind. I walked the streets, no different from any of them.

Time, blood, battles, tears—nothing could stop this city from being my home. I still fit here. Much more than I ever had in any rebellion.

The path in front of me led south into the heart of the market. I had walked it countless times as a boy. This time I strayed and took the route that would lead me past Rena's stolen home. It wasn't the first time.

The temptation to catch a glimpse of her was too great. Looking at a building never harmed anyone, and I had spent too many nights wondering what Rena might look like now. It felt strange to despise the child in my dreams. But no matter how many times I had loitered outside her home, I hadn't seen her.

Would I even recognize her if I had?

A set of bells rang, calling the first round of students to class in the makeshift church. Even the oldest of these children wouldn't be able to remember a time before the Gousht. They had grown up on stories from the Writ rather than those passed down through generations of their people.

If our stories were our people, as my mother had so often reminded me, how could we survive losing them? Could this new generation even call themselves Ennean?

The closer I walked to the town square, the busier it became, which itself didn't raise alarms. The shops on the outskirts of the square would be opening. Most paths cut their way through the square. However, the thoroughfare hadn't only grown busier. People began to slow.

In the distance, a crowd began to gather around the caller's stage.

Do the Gousht have stages in their cities? I wondered. *Or did they adopt this bit of Ennean culture for convenience?*

The crowd blocked most of the stage from view. I slipped deeper into the tangle of people until the red-adorned shoulders and head of a priest stood in the gap between huddled bodies in front of me. His stature and posture were far too weak to be my Priest, but I still found my shoulders dropping like they did before I charged into battle. Even if he wasn't the man who had taken so much from me, he was some relation—a fact which had made killing priests over the past few turns far more satisfying.

"*Worry not about the naysayers.*" As the priest projected his voice, it wavered, like he didn't have enough power in his lungs for the task. "*This land is no longer a conquered land. It is an extension of the Empire. Boundaries and borders mean nothing between our peoples in the future we seek to create. The Gousht Empire welcomes you, and offers your children the status of citizens.*"

The people on either side of me looked on with rapt attention as if these lies had any value. Some few faces in the crowd wore their disgust openly, but a disturbing number leaned forward for more false words.

"*We will not force you or them. Why would a gift require force? Everything we have given you—the word of The One True God, the protection of the Empire, the guidance of civilization—has been for your benefit. What would the Emperor gain from sending his followers across an ocean? Our people have died to offer you these gifts, and we are here to offer another.*

"*Your sons and daughters are welcome to wear the Emperor's green and yellow. We will put a blade in their hands so they can fight the righteous battles ahead. They will be the ones to bring our peoples closer together, and spread the warmth of The One True God to every soul across this heathen land.*"

Even six turns ago, the crowd wouldn't have followed his words. At the time, most adults hadn't learned enough of the guttural language to understand this bastard. Now, too many stood enraptured by an ugly offer to turn their children into weapons against their own people.

"*Your children will earn an extra ration for their families, imperial coin, and the opportunity to become a citizen of the greatest nation to have ever existed.*"

Small conversations passed between people in the crowd. An extra ration and regular coin could keep a family through hard winters. Even if the people hated the idea of trading their children to the Gousht, hungry people made hard decisions.

"*My fellow people.*" The voice cut through all the clamor and stabbed me in the heart. It would have been impossible not to recognize it. I had heard it in my dreams. It had filled every quiet moment for the past two moons.

I shouldered further into the crowd until I could see more of the caller's stage. Rena stood there with her arms open to the crowd.

She looked older of course—had grown by at least a head and her sharp features had only grown sharper—but she was unmistakably the same traitorous child who had killed my family. She wore her hair pulled into a single taut braid like Gousht women occasionally wore.

"*Gousht promises are stronger than any metal or wood. Their generosity knows no bounds. I stand here as a witness to the future in which there are no more Enneans. There are only Gousht citizens living in this colony, serving The One and living a fruitful life.*"

If there weren't scores of people standing between me and the stage, I wouldn't have been able to keep myself from charging.

"*Ask yourself this: where did your traditions lead you? What life do you want for your family? For your neighbors? The stories and superstitions of a dying people don't have to be the anchor wrapped around your feet. Help our young people make the right decision.*"

A girl, maybe fifteen, pushed her way towards the stage. "*I'll do it! I pledge my life to the Emperor. Let me fight for him.*"

The crowd erupted into a clash of cheers and jeers. Some young people followed the girl's example, while others backed away from the stage.

A soldier blocked the route of one boy as he made towards one of the many paths leading away from the square. He didn't force the boy to the stage, but he didn't stand aside either.

So much like the Gousht to promise a choice whilst holding a blade to one's throat.

Blood banners would be born today—some out of misguided beliefs and others from intimidation.

I pushed my way through the crowd, away from the town square before I did something foolish. Throwing my life away in a public arena wouldn't change anything.

Killing Rena might.

The scene in the town square created the perfect distraction. No one was on the street as I lifted myself through a window into Rena's office. The window hadn't been locked. What person with any plans on staying on this side of The Mist would ever break into the regent's home, especially with the barracks nearby?

Their assumption of safety relied on one's drive for self-preservation. But I had nothing left to live for, and I had plenty to kill for.

The desk at one end of the room had been lovingly carved from walnut and shined to perfection with protective oils. My father would have admired and studied it for hours to get a feel for the hands that built it.

Papers lay in ordered stacks on the desk beside a quill and an ink reservoir. Apparently, she wasn't a figurehead. The Gousht had actually put her to work against her own people—not that she could consider herself Ennean and make the speech that she had.

It would likely be hours before Rena returned home, which gave me plenty of time. I had ended lives easily enough with my father's blade, but if she brought any guards home with her, it would help to have something more formidable.

A slow clapping noise over heavy discordant hums sang from the floor above me.

At first, I had thought the trapped spirits were screaming from the barracks when I approached Rena's home. And of course there were echoes radiating from that direction as well, but these were closer.

The bitch hadn't only turned on her people—she had started

collecting their spirits as well.

I strode from the office through a large corridor towards the stairs. A beautiful dining room lay to one side of the house and a kitchen to the back. Everything carried the age and craftsmanship of Ennean hands. After all, it had been the family home of an elder stretching back generations.

Rena had stolen too much, and it would end today.

The staircase ended with a small landing and a set of three doors. The crystals called from the room to the right. I didn't bother with the other rooms.

Empty shelves covered three of the walls. My mother had spoken of the elder's book collection with reverence, but it hadn't survived the reaping. Few books had.

Only one of the many shelves held any books, and each of their bindings donned Gousht text.

The sight of Gousht books replacing a library of Ennean texts would have spirited my mother into The Mist if Rena hadn't already killed her.

A rocking chair sat beside the window with a ledger beside it. I could picture Rena relaxing with a glass of Gousht wine as she checked off names of Enneans she had sent to the mines. It sickened me.

But I didn't need to fuel my rage. There would be time to revel in the reasons Rena had to die later.

My search didn't last long. The stones called to me from the top drawer of a cabinet, and I slid it open. Five stones lay in a line wearing their colors with a dull shine: crimson, tawny, violet, azure, and hunter green.

She hadn't finished her collection. Or maybe she carried The Wind with her.

The fragment of The Seed called to me, twisting The Song I had once known so clearly.

Despite countless opportunities since The Priest stole my connection to The Song, I had never stolen The Seed from a crystal. It seemed perverse to hold a piece of his spirit inside me after I had failed to protect him.

A door slammed against the frame downstairs.

I should have had longer. I hadn't searched for any blades, but then again, I had something better.

It took no time at all to pull The Flame from its crystal prison. The thrashing spirit felt like it belonged. Pain suited this moment.

I could have destroyed the others, returned their spirits back to where they belonged, but I hesitated. Looking at The Seed, its color lackluster in its crystal shell, I took it as well.

Its echo sang like a fiddle that had lost its tune—near enough to what it should have been to highlight the many ways it failed to sing the right notes.

A single set of footsteps climbed the stairs.

This was it. After this, if I survived, I would lose Munnie. Killing Rena would sever the last connection I had in this world. But I had given up on the idea of killing The Priest. There were no more paths leading to his blood. Rena wasn't enough, but she would have to do.

With my father's knife in one hand, I waited. The doorknob turned. And in stepped Rena.

She had a knife in her hand as well. Maybe I had left something out of place, called attention to myself somehow, but she hadn't expected me. Her face twisted, and she squinted at me like a question.

Everything—the raging spirits, the consequences, my pain—vacated my mind for a single thought. *For Shay. For my parents.*

I concentrated on the air around her right eye, pictured a bubble in my mind, and fed The Flame's energy into that confined space. The air shimmered. I would burn her like she had burned Shay.

Rena's eyes widened in recognition. She must have played with the spirits enough to understand what was happening. She lifted an arm as if to shield herself, then plucked something from the air that wasn't there, and The Flame's torment vanished from my gut.

Before I could consider what had happened, I jumped back from a circle of boiling air. The explosion that followed caught me mid-leap and threw me onto my back several paces away.

The silvery strand of The Flame writhed in the air, and I grabbed ahold of it before Rena could call the Great Spirit's power again.

Despite the pain crawling along my back and shoulders, I scurried upright. Patches of scattered flames flickered through the room, casting Rena in an ominous light.

"Thief," I said like an accusation.

"Hypocrite." Her answer came more as a hiss through bared teeth.

"How could you? You turned on your people. You're a dancer?"

"A dancer? This isn't a gift like The River or The Wind. No one looks at a thief and thinks about the good they can do. Our people wouldn't accept me, but the Gousht have. They know my worth." She smiled. "Do you know how many hidden dancers I've found for them? Shay was the first. You never forget your first. I can still see you wailing like a baby over her body."

I released my grip on The Flame. Rena would only rend them from my grasp if I attempted to call on them. My father's blade would have to be enough.

As I closed the gap, Rena drew a foot back and found her stance. With each swipe, she sidestepped or twisted about, making me fight the air. She shifted her feet, angling away from every blow like an agile cat. She only used her blade to parry mine when she didn't move quickly enough.

The Gousht had trained her well. Each step found solid purchase. She understood how to move her body to steal the power from a forceful strike. But she didn't respond with her own attacks. The Gousht had fought too many battles for her.

I had clashed against far better—warriors more experienced, more agile.

With a feigned thrust towards her midsection, I forced her to angle away. I shifted as she dodged and struck again. My blade kissed the length of her off-hand forearm.

It was better this way. If she had died too easily, I wouldn't have been able to track the slow progression of fear across her face. It started as she lifted her brow.

My rage spread with the fire. It crawled up the empty shelves. An orange glow bathed the room with a promise of destruction. I wanted to unmake the world, starting with Rena and her stolen home.

Again and again, I feigned and shifted. What few attacks found purchase only scratched at exposed skin and cloth.

"Your death will mean more to our people than a single breath of your life ever could." I spat on the ground.

"This is the great Hero of Anilace? You may have a pretty story, but they will always hate what you are. A dirty thief."

The small fire was no longer small. It filled the room with smoke. Time was running thin. The air grew harder to breathe. In the gleam of dancing flames, her fear turned on itself, and her face narrowed into a harder expression—exactly what I had been waiting for.

I dashed through the gap, but instead of feigning, I put my weight into the attack.

Manipulative people liked to believe they understood how others thought. Their confidence assured them of the future.

Rena moved to counter, assuming I would pull back and strike at a different angle as I had with each preceding attack. My blade found purchase in the center of her gut, and my momentum lifted her from her feet for a moment before we both crashed to the floorboards.

Our faces were intimately close. Her desperate breaths whispered on my cheek, and her eyes searched the roof over my shoulder, wide and disbelieving.

I wrenched the blade, and her face twisted along with the metal.

"Does it hurt?" I whispered, still close as lovers. "Do you feel the regret flooding in now?"

She only answered in arrhythmic gasps.

This pain was not and would never be enough.

The fire had claimed the southern wall and began to crawl onto the ceiling. The smoke grew denser, and the scent of burning lacquer filled the room.

"I'm not going to kill you." I smiled, searching her eyes for understanding. "You Gousht fucks love your funeral pyres, don't you?"

With whatever defiance remained in her bones, she wrinkled her nose into a snarl.

"That's her," I said. "That's the murderer."

I stood up, pulling my father's blade from her gut. The rough air fought with my lungs, and I coughed. Either she would bleed out, choke on the smoke, or die burning.

The crystals remained tucked away in the cabinet drawer, all with a dull glow save The Seed's prison. I cradled them in my arms and turned back to Rena. Before I broke the crystals, I made sure I had her attention.

She made no indication whether the disintegrating stones came as any shock.

The stolen fragment of The Seed still raged at me from within. I began to let it go, then hesitated. If I had any chance of making it out, I couldn't rely on making it back to the hidden entrance.

A part of me wanted to wait for the flames to crawl closer to Rena, to see the knowledge of impending agony settle into her. But the fire would have already caught people's attention.

I darted from the room, down the stairs, and out the window I had come through. A crowd had begun to form, several soldiers making their way to the house.

They must have seen me escape the window along with the smoke. Gousht voices demanded for me to stop with a variety of colorful words, but I ran, buoyed with the knowledge that I had finally killed the blood banner who murdered my family. If I failed to fulfill any other debt of blood, at least Shay and my parents would have theirs.

I reached the tree wall and used The Seed to let myself out before blocking the path yet again. The soldiers had no chance of catching up.

CHAPTER FORTY-THREE

A part of Tayen reveled in the thought of Rena dying the way she had, but she knew what it meant. There had been a reason Kaylo lived in the forest alone.

"I didn't dare return to Munnie. She had made it clear, and I had crossed the boundary she set," he said, confirming the ache Tayen expected to come. "At least I had done something right. With so many mistakes behind me, I felt proud of what I had done to Rena. I had taken blood for blood, and saved the people of Nomar from her manipulations.

"Of course, in hindsight, it likely hadn't improved anything for people in the city. Maybe it reminded a few people we weren't born subservient. Maybe it made some think twice about wearing the Emperor's green.

"Eventually, I found the isolation I thought I deserved in the Kenke Forest. It took me days to build the hallow with the stolen spirit I kept. It screamed and fought the cage I had become all the while." Kaylo's voice dimmed. "I jailed a spirit of forgiveness for two turns before I thought better of it."

He turned to Tayen with a pained smile. "There it is. My story—as true as I can tell it."

"What about the twelve turns in the forest? There's more." There had to be more. He had been telling her pieces of this story for a turn. Little by little, she got a better sense of her kana. It was the way they had connected. It couldn't be over.

"I told you in the beginning that my mother taught me how to tell a story. Where it ends is just as important as where it begins," he said. "There's not much to learn from the quiet days. My anger grew dull, just like my wits.

"I didn't even know how selfish my self-imposed isolation was until I met you. Little shade, I could have done more. Instead, I mourned myself and faded away into the routines I created."

His lips raised into a heavy smile as he shook his head. "You were right when we met; I had been hiding out in a treehouse."

"Maybe you were healing—biding your time."

"No." He lifted his eyes to meet hers. "I didn't start healing until you came along. Every step of this journey, I discouraged you from involving yourself in the world's mess. I had become too obsessed with my own mourning to see that fighting back was the best thing I could have done.

"When I look back on my story, I'm not ashamed of the times I chose to fight. Even when I made mistakes. Even when the wrong people died," he said. "I am ashamed of the times I ran away. I am ashamed of the turns I spent hiding."

As heavy and worn as his voice sounded, he straightened his back.

There had been times when Tayen had seen two men within Kaylo: the hermit and the warrior. The defiant warrior only used to come out when he fought. But the longer she had known him, the more pieces of his guilt-ridden shell broke away. That isolated, retreating part of him still existed, but it no longer hid the truth from view.

Kaylo was a warrior. He had just forgotten it for a while.

According to Liara's runner, Jani elders and Uprising commanders were meeting around her map, and it was time for the wandering spirit dancer to join them. Not that Kaylo would have much to offer. But it was nice to be invited.

Outside his tent, the encampment swarmed with activity. Swaths of warriors and Jani had started arriving by midday just as the rebels had begun to dismantle the camp. They would all be sleeping under the stars tonight. In the morning, the march to the Last Wall would begin.

The child within Kaylo jittered with excitement. He had only seen the Stone City from afar oh so long ago. The fact that they meant to infiltrate the city, likely dying in the process, only slightly dulled his anticipation.

It would be quite the sight before the blood.

Even the chaos of breaking down the encampment moved according to a design. Assembly lines of warriors loaded rows of carts for non-combatants to travel north to the freecity of Aerolyne. Though, if the plan failed, it would hardly matter where they fled.

Kaylo kept that thought to himself, wishing he could somehow convince Tayen to travel with them.

As he pushed through the entrance of the command tent, the buzz of activity petered out. A dozen battle-weary warriors and time-tested elders stood around Liara's command table. They lifted their gazes from the map laid out in front of them to see who had interrupted their conversation.

Before Kaylo could flee, Torrel broke away from the table and crashed into him with a firm embrace. Kaylo allowed himself to reciprocate, despite how strange it felt to think of Torrel as a friend.

"Join us." Torrel released Kaylo from the embrace and clapped him on the shoulders. "There is much to discuss."

None of the other faces around the table looked pleased to see Kaylo, especially a well-muscled Tomakan woman on the opposite end. The head of her broadaxe stuck out above her shoulder from the harness on her back.

"Who invited him?" Talise demanded.

"For those of you who do not know him, this is Kaylo, one of the founding members of the Uprising." Liara waved him forward. "I have invited him here because he has information you all need to hear."

"It's good to see you, Talise." And it was. Despite all that had transpired between them, seeing anyone from his past who had survived the turns lifted a bit of pressure from his chest.

"You have something to say, say it." Talise placed her hands on the table and leaned over the map. "Otherwise, get out of here before I make good on a dream of mine."

The instigator in him wanted to comment on how nice it was that she still thought of him, but the part of him that enjoyed breathing decided against it.

"You need to get rid of the Gousht's supply of spirit crystals. It would be easier to break them from a distance. It would also be impossible."

"What are you talking about?" Talise asked. "I saw you do it at Oakheart."

"How many hours have your spirit dancers tried it? Has it worked once?" Kaylo asked, matching her tone. "You saw The Balance break the crystals in Oakheart. She used me to do it, but it wasn't me. She told me herself only a few days ago. And she doesn't seem to be interested in doing it again."

Talise scoffed. "So both you and The Thief are useless."

"Talise, we aren't children anymore. This needs to stop." Liara peeled back the map of Ennea to reveal a map of the Stone City. "There are three caches of crystals throughout the city as marked on the map."

One of the regiment leaders placed a figurine on each location as Liara continued.

"Although it would have been easier, the plan never relied on someone recreating what happened at Oakheart. This is a precision attack. Three teams will infiltrate the city through the smugglers' tunnels, each with at least one spirit dancer.

"Messages have already been sent to our contacts in the city resistance. Once the first cache is destroyed, the resistance will rise. They will open the gates for our main force to charge in." Liara spoke with a confidence that filled Kaylo with unearned pride. "Between our infiltration teams, the resistance, and our main force, the Gousht won't be able to hold the city long."

"And if the infiltration teams fail?" Talise asked, staring at Kaylo.

A collection of eyes filled with trepidation fell on Liara. Even if the gathered leaders around the table hadn't been relying on a miracle, they had been hoping for one. That much was clear. Talise's questions chipped away at their resolve. Shoulders began to droop ever so slightly.

If the shifting postures around the table affected Liara, she didn't let it show. "We don't need to clear all the caches to swing the battle in our favor. Once dancers in the resistance regain their abilities, their forces will be ready."

"How do we even know the spirits trapped in those caches belong to the dancers in the city?" an elderly Sonacoan woman in Jani robes asked.

"The city resistance has been fighting against the Gousht since the city fell. They know what happens within the walls. These are the largest stores of spirit crystals on the continent. We destroy those caches, some dancers will regain their connection to The Song, and the Gousht won't be able to arm their soldiers with our spirits."

"How many spirit dancers do you have?" Torrel asked the question slowly, as if scared of the answer.

Liara's delay answered the question before she did. The light of the braziers swayed across her cheek. "With Kaylo and Nomi, we would have five."

Kaylo closed his eyes and took a deep breath. It was too much of an ask. And to ask it here amongst this collection of leaders—Liara had always been strategic.

"No. You don't need her. There are three caches. You have enough without her," Torrel said with an edge.

"Yes, we do. If that is your decision, I will honor it. But the more spirit dancers we send, the better our chances," Liara said.

"Why don't our earth dancers just open the wall?" Torrel offered.

"Certainly, it would be easier than sending in a bunch of infiltration teams."

"We don't have the numbers to meet the full host of soldiers head-on, especially not with spirit crystals," Liara said. "We need to take their strongest weapon from them first."

She placed a wooden figurine on the map beside the city stronghold where the Gousht's leadership slept. "Kaylo will lead one team. Two of our dancers from the Uprising will lead another to the eastern cache, and the last dancer will head to the cache along the west mountain border."

As she placed the next two figurines, she took a moment of quiet. "This plan has always been riskier than any of us would've liked. But if we fail, Ennea's hope fails with us. Nomi is strong, Torrel. She could shift the tide."

Torrel met Liara's eyes, then turned to see everyone else looking in his direction. Too many Jani had committed to risking themselves and their loved ones for him to say no. It would send doubts rippling through the ranks.

"If she goes, I go with her," he said. "I need your word. The team is mine."

"And Tayen will be with me," Kaylo said. He hated the idea of bringing her, but the idea of her fighting outside of his supervision was worse. "She's good in a fight, and it won't hurt to have the shadows on our side."

"Any more demands?" Liara asked of the group, daring anyone to speak.

Talise leaned forward to meet Liara's challenge. "I'll lead the team going after the western cache. This is too important. I want my axe there if anything goes wrong."

Liara shook her head, and smiled. The gravitas of the moment faltered. For an instant, we became our younger selves, and Liara had never been able to stop us even if wisdom was on her side. "If that's the way it must be," she said.

"Once the crystals are destroyed, I don't want any of the infiltration teams going off to find a fight." Liara stared at Kaylo with an accusation. "Wait until the main force reaches you."

Kaylo half listened to the rest of the plan—who would lead which regiment through the gates, what their priority targets would be, how they would secure the wall after the battle. He couldn't pry his attention away from the rendering of the stronghold long enough to get the details of the plan.

The Stone City stronghold had served the Sonacoans since the Hundred Turn War, until the Gousht claimed it as their own. Now he and Tayen were supposed to plunge into the most secure city on the continent and break into the most heavily guarded building in the city with a small team of warriors.

Tayen had been adamant. She wanted to fight for a free Ennea, and by some trick, she convinced him to support her foolish errand. However, she wasn't ready for this. Blessed Mother, he wasn't ready for this.

By the time the meeting wrapped up, Kaylo had imagined the blood spilling out of Tayen's body in twenty different ways.

The others began to withdraw from the tent, but Talise hadn't moved.

"Bringing your toka with you?" She sucked her teeth. "You going to abandon her in battle too?"

"Talise, that's enough," Liara said.

Talise didn't make any sign she had heard Liara. She continued staring into Kaylo's eyes. "You shouldn't have come back."

She slapped the table, and those who hadn't left snapped their heads towards the interaction. Then she directed her ire toward Liara. "You shouldn't have let him come back."

Before anyone could respond, Talise removed herself from the tent.

Liara turned to Kaylo and opened her mouth, but he waved her off. "She has her reasons. At least she didn't hit me."

"You've also earned a little understanding," she said. "I'm glad you're here."

The last of the commanders left the tent, and Kaylo found himself alone with Liara. She stood at the opposite end of the table, resting her hands on the edge. The map lay in front of her as if she were overseeing the whole of Ennea.

"You did good," he said. "You know how to command a room. It's good to see."

She smiled, and the guarded posture she had been wearing fell away like discarded armor. "There's someone I want to introduce you to."

Liara led the way out of the tent and through groups of rebels dismantling the encampment.

On the far side of the organized chaos, a collection of families had gathered to eat dinner. Several rugs had been laid out. Meager meals sat upon them.

As Liara got closer, a young girl jumped up from the ground and ran towards her. The girl's hair had been pulled back into two buns of thick red puffs. The bundles of curls bounced as she threw her full weight into Liara.

Liara bent down and hoisted the little girl into her arms. "Kaylo, this is Kaini. Kaini, this is my old friend, Kaylo."

Kaini turned away and buried her head in Liara's shoulder.

An endless river of thoughts swept through Kaylo's head. Liara held this child so gingerly. Despite how hard she had appeared only moments ago, she transformed into a cradle for this young girl. It didn't look unnatural either. This was as much Liara as any command briefing she could give.

"She's glorious, Liara."

A Sonacoan woman walked over with a slightly older girl in tow.

Liara reached towards the stranger and held her hand. "I want you to meet my wife, Lleta, and my eldest, Celee."

Celee, a lithe girl with umber skin and baby locs growing from her scalp, reached out her hands in a traditional greeting. "Mommy told me stories about you."

Kaylo's hands enveloped the girl's as he accepted her greeting. He could have been jealous, and he probably would find time for that later, but for now, his breath came easy. This was something good.

"I hope they were good ones," he said.

Kaylo reached out in greeting to Lleta, but the full-bodied Sonacoan woman pulled him into a hug. "It does her good to know you made it through," she whispered into his ear.

"She is pretty amazing in that command tent. Everyone jumps at her word."

Lleta pulled back, her warm smile fighting off the rising moons. "I'd be surprised if you told me it was any other way."

"Why would I lie to you?" Kaylo said with a wink.

"Okay, that's enough," Liara said. "I'm having second thoughts about introducing you two. I don't know if I like you talking about me in front of me."

"We could go off and have a private chat—swap stories," Lleta said, her smile turning from welcoming to mischievous.

"Kaylo really should be getting going." Liara put Kaini down, and the little girl clung to her leg.

"Let the poor man stay for a meal at least," Lleta said.

"She's right. I have a young one I'm watching over as well. Not this young, but she will want to hear the plans," Kaylo said, the thought deflating his mood.

Liara placed a hand on his shoulder. "It's a good idea. Tell her she can stop collecting arrows."

Chapter Forty-Four

CURRENT DAY ENNEA

In the valley of the hill's slope, firepits glowed in the night. The small patches of light stretched into the forest far beyond what Sosun could have imagined. She had been an ignorant fool to think that she could stop this power, even slow it.

"We could leave," Nix said. "You don't owe the Uprising anything."

"*No, but I owe the servants,*" Sosun signed. "*They deserve a chance to do something other than serve the people who'd beat them for speaking. They gave me my words back.*"

"What's the plan then?"

"*You can't pass for a warrior without the right robes.*" Sosun stood. "*I'm going to get you robes.*"

Nix's fingers wrapped around Sosun's arm in a too-tight grip before Sosun could take her first step down the slope. "This is a bad idea. I can just kill the next sod who walks off for a piss."

"*When their friends notice they're gone, what then?*" Sosun signed as best as she could with one arm in Nix's grip. "*This way, no questions and you get cloth that fits. We always packed extra robes for the expeditions. A war march will have scores of extras.*"

Nix's grip relaxed, then released. Sosun's arm tingled with the lingering pressure of Nix's fingers. It was good. Having someone to push against forced Sosun to stop doubting her next steps.

Her feet stumbled on the slope of the land, then she caught herself. Mistakes would mean more than death. Mistakes would mean failing, maybe allowing King Shonar to succeed. That would be unacceptable.

She trudged down the rest of the hill with sure feet below her.

Uniformity separated a piss-poor war camp from a functional one. Everything had a place, which the whole of the army would be able to find. It also made one segment of the camp nearly indistinguishable from the next.

Sosun picked up a clump of mud from the ground and smeared it across the south-facing wall of the first tent she passed. Her turns within the cavernous underbelly of the Citadel had taught her to remember the details as she walked. A lost servant risked more than time.

If she wanted to turn back, this would be her last chance.

Within the first collection of tents, a group of warriors sat around a firepit laughing and tipping back their ale as if they weren't on the march towards a battle that would decide the fate of Ennea. Or maybe this was how people acted when they were the ones who carried blades.

She watched them. These folks weren't so different from those gathering in the Uprising encampment. Not on the surface, at least.

"Oy, nameless girl." One of the warriors met her eyes, and she threw her gaze to the ground, remembering far too late how to play her role.

"We really should give them names. It's harder to order them around without something to yell." The man laughed at his own joke, and his friends joined him.

"You, yeah you. We're getting thirsty. Go grab us more ale and be quick about it."

Sosun nodded as experience had trained her to, then turned to walk further into camp.

"I get why we take the tongue, but those nameless fucks are creepy, walking around like specters. We should strap a bell to their necks or something." The man's voice trailed off as she walked farther from the light of their fire.

Thousands of similar jibes and jests had fallen over Sosun like snowflakes over the turns. They began to be familiar and expected, but winter had ended. She would no longer slink away and continue trudging through the snow.

The first thing she needed to do was find a servant. If she meant to bring the war march to a grinding halt, she would need help.

Finding a servant in a Lost Nation vanguard never took much time. One only had to know what to look for. Whoever oversaw the storerooms would know the inner workings of the march even better than the generals supposedly leading it.

She passed several small gatherings of warriors assembled around campfires, but no one else gave Sosun any mind as she made her way to the nearest storeroom.

Through the threshold, she found sacks of grain, barrels of ale, foodstuffs strung tight in hemp sacks, and many supplies she could not name without investigating. A small Tomakan servant lifted his head, the sleep dragging on his eyelids. Then his smile broke something within Sosun.

How could she ask so much of her people?

She rushed towards Einol, throwing herself to her knees and reaching out for his hands. His warmth radiated into her palms.

Holding hands like this, when neither could speak, meant words weren't necessary. At best, a greeting would fumble the meaning they shared with a simple pair of grasped hands. All that needed to be known was known.

When they released each other moments later, Einol spoke first. *"What is it, child?"*

Nix and the others had always tried their best to learn to speak with her words. Their hands slipped around signs and fell in the wrong placement. Seeing Einol speak brought her home.

"Uncle, I need your help."

"Anything, sweet one."

"First, do you have any spare warrior's robes?"

She explained everything as best as she could to Einol. He listened. He nodded. Then he handed her a set of robes.

"You are not the only servant fighting back," Einol said with a smile. *"I fear the King has overestimated the power in his threats. We are silent watchers no more."*

Sosun had carried an ache in her gut since she made her declaration to the Uprising. It finally lightened. She hadn't misplaced her faith. She knew she hadn't. Her people were strong, and they were ready to prove it.

"So you'll help me?"

"Child, we all will. I will spread word, and by the morning there won't be a servant about camp who isn't ready to carry a piece of the burden."

"I have to get back to my friend," she signed, then reached for the robes. But she stopped before she picked them up. *"I also need some ale. And would you happen to have any orris root?"*

With the robes in a sack and a small barrel of ale, Sosun retraced her steps back to the firepit where she had been summoned.

"Finally. Did they cut off your feet as well as your tongue?" the warrior shouted when she stepped into the light. His companions broke into a fit of laughter.

Everything in her wanted to throttle the man, but she kept her head down and placed the half barrel in front of him, the orris root already leaching into the ale.

Given time to dry and sweeten, orris root could add a lovely floral taste to tea. The bureaucrats in the Citadel loved it. But too much before properly dried would have these assholes wearing brown stains in their pants by midday tomorrow.

The loudmouth warrior snatched the barrel from the ground as soon as she placed it down, and Sosun walked off to find Nix.

"Cheers to ya!" the warrior shouted, and the sound of ale sloshing into mugs followed.

Nix held her short sword free of its scabbard, tapping the flat of the blade against her leg. The girl should have been back by now. This was more than a fool's errand. This was an elaborate suicide.

Sosun couldn't fight. She couldn't scream for help. Even if she tried, running would only get her so far. Speed and coordination weren't high amongst her strengths. And not even the cleverest of minds could match an entire vanguard marching to war.

Protect their freedom. There is freedom in the choice to fight back. Her little lecture to Kaylo had brought them here and put Sosun's life in danger. How ignorant could she have been? There wasn't much freedom in being caught, chained, and hanged.

Then again, a hanging would only slow their march. Most likely, they would bleed her and be done with it.

A twig snapped, and there was Sosun, climbing the hill like the clumsy fool she was.

Sosun reached the top of the hill, smiling—oh so proud of herself.

"You got a set of robes. Good for you. It will take a lot more to slow down the vanguard."

"That's not why I'm smiling, asshole," Sosun signed. *"Put these on and make your way into camp. I have to meet with some more servants tonight. They are going to help us."*

"What am I supposed to do down there?"

"Blend in." Sosun smiled and tossed the sack to Nix before heading back down the hill.

At least the girl had been scared before. Without fear, Sosun was going to get herself into trouble. Not that Nix could do anything about it now.

"Time to make a loud end to this shitty life," she said to herself, then set to changing into her new robes.

The fabric hung looser than she would've liked, but it would do. She grabbed a handful of dirt and ran her hand over the robes, giving the fabric some wear. Her cheeks weren't covered in enough ink to justify clean robes.

A quick walk down the hill, and Nix found herself on the edge of a horrible decision. There had been a time when she would have walked away. Following people into their poor choices didn't make one brave or loyal. It made them stupid.

The whole of the vanguard camp lay before her under the light of The Two Daughters.

She took her first step beyond the perimeter of the camp, choosing to be a fool this time.

A group of warriors sat beside a fire, drinking and speaking far louder than necessary. It would be easy to fall in beside them and become a part of the drunken mess, but she had chosen to be a fool, not torture herself.

She continued until she found a dying fire, the last few embers fighting the inevitable. Snores circulated through the tents surrounding the firepit. Evidently, some warriors had decided to take the upcoming battle more seriously than others.

They would be the problem down the line.

Flint and knife in hand, Nix sat beside the fire and helped it back to life. The heat of the flames thanked her, and she settled in. Nothing needed doing. And forcing a thing usually drew more attention.

She rifled through her travel sack and pulled out a whetstone. Too many thoughts in her head demanded her attention, so she quieted them with a simple task. Her blade needed care anyways. She had been neglectful as of late.

The blade washed over the whetstone like a wave, even gave noise to the gentle push and pull of the shoreline.

"Now, there's a sensible warrior." An older northman sat across the fire from her, his curls more gray than black. "Warriors your age like to beat back the knowledge of coming blood with ale. If they thought twice about it, they'd realize they are only making it easier on the enemy. A sharp mind is better than a sharp blade, but I'd take both if I had my choosing."

Too many people assumed she would be interested in the jabbering for some reason. Maybe she had a welcoming face. Curse her mother for making her approachable.

She continued sharpening her short sword as if the northman hadn't said anything.

"So where you hail from? Are you from Astile or did you have to travel to be on the right side of things?"

"A small farming village a day's walk beyond the stormwoods," she said, keeping it simple—keeping it true. Truth, or near-truth, was always easier to remember when lying might be involved.

"Doesn't matter at the end of the day. You found your way to Astile," he said, leaning forward. "You know, we march with The Mother's blessing."

"How'd you come to that conclusion?"

The northman scoffed. "Isn't it obvious? We outlasted every other nation. We built the strongest army to ever walk this land. When the other nations fell, we stood taller. If that ain't The Mother's blessing, I don't know what is."

"You see this?" Nix raised her sword and whetstone. "This is like prayer to me. This is my time to connect with the edge of the blade— that fine line that separates me from The Mist. Truly an act of silent reflection, wouldn't you agree?"

She began refining the edge of her short sword once again.

The northman looked at her for a long moment, wrinkling his nose as if trying to decide if he had been insulted. She had been too subtle. Usually, people knew when she meant to insult them. It was one of the things she most enjoyed about herself.

"Sorry for my intrusion," he said, then walked off.

Nix could handle the subterfuge of pretending to be a warrior in the Lost Army, but she drew the line at small talk.

CHAPTER FORTY-FIVE

Sosun walked amongst a group of servants as the vanguard traveled west. Even as they actively sabotaged the war march, the company of her people calmed her spirit.

Before the Citadel, she'd had her mother and brother for a time. But once her brother passed, her mother left her in every other way but physically. She had never known community.

Strangely, it was the Astileans and their abuse that had given Sosun a sense of belonging. They gave her a people. Though thanking them would be like thanking the Gousht for breaking down the barriers between the nations.

Beside them, a pair of horses pulled a cart loaded with provisions. They had everything they would need to set siege to the Stone City for as long as it took. The Lost Army had made large-scale travel an art form.

A pair of warriors would be out front creating a travel path for the vanguard with stolen spirits. And as the trees fell, the army would carve their scar into the land, leaving it bare and muddy in their wake.

A crack ripped through the forest, followed by a crash, wild neighing, and a scream.

The front end of the cart lay embedded in the ground while the horses bucked and whinnied, trying to get free of their harnesses. The cart driver had fallen to the ground only to have his leg crunched under a horse's hoof.

Chaos whipped around the cart as warriors drew their blades and bows. Two warriors seized the cart driver, pulling him free of the horses, safe but still screaming in pain.

"On your guard," someone shouted, but the sound broke apart in the tangle of noise.

Sosun and the other servants huddled close to the ground, despite the lack of danger.

No one had attacked. There were no soldiers waiting to pounce. Though, the axle had taken longer to break than Sosun thought. Maybe she would have to leave a deeper cut in the wood next time.

A woman upon a horse dashed into the scene, wearing an artfully designed sannil vest and holding her spear aloft. "Ranks," she bellowed. "Ranks, now!"

The warriors fell in line to either side of the cart as the horses continued to fight their harnesses.

"Warrior, shut those horses up," the woman said as she dismounted.

Once on the ground, she drove the tip of her spear into the dirt and marched towards a commander. "Report, and make it quick. Why has my vanguard stopped, and why are my warriors chasing their asses about like they don't know which way is west?"

"General Tanis, we've had an incident with the cart," the commander said, his voice shaking.

"An incident with the cart? Is that the best you can do?"

"The front axle looks to be broken, General," a warrior next to the cart said. "It looks like too clean a break to be an accident."

A jolt of fear ran down Sosun's spine, but she continued cowering with the other servants. The warriors were bound to catch on sooner rather than later, but the General unnerved her. The woman commanded attention and respect with ease. Hopefully, she would be too arrogant to look as far beneath her as the nameless.

"Sabotage? You allowed sabotage on your watch, Commander?"

"I will look into this immediately."

"No, you will move the provisions to other carts and remove this damaged wreck from my path. Do not delay me further," Tanis said. "And do what you can to make sure your warriors know the difference between an ambush and a broken axle."

"Yes, General." The man scrambled to the cart and dispensed orders.

Warriors formed lines to move the supplies between the next two carts.

Another two fine-looking officers trotted in on their horses and stopped in front of Tanis. "Your orders, General?"

"We have traitors in our ranks. First off, they have half the war party shitting their pants like babes. Now, they've moved on to sabotaging the carts." The General hoisted herself onto her mount. "Find them, and bring them to me."

"Understood, General."

Sosun hid her smile. She knew the orris-laced ale had been passed about the war party, but half? It wouldn't stop the vanguard from continuing. It would, however, make their trek very uncomfortable.

"What are you doing?" A commander stomped up to the group of servants. "Be useful and start helping unload the cart."

Sosun and the servants nodded sheepishly as they had been trained.

The disobedience of their small acts of sabotage made the orders easier for Sosun to stomach. Hopefully, the others felt the same.

Sosun had given her people a chance to push back, and they had taken full advantage.

Hours later, Nix hunched beyond a tent as the lantern light passed her by. Another night meant another petty crime against the King.

It would have been fun if the threat of execution didn't hover over her like the moonlight.

Tanis had ordered constant guard patrols, which meant Sosun's disruptions were having the desired effects. Though Nix had a difficult time appreciating the affirmation. Something about the noose getting closer made her neck itch.

As the lantern light passed into the dark, Nix strode over to the horses to cause a bit of trouble.

Sosun's little trick with the ale had done a good deal of damage to the Lost Army uniforms, not to mention their morale. But a war march this large and well organized could overcome a few leaky backsides. Losing their supplies, on the other hand... An army needed to eat.

The horse whinnied as Nix approached, and she set a calming hand on its side. "Easy now. Wouldn't it be nice to stretch your legs a bit? This harness can't be too comfortable."

The next patrol would be along soon. So Nix set to work easing the leather strap of the horse's harness from its latch.

The first strap came free easily, but the second kept slipping from her grasp. Whoever had strapped the horse in had latched it far too tightly. The horse must have been wildly uncomfortable.

As if to confirm the thought, the horse reared its neck and tried to bite Nix.

"Fuck you, you stinky beast. I'm trying to free you."

"You're going to have to loose a lot of horses to keep the carts from moving," a voice said from behind Nix. "They have more, and they'll run them harder."

In a single motion, Nix pulled her sword from her belt and spun to find the prick who had snuck up on her. Her blade stopped at Daak's throat.

The boy's nose had gone crooked and his right eyebrow dropped lower than it should have, but it was unmistakably Daak. Tayen had done beautiful work, helping his outsides match his character.

"If you want to slow the vanguard, add some bluebell to their feed," he said as if unbothered by the blade at this throat. "It won't kill them, just mess with their stomachs a bit. Kinda like whatever's going through the warriors."

She kept her blade level, waiting for the boy to justify his death. "What do you want? I've known you since you were a little pup. Can't say I've ever liked you. You've got some angle. What is it?"

"I always blamed everyone for holding me back. I was supposed to go off and fight," he said. "It turns out I'm just inept. No one's fault but my own. I'll die on the front line and better warriors will walk over my body."

"Oh, so that's it. You're scared. Why not run off? They can't chase you down now. They've got a war to wage."

"You're right, I could run. No one would notice," he said. "I thought that would be different in the army. I thought I would mean something. All I had to do was be cruel enough to matter, and I tried. I hurt people. It didn't feel right, but I did it anyway."

"What am I supposed to do with your little confession? Let you go flap your chapped lips about what you saw here?"

Killing him would be easy. Messy, but easy. The mess would be the hard part. The next patrol would come through any moment, and a dead body would be hard to explain. Not impossible, but hard.

"I don't want to be the person I was anymore."

His eyes looked deep into hers. He was shaking, but every word had been true.

"You know where we can find bluebell?" Nix asked.

When the boy nodded, she sheathed her sword. "I never considered we would sabotage the war march with a river of shit, but it's as good an option as any."

CHAPTER FORTY-SIX

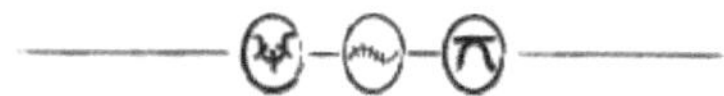

Lying on his back, Wal ran his fingers over his cheek. Smooth, unmarred flesh abruptly transitioned into raised, rough scar tissue. The beard he had been growing against his will stopped at the edge of his scars.

The day he received his first tattoo, he and Rēlan had waited in line with the rest of their regiment. Their first battle had been a minor skirmish, but nothing could deflate the sense of pride he felt as he waited for his turn to officially join the ranks of the Astilean Army.

That moment had been one of the highlights of his underwhelming life.

He had only received three marks that day: one for the battle itself and two for each of his kills. The sweet sting of the spines tingled along his cheek as the field medics tapped the ink into his flesh. He should have been counting his kills all along, immortalizing the blood he had taken on behalf of Adēan, Jolrin, his parents, and all the other Enneans who had been stolen from The Waking.

He had caught a glimpse of a senior warrior that day. Her cheek had been covered in ink. The lines almost ran together into a singular mark. She hadn't earned a command, but that didn't matter. She had taken enough couta fucks from this plane to end bloodlines.

Back then, he had no grand ambition. Command hadn't been a

shadow of a dream in his mind. His grief was still too fresh. All he had wanted was to fill his cheek with tokens of his kills.

Wal could blame many of his poor decisions on the Gousht and the King, but he had to accept his role in his life. He had dozens of memories that would make him ill if he thought about them too long—stealing children for the army, lying and maneuvering for power, condemning people to forced servitude for not having enough fight in them. Maybe he hadn't earned his cell for the reasons Tanis had thrown him in here, but he had done plenty to deserve it.

"Commander, have you fallen asleep? I don't hear the usual knocking about of stones or grunts of what I hope has been calisthenics," Lanigan said.

"Please don't call me Commander anymore."

"Mmm, very well. Are you doing alright in there, Wal?"

"Compared to what?" Wal chuckled to himself. "We are in cold, dank, dirty cells. In general, I wouldn't call it an advantageous position to be in. However, I don't feel as many aches and pains as I could. What should I measure my wellbeing by?"

"It will not always be this way, my friend."

"No, one day I shall die," Wal said. "Poet, how do you think the spirits I've lost will see me after everything I did in their name? Especially the things I claimed in their name that were merely my ambitions?"

"There are still choices in front of you—opportunities to be better than you have been. What will you do with them?"

Wal sat up as if to look at the poet, only to face a stone slab. "What are you going on about?"

> *A stone changes shape*
> *Though it may seem otherwise*
> *It will not be the same tomorrow*
> *It will have lost part of itself*
> *Or that is one way to look at it*

For this loss it may become
Softer to the touch or cut a more jarring edge
The fact of its changing is meaningless
Change will come
What shape it turns into is a far more interesting question

"So I'm a stone now?" Wal asked, failing to hit his typical sarcastic tone.

"After everything that you have been through, would the person you are today choose power or to side with your people?" Lanigan asked. "You will have to choose."

"What are you on about? This is even more off-kilter than your usual nonsense."

"Guard!" Lanigan's voice rang through the cavern. "Guard!"

"Stop that. What the fuck are you doing?"

"Guard!"

"Do you even know if someone is there?"

Lanigan's shouts continued to grow louder.

"Have you finally cracked?" Wal asked, having got up and pressed his face against the bars, as if it would make a difference. "Is this some attempt to get yourself killed? Ask the servants. I'm sure they'd slip you a knife. Leave the guards out of it."

"Guard!"

A slamming noise rebounded down the stone corridor followed by rushed footsteps. "Shut it! Unless you want a boot to go missing up your backside, shut your mouth!"

A red-faced warrior broke into the light, barreling towards Wal. He looked to be running fast through his sixth decade, but that wouldn't stop him from beating the scar tissue off Wal.

Wal backed away from his cell door immediately.

"Guard, I need to speak with you," Lanigan said, voice hoarse from yelling.

The warrior stopped before reaching Wal's cell and turned. "What do you want, you old fool?"

"I've rethought my position and would like to speak with my old friend, King Shonar."

It was worse than Wal could have imagined. The poet had broken after over twenty turns. For all their talk of escaping into their mind, this shrunken cell had proven too much for them.

"Do I look like I got dropped from the wrong branch of my family tree? Why would I ever allow that to happen?"

"Bring me your superiors. I'm sure they have instructions that I am to be given any and every opportunity to recant. I would like to recant, and I know my oldest friend, the King, would like to hear it. He has been waiting for twenty-one turns," Lanigan said. "I honestly never thought it would come to pass, but I believe Astile will unite the nations. Ennea will be one and rid this land of the foul-smelling, baby-killing Gousht."

It had to be a trick of some kind. After all the poems and lectures they had spouted about the importance of self-determination for all nations, they couldn't have flipped this drastically. They could have recanted twenty turns ago and saved themselves. Why now?

"I need to go to my superiors." Doubt hid within the guard's voice.

"You could, and it would be a sensible thing. Or you could be the one to unite the King with his oldest friend—the one who helped snuff out the King's shame," Lanigan said. "I know what they call me, but I see now that I earned the moniker. I have apologies to make. Please help me end the King's shame."

All their talk of opportunities to come—would they beg for the King's leniency for Wal? They bore no responsibility for his freedom. This couldn't be for him.

"I don't know," the guard said. "You try anything, and I won't hesitate to put you down. I won't be made a fool."

"Look at me. Do I look like I could fight a fly for food?"

Several long-held breaths passed, then keys rattled. "Back away from the door."

"You are doing the right thing. Those in the King's service have always been wise."

"Stop talking if you don't want to get smacked. I don't think the King would mind seeing you with a broken lip after so long and all the grief you've caused."

The warrior swung open the door, then feet scuffed against stone.

Wal rushed back to his cell door as Lanigan passed by. The poet had a slight frame but stood taller than Wal had imagined. Tangled strands of matted black hair hung from their head, draping over their face.

Lanigan smiled as the two of them saw each other for the first time.

"What are you doing?" Wal mouthed as clearly as he could.

The poet winked and followed the path towards the corridor.

The stormwood cell door jumped as the guard slammed the flat of his hand on the other side. "Back up, traitor, before I decide to come back and spend some time with you."

A myriad of suggestive comments ran through Wal's head, but he did as commanded. The momentary pleasure of embarrassing the older warrior wouldn't be worth it.

That's growth. Maybe I am a stone, Wal thought as he watched the two figures fade into the dim corridor.

Chapter Forty-Seven

The Uprising's full force waited for Sokan to fall. It felt like an oddity to Kaylo, planning on tragedy. There was a reason for it like usual. But the strategy of death and killing seemed a poor way to save a life.

He looked on as Tayen jabbered away with Nomi beside the cookpot of stew.

It had only been a turn since he made the irrational decision to save some whelp running through his forest. It seemed impossible that those small moments had changed his life so drastically. She had woken him from his self-imposed grave.

"Tayen." Her head whipped around when he called. "I need a moment."

She rolled her eyes and made a show of her exasperation as she left her conversation with Nomi.

As annoying as she could be, he had come to enjoy these moments more than anything. She rarely got to be a child, which made her small acts of childish rebellion all the more important. This turn had aged her as much as his tragedies had aged him, but something of her childhood remained.

"What is it, old man?" she said as she sidled up to him.

"Walk with me." He didn't wait for a response before he walked away from the hastily made war camp.

Sunlight filtered through the poplar and birch trees to the red-hued soil beneath their feet. This forest had seemed so foreign once. Now it felt like a part of his home—another piece of Ennea.

"You know, it's kind of fun to meet the people from your stories. I get to compare them to the images I made up in my mind. I was completely off about Talise. You never said she looked like a shaved bear."

"Tayen," Kaylo chided.

"Come on, she's huge," she said. "I was closer with Tomi and Liara. When do I get to meet Annit? I want to see if I was right."

Hearing the name made the muscles in Kaylo's gut tense. "Annit's not coming."

"He can't be that old. I've seen plenty of white hairs on the march."

"Tayen, Annit died several turns back. Not every story has a satisfying ending. Some apologies don't get said. People die and everyone has to go on living. That's sort of what I wanted to talk to you about."

Kaylo continued to walk as if he could outpace the horrible way he had tried to start this conversation. He may have remembered some of his social graces since Tayen had dragged him from the hallow, but he still stunned himself with his awkwardness on occasion.

"If you are bringing me out here to try to talk me out of the mission, you are sending some conflicting messages. You're the one that volunteered me to go with you in the first place."

A fallen poplar blocked his path forward. From its trunk, three trees rose into the sky. Their roots had tangled around and sunk into the fallen tree.

"Do you know what it's called when trees do this—grow from the body of one that's fallen?" He paused for the length of a breath, but she didn't respond. "We call it an ancestor tree. The fallen tree nurtures the next generation with its decay."

"I know you like to do the whole cryptic wisdom thing like Munnie, but you didn't answer the question. You know I'm going through the wall with you, right? You won't be able to stop me."

Kaylo placed a hand on one of the poplars rising from the ancestor tree. "When I was younger, I used to think the warriors who lost the Invasion War failed. Part of me hated them for not protecting us from the Gousht. That was their job.

"But we're here aren't we? We are here because those warriors gave those of us who survived enough time. The Gousht could have run over our lands and destroyed everything like they've done before. Instead, those warriors fought and died for our survival. They may not be here any longer, but our lives have grown out of their deaths."

Tayen nodded. "Still would have been nice if they won the war."

"Sometimes winning is making sure there is a tomorrow for someone else," Kaylo said.

This conversation wasn't fair. Tayen hadn't seen her sixteenth turn. This weight didn't belong to children, but she rose to bear it nonetheless.

"Tonight, we are charging into the seat of Gousht power in Ennea. People will die. I may die. You may die." The words tasted of soot on his tongue. "You have to know that. Tonight cannot be about spilling blood or personal victory; it has to be about those who will come after. We do this so that others will have a chance at freedom, even if we can only see it through the veil of The Mist."

"Do you really think we're going to die?" Her voice sounded as soft as he had ever heard it.

"I think that...I will fight like the spirits to keep you alive." He looked down at the roots of the poplar tree he was leaning on. Its roots and the trunk of the ancestor tree weren't separate things. They couldn't be disentangled. "You need to promise me that you will listen to me in there. If I tell you to run, you need to run. It doesn't matter if you have to leave me behind."

"That's not happening."

"Tayen," he said with too much force. "I need you to promise me."

Her lip twitched as she looked at him, as if she was fighting the urge to call him out of his name. She mumbled a promise.

"Tayen, promise me. Make sure The Mother and all her seven can hear you."

"Fine. I promise. But you better not send me off running at the first sign of trouble."

The strength this child had humbled Kaylo. He had just told her that one or both of them would likely die in several hours, and she stuck out her chin to tell him to let her fight.

It could have been naivety, but he didn't dare steal her bravery away by dismissing it as such.

He stepped towards her and roped her in to a hug. Her head settled into his chest. "Thank you for taking me from my treehouse."

The last time Kaylo had seen the Stone City, he hadn't been able to move. The sight of it— the broken wall and the Emperor's seal hanging from the eaves of the tallest structures—had been too much. He had run away.

This time, he couldn't run no matter how much he wanted to. He had promised Tayen.

The stone wall protecting the city loomed large in the distance. An oversized banner bearing the Emperor's seal hung draped over the top and down the center of the wall. The snake in the middle of the field of green fabric constricted around the lion's neck.

The gash that had broken the wall in two no longer existed. The seam between the old and new stone stood out even at this distance. Whoever had repaired the damage cared nothing for the art of the wall, only its function.

It still stood large and imposing, but the signs of repair broke the illusion. The city was not impenetrable.

"It's quite amazing, isn't it?" Liara settled in beside him, looking down at the city in the valley.

The stone buildings growing from the earth created lines running through and across the city. It looked as though Kaylo could rub his thumb over the image in front of him and feel the texture of stone rising and falling.

"To think you once lived there," Kaylo said. "Is it as beautiful from inside the wall?"

"On the rare occasions I could forget about the soldiers, it shocked me what our people had made," she said. "Then I'd see a green and yellow uniform, and it became a prison again."

"Their color scheme really puts a damper on the aesthetic."

Liara's echo whisked around them, slow and bending. That sound— the distinct way The River refracted through her—had never left him. In one hundred turns, he would still know her by her echo.

"I am assigning you a spearwoman and two of my best archers," she said. "Between their training and Tayen's shadow craft, you should be able to slip in unnoticed."

"What about my experience and expertise?"

"Back when you gave the orders, something usually went wrong."

Kaylo chuckled and shook his head. "You may be talking to a dead man. Lie a little."

"No lies. No quips. We both know who is on the other side of that wall." She turned his shoulder to force him to face her. "I need to know you can follow the plan—you won't run after old blood debts."

Something about her calling it an 'old blood debt' rankled him to the marrow of his bones. It had been nearly two decades since The Priest destroyed the Jani encampment, beat him, and stole The Seed from him. But his vengeance hadn't aged a day, even if it no longer controlled him like it had.

"I have something much more important to worry about," he said, looking over her shoulder to where Tayen sat.

Liara smiled and the tension in her jaw dissipated. "You may not be her father, but you did good with her. I'm proud of you."

"Don't make this sound too much like a goodbye. It comes off like you aren't expecting me to make it."

"I—" She stopped and her chest rose and fell with a deep breath. "I don't expect many of us will."

"Is everyone ready?" Kaylo asked. "Sokan will be resting before too long."

"Torrel's and Talise's teams are prepared, though Torrel is still bitter about Nomi going through the wall," she said. "Kaylo, I know we haven't talked about you leaving, not directly. But I want to thank you for coming back."

"You don't have to—"

"No, I don't have to do anything, but if this is it, I want you to know I'm grateful. This is the fight we used to dream about. It wouldn't have felt right without you here."

"Don't die," Kaylo said.

Liara yanked him forward into her arms. They hadn't embraced like this since they were little more than kids. A well-earned strength ran through her arms. He held back, unsure of what to do. Everything he wanted was too far from reach. He didn't deserve her gratitude or closeness.

When he couldn't fight the pull any longer, he wrapped his arms around her and settled into the embrace. "Thank you, Liara. Thank you for not hating me. Thank you for being stronger than I could've been. Thank you for finding happiness."

She kissed his cheek through the thickness of his beard as she let him go, and gave him a soft smile. He remembered that smile. The curve of her lips lifted like bittersweet tea.

"Tonight is not about revenge or reclaiming a stolen city. This is our chance to remind them who we are," she said. "Kaylo, remind them we are the promise of our ancestors."

Kaylo nodded. What could he say to her? The truth, filled with apologies and regret, didn't belong in this moment. This moment was an opportunity to stop making his life about the past. Tonight had to be about the future, whether he got to see it or not.

With a final too-long held glance, Liara left to see to her own preparations. She had a battle to wage. All he had to do was destroy a few crystals.

Tayen waited beside Torrel and Nomi, all three facing the legendary wall. Beyond them, Jonan sat against a tree, sharpening his sword.

"So the boy is getting what he wanted?" Kaylo asked.

Torrel spun around, shaking his head with resignation. "I spent my life as a Jani, preaching non-violent service to Ennea. Not that I always managed the non-violence part." He tilted his head with a flare of his brow as if the assault had become an old joke between them.

"And now, I am leading both of my children into an occupied city, inciting armed rebellion. Kaylo, what am I doing here?"

"Don't ask me. I hid away in the densest part of the Kenke Forest for twelve turns to get away from this war, only to be charging into the heart of it. I think we both messed up somewhere along the way."

Torrel chuckled, but it sounded hollow. "I saw you over there with Liara. Are we ready to get on with the most foolish decisions of our lives?"

"Once Toka rises two fingers above the forest canopy."

"What do you say to someone when it might be your last chance?" Torrel asked.

"Usually, you don't acknowledge that it might be your last chance. Tends to be a bit depressing."

"In that case, see you after the fighting is over—this side or the other."

Kaylo reached his hands to Torrel, and they said their goodbyes in the ways of their ancestors. "By the spirits great and small."

Nomi and Tayen had turned to see the end of their goodbyes, waiting expectantly. Neither girl had the turns or the size to carry as much weight as had been placed on their shoulders, but neither wore the fear of it on their faces.

"Nomi, be as brave as your namesake, and you'll have nothing to worry about." Kaylo nodded to Torrel. "Watch over this one."

Nomi nodded.

"Tayen, say your goodbyes and meet me by the mountain entrance."

Kaylo walked off before she could give a response. He had finally settled into some sort of peace with this plan. More conversation would only rekindle his doubt.

Before he made it twenty paces, a shadow of a figure blocked his path. Talise stood with her hands at her sides, her broad axe protruding over her shoulder like a specter.

Tayen was right. She did have the build of a shaved bear.

"I've been meaning to find a moment to speak with you."

She raised her hand to cut him off. "Try not to leave the girl behind this time."

"I..." he trailed off as she walked away.

Talise had always been good at leaving before he could defend himself.

A young Kaylo would have obsessed over what she had said. He would have denied and lashed out, his anger turning their mission into his way to prove her wrong.

Another version of Kaylo would have sunk into shame. He had a lot to be ashamed of, but nothing more so than leaving behind people he cared about.

He couldn't do either this time. This fool's errand couldn't be about old wounds. He had failed. Again and again, he had failed. But he had tried. Every time he ran away from the pain and the insurmountable obstacles, he had returned.

The past was nothing more than a story. And like a story, it had ended. Right here and now, he could begin a new story. Kaylo could make this story something different. For Tayen, he had to.

He made his way to the meeting point. The warriors Liara had assigned to him were already waiting beside the crack in the base of the Conca Mountains. If everything went as they hoped, the smugglers who had constructed these passageways would become unspoken heroes.

A young northman with a longbow slung across his shoulders stepped forward. "Tis Vicna and Mitral," he said, pointing over his shoulder to the two Sonacoan women behind him, his accent shifting his words into one long unbroken phrase. "I'm Binãe. We will be escotin cha ta the stronghold. We were told tha tere would be a little girl wit cha. Where's she?"

"Tayen will be here," Kaylo said. "I want to be clear about something before we go. We will move with Tayen's shadows. We will move as one, and you will need to follow my orders. If you have a problem with that, stay behind. There will be enough risk without arguments on the other side of this tunnel."

Kaylo looked directly at Binãe. The young man carried himself taller than he stood. His broad shoulders and quick tongue called Adéan's spirit forth. If he had half the skill and command as Adéan had, Kaylo had to make himself clear quickly.

Binãe smiled. "Cha may ave stories wit cha name, but we know what we're doin. We will follow cha lead, we will fight, and when ta bleedin starts, we will show cha how we earned ta right ta be first through."

"Vicna? Mitral? You ready to write a story?" Kaylo asked.

Vicna nodded, her lips pursed tightly as if the conversation was a waste of words.

"Should be fun," Mitral said.

Tayen's echo drew closer. Toka rose higher above the trees.

He bent down, kissed three fingers, and planted them on the stone. "Blessed Mother, be our guide. Tonight, we take the Stone City back for you and your people."

———

Inside the mountain crevice, The Shadow's song shifted. Tayen searched for shadows, but despite the darkness, there were none. No light filtered into the hidden tunnel to cast shadows about. The Song pulled further away.

A dripping noise cut through the silence, followed by the acrid smell of firestarter.

Each spark of flint against steel flashed into the darkness and breathed life into The Song. Then the torch caught fire, and The Shadow bellowed. Its closeness gave Tayen permission to breathe.

Once they made it through to the other side of the smugglers' passage, her life could be snuffed out easier than their torch. She had her knife and short sword, but against an army, they meant nothing. The Shadow, however, could withstand.

The Shadow had been the first Great Spirit to give a piece of herself to someone. Shunanlah protected her people with The Shadow, and Tayen would do the same.

Their boots tapped an inconsistent pattern against the rough stone path through the mountain. The sound rebounded off the walls.

Kaylo had been clear—speaking would be a quick way to die. They might have the element of surprise, and the Lost Army might be drawing the empire's attention, but more soldiers resided within the Last Wall than any other occupied city. No one was to speak unless doing so could save a life.

The tunnel wound and shifted lower and lower into the stone. The empty, endless gray walls stole Tayen's sense of direction. Her feet told her she was walking down the slope. That would have to be enough.

Part of her wished she and Kaylo had gone into the mountain on their own. When she arrived at the tunnel's entrance, the rebel warriors had looked at her as if she would be a burden. They didn't know what she was capable of. She could fight. She had killed before. Twice.

This time she would kill as many as necessary. She wouldn't cry over them. They didn't deserve her tears.

The tunnel closed in little by little until the walls hugged each of them. Then the procession stopped.

Everything in Tayen wanted to demand answers. Instead, she clenched her jaw, barring her questions behind her teeth.

A creaking sound replaced the silence. The woman in front of Tayen moved forward, stepped over the edge of a drop-off, then made her way down a ladder.

We must be close, Tayen thought. *This is what I chose. This is the path forward.*

With a deep breath, Tayen followed and settled her feet on the first rung of the ladder.

Once she reached the bottom, the tunnel expanded into a small cavern. Baskets, sacks, and crates lined the walls.

The smugglers had been busy.

Kaylo marched towards Tayen. "Once we get to the surface, thicken the shadows. Do not blot us out behind blackness. Just make them work to see us. Understand?"

Tayen nodded. If she started speaking now, she wouldn't be able to keep her silence when she needed it.

He touched her shoulder. These small gestures of affection had gotten better with time, but he still applied too much pressure and pulled his hand back like he had been burned.

Kaylo still being Kaylo settled her.

If he didn't have to become something else to fight, she could be herself as well. She knew how to use a blade and bend the shadows. She would do.

A second ladder awaited them at the far end of the smugglers' cavern. Kaylo charged forward and everyone fell in line. He pushed through the wooden door built into the rocky ceiling, and a soft light washed down.

One after the other, they climbed into the living quarters of a small home, leaving their torch to burn itself out in the tunnel below. A hearth fire flickered away within a small stone structure, the smoke funneling up through the ceiling. A Sonacoan man far into the late turns of his life nodded at them from his chair beside the fire.

This man couldn't have been a smuggler. Maybe someone in his family was, or maybe they used his home for their discreet operations. Whoever he was, Tayen would have to place a certain amount of faith in the city's resistance. They wouldn't have suggested a path if they didn't trust those watching it.

Kaylo led the way out of the front door with only a nod to the old man, then stopped in the middle of the road, turned, and froze in place. His shoulders drooped and his mouth hung agape.

Tayen and the others charged out after him, reaching for blades and bows, then they stopped as well.

The stone road swept down through rows of buildings before ending at the base of the Last Wall. This slab of stone had two hundred turns worth of stories built into its foundation.

Tayen's father liked to tell her of the earth dancers who called forth the mountain and chiseled it into a wall, running from one peak of the Conca Mountain Range to the next. He had always focused on the dancer who failed to honor his deal with The Mountain and lost himself in The Mist. It had been his way of telling her to follow through on her promises.

But she liked imagining the wall itself, and how dancers had made something that hadn't been there before. Her shadows were impermanent. This wall had lasted more than two hundred turns.

She jumped as a hand clamped down on her shoulder.

Kaylo shushed her, and signaled around them.

Without a word, she pulled on The Song. Elongated shadows fleeing the falling moonlight came to her. She pushed and pulled with each hand in turn, swaying with the movement in The Song. Shadows shifted and thinned into sheer cloth she draped over them.

To anyone watching, they would have become a blur in the night.

The warriors looked at Tayen differently. The burden she had seen in their eyes shifted to something resembling approval.

Before she had a chance to appreciate the change in their attitude, Kaylo began walking the upward slope to the stronghold, and everyone fell in line behind him.

CHAPTER FORTY-EIGHT

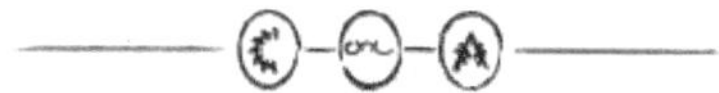

Sosun dug her knife into the seam between two slats forming the hull of a water barrel. She leaned her weight behind the knife. The copper rings had been securely fit to hold curved planks in place. The blade slowly crawled between the wood, and drips of water rolled down the length of metal.

It would have been simpler to pour them out. Nix had told her as much. But this would wreak more havoc.

If she and the other servants could damage enough barrels, the vanguard would be forced to fix them or make more frequent trips to gather water. Either way, their pace would slow.

Between the spiked barrels of ale, the contaminated horse feed, the sabotaged carts, and the dwindling water supply, they might have slowed the war march enough. The Uprising only needed another day or two.

Several other servants worked with stray bars of iron, chisels, or whatever they had gotten their hands on. If any of them were caught, they would be executed after violent interrogation. Maybe they couldn't talk, but the General would find ways to pry the information from them.

No one here held any illusions. If they continued to undermine the war party, they would die.

The seam between the slats finally gave way to Sosun's knife, causing her to fall forward and clang into the barrel. Water rushed out as if she had opened a spigot and soaked her torn servant robes.

"Shhh," Daak said as he watched the long stretch of carts and campfires for any movement. "Who would've thought a bunch of servants who couldn't speak would be so loud?"

Sosun flashed the boy a rude gesture that he could understand.

Why Nix had allowed this baby of a warrior in on their plans baffled Sosun. This was the same boy who had killed Tayen's friend. Tayen had left him wearing her wrath for a reason. Even if he seemed sincere about helping, it didn't make him pleasant to be around.

Sosun moved to the next barrel.

The work moved far slower than she had hoped. The moons continued to slide down the sky as she and the other servants struggled to sabotage a few barrels. If they hoped to do any lasting damage, they would have to work through several other cartfuls of the vanguard's water supply. The Lost Army hadn't left Astile unprepared.

A barrel toppled into another as a young Tomakan servant named Hilse fell forward. The sound made each of them freeze in place.

Daak pulled his knife and walked further into the light to see if anyone had heard them or cared enough to investigate. The farther he walked, the more the shadows and firelight turned him into a silhouette.

Sosun hadn't felt her heartbeat in her ears like this since Pana and the other guard burst in on Tayen trying to rescue her. She forced her lips into a tight circle to slow her breath in and out. If she lost her wits now, the spirits would be greeting her on the other side of The Mist.

Moonlight caught the other five servants with her in a similar frozen stance, save Hilse, who lay partially atop one of the upended barrels. She pushed herself up slowly, the barrel gently clanking against the other as she righted herself. Spilt water darkened her robes.

A slight smile crept over her lips. *"These warriors are too drunk to notice anything,"* she signed.

"If you can't be quiet, go!" a northman in his middle turns signed with

a flourish. *"Some of us intend to—"*

The servant dropped his hands along with his jaw.

Sosun turned in time to see a pair of silhouettes appear behind Hilse. A shadowed hand rose and crashed into Hilse's head, sending the girl into the fresh mud her accident had created.

"What the fuck is going on here?" A young soldier stepped forward, the moonlight showing the snarl twisting his face. He nudged Hilse with his boot, and the girl groaned. "Nameless? A bunch of nameless are causing all this trouble?"

"Should've taken more than your tongues, you little piss pots." The second warrior strode forward, her voice slick with false amusement. "I don't know if General Tanis will be pleased to know we found you, or sick that it was a bunch of worthless cunts slowing us down."

A shadowed figure darted through the night and slammed into the snarl-faced young warrior. Wood clanked. Warriors grunted and yelped. None of the servants dared to move.

A blade flashed in the moonlight as Daak found his feet. "What are you doing? Run!"

The other servants did as they were told, but Sosun couldn't do it. Hilse lay sprawled out on the dirt, and the second warrior leveled her blade at Daak.

Metal clanked. The hurried sounds of more warriors rushed towards them.

If Sosun stayed, it wouldn't save Hilse or Daak. She had a knife, but even the barrel had been a match for her. She had to find Nix.

As she turned, Daak cried out in pain. He had sacrificed himself. The foolish little prick shouldn't have done that.

"Get the servants. They're the fucking traitors!" a warrior shouted behind her.

Sosun cut between a pair of carts and rushed through a series of tents, staying as far from the myriad of firepits as she could. Nix had been off working on her own scheme. She had to find Nix. If anyone could get her out of this, it would be Nix.

More and more warriors stirred from their tents as shouts carried after Sosun. She hadn't seen any of the other servants. Maybe they had raced into the forest, which was exactly what she should have done. But she had a mission.

Firelight cast silhouettes of warriors carrying weapons against the tent canopy in front of her. She angled herself away from them and darted towards a supply cart. Hiding was the only option she had left.

For all of her bravado, all she could think was that she didn't want to die.

The collar of her robes stretched taut against her neck. Her feet slid from under her and she crashed to the ground, the back of her skull smacking the earth.

A coughing fit ripped through her throat. She tried to reach for a breath but only found fire in her lungs. The pain stretched in a circle where her collar had dug into her neck.

"Where you running to, nameless?" A cedar-skinned man with long gray braids stepped over her, grabbing her roughly by the arm. "You all failed the trials. Now, you've failed in your service to the King a second time?"

Maybe she had done enough to give the Uprising the time they needed to secure the city.

The rush of thoughts slowed. Her self-concern vanished when she realized what had just happened. She didn't even know how many servants had ridden with the vanguard. Whatever the number, she had forfeited their lives.

Despite the raging fire in front of Sosun, the darkness was too great to count the rows of servants the warriors had lined up. She knelt in the front, shoulder to shoulder with her people. A line of pain burned around her throat. The warrior had been rough with her, and from the bruises and cuts on the other servants' faces, she hadn't been the only one.

Warriors circled the firepit while General Tanis paced. She wore a short sword on her hip, firelight shining off her leather sannil. Despite how angry she had been when they sabotaged the supply cart several days past, her expression remained calm.

She could kill every single servant, and probably would. There were enough warriors to tend to their needs. They wouldn't perform their duties as effectively, but their work could be trusted.

Ironically, the servants' deaths might be the key to slowing the war march. Sosun fought a smile at the thought of accomplishing her mission by dying. If it had been that easy, she might have tried it from the beginning.

Daak and Hilse knelt closer to the flames, apart from the rows of servants, their hands bound in rope. They each wore welts, cuts, and fresh bruises. Daak's right shoulder hung limp where a haphazard bandage collected a patch of blood.

The scene held a poignancy—two young Tomakans broken and kneeling, surrounded by a crowd of Lost Nation warriors. This would be Ennea if the Uprising failed and King Shonar found the power he desired.

"Who are you working for?" General Tanis said, her conversational tone disquieting.

No one responded, though she and her ilk had removed the tongues of each of the servants before her. She couldn't have expected much of a response.

She strode toward Hilse and flicked her short sword across the young woman's throat. Blood spurted from the wound, and Hilse fell without making a sound.

"Who are you working for?" General Tanis asked Daak.

The muscles in his jaw clenched as he shook and said nothing.

"We have all night, and plenty of nameless." Tanis nodded to a warrior at the far end of the front row of servants. The hulking northman slit an elderly man's throat. "Maybe we'll find one you care about."

Whimpers and moans ran through the rows of servants. Some bent forward, touching their foreheads to the dirt as if to hide themselves from the scene.

"Silence!" Tanis yelled, breaking her calm. "You've no right to those tears. You are here for one reason—to serve. You've failed."

A servant towards the back shot up and ran away from the gathering, his unsteady gait creating a jagged path. Then he fell with an arrow sticking out from his back.

"It pains me to damage the King's servants, but I will be obeyed," Tanis said. "Do not interrupt me again."

The whimpering simmered but did not completely subside.

Sosun had done this to her people. All her thoughts of making a difference and fighting the war her own way had condemned them.

Tanis lifted Daak's eyes back to her with the flat of her blade under his chin. "How many will you kill before you die? Because you will die. Don't doubt that for a moment, young one. The only question is how many will pave your path into The Mist?"

Tears streamed down Daak's face. "Please, don't do this." Saliva dripped in strands from his lips.

Tanis turned back to her executioner.

"Stop!" Nix shouted, pushing her way through the crowd.

Sosun grabbed fistfuls of dirt to keep herself kneeling and quiet. Nix hadn't been caught. It was the single blessing underlying this bloody mess, and now, she marched her way into a fucking crowd of people looking to kill her.

Warriors moved aside, making way for Nix to join the center of the gathering. Her sword hung at her waist, but it couldn't amount to much in a sea of blades.

Tanis removed her sword from Daak's chin and rounded on Nix. "You look familiar. Do I know you? Are you responsible for all this inconvenience?"

"I can't say we've met before, but I've had a bit to do with it."

The calm mask General Tanis wore shifted into a smile and her brow furrowed in confusion. "Why? Sick stomachs and runny shits won't keep us from winning this war. What are you after?"

"You'd have to be wearing your ass as a scarf to think I would tell you why."

"Then why reveal yourself?" Tanis stopped herself. Her brow lifted. "Wait. Now I remember. You were Wal's little pet. The one he tried to use as a spy against the thief. What does any of this have to do with you?"

"Just fulfilling promises," Nix said.

"You have to know I'm going to torture you now. I might as well kill off this sniveling—"

An explosion erupted from the north side of the vanguard. Light flashed in the distance, creating a portrait of trees backlit with a yellow-orange haze.

The crowd's attention shifted toward the explosion, then a second blast rang out far closer if the volume of the blast could be trusted.

Several warriors fell to the ground. Others unsheathed blades.

Nix smiled, and pulled a small wooden cylinder from her belt. "You should probably get down."

The fire at the center of the gathering flared, and the world flashed white as the cylinder Nix tossed into the pit ignited.

Bodies surrounded Sosun as she pawed her way back to her knees. A screeching pitch sang in her ears, and the ground wobbled this way and that.

Muffled screams and shouts rattled amongst the chaos. A hand gripped Sosun under her arm, dragging her upright. She fell, and the hand snatched her again.

Nix was there, yelling something.

Sosun's feet slipped on the unstable earth, but Nix's hand refused to release her.

Had a dancer broken the ground below them?

Everyone was running. A warrior crashed into a servant beside Sosun. Blood ran from the back of her sister's purple robes, a spear pinning her to the ground.

Spots of light painted Sosun's vision, but she continued to run with Nix dragging her along.

The earth settled. Sosun, Nix, servants, and a sea of warriors plunged into the thick forest.

CHAPTER FORTY-NINE

CURRENT DAY ENNEA

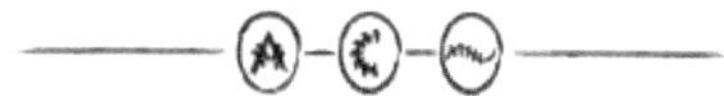

Wal clung to the small stones he had collected from the floor of his cell. Another crash—dulled by stone and distance—broke into the cavernous dungeon. It sounded faintly of metal clanging against metal, but he couldn't be sure.

In all his uncountable days at the bottom of this fucking mountain, he hadn't heard a single sound from beyond the corridor. Bureaucrats weren't ones for loud noises. Even back when he had a proper room in the Citadel, silence marked the hallways.

The poet hadn't returned, which meant two things: Lanigan would be vulnerable to whatever mayhem was loud enough to travel the distance to their cells, and Wal would be forced to wade through this mess in solitude.

Wal had never liked being alone. He had spent turns talking to keep the void at bay. It annoyed people, but they never forgot him. People could hate him, love him, fear him, but they would not feel indifferent. They would not ignore him like his father had.

As much as he complained about the poet, Lanigan's incessant rambling had kept him alive.

With Wal's luck, whoever was in charge of bringing down his bowl of slop and spit had found themselves in the middle of the chaos. He would be forgotten, longing for his tampered-with meals as he withered away with only his thoughts to distract him.

He threw a rock against the stormwood door. It ricochetted and struck him in the shin.

"Blessed Mother! Why do I keep doing this?" he yelled, hopping around on one foot.

Kaylo and all his bloody mercy had condemned Wal to this.

A cascade of clanging sounds carried through the corridor. Closer. Much closer than before.

Whatever was happening beyond his cell had come to find him. It should have made him tense in fear. Instead, the muscles in his shoulders and back relaxed. He hadn't been left alone. Even if it meant his pathetic life would end, he hadn't been forgotten.

The corridor door swung open and footfalls clapped against the stone, growing louder and louder.

A familiar face appeared in the lantern light—a servant who Wal had seen spit in his meals on multiple occasions. He appeared to be a good deal past his middle turns. His gray hair had thinned to a ring around his head. The scars on his face most likely told the story of his long turns serving the Citadel.

"Dinner time?" Wal asked, but the servant didn't respond to the levity in his voice.

Blood stained the sleeve of his robes and spotted across his chest and face. He held a warrior's short sword.

Wal backed away from the door, thumbing the stones in his hand. Three remained.

If murder wore a facial expression, this man had stolen it. Whatever relief Wal had felt about not dying alone flittered away like a fart in the wind.

The distinct sound of keys rattling on the other side of the door made everything clear. Wal would have to scrape and claw his way through this if he wanted to stay on this side of The Mist—and given his wonderful accommodations, who wouldn't?

The stormwood door creaked as it opened.

"We don't have to do this," Wal said. "I'm warning you; I have rocks."

The servant continued into the room, the sword still at his side. This would be Wal's only chance. The servant hadn't passed the trials. He hadn't settled into a fighting stance.

Wal bent his knees, but before he could lunge forward, the servant turned the sword around. He gripped the blade and held out the hilt.

"What are you doing?" Wal asked, surprisingly angered by the situation.

This man was supposed to attack him. Give him something to attack.

Wal had seen plenty of people who wanted him dead. The sheer number of people he had driven to homicidal intent had become a point of pride at some point in his life. And this servant's expression spoke clearer than any words could. He wanted to kill Wal.

The stones in Wal's hand bit into his palm. "No more games! Do it!"

The servant dropped the sword to the ground with a clang that reverberated through the cell. Then he pulled a folded piece of parchment from his tattered robes.

If he took the note, dropped his guard, and the servant ended up sticking a knife in his neck, he would have to use his last breaths to laugh. Creativity deserved all due credit, even if it killed him.

The servant didn't move when Wal bent to take the parchment. Wal waited for the man to spring his trap. When nothing happened, Wal unfolded the paper.

> *The King is dead. Now is your time to choose:*
> *those in power or the people.*
>
> *With regards,*
> *Lanigan*

Wal turned the parchment over, looking for something more. Lanigan had never used so few words in all their time imprisoned together, and they had chosen now to be succinct.

"What is this?" Wal demanded. "The King is dead. Is that some kind of joke? Who killed him? Lanigan couldn't snuff out a fire, much less the King of Astile."

It couldn't be true. If it was, that would mean the army was beyond the Lost Forest and no one of much consequence remained to control the city—the nation. Astile would fall, and the last nation would be unable to hold back the Gousht.

He bent down and picked up the sword, keeping an eye on the servant all the while.

If he helped whatever force remaining in the Citadel retake control, he could take command. General Tanis might hate him, but she could never execute him after he saved the city. He could keep the dream of Astile alive.

But did he want to?

In front of him stood a Tomakan man, scarred and battered. His tongue had been severed, and he had been forced into servitude. As much as the dream of Astile represented an Ennea free from the Gousht, this had been the cost.

King Shonar had been cruel and ambitious in his own right, but he restrained the more radical ideas Tanis put forth. Without him, Astile's cruelty would only grow.

Wal gripped the hilt of the sword tightly. It felt good to hold a sword again.

Regardless of the orders the servant in front of Wal had been given, he hated Wal. He hadn't tried to mask it for a moment. Still, he had handed over his blade.

What had made Lanigan believe in Wal so much? What made the servants believe in Lanigan enough to carry out a rebellion? They spoke in pretty phrases, but a poet was neither a warrior nor a ruler.

If Lanigan had played the long game for power, it had been an immaculate performance.

Wal chuckled at the idea of Lanigan as a masterful tactician plotting for twenty-one turns.

Regardless of the decisions Wal had made in the past, he couldn't bring himself to hurt or even threaten the servant in front of him. There were no decisions left to make. There was one path.

"Where do we go from here?" Wal asked the servant.

Chapter Fifty

The closer Kaylo's unit got to the stronghold, the more Gousht soldiers they passed. Guards patrolled the streets while archers waited in their perches on the rooftops above.

Even if they managed to take all three spirit crystal caches, Ennean blood would run through the streets like a river.

The old voice in the back of Kaylo's head told him liberating the city could never be worth the lives lost. It was the same voice that spoke of shame as a necessity. He had learned to blame himself too readily with that voice.

He couldn't dismiss the spirits that would move on before Sokan rose in the morning. However, Nix had been right. Just like he couldn't protect Tayen from all danger without stripping her of her freedom, the path to Ennea's freedom walked through dangerous lands.

People would die, but if they succeeded tonight, the survivors would have a chance at something closer to the lives they were born to live. That had to be enough.

Their unit hugged a building, the fog of Tayen's shadows obscuring them as an archer looked over the edge of a roof. Kaylo placed his hand on Bináe's arm as the young man nocked an arrow.

After several tense moments, the archer receded from view, and Bináe stowed his arrow with a glare for Kaylo.

Bloodlusts would be quenched, but they needed to wait until violence became absolutely necessary. Caution over speed. The mission mattered far more than any number of soldiers they could kill along the way.

The stronghold grew larger and larger as they traveled towards the cache. The huge stone structure lay within the fall of the mountains lining either side of the city like a bridge connecting peak to peak. It rose higher than any other building Kaylo had seen before, and the Gousht bastards had draped their symbols over it as if they could claim it.

From here, the broken circle—the symbol of their false religion—looked like a target wrought in iron.

It would fall tonight.

Kana had reached its peak in the sky by the time they made it to the stronghold entrance. Two archers guarded the oversized doors from above in addition to the two spear-wielding soldiers standing on either side of it.

"It's time," Kaylo said. "Take out the archers and Mitral and I will take out the soldiers below. Tayen, I need you to get us close."

Tayen nodded.

"Liara said you were two of the best archers she had." Kaylo focused his attention on Bináe. "Let's see."

As vocal as he had been, Bináe only smiled.

If anyone failed, and one of the soldiers called out, they would learn very quickly what it meant to be in the most fortified city on the continent.

Bináe and Vicna found positions in the shadows of an alleyway, nocking their arrows.

Tayen's echo sharpened as she thickened the shadow fog and broke it in two pieces. Her fingers moved while she danced as if she were stitching the shadows with an unseen thread.

Mitral and Kaylo found their positions against the stronghold near their targets.

The dull warning that had walked with him through the city stopped. Consequences be damned. He knew how to kill.

A pair subtle thwips, so alike in sound and close in timing that they could have been a single bowstring, announced the beginning of tonight's war.

Kaylo darted from the shadows without a moment to wonder if the arrows had found their marks. The time for caution had passed.

His target's eyes grew wide as he appeared from the darkness, his blade aimed at her throat. Her stance shifted as she tried to level her spear. Then his father's knife crunched through her windpipe, and blood marred her sickeningly pale skin. The flat of his blade cut off her last breath, her body collapsing to the floor.

It should have been harder to stomach the killing. This soldier hadn't had the turns to question her decisions. But it didn't matter. Spending his energy on remorse for the Gousht would be a waste.

Her comrade slumped into a similar pile beside her with a spear still protruding from his chest.

Liara had given him solid warriors. If either arrow had gone wide, a swarm of soldiers would have already descended upon them. He might have been laid out beside the Gousht woman he had just killed.

They had passed their first test of the night. There would be many more to come.

Without a word between them, Kaylo and Mitral propped open the door and dragged their kills into the stronghold. The Gousht would know they were there soon enough, but it needed to wait. The mission needed a bit more silence.

All the fables of the Stone City waxed poetic about the Last Wall, marveling at its immensity. No one ever spoke of the beauty within the stronghold.

Where the facade of the building had been as plain as it was grand, the hall they stood inside was a magic his whittler's fingers could only dream of. A mural inscribed into the stone entryway ran the length of the corridor. One image led to the next, telling the story of The Mountain gifting her descendants the power to call forth the stone that would become the city.

When his mother told him the story, and for most of his life thereafter, Kaylo had assumed The Mountain's gift had been more metaphorical. Dancers did not need The Great Spirits' direct help to wield The Song. That was what made them dancers. That was before The Balance confessed what she had done at Oakheart.

Maybe the stories he had dismissed as myth or embellishment carried more truth than he gave them credit for. Maybe the spirits had done more than people knew. If he survived the night, he could give the thought more time. For now, he needed to focus on the task at hand.

Wall-mounted lanterns lit their path forward. Each step they took rebounded off the walls, creating a rhythm to their movements no matter how lightly they tried to step.

Echoes of trapped spirits sang from all over the stronghold, but the bulk of them sang from the south. The city's resistance had been right.

Kaylo waved the others to follow, chasing the mass of echoes to its origin.

Though the mural had stopped after the first corridor, small sculptures and drawings lay embedded in the stone, breaking up the flat gray walls. Several sculptures had been vandalized, but the art was too much a part of the structure to completely destroy.

After twists and turns through the stronghold, which felt far bigger than the facade had suggested, they came to a locked door. The trapped spirits sang a chorus of bitter wrath that stung the closer Kaylo listened.

Mitral went to the business of picking the lock.

Sifting through the echoes, Kaylo attempted to count the spirits. There weren't enough. The reports suggested the abundance of crystals within the Stone City would make other collections feeble in comparison. But he had stolen more crystals from caravans. Even if two other caches held similar collections elsewhere in the city, the sum would barely arm a well-stocked outpost.

Every other piece of information they had been given had fallen into place.

Kaylo closed his eyes and listened. Echoes moved about the stronghold without a pattern. The angry shade of The Song didn't rush towards them. The echoes didn't cling together like those behind the locked door. If there were an ambush, the soldiers had left their crystals behind.

The cache hummed, small but not insignificant. Their mission had not changed. Regardless of the size, they would steal back the spirits on the other side of the door.

An echo amongst the cache carried a familiar weight. He hadn't heard it before, not like this. The sound whispered to him like a forgotten thought. It sang alongside the others—no different. Yet, still it stood apart. Then, for the briefest of moments, it sounded like a dandelion sproutling pushing through dirt towards the waiting sun. It sounded like a song he had never heard outside of himself.

The lock popped. Mitral removed it and lifted the bar.

Kaylo's words didn't come fast enough. He thrust forward towards Mitral just in time to see a line of green come into view as the door swung open. There was no time for choice. Instinct took over. He reached as wide as his arms would allow, grabbing for fabric, limbs, whatever he could clutch as he threw himself to the stone floor.

An arrow flew over top of him. Someone took in a sharp breath, then fell beside Kaylo and the clump of bodies he had pulled to the floor.

Bināe's lifeless eyes stared past Kaylo towards the waiting soldiers. The boy's mouth hung limp with the shock of his own death.

"*Ceasefire,*" a familiar voice called out in Gousht.

Kaylo retook his feet, but he knew better than to reach for either of his blades. He stood in the middle of the door frame with a dozen green-wearing, pale-faced soldiers who held their bows at their sides. Arrows were nocked and ready. The others were in various states of standing. One—maybe two—of them could make it if they ran. Even then, what would he do? They were trapped in the stronghold.

"I hoped it would be you," The Priest said with his accented common tongue. "Please step into the chamber."

Behind the red veil of his priestly robes, The Priest had undoubtedly aged. Time spared no one. However, the veil made him ageless.

Kaylo had convinced himself that he had found a way to control his rage. It seemed laughable now. Bile stung the back of his throat as he listed The Priest's trespasses: Nomi, Junera, Soca, Boda's left eye, Sionia, Adéan. The bastard had orphaned thousands and stolen centuries of history. And all the while, the spirit of The Seed—his spirit—sang a tormented tune.

"If you hesitate any longer, I cannot promise my soldiers won't get nervous and release an arrow or two," The Priest said with genuine welcome in his voice. "Please join me."

Kaylo stepped into the chamber, and the others joined him, leaving Bináe's body in the corridor alone. He felt the heat of Tayen beside him without a glance and sidestepped to cover her as much as he dared.

Cool head, he thought as he slowly formed letters Sosun had taught them both at his side. *Keep a cool head, little shade.*

"Welcome." The Priest's words reverberated through the chamber. Ever the performer. "I am glad you accepted my invitation."

Of course, it had been a trap. They had taken a too-easy stroll through the most heavily guarded city on the continent and convinced themselves otherwise. So they had killed a few soldiers. The Priest wouldn't have hesitated to sacrifice a full regiment and their families in service of killing the Uprising.

And if this cache was an ambush, the others most certainly would be as well. Talise. Torrel and his family. Kaylo should have never agreed to this plan.

Across The Priest's red-robed chest, he wore six crystals. A dull forest green stone hung in the center of the bunch. The Seed's song had been twisted, but Kaylo's stolen spirit pierced through the haze of noise surrounding him.

The Priest bowed his veiled face and wrapped his hand around Kaylo's trapped spirit. "Ahh, you must miss it. The Seed might not be the most powerful of spirits I've captured, but I must say, I have a certain fondness for this crystal."

Tayen's echo jumped like a penned stallion. She needed to calm down. Her anger would only get in the way of their chances. He tapped his leg and began signing the letters again, taking time between each movement so as to not draw attention.

"How?" Kaylo asked, keeping emotion from his voice. "Did someone betray us?"

"He speaks! You have grown, but you still make demands when you have no leverage. Why would I tell you such things, thief?"

The lanterns on either side of the chamber provided plenty of light—and consequently, shadows. Tayen's echo moved with focus.

"You want to. The only reason my blood is still in my skin sack is because you want to share your brilliance. So, say what you have to say. I'm ready to die."

"Oh, come now. You earned quite a name for yourself before you vanished. You've fought to live this long. Don't pretend you don't have something to live for." The Priest's veiled face nodded in Tayen's direction.

"Do you have blood banners in the Uprising? Informants?" Kaylo asked, failing to restrain his anger.

"Nothing so simple." The Priest's fingers stroked the forest-green crystal. "Do you think I would allow a resistance to form in my city without knowing about it? It was easy to feed them the information. As soon as you lot began moving from all your little hidey holes around the continent, we simply picked up a resistance leader and the interrogations started.

"If it makes you feel any better, she lasted much longer than you did,"

The Priest said, "Do you have any other questions before I kill you?"

The small shadows under Tayen's control shuddered in the light as she held them in place. If he dragged out the conversation too long, one of the soldiers would take notice. The Priest wouldn't have surrounded himself with fools. But the moment he moved, they would likely fall beside Binãe, whose blood pooled only steps behind them.

"Do you remember what you told me after your long-winded story about your brother who got the crown you assumed would be yours?" Kaylo asked.

"Hmm, I thought your people appreciated a good tale." The Priest's hand settled into a grip on the green crystal. "I told you several things. You'll have to be more specific."

"You told me, 'No matter how tightly you grasp it—'" Kaylo signed the letters behind his hip. *E-Y-E-S N-O-W.* "'—your power can be taken away.'"

The small shadows that Tayen had moved into place flashed into a curtain of solid black between the soldiers and them.

Kaylo dragged Tayen to the side of the chamber as a barrage of haphazard arrows soared out from beyond the curtain.

Mitral fell with an arrow in the stomach and the throat, but Vicna managed to tuck beneath the deadly storm. She raised her bow from the ground, beginning to loose arrows into the blackness.

"Kill them!"

The Priest's anger-broken timbre might have given Kaylo the most satisfaction he would find before he died, but he would take what little he could get.

"Stay alive," Kaylo said to Tayen, before diving for Mitral's fallen spear.

An arrow crashed into Vicna's shoulder and turned her shot as several of the soldiers rushed through the shadow curtain with blades drawn.

Kaylo launched the spear into a bastard at the front of the pack. His battle cry twisted in his throat as the momentum of Kaylo's spear crashing into his chest lifted him from his feet.

Looking back on his life, Kaylo had never believed the Uprising would end the occupation—not truly. He had wanted it to. With each victory, he had tried to convince himself it would work. But he had never been optimistic enough to actually believe his own words.

It also hadn't been purely about vengeance. That had been part of it, but only on the surface. No, if the Gousht were going to take his life from him, the Uprising would allow him to die fighting.

He brandished his sword and his father's knife and met the next soldier in the charge.

Strike. Parry. Sidestep. Thrust.

His body had not forgotten the training he had seared into his flesh. He opened a soldier's throat with his father's knife before catching another's hand axe with his sword.

A pair of arrows whispered as they zoomed past him into the Gousht ranks.

Tayen had taken Bināe's bow, and both she and Vicna were drawing back another nocked arrow.

A sword slipped through Kaylo's guard and sliced along his ribs as he stepped aside too slowly. The soldier smiled at her small victory and was rewarded with an arrow in her chest.

If he had any chance of surviving, he couldn't spare a look to check on Tayen again.

A pair of soldiers rounded on him, one with an axe and the other with a sword.

Metal blades flickered in the lantern light as Kaylo parried the sword, shuffling to the right to put the sword fighter between himself and the axe-wielder.

"Tayen! Lights!" Kaylo called out.

Less than a breath passed, and shadows engulfed the whole chamber.

Kaylo rushed at where the sword fighter had been, shouldering him into the axe-wielding soldier behind him. The resulting grunts and clanging metal gave him something to aim for. He stabbed into the darkness twice before finding flesh.

"Tayen!"

Shadows ripped back to their rightful place in an instant, and Kaylo blinked away the spots from his vision.

The axe-wielding soldier—a man around Kaylo's age with sharp features and long silver-white hair spilling out from his helm—lay pinned beneath his comrade's body. He pushed himself backward, trying to dislodge himself from the dead weight.

Bodies lay scattered across the chamber floor. The door hung open. The Priest was not amongst the fallen. Tayen had an arrow drawn with Vicna laid out flat beside her.

The chamber had become a burial site.

"Let me up. Fight me like a man," the soldier said with a growl in his voice.

"Fighting isn't about fair." Kaylo knocked the man's axe aside with his sword and fell to his knee, driving his knife into the soldier's chest.

The soldier's body twitched several times before coming to a rest. Kaylo dislodged his knife from the man's chest.

"Are you alright?" Kaylo called out, checking the Gousht bodies for signs of life.

"Vicna's dead," Tayen said.

"I asked if you were alright." Kaylo nudged a soldier with his boot. The woman's eyes remained wide open. They almost seemed to follow him, but she wasn't breathing.

"I'm fine. What do we do now?"

Kaylo made his way to a sack, several dozen echoes emanating through the rough material. The Priest had known to bait the trap with crystals. Had another spirit dancer told him they could hear the crystals, or had Kaylo said as much during his torture?

"You are going to stay here, and I am going to end this." Kaylo leaned over the stones and gathered the strands of translucent light connecting the crystals to The Balance. With a small tug, the bag collapsed with only granules left behind.

"No way," Tayen said. "You promised Liara you wouldn't make this about vengeance."

"This isn't about vengeance, little shade. The others are all falling into the same trap. They are most likely dead by now, definitely by the time we could reach them. The best I can do is take The Priest's life—take away their general and give the Uprising a fighting chance."

"Then I'm coming." Tayen leveled him with a stare he had grown to know well. He would have to lash her to a dead body to stop her.

The collection of six echoes bounded deeper into the stronghold. He had to move quickly.

"At my side, the whole time. Obey every order."

She nodded, and he strode to the open door.

CHAPTER FIFTY-ONE

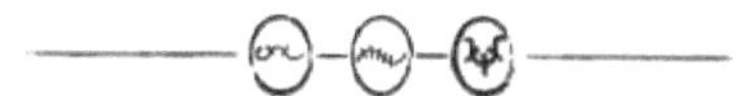

Torrel rounded the corner and waved his children into an alleyway.
Everything had gone so wrong so quickly.

The archer and the other spirit dancer Liara had assigned to their unit
fell in the first volley, before Torrel could call on The Wind. More arrows
than he'd had time to count protruded from their corpses. They had
been relative strangers, young and assured of their cause. And Torrel had
left them behind.

Jonan helped his sister around the corner. The arrow in her side might
not kill her immediately, but it would slow her down. And they needed
to move faster.

The mission had been a trap. Their rebel army wouldn't be coming.
They had to find their own way out.

An archer leaned over the edge of a building with his bow drawn,
and the rage Torrel had known in his youth fed the pace of The Song.
The Wind became a swarm of staccato tones, hectic and wanting. A gust
burst over the rooftops as he shifted and threw his weight forward.

It took longer than expected for the ground to stop the archer's fall
and his screams. Torrel didn't have the time to worry about the curiosity.
He turned the corner and bounded after his children.

They would be hunted anywhere they went in the city. If they attempted to go back through the smugglers' passage, there might be soldiers waiting for them. He needed to find a place to hide out and patch Nomi up. He would have dropped to his knees to beg The Mother for time if she possessed the power to give it.

Ahead of him, Nomi limped as fast as she could down the tight alleyway, a hand holding her wound. Small winces and moans lingered in the air as he chased after her.

He never should have allowed Liara to volunteer his daughter. Nomi never craved the fight like he had—or like Jonan did. She came because her father had asked her to.

An orange glow filtered around the corner behind them. The green bastards were too close behind. Jonan and Nomi would never outrun them, not like this.

"Keep moving," Torrel hissed at them.

Jonan did as he was told. The boy might have struggled to control his rage, but family always came first with him. For his sister, he wouldn't look back. Nomi did, but was in no position to do anything but limp forward with her brother.

Torrel should have praised his son more for his heart. He knew the rage Jonan carried with him better than anyone. Instead of understanding, he had only criticized. His son deserved to know how proud he was. The way the boy had cared for Jonac. The passion he felt driving him to do what was right. Jonan had always been more than his anger.

The orange glow shifted into a yellow heat as the first soldier rounded the corner of the alleyway holding a torch.

Undertones within The Song urged the tempo forward, but Torrel pulled back and coaxed the melody into place.

The Gousht liked to act like masters over the spirits because they could imprison them. They could wield the spirits to their design. But they didn't understand the spirits they wielded.

Torrel had danced with The Wind his whole life. Jonac taught him to study how it moved—to focus on the most minute details.

Wind not only affected the way air moved; it affected the pressure in an environment. If the air pressure lowered enough, their lungs wouldn't be able to draw a single breath. They would drown in the air.

The soldiers raced towards him, unaware of their fate.

It started with a subtle breeze as Torrel shifted his arms back and forth, breathing like a bellows. He fed The Song his breath.

The torchlight flickered out as the wind began to blow in earnest. Soldiers steadied themselves with hands on the alley walls as they continued forward. Then Torrel urged the wind faster.

It was never a command. The Gousht would never understand that. Torrel asked or invited. He never demanded. And The Wind acquiesced.

His robes flapped as he called the gust to pick up more and more speed. A soldier slipped to his knees. Others stopped altogether and reached for the alley walls as if they could wait out the streaming air.

The soldiers probably thought he intended to batter them with the wind's force or physically push them back. They would have run if they had known the truth.

Shock elongated their faces as they reached for air that refused them. A soldier's helm flew off her head into her companion behind her. The bastards pawed at their throats as if something had caught in their windpipes. They didn't understand what they were facing.

Every barrier Torrel had built between him and his anger broke as he screamed into the wind. The sound of the torrent rang in his ears with pain, which he returned to The Song.

Even as the soldiers collapsed forward, Torrel continued to drive the wind. It took longer to suffocate than most people assumed.

One soldier forced himself upright. The bastard looked pleased with himself as he reached for the crystal around his neck, then the gale took him like a kite. It flung him crashing into the wall before he fell limp onto the motionless bodies of his comrades.

When Torrel let go of The Wind, he waited to see if any soldier would rise. Not a one shifted.

It had probably been excruciating—lungs burning, begging for breath. If scales balanced, they must have had enough time to realize they would die and feel their powerlessness.

Rounding back to follow after his children, his first step faltered, and he caught himself on the stone wall beside him. He hadn't called on that much of his spirit ever before. The sound of the screaming wind encircled him even though the air had settled.

He had no time to recover. He took another step, and another, despite the sensation of shifting earth.

Jonan and Nomi had shuffled to the edge of the next large intersecting street. He picked up his pace.

If they had any chance to survive, they had to find a way off the streets. But who would take on the risk? It had taken him turns to overcome his mistrust of strangers and welcome runaways into clan ranks.

Nomi shrieked, and Torrel's attention whipped from his ambling feet to his daughter. Another figure had crashed into Jonan. The movement and distance blurred Torrel's comprehension. He began running.

His feet slipped, but he continued with a hand on the wall to steady himself.

If someone had to die, it needed to be Torrel. Jonan hadn't had a life yet. The turns hadn't pushed him around enough to figure himself out. He needed time. He deserved time.

A soldier pushed Jonan's back against the wall and chopped at his head with an axe, sparks flying when he missed.

In the darkness, their figures conformed into a single shadow, stumbling between one side of the alley and the other. Then one slammed the other's head against the stone, again and again.

Jonan settled into view, his teeth bared as he continued to thrash the limp soldier's head into the stone wall. Blood splattered over his face and chest.

When he stopped, Jonan staggered away from his kill.

Only now had Torrel gotten close enough to see the dagger jutting out from his son's gut. Jonan slumped, and Nomi rushed to his side.

From where Torrel stood, it could be a battle wound—something he could recover from as they found shelter. If he moved closer, it might prove to be different. He hesitated.

He should have never agreed to bring either of his children. They hadn't reached their swearing days. It was his responsibility to choose.

Each step forward brought the truth closer—either hope or despair.

"I'm sorry, Dad," Jonan said, holding the wound in his gut. "I tried my best. I didn't want to disappoint you again."

"You did well." Torrel knelt in front of his son, brushing a tear from his cheek. "You kept your sister safe. You did what you always do; you protected your family."

"I didn't see him coming around the corner. I should have been looking," Jonan said.

Nomi leaned on her brother's shoulder, her back rising and falling with her sobs.

"They really are tricky bastards." Torrel placed his hands on his son's and pulled them away from the wound to get a better look.

Blood rushed out, saturating Jonan's robes and sputtering around the blade. It had likely punctured his kidney from the placement, and it had gone deep.

Torrel placed his son's hands back where they had been.

"It doesn't even hurt anymore." Jonan and his voice had begun to shake. "I'll be fine. Don't worry. We'll get out of this."

"I've always been too hard on you." Torrel felt the warm tears down his chilled cheeks. "You're so much like me, and that always scared me. But I'm so proud. I hope you know that."

"Dad, it's okay. I know I messed up. I'll do better."

Heavy footfalls sounded from down the street, coming closer.

"Help me up," Jonan said. "We need to get moving."

"I love you, son," Torrel said before stepping into the street to meet the oncoming soldiers, The Wind wailing within him.

Talise rushed forward, crashing the shaft of her broad axe into a
soldier and driving her into the chamber wall. Talise stepped back and
swung her axe across the pale woman's chest, ripping through padded
armor and flesh, striking bone.

The woman screamed as Talise ripped her axe from the wound and
created another in the woman's neck. The scream ended abruptly.

Far too many of the Gousht dressed like soldiers before earning the
title. That's why they would lose. If not tonight, eventually.

A sword swiped after Talise, forcing her to scramble away.

The green-clad twat in front of her hadn't earned her attention until
now. His poor footwork and wild attacks made him less of a priority.

He swung his pretty little sword down at her head like he was
chopping wood. It took a minimal amount of effort to step aside. Then
he squealed like a piglet as she drove the heel of her boot into his knee.

The snap that proceeded the soldier collapsing to the ground echoed
in the chamber and brought a smile to Talise's face.

The prick deserved his pain. He had earned every last second that she
allowed him to linger in.

"Stop your whining," she said, though he likely couldn't understand
her. He had probably lived on their land for turns of his miserable life,
and had never thought to learn the language of the people he had
dispossessed.

With a quick crack of her axe into his skull, she ended the moaning.
Then the quiet settled in.

Brain matter and blood clung to her axe blade when she pulled it free.
Surprisingly, the soldier's head hadn't been completely empty.

If the Gousht had set a trap here, they had done the same at the
other caches. The plan had failed.

She looked around at the bodies, Gousht and Ennean lying in blood and filth. In the middle of it all, a bundle of crystals sat untouched. It held far too few spirits.

Someone had lied.

Talise reached for the door and pulled it open. Luckily, a soldier's corpse kept her from opening it too wide as an arrow struck the other side of the wood. She peered through the small opening and slammed the door back in place.

From the quick look she got, about five soldiers waited for her outside the chamber.

Of everything she had survived, she was going to die to a bunch of archers. A bow and arrow—what a fucking waste of a weapon. Of course it was useful, but you couldn't see your kill's eyes shutter closed from so far away.

If she died, it was supposed to be by a blade.

She took a second peek, and the line of archers waited about twenty paces from the door. They shouted something in their shitwit language, but Talise didn't search for the translation in her head. She had never practiced all that much.

Twenty paces? She could do twenty paces.

She hefted a Gousht corpse and opened the door. Arrows careened into the dead body, each one like a tremor through the cold flesh. After the last tremor, she drove her legs forward through the doorway, gripping the corpse by the padded armor.

"It's been too long," Liara whispered at Tomi, forceful enough to get her point across but soft enough for the warriors not to hear.

"The whole point of an infiltration—the whole point of the plan— was to risk as few lives as possible. If something went wrong, they saved the lives of every warrior who stayed behind. Don't sully that."

After so many turns leading the Uprising's forces, there were still people who pushed back, but none like Tomi. The certainty in her voice grated on Liara's eardrums.

"I'm not saying batter ourselves against the wall," Liara said. "We both know there's another route into the city. We send a single regiment to support the infiltration teams. This could still work."

"There is a reason we didn't choose that passageway. It opens up too close to the western barracks. There's too great a risk of open combat."

Tomi waited, staring at Liara. She was right. Liara had worked on these plans meticulously, and they had never made it beyond a hope. Too much could have and likely had gone wrong. However, they had moved forward with the plan for a reason.

"If we don't send in another team and we walk away, what happens next? This fails and the Gousht and Lost Nation fight it out for who gets to call themselves king," Liara said. "This decision will change the course of everything to come. We have to do whatever we can to keep hope alive."

Tomi bowed her head into her hand as she huffed out a breath. "Hope, huh?"

"You're not wrong, Tomi. But I'm not either."

"I'll get my team together," Tomi said.

"No, you're too important to the charge."

Tomi closed the gap between them and grabbed Liara's hand. "If this is the last strand of our hope, I need to be the one to hold on to it. And don't fight me over this. They need you here to make the right decision when the time comes. At some point, hope will run out, and they will need you to choose their lives over a meaningless gesture."

"Don't you die."

"I've made it this long." Tomi smiled and squeezed Liara's hand before turning to find her regiment.

Kaylo didn't bother to sneak through the corridors of the stronghold.

His boots slapped against the stone floor with every stride. No one would have any difficulty finding him. It did not matter. If the Uprising had a chance, The Priest had to die tonight.

The echo of his stolen fragment of The Seed called to him. It raged and bellowed. The anger transformed it, but the undercurrent of the sound was the same spirit that had walked with him for the first seventeen turns of his life.

At the end of the corridor and through a decorative archway, a stone staircase spiraled higher into the stronghold. If he followed the echo up, there would be no turning back. For him or Tayen.

She had managed to stay close behind, her echo and footfalls ever-present companions.

Maybe he should have left her behind or led her away. The night would end in more blood, and she would be in danger again.

Talise's words whispered in a corner of his mind. "Try not to leave the girl behind this time."

He couldn't protect her, support her path, stay at her side, and finish the mission without compromising something. Had he chosen well? Too often the people he cared for died because of his choices.

He rushed through the archway and up the staircase, wall-hung lanterns flickering along the way.

A stationary echo sang from overhead, growing closer as Kaylo raced up the winding stairs. The Flame waited like a spark jumping off a flint stone, subtle and meager, waiting to catch.

Kaylo didn't adjust his speed as he ran towards the waiting ambush. The only advantage he had in this stone maze was awareness. If he changed anything, the would-be assassin would know and adjust like an opponent sitting on the other side of a field of runes.

Jonac might have been teaching him a game to pass the time and distract his mind, but there had been an inherent strategy in the game. Kaylo had played defensively for too long. Now was the time to attack.

What began as a spark ignited into a roaring flame. Kaylo waited with the translucent thread dangling beside him until the soldier appeared around the bend of the spiral. The air shimmered for a moment, then went quiet as The Flame took root in the cage of Kaylo's gut.

The soldier's confusion dropped as Kaylo plunged his sword through the man's padded armor into his abdomen. All of Kaylo's speed and force transferred into the thrust as he collided with his kill, the both of them falling to the stone stairs.

There would be no room for pity or prayers tonight. He could pray for the dead in the morning.

He pulled his sword, slick with blood, and continued up the curve of the staircase, The Flame simmering within him.

More footfalls joined Tayen's behind him, a collection of clattering boots rebounding off the rounded walls of stone. The noise lashed with The Flame's rageful echo.

In the twelve turns Kaylo spent alone, he had discovered who he was without constant violence. It had been lonely, but he had found moments of peace—at least what he had thought of as peace.

At his core, he was a person who loved growing things. He took pride in the garden he had nurtured. He told himself he was not the person he had become on the battlefield. The blood on his hands had never been in harmony with his spirit.

But tonight, he would be death.

He stopped and waved at Tayen to continue.

She didn't hesitate. She had always been more compliant when her life was on the line. Children were strange that way.

The Flame lent Kaylo a sense of the waiting potential in the air. It ran down the staircase, filling the chamber. Kaylo focused on it, bending back and forth with the rhythm that begged for more. He would give the bastard song all it craved.

As he moved to the wanting call, the air shimmered. Heat rolled back towards him, yet still he fed it. Like a pot set to boil, the air was unmoving until the first bubble popped. Then the cascade of fire raced down the spiral staircase and fed on the air below.

Bootsteps turned to screams. The acrid smell of burning meat rose, but he didn't stop feeding the hunger in The Flame. Not yet.

The orange-yellow heat filled the chamber. Blackened marks of soot painted the stone.

Eventually, the air below had nearly all burned away. Only then did Kaylo stop.

If the Gousht wanted to obstruct their plans, he would make them fight for it. The Uprising hadn't failed yet.

He continued up the stairs with smoke rising at his back. The echo of his piece of The Seed wasn't far. The Priest would burn just like his soldiers.

It took several twists of the staircase to spot Tayen. She had done as he asked. She continued to climb higher.

Pride swelled in his chest. This young girl, who had been so afraid when he first met her, had overcome so much. She had learned to fight a battle for a cause and for others rather than for vengeance. It had taken him a lifetime to separate those ideas.

He didn't deserve this feeling. They weren't blood. Her choices and her growth belonged to her. But he couldn't stop the feeling that he had finally done right.

The stairwell twisted then straightened as it reached a platform and a heavy door. Tayen reached towards the handle.

The echoes surrounding The Priest were on the other side, but they had stopped moving.

Kaylo dashed as fast as he could.

Moonlight broke through the opening as Tayen pushed the door outward.

With a fist full of her robes, Kaylo pivoted and threw her from the doorway.

When he looked out, three archers released their arrows, and Kaylo fell to the stone floor.

Chapter Fifty-Two
Current Day Ennea

The door to Kaylo's childhood home hadn't changed. The etching his father had chiseled into the frame still read, 'Family knows.' Small flourishes made the lettering distinct. If his father ever carved something simple, it was only meant to embellish details elsewhere on the piece.

The grain scratched the pads of Kaylo's fingers as he ran them along the length of the text. They felt like a memory.

Muffled sounds carried through the door while Nomar waited in silence all around him. The city had never been this still.

Kaylo hesitated as he reached a hand towards the latch. The dream that waited for him on the other side could destroy him. But he had to know.

The door didn't offer any resistance. It swung in and the hearth fire greeted him. His father stood over the wood-burning stove turning a ladle about in a pot. His mother sat at the corner desk his father had built. Her pen raced across the pages of her journal.

It was the same journal that had burned in the Missing camp when The Priest found them. He had lost the words she entrusted him with—the last piece of her.

His father looked up and a grin spread across his bearded face. "There he is. Welcome home, 'Lo."

His father's voice broke open memories he had misplaced over the turns. Singing around the hearth, none of them carrying much of a tune. His father bandaging a sprained ankle with his light touch. Scolding him after breaking curfew in the early days of training with Munnie.

Kaylo dashed past the threshold and crashed into his father's chest, locking his arms around his father's broad shoulders. He had never been able to fully wrap his arms around his father before.

"Oh, my boy. It will be okay. You've done good."

"I'm sorry. I shouldn't have left you here that night."

His father pulled away from the embrace and reached a hand up to Kaylo's cheek. "You did what I asked. You survived."

A presence hovered over Kaylo's shoulder, and his mother was there with open arms. She pulled him into her. "We are so proud of you, Kaylo. You made your own stories. We have never stopped being there, watching over you."

"I've got to admit, it got pretty dull during those turns in the hallow," his father said with jest in his tone.

"Dekas," his mother scolded. "Our son has just arrived. You have plenty of time to tease him later."

"Mom, I'm sorry I lost your book."

"You protected my son, and that's all I care about."

"But I failed. The Uprising will fail, and Tayen will be spirited on in no time."

His mother shook her head. "You put too much on yourself," she said. "Speaking of your overabundance of guilt, I have someone who has been wanting to see you."

She turned Kaylo by the shoulders to face the bedroom doors. A seventeen-turn-old Shay stepped into the main room. Her loose red curls fell, framing her dimpled smile.

Neither of them moved for a moment. She hadn't aged a day, yet he stood there with all his thirty-five turns.

"It's good to see you, old man," Shay said.

"Why…I mean, you're still so young?"

"You know how this works. Everything here is perception. This isn't your home or Nomar. That isn't your body, and this isn't mine. But this is the home and the me you know. We thought it would be easier."

"It was Rena," Kaylo said. "She was a spirit dancer and had the soldiers follow you out to the forest."

"I know. I was pissed at first, but I've learned to let it go." She waved it off, then her smile dropped. "But I do owe you an apology. That night, when I found out what you were… I shouldn't have backed away."

"To be fair, you were dying at the time."

She looked at him, past the attempt at humor, and her face remained stoic.

"I know what it did to you, Kaylo. You were more of a brother to me than a friend, and I made you ashamed of what you were. You didn't deserve that."

If this form needed to breathe, it would have been hard to keep the shudder out of his breath.

His mother wrapped an arm around his waist. "We are sorry we weren't there for you when you needed us."

Kaylo looked from his mother, to his father, to Shay. Each of them wore a solemn apology on their face in the subtle downturn of the lips and wrinkle of their brows. "No. You don't owe me any apology. It wasn't your fault. It was theirs—the Gousht."

"Maybe," his father said. "But we are still sorry for the time we lost. Just like you will feel sorry for leaving the girl behind. It wasn't your fault, but that won't change the feeling."

Tayen, Kaylo thought.

He had tossed her to the floor of the stronghold and left her there. The Priest wouldn't just let her leave. The freedom Kaylo was responsible for protecting would be stolen from her, if not her life.

"Can I do anything for her now?" Kaylo asked.

"The Waking is beyond us," his mother said. "If not, we would have reached out for you so many times. We can see everything on the other side, but that gift is a curse as well. Because we cannot do anything about it."

Kaylo almost went searching for Tayen immediately—to see her—to find her. Then he stopped himself. It wouldn't offer any comfort. He couldn't protect her from everything to come. He couldn't do anything in The Mist.

Then again, that wasn't true. He had crossed over so often to try to change The Waking. The hope had always been slim.

"I have somewhere I need to be," he said, looking at the people he had missed the longest.

His father smiled. "You always were determined. Go. We will be here when you're finished."

If Kaylo reached for any more words, he would linger too long trying to say everything that he had wanted to for the past twenty turns. Instead, he kissed his mother on the cheek and strode out of the house.

CHAPTER FIFTY-THREE

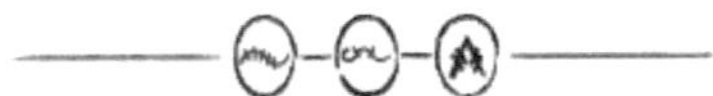

A small contingent of servants followed Wal up the pathway that spiraled through the core of the Citadel, each of them wearing fresh blood splatter. The bodies they stepped over or around were all Ennean, the color and quality of their robes separating them into their respective classes.

Several faces looked familiar—a servant who had brought meals to his quarters, a bureaucrat who managed supplies for expeditions beyond the forest, a warrior he had trained. Each and every name eluded him.

The corpses wrapped in tattered gray robes far outnumbered those in Astilean purple. The turns of living off meager rations in dismal conditions had stripped their bodies to the bone. They were the conscripted who failed their training. Even the weapons lying next to them were largely a collection of repurposed tools.

Wal didn't dare count the dead or consider how many of them he had condemned to servitude himself. They had failed their training, and that had been enough justification for him.

He had always thought of himself as a warrior in the battle against the Gousht Empire, but as he looked over the dead, he wondered if he had done more damage to his own people.

The bodies became more frequent as they rose higher into the main chamber. A young warrior's head and arms dangled over the edge of the pathway.

Any attempted coup would have to do two things: secure the King and secure the armory. Given that Lanigan's note said King Shonar was dead, Wal intended to ensure the armory was under control as well.

Blood dyed the stone floor red as they turned into the corridor leading to the armory. The weapons and spirit crystals within would decide the victor.

Sounds of clanging metal carried through the corridor like a bloody promise.

The servants around him tensed. They had fought well, but several had fallen in their few skirmishes. What remained of the army and the Citadel guard understood battle and how to move in an engagement. But the servants fought with a ferocity that could only come from people who had been wronged.

"If those loyal to the throne take the armory, they will outlast this little rebellion. And all they have to do is outlast," Wal said. "If these soldiers are worth the value of the ink on their cheeks, messages are on their way to every Astilean city, calling for aid. The Citadel will have to be ours before aid comes. That starts with the crystals in the armory."

The servants looked at him with disgust every time he addressed them, and he couldn't blame them. Before his own imprisonment, he had been one of their many tormentors. He commanded them as if they had ceased to be people. If he had aggrieved or abused any of those who followed him now, he wouldn't know it. Who they were and what they looked like hadn't mattered.

"I get it. You hate me. Kill me or move past it. If we don't secure the armory, I'm dead anyway."

Several of the servants fiddled with the weapons in their hands as if considering his offer. Then an older Tomakan man towards the front showed him a rude gesture, and the others followed suit.

"That will do."

Nix yanked Daak up by the arm. The hapless ass would be the death of her. The flood of warriors running through the forest in their wake would saturate the soil with their blood if they caught up with them.

An arrow rushed past her shoulder, and the servant several paces ahead of them tumbled to the ground.

In hindsight, her little display of explosions had only delayed the inevitable. They would die running through the forest instead of kneeling beside a fire.

At least she would die beside Sosun. She owed the girl that much.

Firelight flashed to life behind them, casting a yellow-orange glow against the trees. It rushed over the ground like a predator chasing down a meal. Then it shot past them and extended in front of them like a wall, consuming the undergrowth and forest debris like a daemon with unappeasable hunger.

The servants all stopped in front of the backdrop of flame and smoke as a large contingent of warriors slowed their march forward, falling into a line to finish them off.

Sosun wrinkled her nose as if fighting to restrain her tears. *"I'm sorry for pulling you into this,"* she signed.

"We did what we said we would," Nix signed back. *"I've done a lot wrong with my days. I do not count following you amongst them."*

Sosun reached out and grabbed Nix's hand.

Tanis settled into the line twenty paces in front of Nix. The bitch could have called her archers to take aim and end them quickly, but she hadn't. She wore an expression hungrier than the flames blocking their path.

A throaty cry burst through the silence. A servant, hair white from age, screamed at the warriors with all her rage. There was no fear in it.

Another servant joined the cry, followed by a dozen more, until all the servants shouted at their oppressors in their last act of defiance. Sosun added her unused voice to the wordless chorus.

The servants were outnumbered and largely unarmed, but they would not cower. Then why would Nix?

She gripped her sword and thrust it into the air with a battle cry. Her feet carried her forward before she could think better of it. The cries of the servants ran with her.

They may have failed the trials, but the Enneans beside her measured far beyond the warriors in front of her.

Tanis' brow quirked into a question before she called out to her warriors, the sound of which was drowned out by the rage-filled shouting. Warriors shifted their stances and formed their lines.

None of the servants faltered despite the promise of their deaths.

Nix could think of worse ways to die.

She charged Tanis. The General caught her sword, but the force of Nix's charge pushed her back.

Nix caught her opponent with a kick to the ribs, putting distance between them. Tanis had more experience, but Nix wouldn't concern herself with fighting like a warrior. Warriors had rules and honor. Honor wouldn't save Nix. At least she could die with some blood on her blade.

"This is a fool's errand," Tanis said.

"And this is a fool's blade." Nix thrust the point of her sword towards Tanis's gut. The General parried and sidestepped into the path of one of her warriors engaged with a servant.

Nix stabbed her blade into the side of the distracted warrior, forcing Tanis to watch him fall.

"Your fight is with me!"

"My fight is my own. I will take as many from you as I can."

Tanis bared her teeth and charged forward. Nix blocked and parried as best as she could, but she lost ground with every strike In a straightforward battle, the General would kill her quick. Nix sidestepped, putting a tree between them.

When Tanis rounded the tree to reengage, Nix went on the offensive.

Firelight cast an orange glow over Tanis' golden-brown skin. Smoke continued to billow into the air. Somewhere, Sosun would be fighting for her life if she hadn't already died.

In the last moments of her life, Nix finally had a mission. She had done whatever it had taken to survive all her life, but survival was beyond her now. Tanis would pay for her crimes before Nix crossed into The Mist.

Tomi led her regiment of ten warriors through the Stone City streets. It brought back memories of her childhood she thought she had lost. Every turn and corner looked familiar and new. After all, she was seeing it all from a different vantage point.

Back then, she had been a small wisp of a girl. Now she strode through the streets with a pack of warriors she had trained herself, pointing out archers for them to kill. It felt vindicating, even if they would all probably die.

The smugglers' passage they had taken had brought them closest to Talise and her unit, which worked out. She barely knew the Jani dancer and his children, and Kaylo could die in whatever way he chose best.

The regiment moved with tempered speed. A scout surveyed ahead as the rest of them did their best not to make their presence known.

They had been lucky so far. But luck wasn't an unending well. Eventually, they would find a fight that couldn't be ended with a few well-placed arrows. This was the Stone City after all. The Gousht held it up like a symbol of their triumph and wouldn't let it go easily.

The small ember of hope that remained could die in a weak breeze, which was exactly why Tomi had to be the one to protect it.

Liara's hope had saved the Uprising. When the rebellion could have died or twisted into some self-serving crew of bandits, she led the way through. She showed the people that they didn't have to fight with hate and vengeance. They could fight for a dream of a future that seemed impossible.

She made it all seem possible.

The whole while, Tomi had scoffed at her sister's ideas. She taught recruits to use a bow and led her warriors, but she had never been a believer. For her, every battle was a chance to take back some of the fear the green bastards had forced on her.

At the beginning, Tomi had been against this desperate attempt to steal back the city she couldn't remember. It wasn't until she saw Liara's hope falter as they waited for the Last Wall to open that Tomi realized how much she needed that hope.

Tomi was no different than the countless number of their clan who relied on Liara's hope to carry them through their days. If anyone charged into the city to protect her sister's hope, it had to be Tomi.

The scout signaled for the regiment to proceed with greater caution. Tomi didn't need to repeat the signal. She had trained her warriors too well for that. They each halved their pace and softened their footfalls.

Around the corner, a regiment of soldiers formed ranks in a courtyard. Torchlight illuminated the scene. Several green-clad bodies lay in front of their formation. A line of archers aimed their bows toward a dark-windowed building.

It had to be Talise's unit, but too many Gousht bodies littered the courtyard for it to have been the work of such a small group. Maybe they had joined up with the city rebels.

A soldier with a glowing red crystal stepped forward.

The time for strategy had come and gone. The Wind sang a coming storm, and Tomi grabbed hold of it. Tonight, she would allow herself to hope.

A torrent of wild air burst into the courtyard, throwing several of the

Gousht company to the ground and breaking their pristine ranks. Arrows launched into the night without Tomi saying a word, and her archers struck true.

A half-hearted volley of arrows came back in return, but the protection of the alley walls was all they needed.

Any moment, the soldiers would regain their footing, take proper aim, and call for reinforcements. Now was no time for formations and overly complicated tactics. Tomi had to end the battle quickly.

With a signal, the ground rumbled with her warriors' footfalls as they charged into battle.

They reached their enemy before the bastards had fully recovered. Tomi unsheathed her sword and sliced through a fallen soldier's jugular before he had time to steady his feet.

Another soldier leaped over his fallen companion's body and crashed into Tomi. Apparently, the wind hadn't taken them all so off guard.

She parried his spear thrust and gave herself the room to call The Wind yet again when Talise barreled into his torso. The abruptness unbalanced Tomi for a moment, but she couldn't help her smile.

Talise yanked her axe from the spearman's chest before nodding to Tomi.

"Where are the others? Are they hurt?" Tomi asked as she looked for her next opponent.

"If by 'hurt' you mean 'dead,' then very." Talise blocked an overhead sword attack with the shaft of her axe and twisted the attacker off balance. She had killed yet another soldier without any complication.

"You did this on your own?" Tomi asked, almost as a demand.

Dreak fell at Tomi's feet with an axe in his chest. She had known the warrior since he was old enough to hold a blade. With a battle cry, she surged forward and plunged her sword into his killer before the shit could regain his axe.

"Talk later," Talise said. "We have work to do."

Torrel's legs trembled beneath him. He had never danced with The Wind like this before, never called on such power for so long. The ache traveled through him. He slammed his fist into his twitching thigh.

A building beside him cracked and a soldier screamed as he fell to the ground along with a slab of stone. His scream stopped abruptly.

Nomi removed her hand from the building and resumed holding her belly, buckled over like she would be sick. She had taken on too many angry spirits.

He had brought her here to suffer a painful death. Jonan's body lay on the street. His boy had gone cold as the stone beneath him.

When the Gousht tracked Jonac to the Jani all those turns past, Torrel's mother had fought and died to protect him. He had lived because of her. Now, he had failed to do the same for his children.

The Wind picked up in a chorus of sorrow and rage. It sang the ballad of a hurricane—broken and out of tune, harsh and mournful.

Torrel lifted his arms and swept them to the side, back and forth. Archers fell from the rooftops and crashed into stone facades. He had killed so many, but it wouldn't be enough to save his daughter.

A small pain bit into his shoulder, like a bee sting. A puncture thin and tight, barely noticeable. Then his right arm fell flat against his side, refusing to move.

An arrow jolted clean through his shoulder. It should have been more painful, but he couldn't feel much of anything.

The archer nocked another arrow and aimed for Nomi.

Torrel had already seen one of his children die. He had been too preoccupied to intervene. It wouldn't happen again.

He latched on to the violence within The Song—every dangerous inclination of The Wind lying within the layers of its call—and he pulled. The world spun around him as he twisted the air into a funnel reaching down from the clouds. He and Nomi remained at the center as the tornado took form.

The Priest's guards dragged Tayen from Kaylo's body, through the door, and out to the balcony. Kaylo's blood painted her robes. She thrashed against their grasp, but they only clenched their hands tighter around her.

One of the guards handed Kaylo's knife to The Priest, and the bastard slipped it into his belt, taking another thing that didn't belong to him. How much of Kaylo could one man steal?

"Fuck you, you Gousht pricks!" She hated the way a whine forced itself through her words, but it wouldn't stop her. "I'll kill you! You'll die looking at my face!"

Heavy hands forced her to her knees in front of Kaylo's Priest. She lunged at him, but they forced her back down.

The Song swirled about her, and she pulled at the shadows. She thickened them into an abyss, then pain broke through her cheek, twisting the back of her jaw.

The Priest had his hand raised for a second strike as she lost her grip on the shadows.

"Do that again, child, and I will do worse than bruise your pretty little face."

All the times Kaylo mentioned this man settled into a picture around him. The cadence of his voice broke into a slow, considered rhythm like he expected to be heard and heeded. His shoulders fell back, drawing his chest forward and making him bigger than his size.

The way Kaylo had turned this man into a daemon in his stories made sense now.

"You can't break me," she said. "If you don't kill me now, I will end your bitter little life."

"Bitter?" The word came out with a jovial curiosity.

"Kaylo told me how you moaned over your stolen empire like you were entitled to it. He told me how you liked to make others suffer because your little brother became the man you wanted to be. Does it still hurt knowing you will never be emperor? You will always be subservient?"

The Priest hummed at the back of his throat as if he were considering her challenge. "You will be fun to break. Kaylo never had your confidence, not like this. No, child; you will learn my power."

He reached into the fold of his crimson robes and removed a clear crystal. "I already have a fragment of The Shadow, but I have to imagine you carry something special within you." Even though the red veil hid his face from the world, he spoke as though a smile played with his words.

Breath shook in and out of Tayen's lungs. She ground her teeth to keep the fear from her face. He could take The Shadow. He couldn't have her fear. The bitter old fuck of a would-be emperor didn't deserve her fear.

"No begging? Kaylo begged."

She spat at his feet. The pretty little boots confirmed everything Tayen already knew. The Priest didn't work hard enough to scuff the leather. He was a weak man who knew how to use the power he took from other people.

He held the crystal in front of him as the soldier had done when she first met Kaylo. The familiar chill ran through her. She didn't feel any pain beyond the knowledge of what The Priest was taking from her. She bucked against the grip on her shoulders, only to be pushed back to her knees.

It would be unbearably quiet without The Song.

A faint color twisted beneath the crystal's surface. The pieces of The Song began to blend into a muddled mess. She couldn't distinguish the various shadows within it. It faded and left an unmistakable, yet intangible, hole within her.

The silence that followed was the loudest she had ever heard.

CHAPTER FIFTY-FOUR

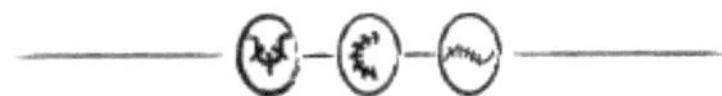

Kaylo knelt in the middle of the town square he remembered from his childhood. He tried to catch his breath after peering into The Waking and seeing the suffering he had left behind. Not that his spirit needed the air.

Nomar's town square had never been this quiet and empty, but every detail down to the imperfect brick of the surrounding buildings made it feel like home. Maybe it wasn't real. But if it wasn't real, then none of The Mist could be.

After all, The Mist existed as a collection of spirits—perceptions projected against an unending plane. He would have to shift his idea of what qualified as real.

Everything he had seen in The Waking had felt real. His friends were fighting for their lives, and he couldn't do anything about it. He had left Tayen at the mercy of The Priest.

He stood up and leaned against the caller's stage. The texture of the wood helped him focus. Tayen didn't need him to scream into a void or rip apart his memory one wooden plank at a time, though he wanted to.

There was somewhere he needed to be.

Even here, in The Mist, a part of his essence belonged to The Balance. He concentrated on that piece. It felt strangely warm and familiar, much like the town square surrounding him.

There was no path to visit The Great Spirits. No anointed walkway or hidden passage. The Mother hadn't laid out The Mist in forests and valleys, rivers and mountain peaks. Distance didn't exist here.

Innately, he knew if he wanted to visit her, all he had to do was gather her in his mind, pull on their connection, and step into her perception of The Mist.

The layers of darkness wrapped around him. The absence in this place reflected his own feelings of powerlessness.

Now that he belonged to The Mist, he felt more in tune with his surroundings. He couldn't manipulate them. This domain belonged to The Balance. However, he could settle into The Mist and sense The Balance coming for him.

And so, despite the rage over what he had seen, Kaylo waited. He didn't call out for her like he had done so often before. She would come. Neither of them could deny their ties no matter how many times they had tried.

Shadows shifted and bent, creating a depth to the darkness that should not have been possible. At the center of the richest black within the void, The Balance walked forth. Her shadow cloak billowed around her. She had not bothered to veil her face with her hood.

They stood in each other's silence for moment, each of them holding the weight of loss about them.

"You weren't wrong," she said.

"About what?"

"The last time we spoke, you said it would be the last time you visited from The Waking." Her porcelain eyes and onyx brow contained a pain. There was no righteousness in her voice, only a tight grief that pinched her tone.

"Are you here to convince me to do...the right thing? You have nothing to offer me. Nothing left to try to convince me. Your little plan killed three other spirit dancers. Another is on the verge of her death as we speak.

"No, I don't need lectures, little thief. Enjoy this plane and make it what you will. You will not be the last of my descendants to die, and you certainly weren't the first. Destroying the crystals won't destroy their prejudice. It was here before the crystals."

"That isn't why I came," Kaylo said.

The Balance swiped her shadow-clad arm through the space between them in a violent motion. "No. I said no. Don't plead for them. Don't ask me for empathy when I have felt them kill me countless times. I am done making choices to appease the people who loathe me for what their stories made me out to be!

"I was made to give them balance! My descendants were meant to help bridge the divide between the marked and the spirit-bound. We did our duty, and they hated us for it! No, I will not bend for them!"

Kaylo stepped forward and closed the gap between them. "I looked into The Waking. The people I love are suffering, and I can't do anything about it. There's no heart left in my chest to break, but the pain won't stop. I said we were the same before, but I was wrong. This is a different agony."

"And you would have me save them because of our connection?"

"No," Kaylo said, waiting for The Balance to meet his eyes before he continued. "Even though he was taken from me, The Seed is and will always be part of who I am. I am a descendant of balance and forgiveness, and I have fought it my entire life.

"I came here to apologize."

"I didn't ask for your apology." The Balance swelled and grew to twice his size.

"I am sorry for believing their stories. I am sorry for hiding you away like a secret. I am sorry for the anger and rage I laid at your feet," he said. "It's been no time at all, and I am being torn apart as people I love are dying. My hands are bound.

"You had to sit by and watch for centuries as people exiled, abused, and killed your descendants. You felt their pain through them. People called you The Thief, even as they stole from you. They told stories and spat on the names of those you walked with."

The Balance stepped back, shrinking to her original size as she did.

"I am sorry for my part in your pain. And I forgive you for what you did. You lashed out at the people who cursed you. There is a balance of sorts in that."

"That's it?" A small challenge lingered in her voice. "No plea for me to act?"

"Would it matter? You will do what you will do. I came here to do what I had to do. I'm sorry for everything, including not being able to show them how wrong they were."

The illusion of perfection in The Balance's mask faltered in the wrinkles about her eyes and nose. She looked as though she were trying to hold back tears, though this was all her projection, and only The Mother knew if The Great Spirits could cry.

Spirit or not, The Balance had endured far too much grief for far too long.

Chapter Fifty-Five

Nix staggered back with her hand covering her new gut wound. It was a poor bandage, but Tanis's blade hadn't penetrated deeply enough to kill. Not quickly, at least.

The two women angled around each other, waiting to close the gap. They moved slower than when their fight had begun. Tanis's off-weapon arm hung loose at her side. It took Nix more effort to plant her next step.

Each warrior had taken advantage of the minute mistakes the other had made, and they wore the evidence on their blood-stained robes.

Worst of all, Nix hadn't been able to keep an eye on Sosun. The distraction would have been the end of her. And if she died, she would be no help to the girl.

Behind her opponent, warriors and servants clashed. The servants hadn't met the warriors head on. It would have been a quick way to step into The Mist. They ran and hid and used the forest to their advantage as best as they could.

The still bodies of fallen servants littered the forest.

Nix would die as well. Even if she killed Tanis, which grew less likely with each drop of blood leaking from her wounds, she couldn't contend with an army.

The fire line carved into the forest with a spirit crystal shined an orange glow against Tanis' face. Even the bitch's scowl had lost energy the longer they fought.

Nix tightened her grip around her sword hilt, took a step forward, and stopped. The glow faded away to nothing. Warriors all around them stood up, staring at their hands like they had lost something.

An elderly northwoman in tattered servant robes rushed forth, swiped her hand over the forest floor, and a plume of fire erupted like a geyser amongst a group of lost warriors. They threw themselves to the ground, beating the flames from their purple robes.

The servant didn't carry a glowing crystal, but she couldn't have been a dancer. The army stole every spirit they could to add to their coffers. It would have been impossible for the northwoman to hide her spirit this long.

Tanis lunged forward, the tip of her sword aiming for Nix's heart. If she hadn't been distracted, Nix would have easily deflected the attack. As it was, she failed to parry the blade and caught its edge with her forearm instead of her own sword.

Pain ripped a line of lightning down her arm as Tanis withdrew her sword for a follow-up attack. Blood spurted from the wound, and Nix dropped her sword, unable to move her fingers.

Tanis pressed her advantage, forcing Nix to stagger backwards with each thrust and swipe of her weapon.

"It was always going to end like this," Tanis said. "I am the superior warrior."

She struck down from her shoulder in a cross-body attack that would have ended Nix's miserable existence if she hadn't thrown herself to the ground behind an ironoak.

The undergrowth picked and pricked at Nix's skin through her torn robes. Her body felt weak. It wanted to lie on the ground and let go, but Nix had never been one to let anything in this world dictate her choices.

Not far off, an elder servant twisted her hips slowly and pushed forward with both of her hands. The gust of wind that followed knocked several warriors on their asses.

Nix had no idea how the servants had regained their spirits. Maybe the Uprising had been successful. Kaylo had always been a lucky bastard.

Even if the servants couldn't win, there was poetry in seeing them bring the spirits to bear on their oppressors.

Nix scrambled to her feet as Tanis rounded the tree, placing as much foliage between them as possible.

Several purple-clad warriors dove to the ground as fire washed over the forest floor behind them.

Sosun might have a chance, Nix thought, and it buoyed her resolve.

Tanis was pompous, entitled, and cruel. If she wanted to kill Nix, she would have to work harder.

With her uninjured arm, Nix hoisted a downed tree limb from the forest floor and set her feet. The world had begun to wobble. Maybe one of the dancers had called on The Mountain, but more likely, Nix's body was ready to shut down after losing too much blood.

Tanis smiled at Nix and her new weapon. Arrogance painted her face. Then she attacked.

Nix parried with the branch once, twice, but on the third attempt, Tanis's blade broke the branch in two.

The short stub of wood wouldn't do her any good in a sword fight, and Tanis knew it. The General stopped to revel in the moment before her killing blow. It would be her last mistake.

Nix threw herself forward, plunging the splintered edge of her tree limb into the General's neck. It tore through the flesh with all of Nix's weight behind it. Blood sprayed as Tanis's head rolled back, and she collapsed to the ground.

"You may be a better warrior, but I know how to survive." Nix fell and rolled over to lie on her back beside her kill.

Suddenly, Sosun stood over Nix like a final vision before her crossing.

Then the girl started yanking on her injured arm. A vision wouldn't have been so careless.

Nix forced herself up, if for no other reason than to stop Sosun from twisting her arm in more pain.

Only a handful of warriors remained, but another round of purple-robed assholes moved through the trees in the distance. The army had marched out with thousands. This small group that had pursued them had only been a fraction of their force, and they wouldn't survive another encounter.

If there had been dancers amongst the servants, there certainly had been some amongst the army's ranks.

A servant, even younger than Sosun with thick gray curls, twisted and turned in the gap between them and the incoming soldiers. She moved with grace and precision. Determination made a snarl of her face.

In her wake, a thicket of thistle bushes grew in a long line with shades of purple and orange visible in the flickering fires.

"Oh great, that will really irritate their shins as they make their way over here to kill us," Nix said.

"Servants adapt. We have to," Sosun signed with a knowing smile tugging one side of her lips higher than the other.

A second servant rushed forward as if to leap over the bushes. She stopped and thrust her arms wide. Then, in a flash, the line of thistles burst into flame, only allowing small glimpses of the warriors beyond to show through.

"They can deal with us or continue their mission," Sosun signed. *"They've always been pragmatists."*

The remaining servants began moving south—running, limping, slinging the wounded over their shoulders.

Between the blood loss and the multiple jarring hits to her head, Nix would have rather lay down. Instead, she cinched her belt around her arm to slow the bleeding and stumbled after Sosun.

Wal sat with his back against the corridor wall, cradling Shiena's head in his lap. Bodies of servants and warriors blanketed the stone floor, but he couldn't bring himself to care about any of them as he held his friend.

He and the servants had managed to secure the armory, but it had come with a terrible cost.

When they assigned Shiena to his training regiment, she had been a skinny little kid. She hadn't known how to grip a weapon, much less plant her feet. But she had anger to drive her.

It hadn't been an uncommon thing. The army was full of angry Enneans who had lost family and friends. The hate drove them like a song they could all hear.

But Shiena harnessed it. She craved instruction, improving every day.

He had asked her once about what she had lost, and she refused to tell him. She said that she would tell him the names of her dead when every couta was either banished from Ennea or dead.

In all his turns in Astile, Wal hadn't told anyone but the poet about Adéan or the moons he had been forced to serve the Gousht.

Shiena's refusal to tell him about her dead made Wal feel instantly bonded to the woman. And he had just killed her.

She hadn't wronged him. She only did what he had trained her to— serve Astile.

Footsteps rang against the stone walls, and the remaining servants stood with swords ready. However, they dropped their arms to the side before Wal had a chance to get up. They parted to either side of the corridor.

Wal placed Shiena's head on the floor with as much care as he could before rising to see Lanigan leading a procession of servants down the hall. Both their forearm and the crown of their head had been wrapped in fabric, now stained with blood.

When they reached Wal, the poet held out their hands. The two had never touched for as much as they had shared. Wal took their hands in greeting.

"I guess you chose the people." Lanigan attempted a smile, but it wore too much mourning.

"You could have been a little less cryptic, poet."

> *Sounds should roam this world*
> *Take shape in time and place, then transform again*
> *If words are truly ideas spoken*
> *Beware the rigid and worship the imprecise*

"You may have to stop speaking in verse if you plan on becoming king," Wal said.

Lanigan frowned and wrinkled their brow in confusion. "You misunderstand me, young man. I intend for there to be no king."

***

Nomi trembled. The stolen spirits ripped at her from within as her father whipped the wind into a tornado about them. The force of it pulled on her robes. The air became thinner and colder. She hunkered down low while bodies and debris were swept up in the racing winds.

She had trained with her father all her life. He encouraged her to learn how to move with every spirit, even lending her his own connection to The Wind.

When she carried The Wind, she understood the immensity of its reach. It felt endless. So the raw power whipping around them shouldn't have surprised her, but her father had always been reserved. The stories of his youth had been incongruous with the man who raised her.

The layers peeled back to show the angry spirit under the surface. Torrel screamed with the twisting air, the rageful bellow of the tornado stealing the sound from his mouth.

His movement slowed with each passing moment. The fluidity in his whirlwind arms stuttered. It took far too much energy to move so much wind, and it would never be enough to stave off the Gousht army.

The tornado died the instant he collapsed to his knees, leaving a silence and stillness in its wake.

She crawled to her father's side. His head lolled as his arms fell limp beside him.

"Dad," she said, but the remnants of the howling wind made her voice small. "Dad, are you okay?"

When he met her eyes, he looked at her like an apology.

"You're going to be okay," she said, knowing the lie of it.

"We shouldn't have come." His voice croaked with a dry thirst. "Jonan should be alive. You should be safe."

"This isn't your fault. Jonan loved you. I love you."

Torrel snapped his head towards a roof of a nearby building, attempting to lift his arms to no avail. His echo sang a farewell.

The wrathful call of The Mountain spirit within Nomi screeched, and she joined it. She pressed her palms to the cold stone pathway beneath her. Its foundation ran deep. Imperfections created gaps within the stone, which she could use.

A crack sank into the stone and ran forth towards the building upon which the archer readied his bow. The stone of the city had all been called and crafted as one. The crack climbed the building's facade, shifting part of the roof as the archer released his arrow.

It went wide, but he regained his stance for another attempt.

She needed to be closer. She couldn't break the building beneath his feet. Not from here. Not as tired and blood-drawn as she was.

Her boots slipped against the stone as she scrambled forward.

It was too far. She couldn't outrace an arrow.

The archer drew back his bowstring, his aim still focused on her father.

She lost her footing and fell to the ground.

The sound of a projectile finding flesh froze her in place. She heard a gargled attempt to breathe. Then the body of the archer fell to the ground twenty paces ahead of her.

A long stretch of ice protruded from his chest.

A figure looked down from the rooftop where the archer had been moments before. Boots slapped against stone, and a crowd of Sonacoans walked through the alleyway towards her.

It had to be the city's resistance. Something had pulled them from their hiding place.

As her heart settled, she heard the shift in the echoes around her. None of them were imprisoned. They sang The Song freely.

How? she wondered, then she whipped around, remembering why she had been running.

Her father remained on his knees, mouth hanging as if he couldn't believe they had survived.

———

Explosions in the distance flashed orange in the purple-black sky as Talise raced through the Stone City streets. The slope drove her feet faster along with the cacophony of boots trampling behind her.

She, Tomi, and what remained of Tomi's regiment made their way to join the resistance fighters at the gates.

Whatever happened to the Gousht's spirit crystals had thrown the soldiers off-kilter, but they would regroup. They still had plenty of blades and arrows. If the resistance couldn't open the gates, the soldiers would overrun them.

Her shoulders ached from all the fighting. Her side burned where a pale giant of a Gousht had slammed his spear shaft into her, breaking at least a couple of ribs. But she had a hope she had never had before.

"I thought your sister's plan was shit," Talise said with a lightness she shouldn't have felt in the middle of a battle.

Tomi smiled. "That's exactly what I—"

An arrow punched through Tomi's chest, and her momentum drove her into the stone street. She lay there, face down, unmoving.

Talise responded on instinct. She grabbed Tomi by the arm and dragged her towards the nearby alleyway. She needed cover to tend to Tomi's wound. It would all be okay if they reached the alley.

Arrows clattered to the ground, and the remnants of Tomi's warriors launched arrows of their own. But none of that mattered.

Talise pulled her friend into the shadowed alcove and flipped her body over.

Tomi's eyes were open. Brown with flecks of green. Her lips waited for her to finish what she had been saying as if time had stopped when the arrow found her.

"No," Talise said. "This isn't the plan. You were supposed to wait out there with your sister. You should be out there. Why didn't you wait?!"

When Talise joined the Missing, all she had wanted was steady food and a place to sleep. She had never killed anyone. Hadn't thought much about it either. But eventually, she got good at it, and that was all it ever was until there were people to protect.

The dead were dead. Killing to balance blood and all that nonsense got in the way of keeping the living alive. That was how she had moved on after losing so many people over the turns, but this was too much.

Tomi had been a little brat ready to fight everyone when they met. If Talise had met someone more annoying, it had been a close race. Then eighteen turns passed.

She could count on a single hand the number of friends still alive after eighteen turns.

Talise hadn't been lying. She hadn't believed in Liara's plan. It had been a slim chance to avoid a worse fate, but it had failed almost immediately. Yet, somehow, it might have worked. And, as ridiculous as it was, it didn't feel worth it in this moment.

She should be dead, not Tomi.

Talise sat with her back against the alley wall and pulled Tomi to her. She wrapped her friend in her arms and didn't move.

Metal clanged, people screamed, and fires flashed, but it didn't matter. The city resistance and what remained of the Uprising would have to open the gates without her.

Tayen had been on her knees grieving The Shadow when the crystal in The Priest's hand and the others around his neck shattered.

The Song flooded back into her bones like the first breath after diving too deep into the water. Each shadow sang within the chorus. The rhythm and harmony created an outline, the clearest doorway through The Mist she had ever experienced.

The guards restraining her loosened their grip from the surprise of seeing unbreakable stones shatter seemingly unprovoked.

Tayen ripped her arms from their weakened grasps and slammed her palms against the stone balcony. The Song paused for the briefest of instances before roaring all around her. Shadows dashed from the balcony, creating space for the surrounding torches to fill with a flash of light.

The dark returned as quickly as it left.

Guards groaned and rubbed at their eyes, but The Priest had not been so easily fooled. Maybe the veil shielded his eyes or maybe he had predicted her move. Either way, he rushed toward her.

He was far larger than Tayen. He wore his size like a warrior beneath the crimson robes. But he didn't have his stolen gifts to rely on any longer.

It took a far defter touch to shape the shadows than to drive them away, but she knew her work well. She painted a thick shade to cover his priestly veil like a blindfold.

The bulky man swiped his arms wildly to grab her, but Kaylo had taught her better. She could not only control the shadows, she knew how to move like them.

She slipped in close. He smelled of roses and barley wine. Kaylo's knife—his father's knife—stuck out from his belt awkwardly. It didn't belong there. It didn't belong to him. So she took it.

Tayen had held Kaylo's knife several times before. It had never seemed like anything special. Well-made and well-kept, of course, but not special. Now, it felt like having Kaylo beside her.

The blade slipped into The Priest's chest easily like it was made to fit the wound.

For all of his verbose speeches and his larger-than-life presence, he shrank to a smaller man. The Priest stumbled back, pulling away from the knife. One knee almost buckled, but he caught himself with the other. Then there was no more balcony left to retreat to. He reached the railing, holding his wound.

Then he straightened to his full height, and reached for the sword at his side.

How? She had pierced his chest. If not a killing blow, it was certainly a debilitating one.

She readied herself for a second attack, then The Priest's head lilted to one side, and his body tumbled over the edge to the city below.

"Get the bitch!" one of the guards yelled, fumbling for his sword.

The closest soldier lunged for her, but he was still squinting and easy to evade.

There would be time to revel in the bastard priest's death later.

It would have been better if she had been able to pull off The Priest's veil and reveal him to the world. The robes made him more than he was. So did Kaylo's stories, for that matter.

But his long fall would have to do.

Tayen wrapped herself in shadows and tore back down the spiral staircase.

Every delayed second made Liara want to sound the charge.

Sending Tomi had been a rash decision. She had already begun mourning until warriors within the Uprising found The Song returning to them.

Maybe Tomi's regiment had made the difference. She had to believe that.

Flashes of fire ignited throughout the city in the valley below. A building crumbled. The street moved with people, but it was too distant to make out anything clearly. The gate remained closed.

For all her need to see her sister safe and charge into the raging battle, she had a responsibility to the warriors she commanded. She wasn't a child anymore. She couldn't risk everyone for her sister's sake.

The gate shuddered. Or maybe it hadn't. The night could be playing tricks on her eyes.

Liara stared at the oversized doors, which seemed much too far away.

The regiment commanders beside her began stirring. The gates shifted, but didn't open. It hadn't been the night. She was sure of it.

Fire flashed through the crack between the doors. A crack wasn't enough.

Liara gripped her spear until her knuckles lightened several shades.

One side of the gate opened wider. Flames illuminated the battle within.

She didn't confer with anyone or deliver orders. She simply ran, screaming, "For Ennea!"

A round of voices mimicked her call and the ground rumbled with their boots.

CHAPTER FIFTY-SIX

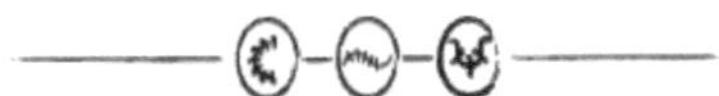

There were no plants growing around Kaylo because of course there weren't. Life—even the projection of life—didn't thrive in The Balance's void. But The Song came back all the same.

He hadn't known whether or not the call of The Great Spirits remained with dancers after their deaths. In fact, he had hoped they didn't. The idea of existing in The Mist for eternity carrying that absence in him had scared him for eighteen turns.

The Seed sang a gentle ringing. It sounded like the morning light slowly burning away dew droplets clinging to a leaf.

For as much as his body wasn't really here, he lost control of it. He fell to his knees and cupped his face.

Every time he told himself he had finished mourning The Seed had been a lie.

He looked up to find The Balance looking at him. Her brow furrowed like she was looking for something in his reaction or waiting for him to lash out as he had so often before.

"Thank you," he said. "I want you to know, I didn't say what I said because I thought it would get me what I wanted."

"You don't have to—"

"No, please let me." Kaylo stood up. "I will never understand it. When

I couldn't do anything to help the people I loved, I got a glimpse of your pain.

"I don't know if the stories will change. Maybe four spirit dancers dying to free the Stone City will be enough for people. Maybe nothing will be. Either way, I am sorry for not seeing you sooner."

The Balance shook her head. "I still don't like you."

A laugh burst from Kaylo that seemed incongruous with the surroundings. "Few people do."

"I'm not people."

Kaylo waved away the comment. "Would you mind if I visited from time to time?"

"You're in The Mist now. You can do what you like."

"Now that all the crystals have shattered and all the fragments have been returned, what will all that rage the spirits felt in their prisons do to The Song?"

"Only The Mother knows."

Kaylo nodded. Even here, so much was unknown.

Strangely, it didn't bother him. His mother was waiting for him.

Just as he had focused on the piece of him that belonged to The Balance, he thought of his mother wrapping her arms around his father from behind as he cooked, her face resting on his back. It was the image that he had always returned to when he needed to see their faces.

The darkness opened, and he stepped back into the home he had left behind so long ago.

Epilogue
Current Day Ennea

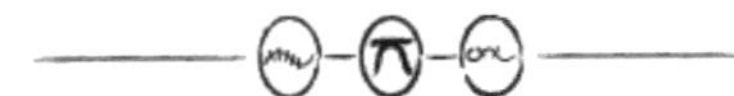

Beyond the walls and hard lines of the Stone City, Tayen knelt in front of the ancestor tree where she had buried Kaylo. The forest was thinner this deep into autumn. Sokan's light scattered over the patch of clover covering the red-hued soil.

It had been six moons, and it still felt unreal. In another six moons, Kaylo would be dead and buried as long as they had known each other.

"Another update," she said. "I know you can probably see all this, but it feels better coming to tell you. Even if it's just me talking to myself, at least it's not so crowded out here. There is not a moment of quiet in that city. How'd you do it with all those echoes refusing to hush for a moment? Maybe I need to go back and find the hallow."

She smiled. "I almost called it a treehouse to piss you off, but it's not as fun without your face getting all red."

A robin landed on one of the limbs of the trees above and started singing as if to laugh at her for thinking she could get a moment of silence.

"The last of the Gousht have been driven into Renêqua. They've got Port Bilãn, but that shouldn't last much longer. If the fucks have any sense of self-preservation, they'll ship off back home like the rest of the cowards."

Of course, it hadn't been as easy as that. To imply as much would dishonor the dead.

The Gousht fought to remain in control even as they lost ground. They had gotten more and more violent, but Enneans had always outnumbered the soldiers. After the spirits returned, the people revisited violence back on the Gousht.

"Liara's in Renéqua with Talise and the rest of the Uprising. Some of the Lost Nation regiments joined them to hunt down the Gousht after the army fell apart, but no one pays them much mind. They are warriors without an army now," Tayen said.

"Liara invited me along, but I've had enough blood, Kaylo. If that was the point of your long-winded story, I got it."

Her fingers needed to move. Every time she visited, she left a tuft of clover leaves picked clean from their stems. In some ways, this place felt like where she belonged. Yet, a voice at the back of her mind begged her to leave. The pain settled in here—necessary and unending.

"Sosun sent a letter. She and Nix made it back to the Citadel—they want people to start calling it Myanack again, but people still call it the Citadel. Nix's wounds have healed, but she can't do much with her right hand anymore. It makes it hard for her to sign, but she does her best.

"Nix says you should've done whatever you did sooner." Tayen smiled. "Talise actually made a similar joke about you dying too late, but it didn't sound like much of a joke at the time.

"Apparently, Lanigan is driving Nix wild with all their 'riddle-talk.' The whole city is a mess, but the servants have started a council to oversee rebuilding it. They even offered Wal a seat on it, but he refused. Instead, he's working beside the laborers like he can sweat away his trespasses.

"Sosun had to hold Nix back from killing him. I know he was your friend—kind of—but I'm with Nix on this one."

If Tayen wanted to pluck any more clover leaves, she would have to move from where she knelt. Instead, she let The Song brush over her and pull at small tones within the larger melody. Shadows moved with her fidgeting fingers.

"Torrel can finally walk well enough to rejoin his wife and the rest of the Jani," Tayen said with a smile that broke her. The first of her tears ran down her face. "He invited me to join them, but I can't leave you alone. You were alone too long already. And I'd make a horrible Jani.

"But if I don't go—I don't have anyone, Kaylo. You were it. And you left. I come out here and talk to the dirt like you can hear me. Maybe you can. I don't know, but I can't hear you."

Tayen slammed her fist on the ground, and the tremor that shot up her arm felt good. The physical pain had always been easier.

"All of my life has been about surviving. Then I thought I needed revenge. Then I had a mission. Now, what? What am I supposed to do now? I never expected to have a choice."

The shadows whipped about like a fury of tendrils. Then they stopped, and she stared at them. They curved unnaturally and looked like anger. The Song didn't deserve that. She had already given it too much of her anger.

"Maybe I should do it. I should just go with Torrel and Nomi. People need help, and the Jani are all about shoving their way into everyone's business. Not a bad fit, right?"

At the other end of The Song, the fragment of The Shadow within her waited. It was a door. She could walk through and find him. She had thought about it nightly, but she wouldn't make it back. If she saw him, her parents, Nita, Vāhn, she wouldn't have the will to return.

Too much needed doing for her to leave.

"I promise, I'll visit." She touched three fingers to her lips then placed them on the dirt to end the prayer. "You know, it's not fair that you got to leave before the hard part."

Tayen nodded to herself. "Of course you do. Family knows."

THE GREAT SPIRITS

 THE SHADOW: The first of the Great Spirits, known for her wisdom. She blesses her descendants with the ability to manipulate shadows.

 THE RIVER: The second of the Great Spirits, known for their patience, and twin to The Flame. They bless their descendants with the ability to manipulate water.

 THE FLAME: The third of the Great Spirits, known for their strength, and twin to The River. They bless their descendants with the ability to manipulate fire.

 THE MOUNTAIN: The fourth of the Great Spirits, known for her constant support. She blesses her descendants with the ability to manipulate the earth.

THE WIND: The fifth of the Great Spirits, known for his foresight. He blesses his descendants with the ability to manipulate the air.

THE SEED: The sixth of the Great Spirits, known for his forgiveness. He blesses his descendants with the ability to manipulate plant life.

THE THIEF/THE BALANCE: The seventh of the Great Spirits, known for her pursuit of power or equity depending on whose story you read. She blesses her descendants with the ability to borrow other dancers' abilities.

GLOSSARY

ANILACE MINES/GOD CAVES: The Gousht's name for Oakheart Mountain, where the first spirit crystals were discovered.

BLOOD BANNER: A derogatory term for Enneans who work with the Gousht as soldiers, spies, informants, and city bureaucrats.

CHANI CLOTH: A light cloth of woven silk. Before the invasion, good chani cloth was worth a goat in trade.

COMMON TONGUE: As the nations developed from tribes and villages, disparate languages and dialects began to merge, resulting in a shared language referred to as common tongue.

CONCLAVE OF SPIRITS: Throughout the Hundred-Turn War, citizens of each nation sought peace from the fighting, taking on a nomadic lifestyle. Eventually, a large group of the nomads representing each nation brought together a meeting of the four nations, where they negotiated an end to the fighting. This was also the origin of the fifth nation, the Jani.

COUTA: A curse that means child of incest. It became a popular slur for the Gousht due to their pale complexion, which Enneans took for sickly.

DANCER: An Ennean who was gifted with the ability to hear The Song and wield one, or in rare cases two, of the Great Spirits' powers. Also known as children of Ennea or spirit-marked.

DAEMONTALE: A make-believe story told to pass down lessons to children.

ENNEA/THE MOTHER: Ennea is the genesis of life. She is the land and mother to the moons and the sun, the spirits, and the people.

FIRESTARTER: A distilled oil that is extremely flammable. Under the right circumstances, it can cause explosions.

FREECITY: A formerly occupied city abandoned by the Gousht after the reclamation war broke out, which runaways and refugees have reclaimed.

GOUSHT PRIEST: Direct descendants of The One True God who serve as leaders of the church and armed forces.

GREAT SPIRITS: Ennea created seven spirits which gave form to The Waking and later gave pieces of their gifts to people in the form of The Song.

HALLOW: A shelter built using The Song and the Great Spirits.

HONORED FIELDS: The burial grounds for Astilean warriors in Myanack.

Hundred Turn War: For ninety-two or ninety-three turns, depending on who was counting, the four original nations of Ennea engaged in a series of wars over territory, which often overlapped. Also referred to as the Great War, Ennea's Reckoning, the Century of Mourning.

Kamani: A being whose spirit is not bound two any single conception of gender.

Kana: Ennea's second daughter, the first moon. This also became a term of respect for a mentor and teacher.

Konki: A tart, sweet fruit with red flesh and a brown husk. The Gousht turned this into a derogatory term for Tomakan people.

Lodestone: The Jani raised these naturally magnetic stones across Ennea as peaceful meeting places during the Hundred Turns War. Traditionally, Enneas relinquish their weapons to the magnetic pull of the stone while they meet.

Lost Forest: A forest of stormwoods the Lost Nation grew to cut themselves off from the rest of Ennea after the Hundred-Turn War. It is rumored to be impossible to navigate without a forest dancer.

Malitu: A corrupt spirit or dancer who uses their abilities for selfish gain or ill-intent. Often referring to spirit thieves, however, it can refer to any dancer or spirit.

Mistwalker: A dancer who is able to send their spirit into The Mist, speak with the spirits, and return to their bodies in The Waking.

GLOSSARY

MOON: A measurement of time based on the cycles of the moons, approximately thirty days long. When Toka disappears from the sky every third span, it marks a new moon.

NAMELESS: A failed recruit in the Astilean army now forced to serve in the capital city, Myanack.

SCION OF THE SHADOW: A title given to the line of royalty in Astile due to the claim they are the descendants of the first shadow dancer, Shunanlah.

SHUNANLAH: Shunanlah was the first person to be marked by Ennea and gifted The Song and The Shadow. The namesake of the autumnal equinox ceremony.

SPAN: A measurement of time equivalent to ten days.

SPIRIT-BOUND: An Ennean who is unable to hear The Song. Their spirit is bound to their body and to The Waking.

SOKAN: Ennea's first daughter, the giver, and the sun.

SUSU ROOT: When it was first discovered, Ennean healers used susu root as a medicine to dull pain. It's addictive and dulls the brain, making people apathetic. In small amounts, it is a powerful and useful sedative. Long-term use can make people irritable and detached. Severe use can be deadly.

TANONTA: A word that grew from a time before the nations, Tanonta refers to the first new day, the spring equinox. It is the celebration of rebirth as well as a transition of life. At night, when the moons are at their highest, those of age pledge themselves to The Mother.

THE MISSING: A rumored group of Enneans organizing against the Gousht Empire.

THE MIST: The spiritual plane.

THE ONE TRUE GOD/THE ONE: The Gousht god. Religious texts say that The One took human form and sired twelve children, the youngest of whom became the leader of the Gousht church and nation-state.

THE REAPING: After the Stone City fell, Gousht priests destroyed everything deviant or unholy in the eyes of The One True God. Soldiers swept through each village and town, burning books and relics, as well as people. Kamani people suffered greatly during the reaping.

THE SONG: Energy in The Mist seeps through the barrier between planes into The Waking. Dancers have the ability to hear a portion of this energy representing their great spirit ancestor(s). This allows dancers to access the power of their spirit ancestors.

THE STONE CITY: The capital city of Sonacoa and the last city outside of the Lost Nation to fall to the Gousht invasion.

THE WAKING: The physical plane.

THE WRIT: The Gousht holy book. Each crowned Emperor, thought to be direct descendants of The One True God, adds a section to the Writ before they stepdown, documenting the history of the Gousht Empire.

THIEF'S NIGHT: A colloquial term for a night sky in which neither moon is visible. People often act erratically on these nights and blame The Thief for their behavior.

TOKA: Ennea's third daughter, the second moon. This also became a term of respect for a mentee and student.

TURN: A unit of time measurement equivalent to four seasons, twelve moons, or approximately three hundred sixty days.

TWICE-MARKED: A dancer who is gifted with the ability to wield two of the Great Spirits' power.

Note from the Author

Among many things, Malitu is a story about resisting colonization and preserving culture when assimilation is demanded.

Throughout history, and continuing through current day, powerful people have used white supremacy and other oppressive ideologies to paint differences as hindrances to progress. When, in reality, it is our differences and our ability to fully be ourselves that allow us to connect with each other and the world around us.

I believe we all have a part to play in dismantling the false narratives that infiltrate our stories. However, I acknowledge that the false narratives of oppression have affected me in far different ways than those they target. I materially benefit from oppression as a white person, a man, an American, and various other identities. My goal is not to center my voice in challenging oppressive narratives, only to play a part.

There are many authors whose works have a closer vantage point when addressing oppressive systems because of their lived experience. I encourage readers to seek them out first, especially when their voices are so often minimized.

Below I have listed some of the authors I have read and enjoyed.

Tomi Adeyemi, Moniquill Blackgoose, Octavia Butler, C.L. Clark, Tracy Deonn, Justina Ireland, N.K. Jemisin, R.F. Kuang, Fonda Lee, Ken Liu, L. Penelope, Nnedi Okorafor, PhD, Kritika H. Rao, Rebecca Roanhorse, Andrea Stewart, Tasha Suri, Moses Ose Utomi, ML Wang, Evan Winters

I did my best to create fully-realized characters who feel human. However, I am well aware that my earnest attempt does not preclude me from causing unintentional harm. This statement is not meant to extricate myself from consequences or critiques. This is a claim to accountability. I believe in and love this story, and with that, I am responsible for its content and impact.

Thank you for reading,
James Lloyd Dulin

No Heart For A Thief

Malitu Book One

No Safe Haven

Malitu Book Two

Don't Bloody The
Black Flag

Malitu Prequel Novella

ACKNOWLEDGEMENTS

Authors can write whatever we want on the page, but no number of words or pages can make a book on their own. Malitu would have never been more than daydreams in a word document without the editors, artists, and readers I worked with.

I won't be able to name every single person who has contributed to helping make Malitu whole, but I will do my best to highlight some amazing people I have worked with.

The first people I have to thank are my wife, Aneicka, and my sons, Sonny and Dominic. They give my life meaning, and without them, I wouldn't be the person I am today.

I also want to thank the readers and editors who helped me refine the rough edges of my story. My greatest appreciate goes out to Taylor Banks, Angelicka Morgan, Rachel Marchesi, and Dominic McDermott. You have no idea what a mess of a story you would be reading without their work.

In indie publishing, even more than in traditional publishing, the style and design of a book is foundational to that book's success. Martin Mottet crafted yet another amazing piece of art for Only a Grave Will Do and my brother, Michael Dulin, made the art into a beautifully designed cover.

However, even the prettiest cover will struggle to find a readership without the support of reviewers. I have been very fortunate to have amazing ARC (Advanced Reader Copies) readers. These readers and reviewers have helped to bring more eyes to my story, and I am forever grateful for that.

To my ARC readers, whether you joined in with Only a Grave Will DO or you were there since No Heart for a Thief, I cannot thank you enough.

Lastly, I would like to thank you for picking up these pages of words and making them into a book. A book needs readers to exist.

If I can ask you to help me take this one step further, please review this book on Amazon, Goodreads, and any other platform you might use. Reviews are the lifeblood for self-published authors. Reviews encourage others to give a book a try, and I want to share this book with as many people as I can.